Victims of a Giant Hoax

This is the quickest I've read a book through in many years! Why ... because I found 'Victims of a Giant Hoax' impossible to put down. Daryl Sahli's latest yarn seamlessly blurs the lines between fact & fiction. From the 'winner takes all' politics of 70's southern Africa to the 'Yes Minister' British bureacracy and the behind the scenes destabilisation by Cuba and Russia; all contributing to an explosive and stirring plot, which I recommend followers of adventure and history read. - Darryl Barber

With his 4th book Daryl has vividly described the build up of Cuban and Russian influence in Zambia. The British have been out manoeuvred. The account leading up to the first Rhodesian viscount atrocity is a page turner. Daryl not only skillfully demonstrates his technical research, but even gives us a delightful love story. I enjoyed Daryl's connection to the fast moving and largely unreported political events of the day. More importantly he provides a far greater explanation of the possible cause of the shooting down of the Rhodesian viscount on 3 September 1978. Finally, there are the Rhodesian 'cross border' raids and covert operations that draw in the reader. Thank you, Daryl. - Clive Cooke

Daryl Sahli was born in Bulawayo Zimbabwe (Rhodesia) and attended Hillside Junior School and Gifford High School ('Tech'). After completing A-levels, he, like all other young men at the time, was called up for national service. The bush war was raging as 163 intake arrived at Cranborne Barracks in Salisbury (Harare). After completing training he was posted to 4 Independent Company (RAR) based at Victoria Falls where he completed his national service.

Daryl completed a B.Comm LLB degree at the University of Natal (Pietermaritzburg) and worked at both Ernst & Whinney (Young) and Arthur Andersen in Johannesburg. After immigrating to Australia, Daryl completed an LLM degree at the University of Queensland. Today Daryl works as a management consultant in his own practice in Brisbane. Daryl is married to Karen (nee Young, born in Ndola, Zambia) with two children Megan and Jason.

Other Books by Daryl Sahli

Rhodesian Bush War Series

A Skirmish in Africa (2011)
Winner of the Bronze Award in the Military/Wartime
Fiction category in the 2012 Independent Publisher (IPPY)
Book Awards in the United States.

Steely-Eyed Killers (2012)

World War II Series

Cocky Lobin over Germany (2013)
A story of 44 (Rhodesia) Squadron RAF

Scorpion's in the Blue
A story of the Long Range Desert Group
(due for release in 2016)

VICTIMS OF A GIANT HOAX

DARYL SAHLI

Northlands Business Consultants Pty Ltd
ABN 75 091 308 146 Trading As

MyStory Publishing
P.O. Box 5336, West End, QLD, 4101, Australia
www.mystorypublishing.com.au

Copyright © Daryl Sahli 2015

The right of Daryl Sahli to be identified as the moral rights author of this work has been asserted by him in accordance with the Copyright Amendment (Moral Rights) Act 2000 (Cth).

This work is copyright. Apart from any use as permitted under the Copyright Act 1968, no part may be reproduced, copied, scanned, stored in a retrieval system, recorded, or transmitted, in any form or by any means, without the prior written permission of the publisher.

National Library of Australia Cataloguing-in-Publication entry:

Sahli, Daryl, author, illustrator.
Victims of a Giant Hoax / Daryl Sahli ;
Maps & contact diagrams, Daryl Sahli;
author photograph, Jason Sahli ; cover design, Despina Papamanolis;
book design, Karen Sahli.

ISBN: 9780987156495 (paperback.)

Zimbabwe People's Revolutionary Army - - Fiction.
Zimbabwe African People's Union - - Fiction.
Southern Rhodesia. Army. Selous Scouts - - Fiction.
Civil war - - Africa - - Fiction.
Zimbabwe - - History - - Chimurenga War, 1966-1980 - - Fiction.

Sahli, Karen, book designer.

Dewey Number: A823.4

ISBN: 9780994244406 (ebook: Kindle)
ISBN: 9780994244413 (ebook: epub)

This book is a work of fiction. Names, characters, places and incidents are either the product of the author's imagination or are used fictitiously and any resemblance to actual persons, living or dead, business establishments, events or locales is entirely coincidental.

Maps by Daryl Sahli
Cover design by Despina Papamanolis
Author photograph by Jason Sahli
Book design by Karen Sahli
Typeset in 11 / 13.2pt Palatino
85gsm creme

To Mom and Dad

I wish to thank my wife Karen for publishing this and my previous books. She provides unstinting support and encouragement. As enthusiastic amateurs we rely on the indulgence and commitment of others to help with perspective, editing and review. Our deepest thanks to Ian Livingstone-Blevins, who convinced me to do this in the first place, Clive Cooke, James Knox, Anthony Lima, Darryl Barber and John Bucknell.

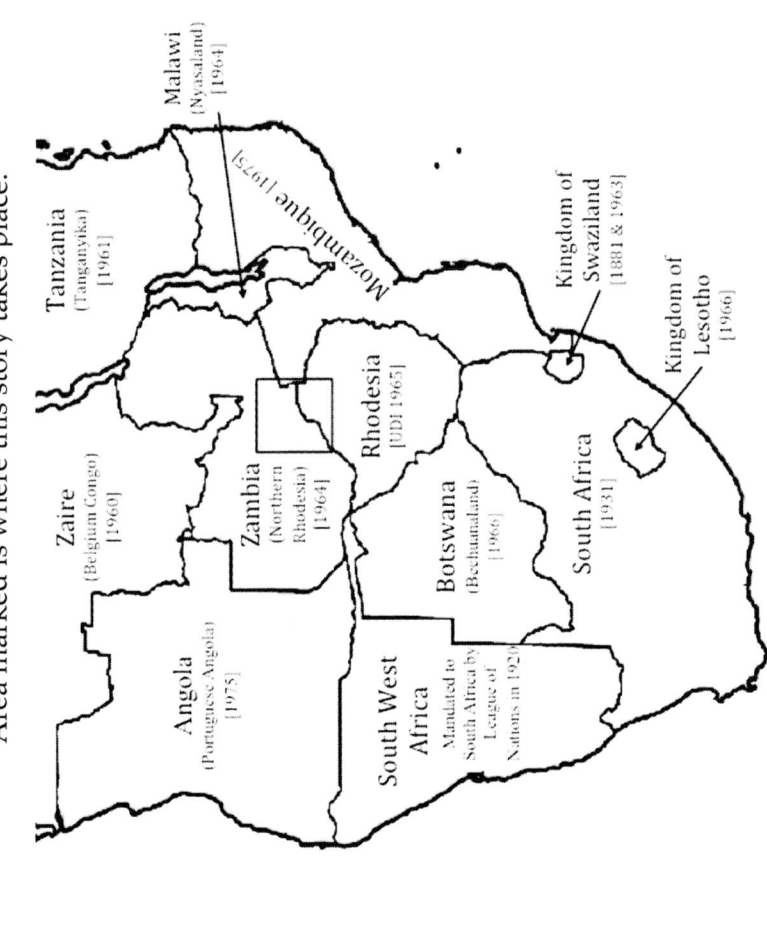

Map 1: *Southern Africa circa 1975 Country names (colonial names) [year of independence]* Area marked is where this story takes place.

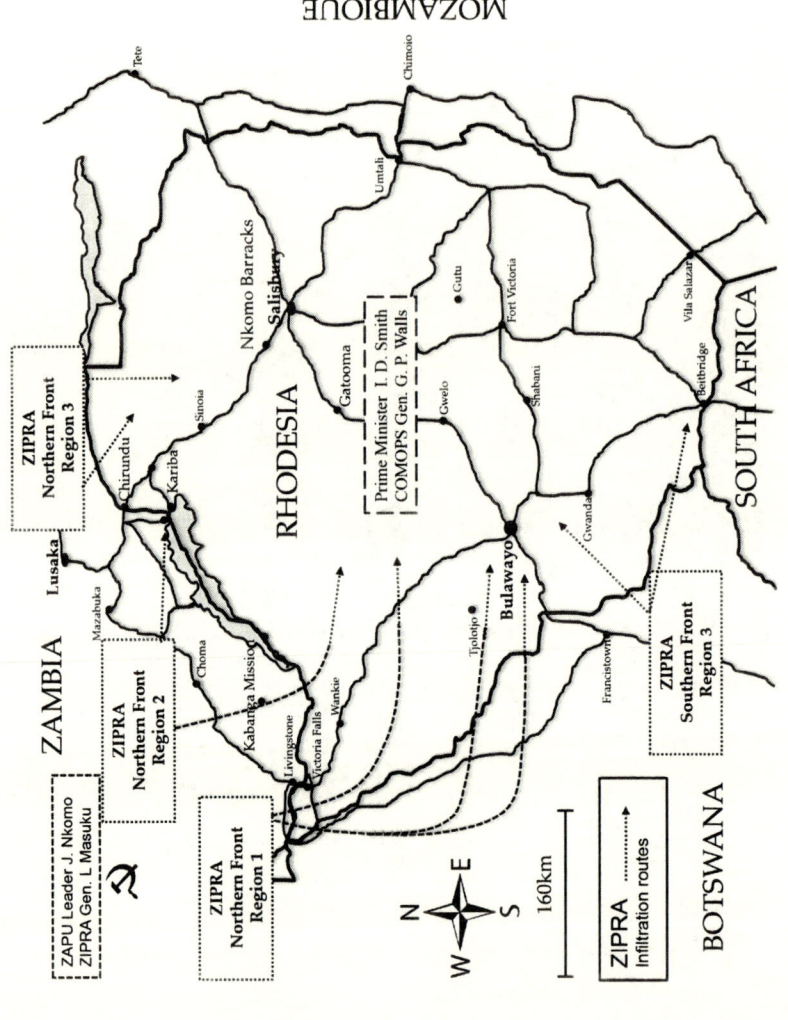

Map 2: ZIPRA Operational Area

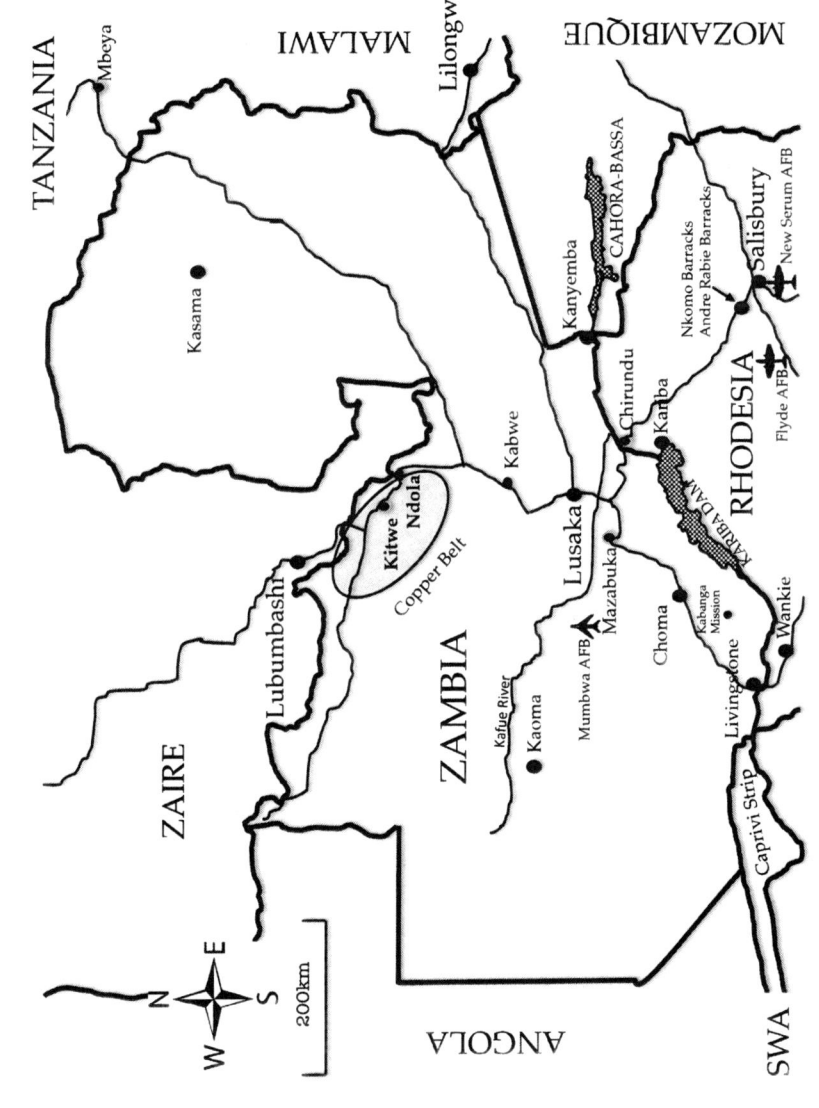

Map 3: Northern Boarder of Rhodesia and Zambia

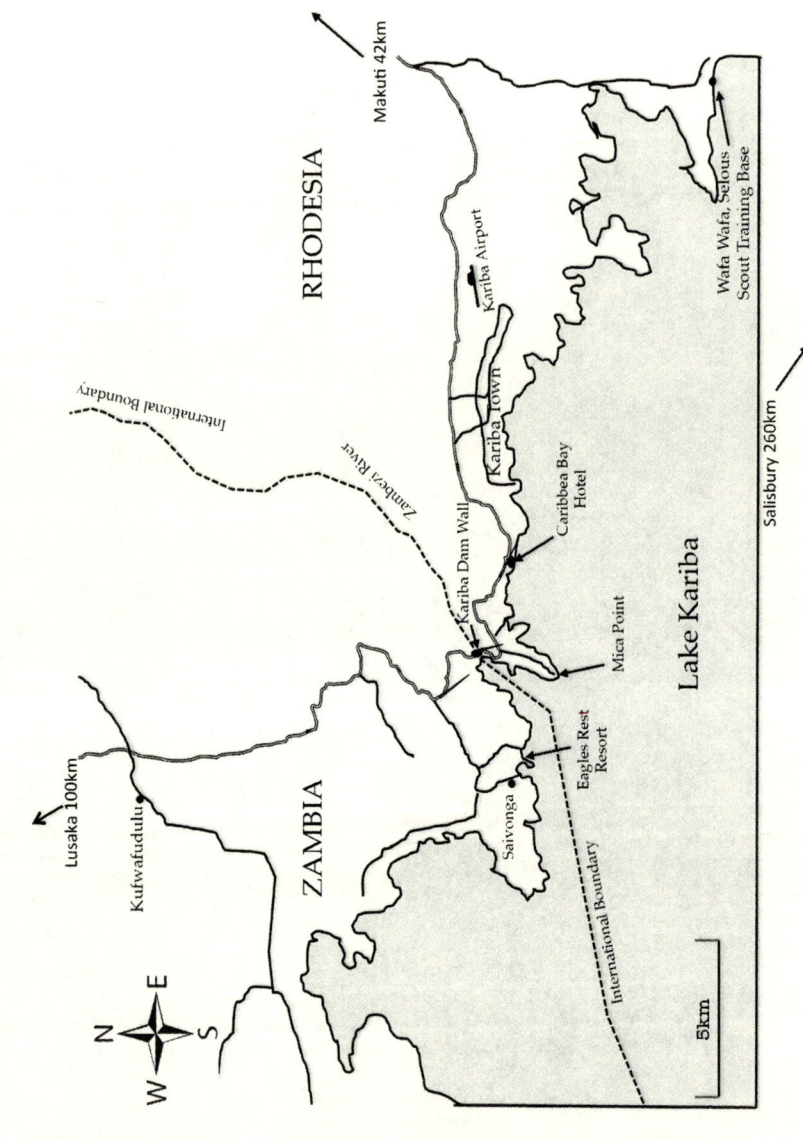

Map 4: Kariba Town and surrounding areas

Map 5: Lusaka and surrounding areas

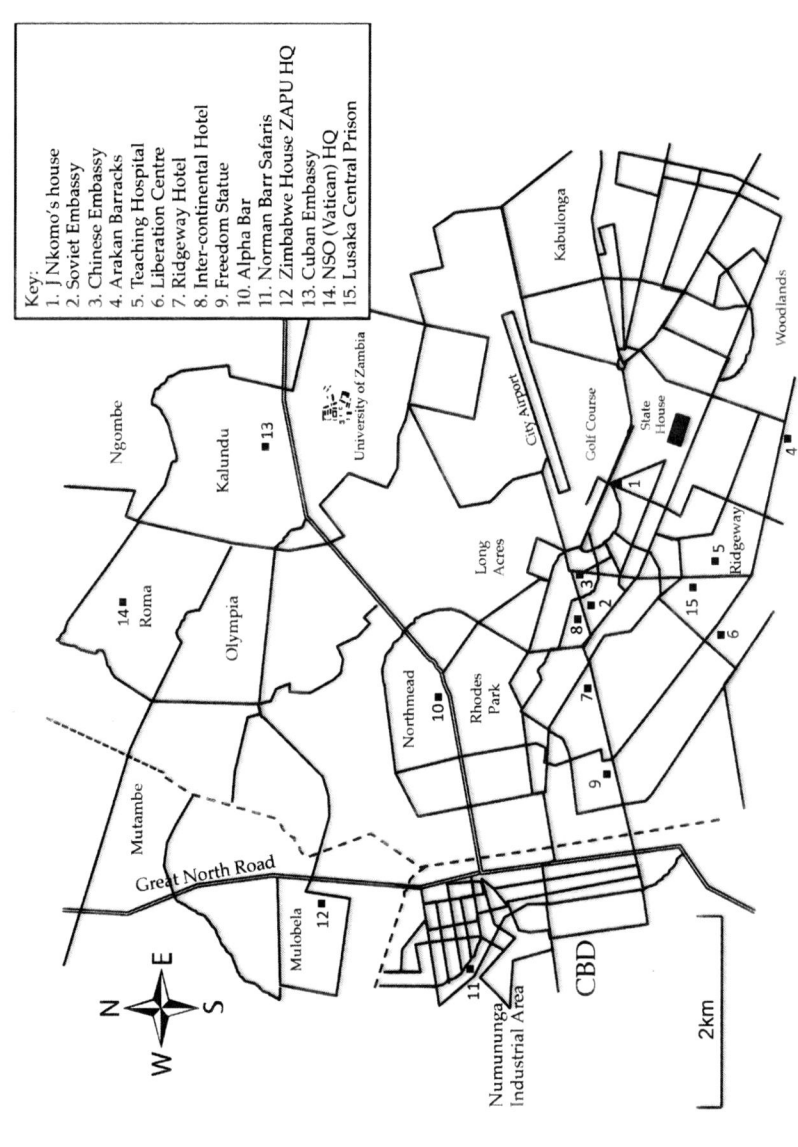

Glossary

2IC	Second in Command
AGL	Above ground level.
AK	AK-47, Soviet Union, (or Kalashnikov), selective fire, gas operated, magazine of 30 rounds, 7.62×39mm assault rifle.
AKM	An upgraded version of the AK-47 assault rifle.
Avtur	Aviation fuel – turbine
BCR	Bronze Cross of Rhodesia, awarded for valour in the face of the enemy.
Big-means	The nickname for the TR48 HF radio.
Bivy	Short for bivouac, a plastic sheet used for creating shelter usually by being strung between trees, low to the ground.
Blue Job	Air force
Brown Job	Army
BSAP	British South Africa Police was the name of the Rhodesian Police Force, a hang over from the pioneer column of the 1890s when the British South Africa Company supplied the police. The British South Africa Company was the company set up by Cecil John Rhodes to exploit the riches of South-Central Africa.
Call-sign, c/sign	Call-sign, Rhodesian voice procedure, the name or number given to a unit, large or small. Personnel issued with a radio would automatically be allocated a c/sign. A c/sign was a vital element of voice procedure.
Canberra	The English Electric Canberra B2, twin-engined, light bomber, supplied to the Rhodesian Air Force in 1959.
Casevac	Casualty evacuation
Cheetah	Augusta Bell 205A (Huey) (UH-1H) helicopter troop carrier (8-10 fully equipped troops), mounted twin .303in Browning MkII machine guns on the left, cyclic rate of fire 1,200 rounds per minute.
Chilapalapa	Hybrid language, developed by the earliest settlers, miners, traders, hunters and farmers to assist with communication with the African tribes of Southern Africa. Words were taken from seShona, siNdebele, Afrikaans and English. The language was in daily use and played a vital role in improving communication between the races.

Glossary

Chimurenga	The liberation war. The ZIPRA called the First Chimurenga the Matabele Rebellion of 1890, ZANLA referred to the First Chimurenga as the Shona Rebellion of 1893, while the Second Chimurenga is believed to have started, by both ZIPRA and ZANLA, with the battle of Sinoia on 28 April 1966 in which 21 Freedom Fighters were intercepted by Rhodesian Forces and killed.
Chopper	American slang - Helicopter
Choppertech	Rhodesian slang, field maintenance technician and gunner on Alouette III G-cars and K-cars.
Combined Operations, COMOPS	The organisation lead by General Peter Walls to co-ordinate the activities of Air Force, Police and Army. COMOPS were also responsible for planning and executing External raids.
Contact	An encounter with the enemy. A battle.
CSM	Company Sergeant Major, in the RLI Commando Sergeant Major, Warrant Officer 2nd Class.
CT	Communist Terrorist, most common voice procedure term used to describe terrorists.
Dak. Dakota	Douglas DC3, military transport version C47, also Paradak for delivering airborne troops.
Donga	Eroded river or streamline, normally dry but a rushing torrent after a rainstorm, often steep sided and boulder strewn with sometimes very thick vegetation along the banks. Most often caused by overgrazing and deforestation.
Kt	Knots, measure of speed 1 knot = 1.852km/hr.
External	An attack outside the country. Rhodesia raided insurgent training and logistical bases in all neighbouring states, even as far as Angola and Tanzania.
Fire-fight	A battle.
FLOT	Forward Line of Own Troops, the line demarcated with smoke grenades or mini-flares to mark the position of ground forces to allow for safe airstrikes.
FN	*Fabrique Nationale* (Belgium), self-loading rifle, magazine 20 rounds, 7.62×51mm intermediate (NATO) round.
Fran, Frantan	Frangible tank napalm bomb.
G-car	Aerospatiale Alouette III, helicopter troop carrier, mounted twin .303in Browning MkII machine guns on the left, cyclic rate of fire 1,200 rounds per minute. 'G' referred to General Purpose, capable of carrying four fully equipped soldiers, plus the choppertech and the pilot.

Glossary

Golf Bombs	Rhodesian made, 460kg pressure bomb.
Gomo	SeShona, hill or mountain. The air force may have used the word to describe major navigation landmarks like the Chimanimani or Vumba mountains while flying into Mozambique.
Gook	American slang from Vietnam, adopted by Rhodesians to describe communist terrorists.
Hondo	seShona, war.
HQ	Headquarters
Hunter	Hawker Hunter FGA9 Mk IX, ground attack fighter, delivered to Rhodesia in 1963.
Indep Co	Independent Company, six in all, part of the Rhodesia Regiment, after 1977, transferred to the Rhodesian African Rifles (RAR).
Intaf	Internal Affairs
JOC	Joint Operations Command, the JOC for Operation Repulse in Victoria Province was located at Fort Victoria (Masvingo).
K-car	Aerospatiale Alouette III, helicopter gunship, mounting one French Matra MG 151 cannon on the left, cyclic rate of fire reduced to 350 rounds per minute, high explosive incendiary shells. 'K' referred to killer, carried the gunner or choppertech, the pilot and the Fireforce Commander. Cannon calibrated to 800ft AGL.
KIA	Killed In Action
Koppie	Afrikaans, hill, koppie is a small hill, words used interchangeably.
Locals	Local villagers, tribes-people.
Lynx	Reims-Cessna FTB 337G, twin-engined, push-pull aircraft, used for close air support, carried mini-golf bombs, 37mm SNEB rockets, Frantan canisters and twin roof mounted .303 Browning machine guns. These aircraft were smuggled into Rhodesia from France in 1975.
LZ	Landing Zone
M962	Fragmentation grenade
MAG	*Fabrique Nationale* (Belgium), *matirueurs a gas*, 7.62×51mm (NATO) round, belt fed machine gun, cyclic rate of fire 650 rounds per minute.
Mig	Rhodesian colloquial reference to Soviet and Chinese supplied jet aircraft.

Glossary	
OC	Officer Commanding
OP	Observation Post
Ops	Operations, Operations Room.
Paradak	Douglas DC3 converted for delivery of parachute troops.
Patriotic Front	Formed in October 1976, after sustained pressure from the Frontline States (Zambia, Tanzania, Malawi and Mozambique), the Patriotic Front was an alliance between Joshua Nkomo's Zimbabwe African People's Union (ZAPU) and Robert Mugabe's Zimbabwe African National Union (ZANU). The purpose of the alliance was to focus on the common enemy the white minority government instead of fighting amongst themselves.
Pom, Pommie	Colonial slang, person from England, can be a term of endearment or derogatory, believed to derive from Prisoner of Mother England - convicts transported to Australia.
RAR	Rhodesian African Rifles.
RIC	Rhodesian Intelligence Corp
RLI	Rhodesian Light Infantry, one regular battalion, made of four airborne commandos including a Support Commando, HQ and Training Troop. The unit exclusively white specialising in Fireforce operations and major external raids, mostly regular soldiers but in later years included national servicemen to boost numbers. The unit included many foreign volunteers from the Commonwealth Countries (United Kingdom, Australia, New Zealand and Canada) but also South Africa, France, USA (Vietnam veterans), Holland and Germany.
RPD	A light machinegun, Soviet Union, 100 round segmented belt in a drum container, 7.62×39mm cartridge, cyclical rate of fire 650 rounds per minute.
RPG-7, RPG	Rocket Propelled Grenade, Soviet Union, hand-held, shoulder-launched anti-tank weapon capable of firing an unguided rocket equipped with an explosive warhead, fired both anti-tank and high explosive/fragmentation warheads.
RR	Rhodesia Regiment.
RSM	Regimental Sergeant Major, Warrant Officer 1st Class.
RV	Rhodesian voice procedure, rendezvous, also RV Point
SAS	Rhodesian Special Air Service (C Squadron)

Glossary

SB	Police Special Branch. BSAP Special Branch.
Scene	Rhodesian slang, a contact with the enemy, a battle
Selous Scouts	The Selous Scouts were an elite unit trained in long-term infiltration of enemy held areas, internally and outside of the country, coupled with highly skilled observation techniques. They were the supreme masters of intelligence gathering through observation. The unit included both white and black soldiers; the black soldiers were mostly drawn from the Rhodesian African Rifles but included policemen drawn from BSAP Special Branch and Ground Coverage.
SF	Rhodesian Security Forces
Shumba	Shona for lion, used to describe Lion Lager beer.
SInf	School of Infantry, Gwelo (Gweru). Also Hooterville and College of Knowledge.
SNEB	Lynx carried Matra 37mm SNEB rockets, Hunter Matra 68mm SNEB rockets.
Stick	A group of 4 men in full operational kit, the maximum number that could be carried in a fully armed Alouette III troop carrying helicopter, G-Car.
Stop, Stop Group	A group of men used to block the escape of terrorists after a contact. In a Fireforce, stops were numbered Stop 1, Stop 2, Stop 3 etc. A Stop Group could be made up of more than one c/sign, as in the case of troops deployed by parachute.
Sunray	Rhodesian voice procedure, Commander, or senior officer.
Sweep, sweepline	The process of spreading out attacking forces in line abreast to flush out terrorists, sometimes in thick bush.
Terr	Rhodesian slang, terrorist
TF	Territorial Forces
TR48	HF radio, the big-means
TTL	Tribal Trust Land
UNIP	United National Independence Party of Zambia
UNHCR	United Nations High Commissioner for Refugees
US	Unserviceable
Vlei	Afrikaans, marshy river line, low-lying area.
White phos	White phosphorous delivered by hand grenade or rifle grenade.
ZANLA	Zimbabwe African National Liberation Army, military wing of ZANU. Leader Josiah M. Tongogara

Glossary

ZANU – (PF)	Zimbabwe African National Union – (Patriotic Front alliance after 1976), Robert Mugabe became the leader of ZANU after the death of Herbert Chitepo in 1975.
ZAPU – (PF)	Zimbabwe African People's Union – (Patriotic Front alliance after 1976), Joshua Nkomo was the leader of ZAPU from its inception in 1961.
ZIPRA	Zimbabwean People's Revolutionary Army, military wing of ZAPU. Leader Alfred 'Nikita' Mangena 1972 -1978, Lookout Masuku after 1978.

Foreword

In the 1960s and 1970s the United States, with its NATO allies, and the Soviet Union reached a point of mutually assured destruction using nuclear weapons. Once both sides had the ability to exterminate each other, and the entire human race, a direct conflict became unthinkable. The two superpowers shifted their attention to war by proxy as they and their allies supported innumerable civil wars in Africa, Asia and Latin America. The flood of Soviet weapons allowed for old grievances to be settled in small regional conflicts many of which had their roots deep in colonial history.

Victims of a Giant Hoax is just such a story set in the time of the civil war in Rhodesia (now Zimbabwe) in the late-1970s. The 'Bush War' between the liberation movements and the Rhodesian regime started in 1966 and ended with the independence of Zimbabwe in 1980.

As the ex-colonial power in Rhodesia, Britain, with the support of the Commonwealth, maintained economic sanctions and an arms and oil embargo. Sanctions were a response to the Unilateral Declaration of Independence (UDI) declared in 1965 by the Rhodesian Government led by Ian Smith. The only other country ever to have made such a declaration was the United States in 1776.

Britain was anxious to ensure a path to black majority rule in Rhodesia but was strongly resisted by the white 'rebel' government. Weak post-UDI British foreign policy regarding its rebellious colony, plus internal pressure caused by the civil war in Northern Ireland, a struggling economy, labour strike action and the oil crisis, left a political vacuum.

Most of this story is set in Zambia, a landlocked country, surrounded by Angola, Zaire, Tanzania, Malawi, Mozambique, South West Africa with Rhodesia on its southern boundary. During these dark years, Zambia played host to a bewildering assortment of communist terrorists - the PLO (Palestine), MPLA (Angola), FRELIMO (Mozambique), ZAPU (Rhodesia), ANC (South Africa) and SWAPO (South West Africa). These revolutionary movements used Zambia as a launching pad for terrorist attacks. The Soviet Union, East Germany, North Korea and Cuba provided military and logistical support in Zambia and supplied huge quantities of weapons.

As this story is mostly set in Zambia it refers primarily to the Zimbabwe African People's Union (ZAPU) and its leader Joshua Nkomo. Joshua Nkomo ran all his operations from Zambia and it was there that his Soviet, East German and Cuban advisors were based. ZAPU was the political wing of Nkomo's organisation while the military wing was called the Zimbabwean People's Revolutionary Army (ZIPRA). For purposes of the story there is little reference to the competing freedom movement led by Robert Mugabe from his bases in Mozambique, the Zimbabwe African National Union (ZANU).

Tens of thousands of people were crippled or killed by Soviet armaments channelled through Zambia. Recruits and kidnapped children from Rhodesia were trained as terrorists in bases throughout Zambia. ZAPU ran concentration camps in Zambia for their own dissidents who failed to join the revolution. Thousands of members of ZAPU were brutally murdered by their own people on Zambian soil. Those who escaped were hunted down by the Zambian police and handed back for torture or execution.

Zambia's history since independence in 1964 has been dark and stormy. The British left over a billion pounds in the bank when they granted independence to Zambia and it was widely hailed as the most prosperous and promising nation in Central Africa. Promising and prosperous that is, until the 'socialist humanism' of President Kenneth Kaunda's one-party dictatorship squandered its abundance with his heavy handed socialism, persecution of opposition, neglect of agriculture, widespread corruption and support of communist inspired terrorism.

In 1967, President Kaunda signed a treaty with China and two years later nationalized all foreign industries and corporations. In 1972, the ruling United National Independence Party (UNIP) became the only legal political party. All others were brutally suppressed. The prisons were filled with political opponents and critics of the President. Zambia then signed a treaty with the Soviet Union. The highest-ranking Soviet officials, including the Soviet President, visited the country. Soviet, East German, North Korean and Cuban military advisors were a common sight.

The year 1978 was a turning point in the war. Ian Smith had accepted the need to negotiate with black leaders, including Joshua Nkomo. The scene was set for an internal settlement. Smith had already passed power to a multi-party interim government and legislation was being passed to remove racially biased laws.

The Soviets were less than excited at the prospect of a political settlement in Rhodesia after their years of support and investment. Britain and the Commonwealth blustered and postured, dismissing the 1978 internal settlement negotiations as 'unrepresentative'. This was primarily because Robert Mugabe the leader of ZANU, based in

Mozambique, refused to participate. Nigeria, Kenya and Tanzania, Mugabe's supporters, called for the war to continue.

The pressure on Rhodesia caused by the military build up in Zambia and the continued British intransigence regarding internal peace negotiations, was building to bursting point. With Cuban and Soviet support there was a real possibility of a full-scale invasion of Rhodesia across the Zambezi. External raids were mounted by the Rhodesians on terrorist bases in Zambia. Spies and assassins were sent into Lusaka to destabilise both the Zambian government and the ZAPU leadership. Rhodesian military aircraft flew over Zambia with relative impunity. Railway lines and bridges were blown up to disrupt the movement of large numbers of troops and equipment towards the border.

President Kaunda of Zambia was equally under enormous pressure. The ZIPRA army, with its Soviet and Cuban leadership, was larger and better equipped than his own. Opposition groups in Zambia were gaining in confidence as the President appeared weak and indecisive. As a result of appeals from the Kaunda government for protection, Britain supplied their latest radar-guided Rapier ground-to-air missile system. These missiles had the potential to sweep the skies over Zambia clear of Rhodesian aircraft. At the same time the Soviets were ramping up arms deliveries to ZIPRA including sophisticated shoulder launched ground-to-air missiles.

This is a familiar story, repeated in more modern times, placing sophisticated weaponry in ruthless, unsophisticated hands ... terrible things can happen.

The situation by mid-1978 was nothing short of calamitous. Cuban advisors, aircraft and troops were dispatched to Zambia to bolster the growing ZIPRA army. Political negotiations were on a knife-edge, it needed only one false move to turn the region into a bloodbath ... *Victims of a Giant Hoax* was just that ... a false move with devastating consequences that still reverberate to this day ...

1

Zambezi / Gwai River confluence, Zambian border with Rhodesia (Zimbabwe), 08:00am, late 1970s

Three Rhodesian Air Force English Electric Canberra B2s flying northwards at 290kts, 1,600ft AGL.

Blue Section

Navigator:	We are approaching the stream (the Zambezi River).

The Navigator was speaking to his pilot from the bomb-aimer's position in the nose.

Blue Leader:	Okay. We're coming up to the stream now. Three-one-eight.
Navigator:	Three-one-eight we've got. We're crossing the stream now.
Blue Leader:	Check.
Navigator:	How's your speed?
Blue Leader:	We're holding about 290knots. Level is sixteen hundred feet.

Blue Leader was leading a loose three-ship V-formation, Blue Section, across the border between Rhodesia and Zambia, passing over the confluence of the Gwai and Zambezi rivers.

It was all business with the two-man crew; they were hardened veterans of external raids into Zambia and Mozambique. Their voices, distorted by the oxygen mask intercom, were measured and professional despite the severe buffeting caused by flying at low level.

Forty kilometres ahead of the Canberras, closer to the target, travelling at 100knots in echelon were two Cheetahs, Bell 205A (UH-1D) 'Huey' helicopters, each carrying eight Selous Scouts. Behind the Cheetahs were four Alouette III K-car gunships and four Alouette III G-car trooping helicopters. Each G-car carried four men from Support Company 1RAR.

The helicopters were flying at 500ft, lurching left and right as the pilots dodged through the rows of low hills.

In the lead Cheetah, Lieutenant Keith Wilson BCR, Selous Scouts, spoke to the pilot, Peter McNeil, through his headset intercom.

'Pete, I make H-hour in four minutes.'

'Roger, four minutes. You ready to rock and roll?'

'Nothing like a bit of killing first thing in the morning,' quipped Wilson. The grim expression on his face belied his attempt at levity.

McNeil, in the right-hand seat, lifted his gloved hand with a thumbs-up. Wilson and McNeil had been at school together, Gifford High School in Bulawayo.

The radio crackled, 'Red Section, Red Leader, drop to treetop level.'

The 8 Squadron Commander, Sqn/Ldr Hugh Fitzsimmons, was flying as Red Leader, in the lead Cheetah.

'Red 2 copied,' replied McNeil as he pushed forward to nose the helicopter down at the same time pulling closer in behind Red Leader.

McNeil was concentrating hard on keeping his formation with the other helicopters. On the left side of the Cheetah the door-gunner (choppertech) sat hunched over a set of twin .303 Brownings.

McNeil swivelled his head to glance at his choppertech, Samuel Jacobs a farm boy from Gatooma in the Midlands. Jacobs was nicknamed 'Samson' because of his huge muscular arms. He had been a star school rugby player at Jameson High School.

Next to McNeil his co-pilot, Air Sub-Lt James 'Dicky' Bird, had a map open on his lap as he traced the route to the target. Dicky was straight out of flight school.

The faces of the helicopter crew were obscured by helmets, oxygen masks and sunglasses.

Inside the Cheetahs the sound from the turbine and the huge blades was deafening. The crew wore earplugs under the noise shielding ear cups in their helmets. Those riding in the back, without a headset, had to yell at each other.

'Let's hope the gooks are still on muster parade,' said Wilson into the intercom with a grim smile. He also had his map open on his lap, following the route to the target with his finger. Map reading to the target was part of Wilson's pre-battle ritual. He found it helped him maintain a mental picture of the target and the task at hand.

'If they are, the Canberra strike will spoil their day,' replied McNeil.

The soldiers in the two Selous Scouts sticks sat impassively watching the trees flicking past only a few feet below.

Wilson, call-sign 73, sat on the side-facing bench seat, immediately behind the pilot. Next to him was his machine gunner Stanley Chiyeka, then Sgt Cephas Ngwenya BCR and Tpr Richard Mundiya.

The second Selous Scout stick was commanded by Sgt Pat Meredith. His call-sign was 73Alpha, with troopers Sibanda, Ncube and Moyo.

The Selous Scouts were wearing weathered Rhodesian camouflage uniforms with matching combat caps, chest webbing, kidney pouches with extra ammunition, medical supplies and two days rations. Each trooper, including Wilson, carried a 7.62mm FN rifle. Wilson had his rifle clamped between his legs in an inverted position. Stanley Chiyeka held the MAG across his lap pointing out the open door while his shoulders were draped in belts for 500-rounds of 7.62mm ammunition. Each of the members of the stick carried a spare 100-round belt in their webbing.

Wilson and Ngwenya were carrying A76 VHF radios in their backpacks. The hand-pieces were clipped to stitched loops on the chest webbing harness next to their left ears.

Chiyeka's face was animated with anticipation. He turned and smiled broadly at his officer, his face alive with the excitement of pending battle, Matabele warrior blood running in his veins.

'Ready to kill *Makandanga* today *Ikhanka*?' shouted Chiyeka into Wilson's ear over the scream of the turbine. Wilson's nickname amongst the black soldiers of the Selous Scouts was *Ikhanka*, the siNdebele word for the Blackbacked Jackal. This described Keith Wilson perfectly, *thin wiry body, well suited to an opportunistic lifestyle in a wide variety of habitats, wary of unfamiliar objects, can live off very little food and water and fiercely defended family groups and territory.*

Wilson had dark coal-black eyes, long jet-black curly hair and an unkempt black beard. His face, chest and hands were covered in thick black camo-cream, making him almost indistinguishable from his black brothers.

'Yes, we will kill many gooks today Chiyeka,' shouted Wilson still smiling. He was fluent in siNdebele, coming from a farming family on a cattle property near Gwanda in Southern Matabeleland. Conversations in the helicopter were impossible so both men returned to their own thoughts.

Wilson was going over the Target, designated C (Charlie), in his mind. His target was one of five to be attacked by different elements of the assault force. Target C was roughly in the middle of a sprawling ZIPRA terrorist base with a total diameter of 3.6km.

The simplicity of his orders belied their difficulty: *1st wave drop east of Target C, clear business centre of any CTs bearing in mind that hierarchy and logistics are likely to be in the area.* He was also tasked to look for ZIPRA radios and documents and hopefully take a high-ranking prisoner.

Sergeant Cephas Ngwenya smiled thinly across at Keith Wilson, all their faces showing the signs of nervousness … it was the same every time … jumping out of a bucking helicopter into … chaos … shit and derision …

Blue Section

Navigator:	Turn coming up, twenty seconds.
Blue Leader:	Onto?
Navigator:	Zero-five-six. Standby … Now …
Blue Leader:	Zero-five-six. Rolling out … We're going to have to drop a bit.
Navigator:	How's our speed?
Blue Leader:	We're holding 290.
Navigator:	Good that's fine.
Blue Leader:	Just check on that road.
Navigator:	Go right … about two degrees. Zero-five-eight.
Blue Leader:	Roger. Level … a thousand feet.

The Canberras had crossed the Zambezi then turned right. While their target was only 74km away as the crow flies, they were planning their approach directly from the east, over a set of low hills, coming out of the early morning sun. Their track would take them northeast before their final turn onto the target. Each of the Canberras carried three hundred locally designed spherical Mk2 Alpha bouncing bombs. The bomblets would strike the ground, bounce up and explode, killing or maiming everyone and everything within an area of 1,000m×300m.

The Alpha bomb was about the size of a large volleyball, with a double-walled steel body. Between the double walls there were small rubber balls that gave the bomb a 'bouncing' capability. Inside the inner wall or shell was the explosive. When dropped, at very low level, the Alpha bombs looked like a swarm of bees coming out of the Canberra bomb bay. They floated down in a huge swathe behind the Canberra as it accelerated to over 300kts. As they bounced off the ground to about 15ft they exploded. As the drop of the bombs was fractionally retarded, the explosions 'moved' forward across the target area in a fast and expanding wall of smoke, sound and shrapnel sounding like hundreds of large, loud, sequenced firecrackers. The Alpha was a very effective anti-personnel weapon, equally effective at defoliation when dropped amongst trees!

The radio crackled in Wilson's earphones.

'Red 2, Red Leader.'

'Red 2 copied,' replied McNeil.

'Turn coming up ... Turn to your west, half a click,' called Fitzsimmons.

'Roger, starting my approach now.'

A large hill marked the turning point towards the target.

'Red Leader, Red 3, we're getting ground fire from the ridgeline off to the west.'

Red 3 was the lead Alouette III K-car gunship flying about 2,000m behind the two Cheetahs.

'I see some tracer coming up,' replied Red Leader.

All the pilots glanced to the west but there was no change in course.

'Two minutes,' called McNeil to Wilson holding up two fingers.

'Roger,' replied Wilson, tapping the pilot on the helmet to confirm.

'Okay *vuka!*[1]' shouted Wilson at the top his voice.

The men visibly braced as if given a sudden electric shock. The reality of battle was now upon them, there was no going back, no time for reflection ... no second thoughts.

Alone with their fears ... the sound of the helicopter turbine, the whipping of the blades above ... all concentration, stomach churning ... muscles aching with pent up anticipation.

Out ahead of the helicopters three DC-3 Paradaks came into view flying in line astern at about 800ft. They each carried sixteen Support Company (RAR) paratroops.

Blue Section

Blue Leader:	White Section do you copy?
White Section:	Roger.
Blue Leader:	We are one minute out ... confirm your position.
White Section:	We are coming up on the IP[2] at the dam in fifteen seconds.
Blue Leader:	Copied.

Blue Leader spoke to the leader of White Section, a pair of Hawker Hunter FGA9 Mk IX, ground attack fighter-bombers, each carrying two pods of 68mm SNEB rockets, two 50gal frantan canisters, plus their four internal 30mm Aden cannons.

The Hawker Hunters were screaming over their Initial Point at

---

1　Chilapalapa, wake up.
2　Initial Point – the beginning of the run onto the target.

450knots, so low that the trees flicked about with their passing. The Initial Point was a small farm dam to the north of the target area. Ripples and fine spray flew up off the water from the jet blast as the Hunters thundered over the water.

Blue Section

Navigator:	Everything is set up and ready.
Blue Leader:	There's a school coming up. Roger, I have 310knots, two-three-nine.
Navigator:	Come left three degrees. IP at the bridge coming up.
Blue Leader:	Roger … Blue Section Go! Blue Section Go!

The Canberras each had a separate target for their Alpha bombs. Blue Leader was instructing them to breakoff to their respective targets. The Hunters of White Section were doing the same but they were tracking more to the north.

Blue Leader was responsible for Target C, a small cluster of offices and storage buildings and what was believed to be a radio communications bunker and HQ building. The main complex was an old school building, an oblong shape with barrack rooms and offices forming a 30m square around a courtyard. At one time, the buildings had been part of the nearby Kabanga Mission compound, now requisitioned by ZIPRA.

Navigator:	I have the target visual.
Blue Leader:	Beautiful. Yes! Switches. Speed up, or is it okay?
Navigator:	Speed's fine. Go right. Steady. Steady. Two-four-two.
Blue Leader:	Roger.
Navigator:	Steady. Steady. Right a touch.
Blue Leader:	Bloody fantastic!
Navigator:	Steady. Steady. Right a touch. Steady. Steady. Steady. Can I switch the doors open?
Blue Leader:	Yes. Switch your doors.

The two airmen were almost shouting over the intercom, a warm shot of adrenalin was now flowing through their veins as the excitement reached fever pitch. They realized that the strike was going to be right on target.

Blue Leader:	Okay. I am on two-four-two. Speed now 300 knots.

Blue Leader:	Road coming up. Shit, we are exactly on time!

A large group of ZIPRA cadres were formed up on a dusty parade ground next to the buildings designated Target C.

Their leader standing in front of them looked up into the clear ice-blue sky …

Blue Leader:	Is my speed Okay?
Navigator:	Yes, it's fine. I have the target! Steady … Steady.

The Canberra was now accelerating onto the target at just over 300knots, 300ft above the ground.

Navigator:	I am going to put the bombs right in the middle. Fuck, they are grouped next to the buildings. Steady … Steady! BOMBS GONE! … Beautiful man, bloody beautiful!
Blue Leader:	Fucking beautiful!

The screaming, reverberating sound of the aircraft, stunned the people on the ground. As they looked up, all they could see was the blunt nose of the Canberra aimed right at them, as an eagle dropping onto prey, talons drawn. The Canberra crew watched the enemy troops break ranks, running out in front as the terrifying high-pitched screeching sound of the bomber passed over them.

It was the stuff of the worst nightmares. As the ZIPRA cadres ran in helpless panic across the parade ground, the aircraft swept overhead, spraying down the Alpha bouncing bombs. The bomblets struck the ground, bounced up and exploded, shredding everyone standing in the open. Their bodies were literally torn apart making them unrecognisable as human beings. Dust lifted in a cloud behind the aircraft as it passed overhead, clods of dirt mixed with blood and flesh lay splattered on the bone-dry ground. The camp buildings were pockmarked with millions of holes; they looked as if they had been spray-painted in red.

As the Canberra climbed away it was chased by 57mm shells from a quad-mounted Soviet ZSU-23-4V1 'Shilka' self-propelled anti-aircraft gun. The weapon was mounted on a tank chassis, hidden in thick bush on top of a low hill overlooking the Target C compound.

The ZSU's flat-faced radar mounted on the vehicle behind the guns swung the four cannons into line, DUFF ... DUFF ... DUFF, DUFF.

The heavy shells punched out bright red tracer rounds, chasing after the Canberra, skimming over the cockpit canopy, so loud the pilot could hear the supersonic crack over the sound of his engines and the radio in his ears.

Blue Leader: ... Fuck me gently! ...

Jinking his aircraft left and right, he dropped back to treetop level to escape.

The presence of a deadly weapon like the ZSU-23-4V1 had not been picked up on reconnaissance photographs.

'Red 2, Red Leader on short final now,' called McNeil when he saw the LZ.

'Keith, get ready to debus,' called McNeil to Keith Wilson on the intercom.

A haze of dust and smoke marked the Canberra strike that had been delivered only seconds before.

Wilson glanced out the front of the canopy, it was a bright sunny day, not a cloud in the sky, just dusty, dirty black splodges lifting into the air from the air strikes going in.

The helicopter was approaching the target from the south along a vlei line, using the terrain to hide its approach. The topography was mostly flat with dry, almost white, sandy soils, criss-crossed by green vlei lines, some with tiny muddy waterholes.

The Cheetah's 1,400shaft horsepower turbine engine, spinning big wide chord main rotor blades, made a sound heard from miles away. Long before the helicopter could be spotted in the sky people on the ground could hear it coming, pulsing, throbbing, and beating the air into submission, getting louder and louder, until the heavy beat could be felt in the chest, the pulsing, thumping WHOP, WHOP, WHOP. It just kept getting louder and louder.

McNeil flared to go in, bringing the helicopter up on its tail to drain off speed. He made a correction, slipping right, lining up on the horizon. Tracers lifted out from the right side in a tree line overlooking the LZ. McNeil ignored the incoming fire, focusing on the horizon, holding the helicopter straight and level.

The K-car assigned to provide cover for the LZ immediately engaged with the 20mm cannon, dust lifted from the impact of the exploding heads.

As the Cheetah lined up to land the tick-tick, tick-tick, sound of bullets hitting the fuselage was as a steel hammer on metal.

The helicopter lurched violently to the right as McNeil again corrected his descent, tracer cracking past the front of the canopy. His left gloved forefinger was pointing down vigourously.

'Get ready to debus ...'

The LZ was pre-planned in a small patch of ploughed land next to the vlei, surrounded by trees and bushes to provide cover.

As the helicopter steadied the final few feet into the LZ, a man appeared on the edge of the clearing carrying an AK-47.

McNeil spotted him, 'Gook left... gook left!' instinctively swinging the helicopter beam-on to give his gunner a shot.

The choppertech swung the Brownings around to bear on the terrorist, firing all the time, trying to 'walk' the bullet strikes towards the target. The man began to fire, the AK jerking into his shoulder, muzzle flashes clearly visible. The pilot slipped the chopper to the right desperately trying to get out of the way. Wilson watched in horror as the rounds hit the perspex canopy ... the helicopter hit the ground hard, dust swirling in a grey cloud, visibility instantly reduced to nil.

'GO .... GO, GO!' yelled Wilson as his men dived out of the helicopter. Ngwenya had seen the CT in the trees now firing his FN in that direction. Mundiya crashed down next to him.

Chiyeka, to Wilsons's right, was firing the MAG. Wilson dived down next to him. The helicopter, suddenly released from its load, lifted as the pilot reapplied full power, nosing forward as the blades bit into the air, turbine screaming, clawing back into the air.

Just as McNeil cleared the tree line with full power on, more tracers arched up towards him. He directed the choppertech on the left side to fire into the tree line and nosed the chopper over, gaining airspeed. Entering a cyclic climb by pulling back speed from 110knots to about 60knots, the helicopter swooped up into the air out of small arms range. Once out of harm's way, McNeil entered a wide orbit waiting for further instructions.

On the ground in the LZ it was all choking dust, stinging the eyes, clogging the throat ... numbing noise from ground fire filled the brain. Acrid smoke was drifting across the LZ from a bush fire caused by the Canberra strike.

Bullet strikes spat dirt into the air.

'Move ...' shouted Wilson as he got to his feet, dashing across the ploughed field towards the tree line the CT had ducked into. The other three scrambled to their feet and ran after him, firing into the trees as they went.

The CT had disappeared.

Wilson reached the tree line just as a K-car spun back overhead, already engaging CTs running from the compound only 80m ahead. He waited as Sgt Pat Meredith's stick ran up next to him.

Above the battlefield at 4,000ft the mission commander, Major David Jackson OC of Support Company 1RAR (call-sign 79), in a Reims-Cessna FTB 337G 'Lynx' was taking stock.

'73, this is 79, do you copy?'

'73, Go.'

'Airstrike was accurate, proceed to your target, hundred metres to your northwest,' called Jackson, his voice calm and measured.

'73, copied,' replied Wilson.

Major Jackson switched VHF radio frequencies in the Lynx to talk to the team attacking Target D further to the west. The Paradak on Target D was beginning its drop in the distance. It was being engaged by the ZSU, Wilson could see the tracer lifting into the sky as chutes popped open.

Once the two Selous Scout call-signs were together, Wilson repeated the instructions from the briefing. In the heat of battle, the mind had a tendency to go completely blank. It helped to repeat instructions over and over again.

'Right, Pat you cover us, we start on the eastern side of the buildings and sweep through to the west ...'

Wilson had his detailed map open so all could see. Each building was planned to be cleared in a pre-rehearsed order. Nothing was left to chance ... *hopefully*.

'Once all the buildings are clear we move to this point here,' instructed Wilson pointing to a line of trees immediately to the northwest of the Target C compound.

Once the buildings were clear, the plan was that they would return to search for intelligence. The choppers would drop a team of policemen from Special Branch (SB) to help with the search ... *a piece of cake*.

The ZSU opened up again. DUFF ... DUFF ... DUFF, DUFF. It sounded so close, right on top of them.

'What the fuck is that?' exclaimed Meredith.

'I don't know but it sounds big,' replied Wilson.

'It is a fifty-seven millimetre anti-aircraft gun,' said Ngwenya quietly. 'We saw them in Mozambique last month at Mabalane. They kill aircraft. I saw one shoot down a helicopter.'

The simplicity of Ngwenya's explanation was enough.

'Well let's hope the Blue Jobs sort it out soon,' said Wilson. 'All right, is everyone ready? On my call ... we go.'

All the men gathered themselves for the danger of clearing buildings. They had practiced long and hard but the real thing was something else altogether. Each man had a pouch full of M962 fragmentation grenades and white phos. Ngwenya had two bunker bombs in his kit for blowing down walls.

'Okay, shake out into a sweepline. Pat, you are on our right flank. We will go first, you cover us,' called Wilson, having to raise his voice above the sound of a K-car orbiting above. Pat Meredith waved his hand to show he understood.

Wilson looked through the trees towards the target; one of the buildings was burning fiercely, a loud explosion shook the ground ... *that must be a landmine in the storage shed.*

'Cephas, you take the left flank,' called Wilson to Cephas Ngwenya, laying only a few metres away.

'*Yebo Ikhanka*[3]*,*' replied Ngwenya, his face a picture of concentration. They had at least 100m of open ground to cover before they reached the main buildings ... *we will go first.*

'Okay when we go, we go fast, no stopping until we get to the building. On my call ... GO!'

The four Selous Scouts leapt to their feet, sprinting out across the open ground, dust lifting from their boots, their webbing pouches and water bottles bouncing wildly, all focusing on the building ahead of them. The copper and brass rounds in the belts around Stanley Chiyeka's shoulders glittered in the bright sunlight.

50m ...

Rounds lifted in the dust in front of Wilson, his brain took a split second to comprehend ... *fuck someone's shooting at us.*

To the east of the buildings was a network of well-camouflaged slit trenches. A band of terrorists had seen the men running across the field and opened fire.

The incoming fire was too intense; Wilson was forced to dive into the dust.

'Down ... Down ... CTs ... two o'clock, fifty metres.'

Chiyeka was already firing, the belts jumping in the breach

---

[3]   siNdebele, Yes Jackal.

expelled casings flying out. Pat Meredith saw Wilson go down.

'73Alpha, 73 do you copy.'

Wilson was lying in the open, his head buried in the dirt, his hand clicking on the radio handset.

'73Alpha copied.'

'I have gooks dug in to my front. You need to flank to the right, to those trees ... seen?'

'Seen ...'

'Go ...' called Wilson.

Behind him, Pat Meredith and his stick took off to the right along the edge of the field, to get into position in a clump of trees where they could suppress the fire coming from the trenches.

'Okay, we can't stay here ... we need to skirmish forward as soon as 73Alpha engages ... *Uyezwisisa na*[4]*?*'

We stay here any longer and we are as good as dead.

Wilson twisted his head to see his men, to make eye contact, to make sure they knew what he wanted. These were hardened professionals ... they understood what was expected.

'Cephas, you and I first ... ' Wilson spoke loudly and precisely to make sure his men heard.

'Yee.'

To the right, Meredith and his men opened with their supporting fire. The collective firepower of two MAGs firing at once at 600-rounds/minute was enough for the CTs to put their heads down.

'Go ...'

Wilson and Ngwenya were on their feet, firing their rifles as they went, the weapon's recoil making it impossible to aim.

Ten metres ... down! Fire! ... roll ... up again sprint ten metres ... down! Fire! ... roll ... up again.

Bullets flew past the four men as they skirmished forward, Wilson could hear the crack as the rounds passed overhead, whizzing and buzzing like angry hornets, each one spelling instant death. His legs shook from the strain of running over the sucking soft sandy soil. Sweat filled his eyes making it impossible to focus, dust spat into his face every time he dived back to ground. Dust and sweat combined to burn his eyes as red-hot needles. He opened his mouth to urge his men onwards towards the buildings but no sound would come, his throat now bone dry ... coughing uncontrollably.

Ten metres ... down! Fire! ... roll ... up again sprint ten metres ... down! Fire! ... roll ... up again.

---

4   siNdebele, do you understand?

Wilson and Ngwenya collapsed against the wall of the building, chests heaving from the exertion, unable to speak ... panting uncontrollably, spitting to clear their throats. Chiyeka and Mundiya were still on their way. Wilson wiped his eyes with the face veil around his neck. His eyes still burning, he turned to watch as his teammates behind him came on as if in slow motion. Withering fire, darting left and right, the very air around them seemed to be alive with bullets.

Chiyeka was visibly slowing, the weight of the MAG draining his strength. He tripped and fell, the gun barrel digging into the soil, wrenched from his hands. Mundiya sprinting ahead of him did not see him fall.

Cephas Ngwenya was up on his feet, dashing back across the open field towards Chiyeka who was now struggling up onto his knees. Wilson aimed his FN around the side of the building and joined the covering fire coming from Meredith's stick.

Ngwenya hefted up the MAG using the carry handle and with his free hand lifted Chiyeka back to his feet. Both staggering forward Wilson urged them on until they crunched down against the wall. Chiyeka sat back ashen faced from the shock of falling, his chest heaved as he tried to regain his breath.

Firing from the trenches stopped.

The only noise was the Lynx 4,000ft above with the K-car orbiting further to the north.

'73Alpha, 73, we will need to clear those trenches before we clear the buildings,' called Wilson.

'Copied.'

Wilson sat on his haunches with his back against the wall. The building was constructed from unpainted rough concrete bricks, the window frames were devoid of glass, and the roof was made of corrugated asbestos sheeting. Wilson ducked his head out to gauge the extent of the trench system. As he did so he saw a CT pop up out of the ground with an RPG-7. Then using the parapet of the trench as a rest the man fired. Wilson did not have time to warn the others as the rocket impacted the edge of the building tearing out a huge chunk of brickwork, showering Wilson and his men with sharp pieces of masonry. All four lay flat on the ground behind the wall covered in brickwork and choking concrete dust.

'Fuck!'

'79, 79 ... 73 do you read!' Wilson was calling Major David Jackson, the mission commander in the Lynx.

'73 ... go.'

'Roger I have Charlie Tangos in trenches to the east of the buildings at Target Charlie. Can you put in a strike? Over.'

'73, standby...'

The K-car returned overhead, the door gunner on the 20mm cannon searching the ground for the trenches. He couldn't see them, the zigzagged trenches were in thick tree cover, each well camouflaged with grass and branches. They had been carefully sited with fields of fire, with part of each trench protected by a matrix of heavy wooden poles for overhead protection.

The CT with the RPG tracked the helicopter with the iron sights on the launcher ... waited ... aimed ... fired. The distinctive sound of the rocket carried to where Wilson and his men were taking cover. The projectile shot out through the trees streaking towards the helicopter. Neither the pilot nor the choppertech saw it coming.

Striking the helicopter on the left side just aft of the choppertech's position, the RPG punching through the paper-thin skin, detonating against the internal framework. The explosion killed the choppertech instantly, shredding him to pieces.

Wilson looked up to see the helicopter spinning out of control, thick smoke churning out of its fuselage. It was only a split second before the helicopter spun into the ground with a sickening thud. The fuel exploded, sending orange flame, smoke and dust high into the still morning air.

The battlefield seemed to hesitate as the enormity of what had just happened sunk in.

'79 ... 79, 73 ... chopper down ... chopper down to my east.'

The helicopter came down only forty metres from Pat Meredith's position. Pat could feel the wave of heat pass over him as the helicopter exploded. There was nothing they could do, just watch in horror as the helicopter burned, the pilot strapped helplessly in position, slumped forward unconscious, his back broken.

'73, 79 standby for Hunter strike ... one minute ... you will have to call him in ... switch to Battle Command Net frequency code Lima-two-zero.[5]'

'Copied.' Wilson pulled his light pack off his back and unclicked the press-studs, reached inside and changed the frequency on the radio.

'White Leader, 73 do you copy.'

The pilot of the Hunter had climbed out after his initial strike and

---

5   The A76 VHF radio could be tuned to different frequencies using two switches one with letters the other with numbers. Wilson was on code J30 (130.3Mhz) for his target, the Mission Commander asked him to retune to 132.2Mhz code L20 to talk to the air force.

was now at 20,000ft looking down at the target area.

'73 go...' came the clipped response. The air force pilots always sounded detached as their voices were distorted by their oxygen masks. They spoke in calm unflappable phrases ... *can you pass the sugar?* The pilot had just witnessed the death of the K-car pilot, a close friend.

'Roger I have a line of trenches stretching a hundred metres to the east of the buildings on Target Charlie.'

'73 ... I can see the buildings ... confirm the trenches are in the tree line to the east.'

'Affirmative ... the tree line to the east.'

'Roger ... on my call, mark FLOT. I will throw fran.'

The Soviet 57mm ZSU self-propelled gun opened up again, trying to hit the command Lynx that was mercifully just out of range.

Wilson contemplated whether he should warn the Hunter pilot who would be flying directly into the ZSU's range envelope.

'White Leader, 73.'

'73 go.'

'Roger, we have a fucking big anti-aircraft gun down here, to my north, can you see it?'

'Fucking big anti-aircraft gun to your north, copied,' was all the pilot said.

Pat Meredith, with his radio to the command net, realised that he was within the kill zone for a frantan strike. The problem was that he was pinned down behind a low drainage ditch ... return fire from the trenches had intensified.

Meredith flicked open a pouch on his chest webbing under his left arm and pulled out a green smoke grenade.

'White Leader ... 73Alpha ... I am only a hundred metres to the south of the trench line ... I cannot move ... do you copy. Over,' called Meredith.

The pilot of the Hunter had already banked into a tight turn to bring him onto an attack path parallel with the line of trenches. He was planning to come in from the west using the buildings to cover his approach.

'73Alpha copied ... stay down ... mark FLOT on my call.'

The pilot, White Leader, was confident that he could make the strike without endangering Meredith's call-sign.

The ZSU opened up ...

A sound of thunder burst in the west as the Hunter pushed through the sound barrier ... it dived out of the clear blue sky towards its target.

'Standby to mark FLOT ... standby ... mark FLOT ... Now!'

Wilson and Meredith tossed their smoke grenades out in front of their positions, green smoke fizzing loudly. The CTs in the trenches saw the smoke grenades pop open and began a hail of fire in that direction. Bullets cracked only inches above Meredith's head as he and his stick buried their faces in the soft soil ... *digging trenches with their eyebrows.*

Wilson's stick, also unable to move, lying behind the wall as a hail of brick and concrete showered over them. The RPG gunner took another shot, this time the round sailing wide to explode against a nearby tree.

The Hunter pilot lined up his aircraft on the trees to the east of the buildings of Target Charlie. Under his wings were two 50-gallon finned frantan canisters. His speed increased to 450knots, 100ft above ground. The CTs in the trenches could not hear the aircraft approaching at such tremendous speed at low level.

Still the ZSU fired, its radar following the incoming Hunter.

In a thundering howl the jet passed over Wilson's position, the two frantan canisters released in unison, striking the ground only a few metres in front of the first trench.

The inexperienced crew of the ZSU did not track the second Hunter following its leader down towards the target. The pilot of the second Hunter could see the bright flashes as the quad-guns pumped out shells, he took careful aim with his own 30mm cannons and fired. The armour on the self-propelled gun was no match, the shells exploded inside the crew compartment, combined with the ammunition and fuel the turret blew off in a violent explosion.

Frantan killed in two ways, by immolation and asphyxiation. Since frantan was essentially an incendiary product, it set fire to any combustible matter it came in contact with. A human being in the open cannot protect himself against it. Frantan acts not only by burning, but has an equally devastating effect consisting of a complicated process whereby shock, absorption of oxygen from the air, smoke and noxious carbon monoxide become lethal.

As the Hunter strike went in, the canisters tumbled, corrected as the fins bit the air, impacting the ground with a bright orange and black petroleum cloud of superheated flame. The death-cloud purged forward over the line of trenches. The CTs hiding below ground were incinerated, instantly turning their writhing bodies into a viscous tar-like, black magma. Those protected from the direct effects of the flames had the air sucked from their lungs replaced by carbon monoxide in overwhelming quantities. Carbon monoxide combining with haemoglobin in the blood is powerful and rapid, occurring within a few hundredths of a second. They died rolling in the dust, holding their throats as their chests heaved convulsively from collapsed, poisoned lungs.

The explosions radiated out in shock waves. Wilson could feel the burning heat pass over him, as if opening the door to a hot oven.

No further gunfire came from the trenches, a thick cloud of acrid smoke hung in the air; the stench of burned flesh mixed with fuel frantan stuck in the throat. Screams of agony came from the few CTs outside of the kill zone, third degree burns melting their skin, their uniforms burnt off their bodies.

'Up ... Up,' screamed Wilson, scrambling to his feet to rush forward towards the trenches. The trees that hid the trenches were burnt to a crisp, those further away were burning fiercely, each exploding into flames as the fire spread.

As the Selous Scouts ran forward they shot at any bodies they saw in front of them, taking no chances that a CT may be 'playing dead'. The Hunter screamed back overhead to check the effectiveness of the strike, the sound of the powerful turbine beat in the chest.

Wilson called Meredith forward after they had skirmished through the line of trenches that stretched for over a hundred and fifty metres. Those few CTs unhurt were running for their lives towards the north. The Selous Scouts killed the few survivors too badly burnt to offer resistance ...

More Alouette helicopters arrived overhead, raging Valkyries intent on avenging the death of one of their own. They hounded the escaping men on the ground, 20mm cannon and .303 browning machine guns cutting down the survivors.

Further to the north, Support Company 1RAR were running into fierce resistance. Heavy gunfire joined supporting mortar fire rolling through the bush. Another Lynx arrived overhead to provide support.

Wilson regrouped with Meredith's stick, all miraculously unhurt, making their way back towards the Target C buildings, avoiding the dying flames that had burnt everything to a cinder.

The ZIPRA command compound was built in an open 40-metre square with barrack room buildings on all four sides. On the inside of the square, covered verandas ran the length of each building with doors leading into the various offices and sleeping accommodation. A tall radio mast that doubled as a flagpole dominated the middle of the courtyard. Entry to the courtyard was via a gate between the buildings on the west side. The gate was thick wire mesh topped with barbed wire.

In the pre-mission planning the Selous Scouts had realised that trying to clear the buildings through the courtyard would be suicide if the defenders were hiding in the buildings. They would be trapped in a cross fire without any cover.

The rear of the buildings had a few unglazed steel windows covered with burglar bars. Crouched over at the trot, Wilson led the men forward until all were safely up against the wall of the eastern side of the compound.

'Okay Cephas, its all yours,' whispered Wilson.

Ngwenya slipped off his backpack and extracted a canvas satchel. Inside was a two-kilogram homemade bunker bomb. Ngwenya expertly slipped out a length of cortex with a detonator clamped to one end. He pushed the det into the plastic explosive and silently stood up to look into the nearest window. It was a tiny room filled with steel filing cabinets. The door onto the veranda over looking the internal courtyard was closed.

Signalling to the others that all was clear, Ngwenya slipped the strap of the satchel over the handle on the window frame so that the explosives sat flush against the wall. They all watched Ngwenya's every move. He took out a cigarette lighter then held up his hand showing one finger ... *a one-minute fuse.*

On Wilson's signal, the Selous Scouts moved along the wall crouching below the windows until they had reached the edge of the building. Ngwenya lit the fuse and followed them.

The tremendously loud thump followed in exactly one minute, throwing concrete and dust high into the air. The bunker bomb knocked a three-foot wide hole through the wall and ripped out the window frame.

'Go ...' shouted Wilson as the men dashed back down towards the opening blasted in the wall. The first through was Meredith shooting into the corners and into the roof space above. Paper, shredded into confetti flickered in the air, the steel filing cabinets lay as fallen dominoes, bent out of shape by the force of the explosion.

Once all eight men were in the room, Wilson and Meredith crouched at the door, looking out into the courtyard. Heavy gunfire continued in the distance, jets were still orbiting above 20,000ft.

There was no movement in the courtyard.

'Okay, Pat, you go left, we go right. Once you have cleared all the rooms on your side we meet at that room across the way, the one with the blue door,' instructed Wilson softly.

Meredith nodded his understanding, this was the way they had rehearsed it.

'Go fast Pat, kill anything that moves.'

Pat Meredith gathered his stick, there was only room for one man at a time through the door onto the veranda.

'Ready,' he called back.

His men all nodded that they were in position. Wilson and his stick would follow as soon as the others left the room.

'Go ...' called Meredith, ducking through the door, crouched down as low as he could. His men followed him, spinning to the left as they ran.

Wilson signalled for his men that it was their turn.

As he reached the door, a hail of small arms fire erupted from across the courtyard. A man yelped in agony ... one of Meredith's stick went down onto the hard concrete veranda, his rifle skidding from his hands from the impact of his fall. A Soviet 'pencil' rifle grenade impacted against the doorframe spraying splinters of brickwork into the room.

It was impossible to move, Wilson and Chiyeka were pinned against the wall on one side of the door, while Cephas Ngwenya and Richard Mundiya, against the other. Bullets zipped through the doorway, biting chunks out of the opposite wall.

Wilson sat back stunned, trying to get his mind around what was happening. He could hear Meredith's stick returning fire outside but he could not get his head around the door to take a look.

Wilson made his decision.

'Cephas, we have to get around to the side of the courtyard. The gooks have barricaded themselves in the rooms opposite ... '

Ngwenya nodded, 'I can set a bunker bomb and blow the wall in.'

'Yes, take Mundiya with you.'

The two Selous Scouts crawled over the toppled filing cabinets, when they got close to the hole they dived through, rolling in the dirt outside to break their fall.

The gunfire inside the compound slowed to a few sporadic shots.

Ngwenya led Mundiya around to the side of the compound, the side with the parade ground bombed by the Canberra earlier. He carefully eased his head around the edge of the building. In front of him was the horrific result of the Alpha bomb strike. Bodies lay everywhere, many had limbs torn off, blood soaking into the sandy soil. A few had dragged themselves away before they died. Muffled moans came from the few survivors who were too injured to move, just lying in the hot sun, flies already settling on their suppurating wounds.

The surrounding bush had been cut back from the buildings leaving 20m of open ground without any cover. Any ZIPRA CT hiding in the bush would be able to kill them very easily. Ngwenya keyed his handset.

'73, 73Bravo, do you copy?'

'73 Bravo go.'

'I am on the north side of the compound ... I will lay the bunker bombs under the two middle windows.'

'Copied ... blow them in three minutes,' called Wilson.

'Roger ... three minutes.'

Ngwenya signalled to Mundiya that he wanted him to cover the bush opposite the building. Mundiya lay down on his stomach with the FN supported on his elbows. Cutting two pieces of cortex to one-minute fuses, Ngwenya slipped the dets into the bunker bombs and waited, watching the second hand on his watch come round.

He was off and running, reaching the first window, he slipped the pouch off his shoulder and placed it against the wall. Working as quickly as he could, he lit the fuses and ran back to where Mundiya was waiting.

The two bunker bombs exploded only a split second apart with a deep resonating thud. A thick choking cloud of concrete dust blew out obscuring the whole western side of the building.

Ngwenya and Mundiya were up, running from window to window, tossing M962 fragmentation grenades as they went. Reaching the last window on the building, Ngwenya had used up his M962s. He reached in his webbing for a white phos grenade, pulled the pin and tossed it through the window, scurrying back out the way.

The white phos grenade exploded with a dull thud, white superheated gas blew out the open window. A bloodcurdling scream came from inside ...

Wilson and Chiyeka leapt to their feet as soon as the bunker bombs exploded, raced out the door into the courtyard, firing their weapons as they went. Chiyeka was firing the MAG from the hip. It was all dust and commotion, a CT staggered out of the room blasted by Ngwenya, his face and uniform covered in white dust, Wilson shot him in the chest ... continuing to fire blindly into dust cloud.

Aware of movement to his right, Wilson swung around ... in the murky light he saw a person dragging another out of a room, across the veranda into the courtyard. He hesitated thinking it might be Meredith. Someone was screaming in agony ...

Blond hair? ...

Blinking to clear his eyes, Wilson could see the person was wearing what looked like a grey flak jacket and a baseball cap.

Chiyeka opened up on another CT trying to escape from the building. Wilson went down on his knees to take aim. He could see that the person screaming was the one being dragged into the courtyard ...

The person with the baseball cap turned, looking straight at him ...

A woman ... with blond hair!

'Help me,' she called out. The person on the ground continued to scream, rolling from side to side.

Bullet strikes appeared in the dirt at Wilson's feet. More CTs appeared out of the gloom, shooting indiscriminately, spraying bullets in all directions. Chiyeka was firing again ... the noise was deafening ... making it impossible to think ... more gunfire came from the opposite side of the courtyard.

Wilson dived to the ground, leopard-crawled towards the woman in the baseball cap sitting crouched over the person on the ground. As he got closer, she slumped over, rolled to one side and lay still.

Chiyeka, joined by Ngwenya and Mundiya were running from room to room in the compound, shooting and tossing more grenades. The explosions were knocking off the roof sheeting, falling into the courtyard in tiny slivers.

Crawling to the two people lying in the dust, Wilson realised that both were dressed in khaki, wearing M69 type flak jackets. The one lying on his back moaned in pain. The other was a woman, her long strawberry-blond hair fallen across her face. The man's clothing was smouldering, both his legs had the clothing burnt off leaving blackened stumps ... *white phos?*

Trying to comprehend what this meant, Wilson spoke to the man who was still conscious, his eyes flicking from side to side.

'Who are you?' he shouted above the gunfire.

The man turned towards Wilson, a confused look on his face, his unfocused watery eyes seemed vacant.

He tried to speak. His mouth moved but no sound came out. He lifted his hand towards the woman who was still lying curled up in the dust.

A loud groan came from the woman who was beginning to regain her senses. She lifted her head ... it was a mass of blood with a deep cut across the forehead along the hairline, running down her face, dripping off her chin onto her clothing. Matted hair stuck across her face.

Green eyes ...

She looked at him, her eyes blinking as if trying to focus on what or who she was looking at.

'Who the fuck are you?' she shouted.

'We are Rhodesian Security forces ... this is an attack on a terrorist base,' replied Wilson, not sure what to say.

'Fucking murderers!' screamed the woman back at him. The effort seemed too much, her head sagging back into the dirt. It was then Wilson saw the camera hanging around her neck, the man had the word 'Press' stitched onto the front of his flak jacket.

'79, 79 this is 73 do you copy?'

'Roger 73, this is 79 go.'

'I have two reporters in the compound Target Charlie ... both require casevac. Over.'

There was a hesitation from the Commander in the Lynx. All Wilson could hear was the hissing sound of the A76 in his ear. The war in the compound died down, replaced by the sound of flames as the filing cabinets, bedding and wooden furniture in the buildings burned. The smoke was getting thicker all the time.

'*Ikhanka*, are you okay?' asked Cephas Ngwenya, who had finished mopping up with Mundiya and Chiyeka. A few surviving CTs had made their escape, running into the surrounding bush.

Wilson scrambled to his feet.

'Sergeant Meredith has lost two men, Sibanda and Ncube ... they are over there,' pointed Ngwenya across the compound to where Meredith was sitting on the veranda with his surviving trooper, Moyo.

'Fuck!' Wilson looked around him. 'Anyone else hurt?'

'No ... who are these people?' asked Ngwenya.

'These are reporters, that woman has lost a lot of blood. We need to put a drip in. This one is burned ... looks like white phos ... we should put a drip into him as well.'

Wilson could see the telltale yellow necrotic wound with the distinctive smell of garlic. He knew from experience that the chances for the man's survival were low, particularly if he had ingested white phos ... *that explained the vomit all over his flak jacket.* The man was coming in and out of consciousness, moaning loudly in agony. Wilson pulled an ampoule of morphine from around his neck, squeezing the vial into the man's upper arm. Taking out his water bottle, Wilson soaked a few first field dressings and placed them over the worst of the burns.

Ngwenya unclipped his kidney pouch on his webbing belt and pulled out a saline drip and drip kit. The man was beginning to shake as his body went into shock.

'73, 79 do you copy?'

'79, go.'

'Roger, we will get a casevac helicopter to you in ten minutes.'

'79, 73 copied, Target Charlie is secured … you can send Sierra Bravo[6]. Over.'

Wilson crouched over the woman. Working quickly, he tied a tourniquet around the upper arm, attached the giving tube to the drip and squeezed until the clear liquid squirted out of the catheter. As soon as he saw a vein pop in the forearm, he expertly inserted the catheter and taped it in place. The drip began to run immediately. The woman groaned softly.

Meredith and Moyo walked across from the far side of the compound. Both watching blankly as Wilson worked on the two injured reporters.

'Mundiya, hold this drip,' called Wilson.

The male reporter was in a bad way, he had lost blood and his burns were severe, Wilson struggled to find a vein as Ngwenya held the tourniquet as tightly as he could. It was no use … he couldn't do it. Switching to the other arm they repeated the process. This time Wilson managed to get a vein; he then squeezed the bag gently to force the saline into the blood stream.

A G-car spun overhead.

'Okay, we will have to carry these people through the gate to open ground for an LZ. Chiyeka, go ahead and cover us.'

Meredith and Moyo shook out a plastic bivy and rolled the man onto it, then with Meredith and Ngwenya holding the feet, Moyo and Mundiya lifted the mans' shoulders. Wilson slung his rifle then placed the drip on the woman's chest putting his arms under her to lift her up. She looked small but as he hoisted her up baby carry she was surprisingly heavy.

The Selous Scouts pushed through the gate of the compound into the open ground beyond. Wilson lowered the woman gently to the ground, popped blue smoke and called in the helicopter.

Heavy gunfire and explosions continued in the north as Support

---

6   SB, police Special Branch.

Company met fierce resistance from well dug-in trench systems. They were on a different radio frequency so the Selous Scouts could not hear what was going on.

'Jake, are you all right?' moaned the woman, trying to twist her head. 'Jake? ...' Her accent was distinctly American.

Wilson lifted her again his chest heaving from the exertion.

After only thirty metres, Wilson had to stop, laying her back on the ground, panting to regain his breath.

'Your friend's badly injured. A helicopter's coming to fetch you,' said Wilson softly. 'Stay still, or you will pull the drip out.'

The woman jerked her head off the ground. He could see that she was confused, trying to assimilate the sweaty, black streaked face looking down at her.

'Where will you take us? Who are you people?' asked the woman loudly. On the front of her flak jacket the name, 'Burrell' was written in black marker pen.

'I told you, we are Rhodesian Security Forces,' replied Wilson softly, holding up her drip.

'Don't bullshit me, you are all black, the Rhodesians are white,' she replied, there was a venomous edge to her voice despite her injury. Her hair was golden blond, but obscured her facial features matted thick with dirt and blood. Only the fierce green eyes shone through.

'We should shoot the bastards,' chipped in Meredith. 'What are they doing here helping the gooks? Fuck'em I say. Fucking reporters ...'

The woman twisted her head to see who was speaking ... *they sounded white!*

'What's your name,' she asked looking at Wilson.

'Keith.'

'Keith what?'

'Just Keith. What's yours?'

The helicopter spun out of its orbit, flared for a landing, dirt kicked up in a thick cloud as it disappeared into its own dust. Wilson leaned over to protect her face from the flying dust.

'Go' shouted Wilson above the whine of the turbines.

As they lifted the two injured reporters, gunfire erupted from the nearby tree line. Bullets whizzed and spat overhead, dust spurted up from bullet strikes on the ground. They were completely exposed.

Chiyeka dived to the ground, firing the MAG in reply, the belts jumping in the breech as he ripped through a belt of fifty rounds.

'GO' shouted Wilson again, sweeping the woman back up,

struggling forward.

Meredith and Ngwenya lowered the reporter to the ground to return fire, rushing across the open ground towards the tree line. Moyo and Mundiya were left to drag the man wrapped in the bivy across the open ground towards the helicopter.

Chest heaving from the strain of carrying the woman, Wilson tottered forward, his legs burning from the effort. One step in front of the other, legs shaking under the weight.

Bullets zipping past angrily, Wilson focused on the helicopter, one painful step after another. The dust thrown up by the helicopter blades stung, filling the lungs, choking, cramming his eyes with grit. It was virtually impossible to see, Wilson squinted, desperately seeking the door. He could see Moyo and Mundiya ahead of him … Moyo went down in the dust.

It was blinding, a white blizzard, destroying all visibility. Wilson glimpsed the pilot waving his arm urgently. The Choppertech was firing the twin Brownings into the bush. The noise was deafening …

More CTs appeared on the edge of the LZ, firing wildly, a bullet struck the perspex right in front of the pilot's face.

Wilson shoved the woman into the doorway, pushing her as far across as he could, the door gunner grabbed her flak jacket one-handed to haul her inside.

Dashing back to help Mundiya, Wilson hauled the reporter Jake's deadweight up shoving him bodily into the helicopter with the almost empty drip on his chest.

Going back again for the stricken trooper Moyo, Wilson pulled him by his webbing. One of the straps gave way and he fell over, bullet strikes appeared in the dust all around. Wilson had the wounded Moyo under his arm, carrying him as he would a sack of potatoes. Mundiya ran back to help. The helicopter was now taking heavy fire; the pilot was screaming, urging them to hurry.

A jet came over, releasing frantan. The bush disappeared into fire and smoke, so close that the heat forced Wilson to close his eyes. The helicopter's blades bit hard at the air as the pilot applied full take-off power, starting to inch forward.

He was at the door again, he and Mundiya lifting Moyo onto the bench seat. The juddering fire from the Brownings was continuous as the gunner tried desperately to suppress the incoming fire.

Its turbine raced to full power, as the helicopter staggered back into the air, banking into a tight left hand turn, clearly visible green tracer following them as they went. Two more jets strafed the surrounding bush with 30mm cannon. A huge pall of smoke lifted into the air from the burning fran strike.

Wilson and Mundiya stood in the middle of the LZ watching the helicopter climb out … the battleground fell silent, just burning bush and thick acrid smoke drifting in squalls, the chemical frantan smell caught in the back of the throat.

Meredith, Chiyeka and Ngwenya emerged from the bush. Ngwenya waved at Wilson through the smoke.

Helicopters orbited above …

… *Burrell?* Keith Wilson felt a shiver down his spine … *who is she?*

Well, I keep on thinkin' 'bout you
Sister golden hair surprise
And I just can't live without you
Can't you see it in my eyes?

I been one poor correspondent
And I been too, too hard to find
But it doesn't mean
You ain't been on my mind

Will you meet me in the middle
Will you meet me in the air?
Will you love me just a little
Just enough to show you care?

*

A few kilometres to the east, on a low ridge, a man stood up from where he had been sitting. A pair of Zeiss binoculars hung from around his neck. He was dressed in khaki with a tattered fishing vest and bush hat. His face was tanned in the way that showed a lifetime exposed to the elements. He made his way down the hill, agilely jumping from rock to rock. At the bottom was a rough bush track. He walked for a kilometre down the track to where a battered lime-green Datsun 1500 truck was parked, covered in shrubbery cut from the surrounding bush.

On the door, in poorly painted black signwriting read the words, 'Scania Trucks & Parts' …

The man looked at his watch … 09:05am

Contact at Target C

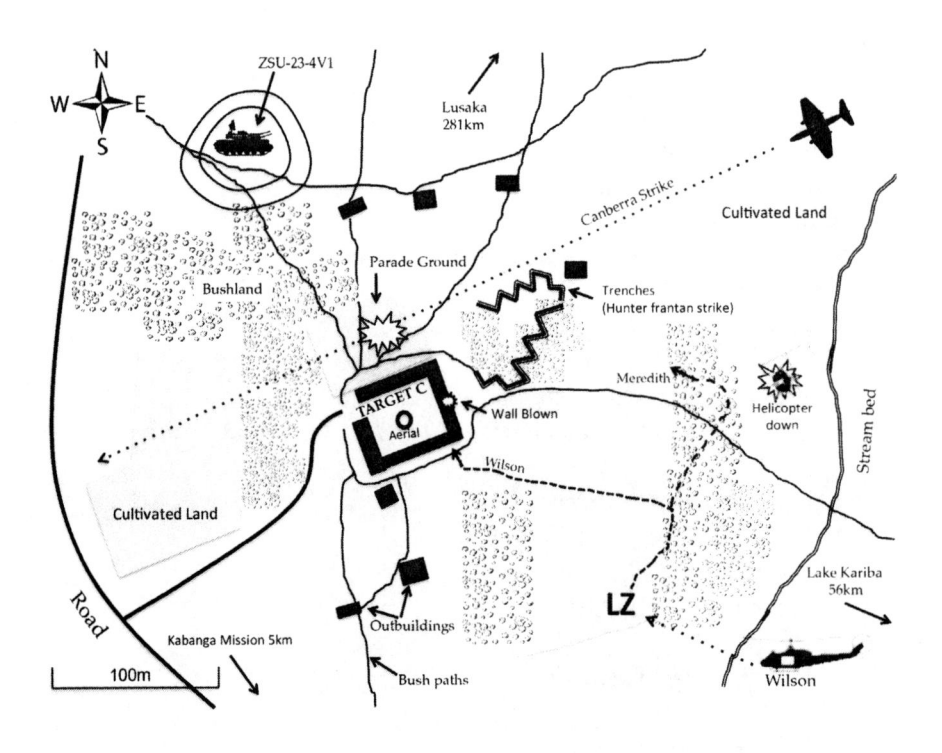

2

Cuban Embassy, Plot 5574 Magoye Road, Kalundu Township, Lusaka, Zambia

Warfare is a means and not an end. Warfare is a tool of revolutionaries. The important thing is the revolution! The important thing is the revolutionary cause, revolutionary ideas, revolutionary objectives, revolutionary sentiments, revolutionary virtues!
Comrade President Fidel Castro, Speech at the memorial service to Ernesto Che Guevara, 8 October 1967.

Comrade Lieutenant-Colonel Julio Ángel Casas sat impassively looking out the window of his office facing Magoye Road in the fashionable suburb of Kalundu in Lusaka, the capital city of Zambia. Casas, in his early thirties, had jet-black hair, cut short, a thick bushy moustache and a dark deeply creviced complexion that showed the ravages of a life spent in the hot sun. He was not a tall man at 5ft 6', but he was lean and physically enormously powerful. As a young man, he had been an accomplished boxer, his twisted nose and deep scar over his left eye made him look menacing, a testament to his commitment. 'Commitment' was a word that described Julio Casas perfectly, his attitude to his family, his work, his country and above all, his glorious leader.

While 'commitment' might have been an appropriate nomenclature for Casas, so too was 'sinister'. He was ambitious to the point of treachery, unrelenting in his quest for power and advancement, nothing and nobody could stand in his way.

As he looked out the window, Casas marvelled at the redness of the Zambian soil and the unrelenting dryness before the rainy season, so similar to his home in the village of San Christobal to the west of Havana. The other similarity with Cuba was poverty and oppression, although in Casas' mind that was the natural consequence of the Revolution. Casas believed implicitly that the people needed Communist-Leninist values. The people needed to be taught what was important for them. Some were slow learners. As the great leader Fidel had said, '...quality of life lies in knowledge, in culture. Values are what constitute true quality of life, the supreme quality of life, even above food, shelter and clothing.'

The similarities between Zambia and Cuba were remarkable.

Kenneth Kaunda and Fidel Castro had been imprisoned for subversive activity. Kaunda was imprisoned for two months in 1955 with hard labour for distributing subversive literature; such imprisonment and other forms of harassment were normal rites of passage for African nationalist leaders.

Both Kaunda and Castro saw themselves as freedom fighters although the closest Kaunda had got to an actual 'struggle' was a few roadblocks and burning down public buildings. Both created a one-party state to exercise dictatorial control over all aspects of political, economic, and cultural life. All political dissent and opposition were ruthlessly suppressed. They both pursued radical economic policies: private commerce and industry were nationalised; sweeping land reforms were instituted; and colonial (in the case of Cuba, American) businesses and agricultural estates were expropriated. For Zambia, the nationalisation of the copper mines had been Kenneth Kaunda's finest hour. Both countries now relied completely on the financial support of foreign powers, the Soviet Union and the People's Republic of China.

Julio Casas was a veteran of the war in Angola, where a 25,000 strong Cuban force had been sent to support the struggle of the Marxist MPLA[7] against forces supported by the imperialist United States. The Portuguese Colony had collapsed in 1975 after a bitter revolutionary war lead by the MPLA's charismatic leader, Agostinho Neto. The USA had intervened militarily, supporting forces from South Africa and Zaire in favour of the FNLA[8] and UNITA[9] opposition groups[10]. It was classic Cold War by proxy, a power struggle between the USA and the Soviet Union, with the Soviets using Cuba as their blunt instrument of revolution while the USA turned a temporary blind-eye to Apartheid South Africa. The expulsion of the South Africans from Angola with their tail between their legs was one of Casas greatest sources of pride. The cost had been high, but victory had been sweet[11]. UNITA and

---

7   *Movimento Popular de Libertação de Angola – Partido do Trabalho* - The People's Movement for the Liberation of Angola – Labour Party
8   *Frente Nacional de Libertação de Angola* - The National Front for the Liberation of Angola - leader Holden Roberto
9   *União Nacional para a Independência Total de Angola* - National Union for the Total Independence of Angola, leader Jonas Savimbi.
10   Cuba had been aiding the MPLA since the mid-1960s, and sent military instructors in 1975. The United States increased funding to the FNLA and for the first time provided funding to UNITA. In response, Cuba sent approximately 1,500 more military personnel, primarily combat troops, by early October to the MPLA. In April 1975, the presidents of Zambia, Tanzania, and Botswana supported Savimbi of UNITA as leader of the Angolan government of national unity.
11   The MPLA indisputably became the major military power in Angola by January 1976; it had the support of approximately 12,000 Cuban military troops and

the FNLA had been chased into the bush where they would rot from disease and starvation.

Casas was the youngest Cuban graduate ever from the General Staff Academy of the Armed Forces of the USSR 'Voroshilov'. It was the senior Soviet professional school for officers. He was one the 'best and the brightest' officers of all the Cuban Revolutionary Armed Forces and therefore selected to attend this most prestigious of all the Soviet academies. His promotion to General was assured. This mission to Zambia was just the stepping-stone he needed to higher honours.

Comrade Casas had been sent to Zambia on a very important mission. To provide leadership and training for the ZIPRA army of freedom fighters that was being built, trained and reinforced for the invasion of the racist rebel state of Rhodesia. The last withered vestige of British colonialism on the African continent.

What Casas had seen on his inspections so far was anything but an invasion force. There was much work to be done.

There was a quiet knock on the door.

'Pasa,' called Casas, snapped out of his reverie.

'Comrade Colonel, we have received a call from the office of the Zambian President. They want to see us urgently,' said Captain Jose Gomez, Casas' *aide de camp*.

'What could those idiots want?' replied Casas, frustrated at the constant interference by the Zambian Government in his mission. All they did was seek to skim money and equipment supplied to the ZIPRA forces by the Soviets.

'They did not say Comrade Colonel, but the person who I spoke to was very agitated,' whispered Gomez, who was fearful of his boss's quick temper.

*

Rhodesian Combined Operations HQ, Milton Buildings, Jameson Avenue, Salisbury, Rhodesia.

Let me say it again. I don't believe in black majority rule ever in Rhodesia, not in a thousand years. I repeat that I believe in blacks and whites working together. If one day it is white and the next day it is black, I believe we have failed and it will be a disaster for Rhodesia.
Ian Smith, Prime Minister of Rhodesia, 20 March 1976

While Colonel Julio Casas hurried across Lusaka for a meeting at State House, a meeting, similar in many respects, was taking place in

---
Soviet arms worth approximately $US200 million.

Salisbury.

Milton Buildings, in Jameson Avenue in Salisbury, was an impressive colonial office block, complete with white plaster and clock tower. Milton Buildings housed the seat of the Cabinet Rooms, the Prime Minister's Office, the Treasury as well as the Ministry of Defence and Air Force HQ amongst other government departments. More recently, it accommodated the offices of Combined Operations; the unit designed for co-ordinating all Rhodesia's activities in prosecuting the war against the Patriotic Front.

The subject of the meeting in Milton Buildings was an analysis of the results of the recent raid by the Selous Scouts and Support Company RAR on the terrorist base near Kabanga Mission in Zambia, code named Operation Valiant.

There were five men in the meeting, all dressed in various uniforms of the armed services, air force, army, police special branch, and a civilian in a suit from the Central Intelligence Organisation (CIO).

An air force officer with Wing Commander stripes on his epaulet brought the meeting to order. In front of him was a 1:50,000 map of the area subjected to the attack, marked with all the targets and the results associated with each.

The Wing Commander cleared his throat.

'Unfortunate business, the dead American reporter,' said Wingco Peter Bowker, addressing the men in the room in a clear authoritative voice.

Peter Bowker was a tall slim man who was a career air force officer and a very accomplished pilot. He had trained at Royal Air Force College Cranwell and was part of the group that brought the first Hawker Hunters to Rhodesia. He was intelligent, resourceful and a good man for tight corners. He had been part of a team that developed the deadly Alpha bouncing bombs as well as refining the now widespread Fireforce quick reaction units.

'They should know better, hanging around terrorist bases. It's a miracle more of them haven't been killed,' replied Major Rob Warner SCR[12], Selous Scouts. Rob Warner had worked his way up through the ranks in the RLI and was a hard-core fighting man. At twenty-eight, he had been selected by Ron Reid-Daly as the head of Intelligence in the Selous Scouts. He was also a veteran of numerous cross-border raids.

'Do we know the news service the dead man was with?' asked Chief Superintendent Jim Winston, BSAP Special Branch – Terrorist

---

12   Silver Cross of Rhodesia.

Desk. Jim Winston was the quintessential policeman, training at Scotland Yard during Federation[13]. He was a supreme gatherer and analyst of intelligence information and had a formidable network of spies and informers throughout the country.

'His name was Jake Gallagher. He was freelance, but the particular story he was working on had been commissioned by Newsweek. He won two awards for work he did in Vietnam. He was accredited with our Department of Internal Affairs, but he was hardly, what you would say, friendly,' replied Deputy Director John Sutcliffe, Branch II, CIO, reading from a file in front of him. John Sutcliffe was in his early forties, thick set, with premature grey hair that made him appear much older than he actually was. As a young man he had trained with MI6, and until UDI[14], was the main liaison with the UK intelligence services.

'What about the woman he was with?' asked Bowker.

'Her name is Sarah Burrell, also freelance, she was working on a story for Associated Press. She is still in Andrew Fleming[15] but will make a full recovery. Interesting ... she was also a veteran of Vietnam, pretty impressive record. Word is she and Gallagher had more than just a professional relationship,' read Sutcliffe from his notes.

'Bastards!' exclaimed the fifth man, Colonel Dudley Coventry, Rhodesian Army Military Intelligence. 'We should string reporters up! Have we given her the third degree?' added Coventry gruffly. He was an old-school army man in his early fifties. Trained at Royal Military College Sandhurst, he had a thick handlebar moustache, twisting it when deep in thought. His intellect was matched only by his arrogant inflexibility.

'I sent one of my female agents down to speak to her, posing as a nurse. That lasted all of ten minutes. She may have a crack on the head

---

13 The Federation of Rhodesia and Nyasaland lasted from 1953 to 1963. Decolonizing pressure from the United Nations, the Organisation of African Unity and African nationalist organisations doomed the Federation to failure. Northern Rhodesia gained independence from the UK as the new nation of Zambia and Nyasaland gained independence as the new nation of Malawi. Southern Rhodesia became known as Rhodesia and remained in political limbo.
14 The Unilateral Declaration of Independence (commonly referred to as UDI) was a statement adopted by the Cabinet of Rhodesia on 11 November 1965, announcing that Rhodesia, a British colony in southern Africa that had governed itself since 1923, regarded itself as an independent sovereign state. The culmination of a protracted dispute between the British and Rhodesian governments regarding the terms under which the latter could become fully independent, it was the first unilateral break from the United Kingdom since the United States Declaration of Independence nearly two centuries before.
15 General Hospital

but she is on the ball ... filthy mouth on her. They had to move her into a private room, her language was peeling paint off the walls,' laughed Sutcliffe. 'We won't get much there I am afraid.'

The men all smiled at the mental image of the American reporter swearing at the CIO officer.

'Right, let's get on,' said Bowker. 'From all accounts we got very little in the form of document intelligence from the raid. The use of white phos grenades and bunker bombs was not conducive to intelligence gathering.'

'Just a minute, we were getting our arses shot off. Who fucked up the int[16] on those trenches ... and the ZSU ... we lost two dead and one wounded,' interrupted Major Warner, raising his voice. His eyes flicked from man to man as if he was about to leap across the table and belt anyone who cast aspersions against the men of his unit. The real risk was that he would do precisely that.

'Steady on Rob, nobody is suggesting your men did anything wrong. It was just that the buildings, unfortunately, were largely burnt out,' replied Bowker, trying to calm Warner down. 'We lost two good men when that helicopter went down.'

Warner grunted a response and sat back in his chair, clearly very unhappy with the implication.

'We got three pretty good captures,' interjected Jim Winston from SB. 'They have been squealing blue murder. It will take us a few more days to get all their jabbering down, but there is some interesting stuff already.'

'Yes?' questioned Bowker, eager to hear.

'Well, the most senior man is a Political Commissar who claims to have been trained at Patrice Lumumba University[17] in Moscow,' stated Winston. He had the undivided attention of all in the room. 'Nice piece of Russian skirt for a girlfriend judging by the photograph in his wallet.' Winston was enjoying spinning out the story.

'Go on please, Jim,' added Bowker gently, hiding his frustration, always the gentleman.

'It appears that the terrorists are about to get some help from

---

16 Intel, Intelligence
17 The university opened its doors in 1960, at the height of the Cold War, providing a training ground for young communists from developing countries. The terrorist Carlos the Jackal studied at this university, along with terrorists and revolutionaries from Latin America, Africa, Middle East and Asia. It was called Patrice Lumumba University, in honor of a first prime minister of the former Zaire, who was killed in a coup blamed on the United States.

Cuba. Our man says that Cuban advisors were expected at the camp any day now. The Soviets apparently refused to supply more men, so the Cubans have stepped in. He tells us that they were going to get a Cuban battalion commander and a few Company Commanders. Interesting …'

'That is a pretty significant escalation,' chipped in Dudley Coventry from Military Intelligence, already twisting at his moustache.

'Yes, he also confirmed what we have known for some time, ZIPRA are being trained for a conventional attack across the northern borders. He identified at least three training camps that we were previously unaware of … we are a little behind the eight ball on some of this stuff.'

'Do we know where the camps are?' asked Warner.

'No, he could tell us the names but not the location with any accuracy, only the rough geographical region.'

'Shit, we are going to have to get onto this ASAP,' said Warner, concern in his voice.

'John, can your agents in Lusaka help?' asked Bowker, addressing Sutcliffe from the CIO.

'We are tasking them as we speak, but it may take some time.'

It was well known in the Rhodesian intelligence community that the CIO operated agents in Zambia, Mozambique and Botswana, in fact, even further afield in Tanzania and Kenya.

'Anything else you can say Jim?' asked Bowker, turning back to Jim Winston.

'Only that the Zambians are getting Migs … but we have heard that for years.'

'Well, lots to think about gentlemen,' ended Bowker.

The debrief on Operation Valiant continued for a further hour before Bowker closed the meeting.

Just as they were preparing to leave, Jim Winston from SB interrupted.

'Oh, by the way, I probably should have mentioned this earlier, but it appears that the Soviet Strela SAM 7[18] is now being introduced to the terrorists in greater numbers,' said Winston, clearly a little embarrassed that he had not brought the subject up earlier.

'Yes, we captured one some time back and the air force has been conducting tests on it,' added Bowker.

'We have now established that the terrorists have fired unsuccessfully on civilian aircraft,' added Winston. He now had

18   SAM-7 Soviet, Strela, shoulder fired, ground-to-air, infrared, heat-seeking missile.

the undivided attention of the others. Winston continued, 'Our investigations show that they had a crack at a RUAC[19] aircraft at Victoria Falls. We have also found undeniable proof of a launch two thousand metres west of runway one-two at Victoria Falls.'

It was possible to hear a pin drop.

'How can you be so sure?' asked Bowker incredulously.

'We found a carry tube for a SAM-7. They are definitely in the hands of a few terrorist bands inside the country. These things are deadly to low flying aircraft. God knows what would happen if they take down a civilian airliner,' replied Winston earnestly.

'Surely they wouldn't do that!' interjected Coventry. 'They wouldn't dare!'

'Let's hope not. We have informed Air Rhodesia and South African Airways of the threat,' replied Winston.

'The air force are already taking steps to shroud the engines on the Alouette IIIs and the exhausts on the Dakotas. I had no idea that the terrorists have made unsuccessful strikes. We have no reports of attacks on our aircraft as yet,' added Bowker, his face showing signs of strain.

The threat of these missiles could not be underestimated ... by anyone ...

'What was Air Rhodesia's reaction?' asked Bowker, turning to face Winston.

'I believe they have instructed their pilots to vary their approach angles and take-off tracks. They have no intention of shrouding the Viscount engines at this time,' replied Winston. 'A little perplexing really, but there it is, they have been warned.'

'What was SAAs reaction?' asked Coventry, the question on everyone's lips.

'They seemed unfazed. I spoke to their Chief Training Captain. He told me that they were designing a few evasive manoeuvres on landing and taking off, but they have no plans to stop flying to Victoria Falls,' replied Winston.

'There would be serious political fall out if they did,' said Bowker. Then trying to lighten the mood he added, 'Those 737 jockeys will have a bit of fun flying at treetop level, most of them are ex-mirage pilots.'

The meeting broke up and the men left the room, all deep in thought.

Major Rob Warner gathered his files, carefully set his beret, with

---

19 RUAC, Rhodesia United Air Carriers (est. 1957)

the distinctive light brown with the silver Osprey badge[20], and left the building. This news needed to get back to his boss Colonel Ron Reid-Daly immediately.

The shit was about to hit the fan …

*

Selous Scout HQ, Andre Rabie Barracks, Inkomo Barracks, 40km northwest of Salisbury

Lieutenant Keith *Ikhanka* Wilson and his team, Sergeant Cephas Ngwenya, Troopers Richard Mundiya and Stanley Chiyeka, stood waiting under a tree next to the Orderly Room at Andre Rabie Barracks. The Selous Scouts HQ was tucked away in a corner of the sprawling military base called Inkomo Barracks. Heat haze shimmered off the corrugated iron rooftops and the tarmac in the carpark as if a lake of cool, sparkling water. It was hot, blisteringly hot, like only the Rhodesian bush can get before the rains set in. The men were all sweating profusely despite being in the shade of the tree.

They were waiting for their instructions for transport back to Bulawayo. Each was dressed neatly in camouflage uniform with Selous Scout beret and stable belt. All wore the ubiquitous soft suede 'veldskoens' that had been brushed clean giving them a distinctive off-white hue. All were unshaven, with long unruly hair, making keeping the beret in place a challenge.

The four men belonged to 3 Group, Selous Scouts based in Bulawayo. Their group specialised in operations against the Matabele-dominated ZIPRA.

As they stood waiting, Keith Wilson's mind wondered back to the woman with reddish blond hair that he had carried to the helicopter. *Burrell* … The whole episode seemed surreal, nothing remotely like it had ever happened before to anyone in the Selous Scouts. A wounded female reporter in the middle of an external raid … He couldn't get the girl out of his mind … he had detected a fire in her … like no other woman he had ever met.

> *Well, I keep on thinkin' 'bout you*
> *Sister golden hair surprise*
> *And I just can't live without you*
> *Can't you see it in my eyes?*

---

20   Osprey bird of prey, in its stylized 'striking' pose. This was the adopted insignia for the 'Scouts', it was most recognized when worn on their brown beret, it could also be found on the stable belt when in garrison or parade.

Wilson had not much experience of women; he had never had a proper girlfriend. His experience, very unsatisfactory sex behind the railway workshops with one of the girls from the typing pool. A few forgettable ships passing through the night since …

Wilson was in his mid-twenties, his dark curly hair, and olive skin was a product of his Greek mother. He was second generation Rhodesian. His grandfather had come out to Rhodesia from England after the First World War. His father Lance Wilson had fought in the deserts of North Africa during the Second World War with the Long Range Desert Group.

At 5ft 11', Wilson had a thin sinewy body, with the enormous strength and endurance of a marathon runner. His wiry beard and curly black hair made him look very similar to Cat Stevens, from the cover of his 1973 album *Foreigner*. A lot of people commented on the similarity, he was happy with the comparison … *didn't Cat Stevens also have a Greek mother?*

Wilson would be described as an introvert. He enjoyed a few beers in the pub with his friends, but he was not a heavy drinker. He had always been a bit of a loner, being brought up on a farm near Gwanda in southern Matabeleland. His childhood friends had been the black kids from the local village. That also explained his fluent command of siNdebele and his encyclopaedic knowledge of Matabele custom. This made him a formidable pseudo-operator. He could literally click from being a white man to a black man as if flicking a light switch.

Being from a farming family, he had been sent to boarding school, Gifford Technical High School in Bulawayo. He hated school and struggled to make friends, happier mixing with the black kitchen workers in the compound at the bottom of the school grounds. He ran middle distance. Running was an escape for him, quite happy to spend hours at the track, his only communication with Mr Grey, the athletics coach who was also his housemaster. Academically nothing interested him other than art and technical drawing.

At the end of O-level, Wilson decided that further study was useless and started an apprenticeship as a fitter & turner on the Rhodesian Railways. As with all young men, he got his call-up papers for National Service but deferred for the three years needed to get his trade completed. Being older than the other recruits when he went into National Service gave him an advantage plus his natural strength and fitness set him apart. He was put up for officer training, as he had a trade.

At the School of Infantry in Gwelo he had, as his Course Officer, the then Lieutenant Rob Warner. The two got on from the very start so it was natural that Warner convinced him to try for Selous Scout selection. Now, two years later, he was one of their brightest stars, having also completed a combat engineer's and demolitions course.

As the men watched, a door opened in the Admin Block. Colonel Ron Reid-Daly walked onto the covered veranda in front of his office. He stood hands on hips, scanning the courtyard between the buildings.

Spotting the men standing next to the Ops Room, he yelled out, 'Lieutenant Wilson ... Sergeant Ngwenya, come here.'

Reid-Daly had come up through the ranks, the first RSM in the RLI. His voice had not lost any of its parade-ground power.

The two men walked briskly across to where their CO stood. The Colonel watched as they approached, a broad smile on his face. They did not salute. He shook their hands firmly.

The Colonel had a personal relationship with all his men, particularly those who had excelled as these had done. The Scouts were not hot on military protocol, most troopers and NCOs called each other by their first names. Reid-Daly was called 'Boss', 'Uncle Ron' or 'Colonel'. He was tough on his men and he was tough on himself. His devotion and dedication to the Selous Scouts and his deep concern for the welfare of his men earned him loyalty and respect. These men would follow him unquestioningly into the 'valleys of death' the Honde, the Save, the Pungwe, the Buzi, the Limpopo and the Zambezi.

'What can we do for you Boss?' asked Wilson irreverently, a mischievous smile on his face. There was little standing on ceremony in the Selous Scouts.

'Come into my office.'

It was cooler inside the office. A ceiling fan was spinning wildly, beating the air like a wayward helicopter. The blades were out of balance making the whole thing oscillate alarmingly, threatening to tear itself from its mountings.

Major Rob Warner was already sitting at a meeting table. He stood up as the men walked in, greeting them with a smile. Cephas Ngwenya had not been inside the Colonel's office before. He couldn't help but look around. There was a strong smell of Cobrawax floor polish. One wall was covered with a large-scale map of Rhodesia with pins stuck in numerous places. A flag of the former Malayan Union was on the opposite wall, testimony to the Colonel's time with 'C' Squadron SAS during the anti-communist Malayan Emergency in 1951 – 1953. Photographs of the Colonel with various people, including group photographs from the RLI and courses he had been on, filled the wall behind his desk. His RLI pace-stick was mounted in a wooden frame immediately above his head.

'Sit down please,' ordered the Colonel pointing to two empty chairs at the table. He made casual conversation sound like parade ground drill ... ... *left, right, left, right ... left ... leeeft wheel!*

The Colonel remained standing, hands clasped behind his back, his chin pushed forward pugnaciously.

'I will get straight to the point. We need to infiltrate a team into Lusaka to recover some vital intelligence,' stated Reid-Daly, never a man to waste words on pleasantries and introductions.

Wilson and Ngwenya glanced at each other unable to mask their shock ... the impact was a slap in the gut. Wilson could feel the blood draining from his head. There was a huge difference between pseudo ops in the bush or cross border raids, and infiltration into a heavily populated city ... in a foreign country. The mind boggled.

Both men chose to stay silent.

'You need to understand that this will be extremely dangerous. I am not ordering you to go, I am looking for volunteers. This is no ordinary reconnaissance. In any external operation we would move heaven and earth to get you out. We would use the whole air force if we had to. But with this mission, if you are compromised, there will be nothing we can do for you. In fact, we will probably disown you. You will be tortured and sent to prison, at worst you will be executed by hanging or firing squad.'

Reid-Daly was clearly uncomfortable with this part of the briefing, changing weight on his feet.

Ngwenya felt a trickle of sweat run down his back. The thought of being hanged made him blanch.

The Colonel barrelled on.

'We have come across some disturbing information on Cuban involvement in Zambia and we can't rely on those pricks at the CIO to come up with the goods ... and of course we know that COMOPS leaks like a sieve. We are going to do this ourselves!' Reid-Daly stood perfectly upright studying the faces of his men. His sentences were delivered as a crack of the whip.

Wilson and Ngwenya remained impassive ... they did not scare easily ... but this was different ...

'You will be disguised as hunting guides, working for Norman Barr Hunting and Fishing Safaris. A mate of mine from C Squadron days runs an operation in South Luangwa ... it will be a great cover for you ... we will HALO[21] drop you into his hunting camp and you will take it from there. He has an admin office in Lusaka which will be your base of operations.' The Colonel now had a beaming smile on his face, clearly enormously satisfied with the plan he had concocted ... it was brilliant!

'How long will we be in Lusaka, Boss?' asked Wilson offhandedly, as if he was asking for the time of day.

'Until the job is done,' clipped the Colonel ... *stupid question.*

'I don't speak the language Sir. I have a little Chitonga,' said Ngwenya almost at a whisper.

'That should not be a problem, they mostly speak English.'

Ngwenya chose not to respond, it was no use, the Colonel had demonstrated the white man's naivety in these matters. While the official language was English, the language of the street was what was important, that was where the information they needed would be hidden. While Zambia had at least 12 language groups, the area around Lusaka was mainly Tonga or Chitonga.

Cephas Ngwenya was not a physically imposing man despite his family name, *Ngwenya,* meaning 'crocodile' in siNdebele. While he was slightly built, he had the hunting instincts of a crocodile, silence, patience, and speed, with the attack vicious and deadly. Cephas was softly spoken, with a more serious attitude towards life but quick to smile. His face was that of a man with honest emotions, the only blemish being two parallel scars on his left cheek from his initiation ceremony into manhood. He was a Matabele by birth being brought up in a district called Tjolotjo about 100km northwest of Bulawayo in Matabeleland.

At twenty-nine, Cephas was an ex-policeman, trained by Special Branch in intelligence gathering and counter-insurgency. His father's time in the police force had inspired Cephas to follow in his footsteps. Cephas had been part of the original 'pilot' pseudo scheme set up by the police Special Branch[22]. When the Selous Scouts were formed in late 1973, Ngwenya volunteered for selection primarily because he had heard that the pay would be more than double what he had been earning in the police. That had proved not to be completely correct, but the danger and excitement provided by the Scouts had compensated to some degree. Sgt Ngwenya had achieved much success from the Selous Scout base in Bulawayo against ZIPRA, including a very successful

---

21 High altitude, Low Opening.
22 Set up by Superintendent Peterson of Special Branch in Salisbury in January 1973. The first few, largely unsuccessful, deployments with the team were in Bushu and Madziwa Tribal Trust Lands.

'snatch' of senior ZIPRA officers on the road between Gaborone and Francistown in Botswana. That mission had earned him the BCR. As with most black people in Rhodesia, he was also fluent in seShona, the language of the majority of the population.

Being the eldest of six children, Cephas had been brought up with a sense of responsibility. It was expected that he would take over the family land and cattle and look after his four brothers and two sisters. He would be described as a man of few words, happy with his own company. Softly spoken, Ngwenya would seldom raise his voice no matter what the provocation. He always seemed to be within himself, with the situation under control. With nerves of steel his was a good man in a crisis.

He had no articulated political convictions other than his tribal and clan affiliations within his district of Tjolotjo. His view was that the terrorist forces were misguided with corrupt leadership. The concept of a democracy where people voted for leadership was foreign to him. In his mind leaders came from tribal law, where chiefs came from ruling families. The tribal chiefs had to negotiate political rights from the white man. That had been the case since the white man came. *These men Nkomo and Mugabe were not chiefs, they did not come from ruling families, what status did they carry? Were not the Council of Chiefs at the forefront of negotiating with the white man?*

Ngwenya's position in the police had given him a good income that had allowed him to raise *lobolo* for his wife, Nomsa. His family still thought he was in the police force; they would have been horrified to hear he was in the Selous Scouts. That information would have put his family in grave danger from the ZIPRA terrorists operating in the Nata region. Tjolotjo was the centre of the Nata TTLs. The fact that he was a policeman and from a respected family meant that the terrorists left him and his family alone. In any event, many of the ZIPRA cadres were friends of his from school; they were neighbours, herded cattle together as children, playing amongst the granite kopjes that surrounded the district. A terrorist landmine killed Cephas's father while out on patrol. Two of his ZIPRA friends had come out of the bush to attend the funeral. The war had so many contradictions - that's just the way it was.

Nomsa was the daughter of a headman and had high status. The cost of the *lobolo* had been high, six cattle, ten goats and $100 in cash. It was still the best decision of his life. He loved Nomsa more than life itself. His son Matthew was only two years old, he wanted to watch his son grow.

He enjoyed the informality of the unit and the freedom of movement it offered during operations[23]. Most importantly, he enjoyed working with *Ikhanka* Wilson, the closest thing to a white brother that Ngwenya could imagine. They had a deep, almost telepathic, understanding. It made them an awesome combination.

'Your primary mission is to establish the location of enemy troop concentrations and logistical bases. You are to establish the Cuban presence and the location of their operations. We will give you addresses, maps, aerial photographs of all known offices and bases of ZAPU and ZIPRA in Lusaka ... any questions so far?'

Wilson and Ngwenya remained stony faced.

'I would like you to try to snatch one of these Cubans ... if you kill a few on the way that would also be helpful. You will be given fake passports, so you will need to swot up on your cover stories,' continued Reid-Daly. 'We will send you in with a TR48 radio so you can transmit sitreps. A set of codes will be used to phone numbers in Johannesburg and Francistown as back-up.'

'How will we get out if we are compromised Boss?' asked Wilson, this was the $64,000 question.

Reid-Daly cleared his throat, glancing across at Warner for a split second.

'By helicopter, Lusaka is in range of our new Cheetahs. We will give you emergency codes ... We will use helicopters to pick up your Cuban once you have got him.'

Wilson kept his face passive, showing no sign of concern. Ngwenya was doing the same, although their insides told a different story.

'I've always wanted an all expenses paid trip to Lusaka. Take in the sights ... should be fun,' laughed Wilson.

The Colonel smiled back. 'Good, Major Warner will complete the briefing, we need to choose a codeword for you, any ideas?'

---

23 The black soldiers in the Selous Scouts were recruited from all branches of the police and army; many came from the Rhodesian African Rifles. The Selous Scouts were trained in so-called 'pseudo' operations. They were taught to pose as terrorists, to infiltrate the terrorist organisation. They were taught how to infiltrate a village, how to approach a band of terrorists in the field, passwords, pass signs, liberation songs and how to collect food from the local population. The skills the Scouts were taught included 'turning' captured terrorists; the unit had already recruited a good many 'converts', who now enthusiastically fought with the Rhodesian forces against their previous comrades.

'No Sir'

'How about Cat Stevens?' joked Warner.

'Sounds as good as any … you leave in two days … good luck.' The Colonel missed the joke completely.

'Thank you Boss,' smiled Wilson.

Ngwenya kept a nondescript grin.

What would become of my family if I am killed?

'That crow that you found in Zambia will make a full recovery,' added Warner, addressing Wilson.

'That is good news Sir, do we know her name?' replied Wilson, hiding his interest as best he could.

'Sarah something,' replied Warner.

'Sarah Burrell.'

'That's it.'

The Colonel moved towards the door. 'Oh, by the way, one final thing. You may be required to execute a special operation with little notice,' said Reid-Daly, uncharacteristically softly.

'What would that be Boss?'

'Killing Joshua Nkomo!'

3

State House, Independence Avenue, Lusaka, the official Residence and Offices of the President of Zambia

> *Some people draw a comforting distinction between 'force' and 'violence'. I refuse to cloud the issue by such word-play. The power which establishes a state is violence; the power which maintains it is violence; the power which eventually overthrows it is violence. Call an elephant a rabbit only if it gives you comfort to feel that you are about to be trampled to death by a rabbit.*
> Kenneth David Kaunda, President of Zambia[24].

Comrade Lieutenant-Colonel Julio Ángel Casas and his aide Captain Jose Gomez, waited patiently outside the office of His Excellency the President of Zambia. Both were dressed in blue business suits, each had a briefcase at their feet and a business hat on their laps. The hats were more in the style of the late sixties than the late seventies.

The two Cubans were seated on high-backed chairs set against the wall in a circular anteroom. There were no windows in the room and the atmosphere was hot and stuffy. The air-conditioning had long since given up the ghost. The walls were all wood-panelled to waist height, adorned with huge portrait paintings of the President. In front of them was an impressive wood-carved double door. The floor was highly polished parquet tiles that shone in the bright light from a skylight in the vaulted ceiling.

Two armed guards standing at parade-rest flanked the double doors, dressed in the light green uniform of the Presidential Guard. Both had British SLR rifles with varnished wooden stocks on brilliant white ceremonial rifle-slings. A secretary sat at a large wooden desk to the left of the double doors. She was dressed in the brightly patterned traditional caftan with a huge elaborate headdress made of the same material. She was typing deliberately with two fingers on a Royal Sabre typewriter with a manual carriage return. This she banged emphatically with the completion of each line.

Tick ... tick ... tick ... tring! was the only sound in the room

Casas studied the guards with the eye of a seasoned military professional ... *I doubt whether those rifle magazines even have rounds in them ...*

The sound of approaching footsteps along the passage carried into

---

24 The first President of Zambia in 1964 as head of the UNIP party.

the anteroom. In swept His Excellency Esteban Lazio the Ambassador of the Republic of Cuba and his entourage. Lazio was a second cousin to the Great Leader and played it for all it was worth. He was a short obnoxious man in a black business suit, with a thick black moustache, his face almost covered by a pair of thick-rimmed dark glasses.

Never before had Julio Casas met a person that he despised more.

'Comrade Ambassador, I did not realise you were coming to this meeting,' said Casas standing up.

'You don't need to know everything Casas!' replied the Ambassador with obvious distaste. The ill feeling between the men was mutual.

Casas chose not to rise to the bait, this pig wasn't worth jeopardising his career for.

A buzzer rang on the desk.

The elaborately dressed secretary leaned over in a disinterested fashion and pressed the intercom. The voice on the other side carried across the room in clear accented English.

'Send them in!'

Not responding or looking up from what she was doing, the secretary gave a vague, dismissive flick of the wrist. That appeared to be enough for the guards, who stretched across and pushed the doors open.

The Ambassador, full of his own importance, marched purposefully through the doors into the room. Julio Casas assumed that he was to follow, Gomez a step behind him.

The room was dimly lit, with more than half of the down-lights without bulbs. A giant wooden meeting table dominated the room, lined in the centre by a neat row of Coca-Cola bottles, stretching uninterrupted into the distance. In the poor light the person at the head of the table was difficult to see. The walls were dominated by paintings of the President in different imperial poses, with an enormous flag of the Republic of Zambia behind the head of the table.

Unsure of which side of the table to navigate, Casas chose to follow his ambassador's entourage, their shoes clicking loudly on the parquet floor.

'Welcome, Comrade Ambassador of the glorious Republic of Cuba,' boomed a voice from the gloom.

As Casas approached, he noted two other men seated at the table.

Hindered by the poor light and dark glasses, the Ambassador was uncertain of the source of the loud welcome. He stopped, twisting his head to one side as if to pinpoint the sound. His sudden halt caused one of his aides to bump into him, followed by a concertina effect as they all tried to stop at the same time.

The man at the head of the table stood up and rushed forward to welcome the Cuban delegation. He was the President of Zambia, Kenneth David Kaunda.

Arriving with an expansive flourish, the President spun His Excellency Esteban Lazio around, then clamped him with a warm embrace as if he was a long lost friend. The enthusiasm of the President's welcome knocked off the Ambassador's treasured sunglasses. They fell to the hard wooden floor with a loud clatter.

Lazio, clearly flustered by such a passionate greeting, stood back searching the dimly lit floor for his sunglasses. The President stepped back, both men studying the floor intently.

An ominous crunch heralded the demise of the sunglasses. Lazio whimpered in distress, they had cost him nearly a month's pay. Ray-Ban Wayfarer sunglasses were Lazio's only submission to decadent capitalism.

One of Lazio's aides dived to the floor to retrieve the sunglasses, passing them back to his leader. Lazio held them up to what little light there was. One of the lenses had a diagonal crack across the length of it. The Ambassador let out a forlorn sigh of resignation …

Undaunted, the President swept his arm in the direction of the other men at the table.

'Comrade Ambassador, let me introduce you to His Excellency Comrade Professor Vassily Solodovnikov, the director of the African Institute of the USSR Academy of Sciences and Ambassador to Zambia, and Comrade Colonel Lev Kononov. Colonel Kononov is the head of the Soviet advisory delegation to Comrade Joshua Nkomo's Zimbabwe African People's Union and its military wing the Zimbabwean People's Revolutionary Army.' The President was on a roll waving his arms in a flourish.

'Comrade Solodovnikov is the architect of the Soviet 'Bridge across Central Africa' policy to train Freedom Fighters to overthrow the white racist colonial regimes in Rhodesia, South West Africa and South Africa,' stated the President expansively, in a booming voice as if addressing a UNIP[25] rally. He was a man who loved the pomp, ceremony and protocol of his high office.

Vassily Solodovnikov smiled and bowed graciously at the compliment. He was a great favourite of the Zambian President, his

---

25 United National Independence Party (UNIP), the only legal political party in Zambia. The constitution was altered and promulgated in August 25, 1973, and the national elections that followed in December 1973 were the final steps in achieving what was called a 'one-party participatory democracy'.

patient, unaggressive style, coupled with an impressive understanding of Africa, put him in good stead.

Lazio introducing the members of his delegation, pointedly leaving Julio Casas till last.

The President was surprisingly tall, with a wide beaming smile, dressed neatly in a dark brown Chinese *Sun Yat-sen* suit, with turn-down military-style collar, four patch pockets and five centre-front buttons. He wore these suits as a 'uniform', a gift from the People's Republic of China, his greatest benefactor.

The four pockets were said to represent the Four Cardinal Principles cited in the classic *Book of Changes*[26] and understood by the Chinese as fundamental principles of conduct: propriety, justice, honesty and a sense of shame. The five centre-front buttons were said to represent the five powers of the constitution of the Republic; Executive, Legislative, Judicial, Examination and Control. The three cuff-buttons were to symbolise the Three Principles of the People; nationalism, democracy and the people's livelihood or socialism. Casas was convinced that the President had no idea of the symbolic significance of his uniform, nor did he subscribe to its philosophical principles.

Casas stepped forward to shake the hand of the President, the contrast between his broad smile and warm welcome and his touch was shocking, sending a shiver down his spine. The hand felt limp, unresponsive and clammy. Casas shook the proffered hand, fighting the urge to recoil.

Waved to the seats around the table, the Cubans sat down. Two empty Coke bottles were in front of the President, he leaned forward to grab another, flicking off the top expertly with a silver bottle opener emblazoned with the British coat of arms. The bottle opener was passed around the table to allow others to partake in this elixir of the gods, warm, straight out the bottle.

Poor Gomez chose a bottle that had been given a 'fright', bursting foam and spray over his white shirt as he opened it. Gomez feverishly tried to mop up the spill with his handkerchief.

The President burst into laughter at Gomez's distress. Casas suspected that the President had given the bottle a good shake, for just this outcome. Still laughing, the President passed down a white handkerchief to help Gomez clean up the mess.

'Young man how old are you?' asked the President addressing

---

26 The *I Ching* or *Book of Changes* is one of the oldest of the Chinese classical texts. The book contains a divination system comparable to European Middle Ages geomancy or the West African *Ifa* system; in modern East Asia, it is still widely used for this purpose.

Lazio.

'I am forty-six, Comrade President,' replied Lazio, clearly perplexed by the introductory question.

'Full of wisdom, full of experience, full of commitment following Fidel Castro's programmes and activities,' said Kaunda waving his hand towards Lazio, another white handkerchief wrapped around his left wrist. 'The West can call Fidel Castro ugly names but we stand by you because we know where we come from and all we have in common. Zambia is very grateful for what Cuba is doing for Africa and in particular Zambia. Cuba has assisted us in the fight against colonialism and imperialism.'

Ambassador Lazio was unprepared for such a speech, his eyes intermittently flicking from side to side as a frightened schoolboy in front of the headmaster. The Soviets across the room sat impassively, all eyes on the Ambassador, waiting for his response. A flicker of a smile crossed Vassily Solodovnikov's face.

Gathering his thoughts, Lazio rose to his feet. Drawing himself up to his full 5ft 5' he began …

'We the people of Cuba extend to you a brotherly greeting, an embrace from the bottom of our hearts for a colleague in the struggle for justice, a symbol of the African struggle for independence. You are a symbol for all of Africa, a living symbol for all those African heroes who fought like you and you are also the symbol of the bond between Cuba and Africa and Zambia in particular,' stated Lazio in a formal response, quoting his speech given at the occasion of the presentation of his credentials. He returned to his seat, staring defiantly across the table at the two Russians.

Take that sports lovers!

'Well said Comrade!' applauded Kaunda, in obvious delight, enjoying himself immensely. 'Where would we be by now if Cuba had not given a hand to these African countries in the fight for their freedom?' he asked rhetorically. 'How can we thank you sufficiently except to support you and to tell your people to continue the fight.'

Casas could not believe what he was hearing, he had been called to a meeting that was turning into the mutual admiration society. He glanced across the table to where the Soviets sat deadpan.

Not yet satisfied, President Kaunda continued in the same impassioned vein, 'We cannot forget to mention that great son of Cuba, a great son of Africa as well, Fidel Castro. He has guided Cuba well towards assisting Africa in a big way. And we thank you, the Cuban people, for supporting us, through One Zambia, One Nation. Now I say One Cuba, One Nation… we must continue to stand together as Comrade Fidel Castro taught us. He has given us a good example of working together, in full solidarity for the good of humanity. Cuba has done wonderful things. I can only pray to God for your continued guidance.'

Here it comes … thought Casas.

'We must defend ourselves from our enemies. Many persons in Zambia feel it is too much. I am a believer in non-violence, it was one thing to attack combatants but another to attack civilians and infrastructure. My students at University of Zambia are demonstrating … they want guns! … They want war! They have marched to State House. I have announced the mobilisation of my army and activated the reserve and Home Guard.'

The President was in full voice now using his hands expansively to make his point.

'We need your soldiers to train our people, we need your pilots for our aeroplanes … we need your missiles to shoot down our enemies, the racist colonial pigs to the south,' wailed Kaunda, pointing to the metaphorical 'south', gazing evangelically towards the ceiling as if the ghostly enemy aircraft were overhead at that very moment. His voice became wracked with emotion, as if delivering a Shakespearian soliloquy. 'We cannot defend ourselves against their aggression,' he pleaded, dabbing his misty eyes with his handkerchief.

Lazio sat bolt upright, riveted to his seat, his mind racing for a suitable response to this passionate appeal.

The Russians gazed fixedly ahead.

'Comrade President, didn't the British already send you missiles?' enquired Lazio, gathering his thoughts.

'Yes they did. Now, what were they called?' the President sat deep in thought. 'Cat something … Tigercat, yes that's right Tigercat[27] … but alas they are all broken. They needed the little wire out the back that was too difficult for my people. We need automatic missiles!'

'Comrade President, why don't our brothers the Soviets supply new missiles? After all, our missiles are their missiles,' asked Lazio, conspiracy in his voice, he faced the Soviets across the table.

Professor Vassily Solodovnikov almost leapt out of his chair.

'Comrade President!' urged Solodovnikov, 'our commitment is to the freedom struggle of the people of Zimbabwe, to Comrade Joshua Nkomo and his brave forces. This is our immediate priority.'

'But we are being attacked. They fly over my land and the land of

---

27   Wire-guided missile.

my ancestors. We must stop them!' pleaded Kaunda, dabbing his eye again.

As Casas watched in the gloomy light he was certain the President was crying.

'Comrade President, once we have attained victory over the rebel regime in Zimbabwe, there will be no need for missiles. That must be our priority,' said Solodovnikov, softening his tone. Then changing his intonation to one of collusion, 'Comrade President, is it not the obligation of your previous colonial masters to provide for your defence?'

'What do you mean?' asked Kaunda sharply.

'The freedom struggle in Africa is the priority of the Soviet Union and the Republic of Cuba. You have your freedom Comrade President, it is up to Britain and the United Nations to protect you,' replied Solodovnikov with a clear note of authority in his voice. He had many years of experience as a diplomat in Africa, his true role being that of a senior KGB officer.

'How can Britain help me?'

'Ask them for their latest missiles Comrade President, they have an absolute obligation to protect you.'

Kaunda sat back in contemplation, ... he was thinking, his fingers splayed in front of him in open prayer, the tips being tapped together. His eyes lit up ...

'You are right ... they are the ones ... they must protect me and my people.' Kaunda's voice rose up again as he grasped a solution.

Not to be overshadowed by his Soviet counterpart, Lazio interrupted, 'We the people of the Republic of Cuba will supply pilots for your aeroplanes and training for your army, Comrade President.'

Lazio stared defiantly across the table at the Soviets, challenging them to respond.

'Comrade Colonel Julio Casas will make the arrangements,' snapped Lazio, waving his arm towards Casas.

'So be it. Thank you gentlemen,' said the President, getting to his feet. 'We have not a moment to lose. Then turning to the Soviet Ambassador, 'Comrade Solodovnikov can you help me draft a letter to the British Government?'

'By all means,' smiled the Soviet Ambassador, his face now cracked in a broad grin, like the cat that had got the cream.

Casas shook his head in disbelief ... putting sophisticated ground-to-air missiles into the hands of these idiots was a huge mistake!

The meeting broke up, Casas picked up his briefcase, turning for the door.

'Comrade Casas,' called Lazio softly.

'Yes Ambassador?'

'You have new orders from Havana. Your mission is being placed under the command of the Soviet mission in Zambia, you will report directly to Comrade Professor Vassily Solodovnikov from this point onwards,' smiled Lazio, revelling in the obvious discomfort of Casas at this news.

As Julio Casas glanced across the room, both Vassily Solodovnikov and Lev Kononov were smiling at him … Kononov nodded his head in acknowledgement.

Comrade Colonel Julio Casas did not respond, turning on his heal he left the room in disgust … muttering Spanish swear words under his breath … *fucking politicians!*

*

SAS HQ, Kabrit Barracks, Seke Road, Salisbury

The Rhodesian SAS Head Quarters at Kabrit Barracks[28] on the southern end of the main runway at Salisbury International Airport was a highly secure 100-acre compound. In pre-war days, it housed the Kutsaga Tobacco Research Institute, explaining the opulence of many of the buildings[29]. The entrance to the compound on Seke Road was through massive wrought iron gates flanked by impressive white pillars. Seke was the main road to Chitungwiza Township, another 6km down the road.

There was no outward indication that this was a military base, other than the two uniformed guards at the gate that was kept shut. Inside the gate, hidden by trees was a guardhouse that doubled as an orderly room.

A white Datsun 120Y travelling at high speed came down Seke Road from the direction of Salisbury. As the female driver saw the main gate, she braked hard pulling off onto the shoulder of the road skidding in the dust. This impressive arrival drew the attention of the two guards who slipped their FN rifles off their shoulders.

The driver executed a neat U-turn, spinning the wheels on the gravel shoulder, and pulled up in front of gates giving a loud toot on the hooter.

---

28 Named after the village near the original SAS base set up by Colonel David Stirling in Egypt in 1941. The village of Kabrit was in the Suez Canal Zone some 160km south of Cairo.

29 Tobacco was Rhodesia's main export crop.

A woman stuck her head out the window and shouted, 'Open the gates!'

One of the guards unhitched the latch on the gate and eased his way through, walking around to the driver's side. The guards to the SAS compound were not qualified SAS operators themselves, instead they were men who had either just passed or were waiting for selection. A few national servicemen boosted their numbers.

'Can I help you?' asked the guard politely, taking in what was a very impressive sight.

The woman was wearing a bright floral dress, with long strawberry blond hair in the style of Farrah Fawcett-Majors from *Charlie's Angels*. The dress was cut in a round high neckline with narrow see-through shirring in front, button-trim down the front, with long raglan sleeves elasticised at the wrists. She had green eyes, accentuated by green eye shadow, bright pink lipstick and a smile that could melt hot metal.

The radio in the car was blaring Linda Ronstadt's *It's so Easy*.

> *It's so easy to fall in love*
> *It's so easy to fall in love*
> *People tell me love's for fools*
> *Here I go breaking all the rules*

The woman turned down the volume on the radio.

'I'm here to see Keith,' she said brightly with a posh English accent.

'Keith who?' asked the guard, not sure of such an incongruous request delivered by a supermodel.

'I don't suppose you know him. This is the SAS isn't it?' she asked still smiling.

The guard was clearly out of his depth. What he did know was that he could not let anyone in to the base without ID and special orders. Just then an army Land Rover pulled up on the inside of the gate.

The Datsun was parked directly in the middle of the driveway blocking the entrance.

'What's going on here?' shouted a man from the driver's seat of the Land Rover.

The guard walked back through the gate saluting the officer smartly.

'This woman is looking for Keith, Sir.'

'Keith who?'

The guard realised he hadn't got an answer to that question, blinking back towards the woman.

The woman opened the door of the car and stepped out into the road. All three men gaped at her, spellbound.

She was magnificent. The dress was cut just below the knee, the shape of her slim calves, accentuated by healed sandals … stunning! As she walked, the light passed right through the light material revealing exceptional promise beneath. The dress seemed to flow around her body when she walked, the bodice loosely covering a set of perfectly rounded breasts, unrestricted by a bra.

'Is Keith here?' asked the woman loudly, walking up to the gate, still holding a broad smile, revealing a set of pearly white teeth. She stood at the gate, feet slightly apart, allowing the light breeze to flutter her skirt.

The man in the Land Rover, with three pips of a captain on his shoulder, stepped forward. He was not wearing a beret or stable belt.

'Why do you want to see him?' asked the officer.

'I met him at a bar in Salisbury and he left his camera behind, I wanted to return it to him,' replied the woman, her head tilted to one side. She made to squeeze through the gap between the gates.

'You can't come in here!' called the officer, blocking her way.

'Why not? Have you got something to hide?' she replied disarmingly, her smile now taking a more mischievous bent, her eyes flashing provocatively. Her accent was delivered in clear precise King's English.

'There is no Keith here, you must have the wrong base,' stated the officer, trying to maintain his composure in front of the two guards who were watching the exchange with deep intent. As the men watched, two enticing nipples made their appearance from beneath the bodice.

'He must be here. This is where he told me to come,' said the woman, her voice displaying the faintest hint of irritation.

'What does he look like?

'Well when I saw him he had long black curly hair, dark brown eyes … a black scraggly beard … he was black.'

The officer was completely flummoxed, there were no Black soldiers in the SAS. *How could such a beautiful white woman have dated a black man in Salisbury! It was impossible!*

'There must be some mistake,' said the officer, lost for words.

Continuing to smile playfully, the woman bent forward to within a few inches of his ear. He noticed she had a plaster strip across her forehead under her fringe. Her perfume hit him in a wave, the close proximity making him blush.

'Well Captain,' she whispered softly, 'There's no mistake, he fucked me silly ... I would like some more of where that came from ... you tell him to call me, Sarah Burrell. I'm at the Red Fox Hotel in Greendale.' She lingered on the word 'fuck', delivering it with clear intonation, leaving no doubt about what she meant.

Turning on her heel, she floated back to her car. Slapping it into reverse, the wheels spun on the smooth tar as the car skidded backwards, performing an expert handbrake turn aiming back in the direction of Salisbury, accelerating away to the smell of burnt rubber.

The three men watched her go ... the Captain, a fearless veteran of numerous external raids, was blushing brightly ... *fuck me gently!*

> *My heart can learn*
> *Oh it's so easy to fall in love*
> *It's so easy to fall in love.*

*

Muramba Road, Chilenji Township, Lusaka, Zambia

A light blue Volkswagen Beetle drove slowly down Muramba Road. It was just after 11:30pm and the road, extremely busy during the day, was deserted. While lined with streetlights, none were working.

Sitting in the passenger seat of the 'Volksie'[30] was a tall thickset man dressed in a black boiler suit with blackened Bata 'takkies'[31]. His broad shoulders seemed to fill most of the front seat, his head only an inch from the roof. His black hair was cut short but not military-short.

'What do you think Jock?' asked the driver anxiously. He was a much smaller man with a slim sinewy build. He was gripping the steering wheel nervously with both hands, his knuckles white.

Both men were studying the opposite side of the road as they travelled to the east, Muramba Road was one of the main east-west arterials in the city.

'Looks good,' replied Alan 'Jock' McLean, his thick accent reflecting his hometown of Clydebank to the west of Glasgow. 'Keep going to Tutwa Road ... we will reassess there.'

The two men had studied Muramba Road and their target for over a month. They had followed their quarry all over Lusaka, noting carefully the address of his stops, the people he met, their descriptions, vehicle registration numbers and, where possible, they had taken photographs. They had compiled an impressive dossier of people and

---
30 Volkswagen Beetle.
31 Tennis shoes

places, all requiring further investigation.

Unlike many of the other military and political leaders that they had followed, the target did not have a bodyguard. Choosing instead to remain incognito, living alone in a quiet residential suburb.

The Volkswagen carried on its noisy way, headlights on, but travelling just fast enough to avoid attention. Each man scanned his side of the road looking for any sign of changes from the previous reconnaissance.

On his lap, Jock Mclean was holding a large *El Rey del Mundo* Cuban cigar box[32], the tin used for carrying a half-dozen smaller cardboard boxes. This particular box carried an extra wallop, well in excess of the best of *El Rey del Mundo,* four kilograms of Pentolite explosive. It was more than enough to spoil someone's day.

As luck would have it, their target also drove a Volkswagen Beetle so the two men had been able to experiment with different places to set the charge. They had settled on the space behind the right front wheel, where they could wedge it into position using a chunk of wood they had cut for the purpose. Pentolite, although brittle, is stable. Jock had gouged out a hole in the middle of the Pentolite and packed it with plastic Semtex H explosive. This would allow for the placement of the two detonators. He had thought of using a Soviet plastic explosive in case a detailed forensic investigation took place, but decided on a South African product because of its reliability. There was no room for mistakes.

Alan 'Jock' McLean, secret agent, was no ordinary man. He was a veteran of A Squadron, 22 SAS, serving in Borneo and Aden, then assignments with 'The Firm' Watchguard International, MI6's dirty tricks department. His partner, Ian Southwood, had no such military pedigree. He ran the local Scania trucks agency, hence Jock's cover as a truck salesman, offering spare parts and service. The truck business was run from a small farm to the west of Lusaka. They were an unlikely but effective partnership.

On reaching the Tutwa Road intersection, Southwood slowed down and then performed a neat U-turn. The road was quiet, no pedestrians or vehicles, not even one of the ubiquitous stray dogs. They had found no difficulty driving around the Lusaka townships at night. Police presence was limited and roadblocks or vehicle inspections were a rarity. In a moving car at night, it was impossible to determine whether the occupants were black or white.

Southwood eased the car into third gear and returned down

---

32   23cm long, 12cm wide and 6cm deep.

Muramba Road, passing number 130 on the right. The house in Chilenji South was typical of the semi-detached cottages found in the Lusaka townships. It had a tiny front garden, no more than ten by five metres square. The whole property was surrounded by a wire mesh security fence, with two strands of barbed wire at the top. This was not unusual in Lusaka where unemployment fed a rampant crime rate. A double gate at the front allowed a single car to be driven in and parked on the tiny driveway. The yard was swept clean, not a single blade of grass, except the few resilient patches surrounding the downpipes off the roof.

Their target had arrived home at his usual time; he was a man of discipline and habit. He had followed the usual route home from his office at 'The Rock'; the military headquarters for the Zimbabwean People's Revolutionary Army, 10km to the north.

As the two men passed the house, they could see the target's car parked in the driveway. The target followed a regimented routine, entering the house, turning the lights on, and switching on the transistor radio. He listened to the 9 o'clock news from the BBC World Service over his dinner. He lived alone, spending most evenings sitting at the dining room table writing. Between 9:30pm and 10pm, he retired to bed and the lights would go off. He arose early in the morning, took a shower and drove back to his office ready to start work at 8am sharp. The route to and from home was identical.

McLean and Southwood had driven in from the farm earlier that evening to dine at the Inter-Continental Hotel. This was to establish a cover story if they were stopped by police. Establishing an alibi was part of their practiced *modus operandi* as two whitemen driving the streets of Lusaka in the dead of night was unusual.

'Let's get on with this,' said McLean in a whisper.

Southwood drove on 200m past the target's house then pulled off the road. This spot under a huge *Mpapa*, Pod Mahogany tree[33], had been identified earlier. It provided deep 'shade' from the bright starlight.

McLean pulled a big Afro wig over his head, then gently opened the passenger side door, careful not to make any noise. The wigs were essential as they could not use black camo-cream in an urban area. Removing the stuff was hugely difficult and even the slightest hint of it in an ear or hairline would arouse suspicion. He grabbed the folding-butt AKM that had been wedged next to his leg and slung it

---

33 *Fabaceae* (subfamily *Caesalpinioideae*) Common names : pod mahogany, lucky bean tree.

over his back. The bomb was carefully placed into a canvas backpack.

Southwood slipped his AKM onto his lap and signalled a thumbs-up to his partner.

In their carefully rehearsed routine, McLean knelt down next to the car, looking back down the road towards the target's house. He sat rigid for 30 minutes not moving a muscle. Patience in this line of work was the difference between life and death. The plan dictated that if lights were turned on in any of the surrounding houses the mission would be aborted.

When McLean was satisfied they had not disturbed anyone he set off. It was hot in the boiler suit with his dinner clothing on underneath. After only a few metres, McLean was sweating profusely; a combination of the two layers of clothing and the stress of a mission.

Reaching the security fence outside the target's house, McLean took out a pair of razor sharp wire cutters then carefully and methodically cut a hole through it. Waiting between each loud CLICK, meant that the process took ages. His eyes filled with sweat forcing him to constantly wipe his face with his sleeve.

Once the hole was cut, he slipped through, waiting again on the other side. Taking to the ground, he leopard-crawled the few metres to where the car was parked. Carefully easing around to the front of the car, McLean lay on his side. Then, as he had practiced, he slotted the cigar box with its explosive charge into its planned position behind the front wheel. Inserting the wooden wedge, he jammed the box in place.

After much thought and debate in the planning, he had decided to initiate the device by placing a matchbox behind the car's front wheel. It would be crushed the moment the car rolled back. An electrical contact, connected to torch batteries, would be made by pushing together two 4 inch nails fastened to the positive and negative leads.

The matchbox initiator was pushed into place behind the front wheel and concealed by pushing loose sand over it. The wires leading from the matchbox were pushed around behind the wheel out of sight.

Pausing for a moment to take stock, McLean relaxed, resting his head on the ground.

The light went on in the target's bedroom only two metres from where he was lying.

McLean froze ... the man was moving around in the room behind the curtains. A shadow passed in front of the window. He eased the AKM off his back holding it across his body as he lay on his side facing the car. His mind raced through the options ... if the man came out the front door McLean would have no choice but to gun him down and make a run for it.

The toilet flushed.

The bastard's just gone for a leak!

McLean lay perfectly still, controlling every breath.

Ten minutes went by … then fifteen … then thirty.

Lying in such a cramped position was making his muscles twitch, he could feel the pain building in his neck and his hamstrings. Eventually he relaxed after giving the target enough time to get back to sleep. Double-checking his handiwork, McLean pushed a pencil into the plastic explosive to make two holes, then inserted the detonators. All was complete … the bomb was ready.

It was all up to the target now.

Slipping an AK47 magazine out of his pack, he placed it next to the back wheel. It had the word 'ZANLA' scraped into it, the military wing of Robert Mugabe's ZANU party.

'Everything all right?' asked Southwood when McLean got back to the car. 'I was shitting myself, why did you take so long?'

'Prick went for a piss. I had to wait for him to go back to sleep.'

'Fuck … '

Southwood was visibly shaking from the stress and the adrenaline rush.

'You got my wire cutters?'

'Oh shit, I must have left them next to the fence. Not to worry, nobody will notice them after the shit and derision that will be spread tomorrow.'

'Fuck that … those things are like rocking-horse shit. Go back and fetch them!' demanded Southwood.

'Don't be daft, it's too late to go back!'

'I'll never get another pair like them. I'll go.'

Southwood turned to open the car door.

'Stop, this is bloody ridiculous. I'll buy you another pair when I am next in Jo'burg.'

'I don't care I want those cutters!' hissed Southwood. He was determined.

'Shit!' spat McLean. 'Wait here.'

He climbed back out the car and walked briskly back to the fence. The lost cutters were just inside. He scooped them up and returned to the car.

'That's better!' smiled Southwood.

The two men drove back through the deserted streets to the farm, feeling immensely pleased with themselves.

4

130 Muramba Road, Chilenji Township, Lusaka, Zambia

Comrade General Alfred 'Nikita' Mangena woke earlier than usual. He had a busy and complex job that sometimes made sleep difficult. This was a consequence of being the Supreme Military Commander of Zimbabwe Peoples Revolutionary Army (ZIPRA), member of the Revolutionary Council, the main political and representative body of ZAPU-PF outside of Zimbabwe, and member of the War Council.

The dream he had most often was of the day he would march back into his home village of Belingwe in Southern Matabeleland at the head of a victorious army ... to make his family proud of his achievements.

Alfred Mangena was a good-looking man, medium height, slimly built, with a kindly face and a neatly trimmed beard. His lean stature gave the impression that he was much younger than his thirty years. He had bright brown eyes, a ready smile and a pleasant disposition that drew people to him. Alfred Mangena was also a modest man, achieving his rank through dedication and commitment, not relying on political patronage and intrigue. He had not yet taken a wife as his only focus was winning the war against the white racist regime ruling his beloved homeland.

Comrade Mangena would not have described himself as a fanatic, but in the sense that he lived and breathed the freedom struggle, consuming his every thought, he most definitely was. Mangena had been recruited by ZAPU while he was at Catholic mission school in the early sixties. He had escaped from the country at his first opportunity and his energy and enthusiasm led to his selection for training in the Soviet Union where he was a keen student of Marxist philosophy. His dedication to the Soviet ideals had earned him the nickname 'Nikita' by his Russian teachers after the great Soviet Leader, Nikita Sergeyevich Khrushchev.

Mangena hated colonial oppression, where the 'Settlers' put themselves apart from the indigenous population. It was not to say that he hated white people, 'We are fighting against a system' he would say, 'not white people'. What he hated was that his nation were denied their political rights, first by the British colonial power and, thereafter, by the ridiculous Unilateral Declaration of Independence by the Smith regime. In his mind, the natural outcome of a democratic process in the country would result in black majority rule. It was the injustice of the situation that Mangena hated; it gnawed away at him, a throbbing pain, deep in his gut.

Being a military man, Mangena had a strict routine. He showered and dressed in the usual non-descript civilian clothing. None of the ZIPRA leaders wore military uniforms to avoid attracting attention. He made some toast and ate it while reading the two-day old *Times of Zambia* newspaper. His housekeeper would only come in after he left for the day.

Grabbing his briefcase, he packed away the papers he had read the night before, picked up his sports jacket hanging on the back of the chair and went out to the car.

It was still cold in the early spring morning, a thick layer of dew covered the old Volkswagen. As he sat back into the driver's seat, he looked at his watch, 7:30am, a half hour earlier than usual.

He pulled the choke as the car sometimes struggled to start after a cold night. He pressed the accelerator and turned the key. The Volkswagen gamely turned over, the starter motor giving of its best. He tried again ... coaching the car to start.

It was a miracle that the car still drove at all, it had not had a service in the past 5 years. What point was there? There were no spare parts in the country anyway.

Climbing out the driver's seat, Mangena called two teenage kids walking along the road to school ... they were going to have to push.

The two youths smiled and joked with Mangena as he explained that they needed to push the car out into Muramba road.

The Volkswagen Beetle is not a heavy car, that was one of its great strengths in Africa. It could handle poor roads and thick sand and could skip effortlessly over corrugations. It was a remarkable piece of German engineering, subsisting on low maintenance and harsh treatment.

The two young men took up station in front of each headlight fender where it was possible to get a grip on the slippery metal. Then, on Mangena's call, they gave the car a firm push.

A brilliant flash followed by a loud rumble carried across Lusaka. Many people in the streets looked up, thinking it was a clap of thunder. Out towards the south of the City a thin pall of black smoke lifted into the still, cloudless sky.

What was left of the Volkswagen lay on its back, the bonnet and front suspension had been torn apart as if it had been attacked by the jaws of some primordial monster. The front room of the house had been blasted inwards, with the asbestos roof sagged on the supporting timbers.

Comrade General Alfred 'Nikita' Mangena was dead, his body smashed beyond recognition, the two young schoolboys ... vapourised.

*

Foreign and Commonwealth Office, King Charles Street, City of Westminster, London

Lord Baron Goronwy-Roberts of Caernarfon, Minister of State, Foreign and Commonwealth Office, Deputy Leader of the House of Lords, at 65 was at the height of his powers. He was a veteran Labour Party man from Wales and proud of it. He had survived changes of Government, political reversals and vicious internal party machinations. He witnessed the victorious Labour Party rise from the ashes of the defeat of 1970. Despite losing his seat in the elections of 1974, his loyalty to the Labour Prime Minister, James Callaghan, won him a peerage, a seat in the House of Lords, and a ministry.

One thing Lord Goronwy-Roberts shared with his Prime Minister was his distrust and intense dislike of the Rhodesian Prime Minister, Ian Smith. The rebel leader had outwitted and outmanoeuvred them at every turn. When Lord Goronwy-Roberts received the request from Zambia for ground-to-air missiles and military assistance, he was favourably disposed. He so wanted to teach the confounded, upstart rebel leader a lesson.

The Minister had gathered his team from the Africa Desk to discuss the request from Zambia, but it was not going quite as he had planned. The Minister was becoming impatient as he sat behind the huge mahogany desk in his office on the third floor of the Foreign and Commonwealth Office. His window overlooked the inner courtyard and carpark.

The Minister had the letter from the Zambian President in his hand, waving it about excitedly above his head as if it was an order for shares on the floor of the Stock Exchange.

'When the Prime Minister and I met President Kaunda, the President asked for our help in dealing with Zambia's economic problems and for military assistance, making it clear that he was turning to us in the first instance, as a fellow member of the Commonwealth, with which his country has had economic and defence relations since independence in 1964,' stated the Minister in his broad Welsh accent, placing the Zambian letter purposefully down in front of his staff as if it was an executive order from the Prime Minister where no dissent would be entertained.

'Yes Minister, but sending him our latest Rapier missiles, will be seen as taking sides in the war. We will get a great deal of opposition to this idea,' replied the Permanent Under-secretary of State, Sir Charles Prior. The two other civil servants in the room nodded their agreement.

Leaning forward, spreading the fingers of both hands on his ink-blotter to emphasise his point, the Minister hissed, 'We have agreed to provide military aid to improve Zambia's defensive capability.' He stopped to glare at the three civil servants daring them to challenge him. When no immediate opposition was forthcoming, he raised the tone of his voice, banging the ink-blotter with his finger tips, 'Some ground equipment and spares have already been supplied strictly for the use of the Zambian armed forces and police. More will follow, after detailed consultations with the Zambians. We will also step up military training for Zambians in Britain.'

Sir Charles Prior ventured a response, 'We have concerns that our weapons will fall into the wrong hands, Minister. You have read the reports of Soviet and Cuban activity in Lusaka. In addition, how can you guarantee that the equipment will not be used to protect guerrilla bases?'

The Minister jousted back, 'The Zambian Government have given us firm assurances that the equipment will be used for no other purpose than the defence of Zambia and will not be passed to any third party. The air defence equipment will be used to safeguard the integrity of the capital.'

'Yes Minister, but, like it or not, there are guerrilla camps in Zambia, some - at any rate, one - not very far from Lusaka. From these camps on Zambian soil, guerrillas enter Rhodesia and kill Rhodesians, black and white. It is surely not very surprising that the Rhodesian forces attack these camps,' parried Sir Charles, being careful to state his position as clearly as possible without antagonising the Minister still further.

Changing tack, Sir Charles zeroed in on the most sensitive subject … money. 'Minister, we have no budget allocation for the supply of this equipment.'

The Minister flashed back, 'When we have established with the Zambians their exact needs, I will immediately tell the House the cost to the Exchequer of the military assistance we are providing. We owe Zambia our protection, that is quite clear.'

Feeling totally exasperated, but showing an outward calm that was truly an art form, Sir Charles tried a flanking movement worthy of his time in the Coldstream Guards.

'Minister, have you considered the impact of these missiles being misused? What would be the case if the Zambians shot down friendly aircraft? These are very sophisticated weapons. Are you confident you can train the Zambians sufficiently to prevent accidents?'

Sir Charles very pointedly used the word 'you' to highlight the Minister's precarious position. The civil servants studied their Minister's face closely, he had been put on the spot ... *would he crack?* The question of personal responsibility had been raised. Responsibility was something to be avoided, it was as a snake under a rock, it could kill with a single strike. The Minister, like his colleagues in the Cabinet, saw his job more in terms of all care and no responsibility!

The Minister hesitated, gathering his thoughts. He had been thrust into a position that politicians avoided at all cost ... accountability! *God forbid!* Turning his swivel chair to look out the window, he gazed up into the grey sky as if seeking some divine intervention.

These blasted, infuriating, civil servants ... A full minute passed in perfect silence as the Minister pondered. The solution struck him like a thunderbolt ... loyalty!

He spun back.

'If this friendly Commonwealth Government appeals for some military aid, then in principle, it should not be refused. The fact is that President Kaunda is in a very weak position. He has hardly any effective force at his disposal, and he, therefore, cannot prevent the establishment of guerrilla bases in his country even if he wanted to do so. Anyhow, they are there already! Her Majesty's Government has been asked to provide for the military air defence of the capital, Lusaka, but not in any way to give military assistance to the rebels in the defence of their guerrilla bases.'

The Minister sat back in his chair, fingertips tapping together in front of his chest, a smug expression on his face ... *put that in your pipe and smoke it!*

'Are you to send British military personnel to Zambia, Minister? How can we protect them?' asked Sir Charles. He was virtually out of ammunition, the enemy were at the gates, defeat was at hand.

'No British service personnel or aircraft will be stationed in Zambia. The Prime Minister is very clear on this point!'

There it was ... blame could be placed at the door of the Prime Minister if anything went wrong ... no British soldiers would be in harm's way ... the Government could parade their self-righteous defence of Zambia in front of the other Commonwealth leaders ... a perfect political outcome for the Minister.

Sir Charles nodded his acceptance, not his agreement, and stood to leave the room.

As the civil servants filed out, one of them whispered, 'Sir Charles, without our people on the ground how will we ever know where the missiles are stationed?'

'We will never know ... we will have to place our trust in Providence ... Ineptitude and Poor Maintenance,' replied Sir Charles ... a sick, uneasy feeling was rising in his stomach.

*

RAF Lyneham, 10.1 km northeast of Chippenham, Wiltshire, England

With unseemly haste following the decision from the Foreign Office, that very evening, a pair of RAF Lockheed Hercules C1s were loaded with Rapier missile systems. The Rapier system took the form of a wheeled launcher with four missiles, an optical tracker unit, and an all-weather radar unit plus generators and a trailer of stores. The whole system was delivered by three Land Rovers designated as the Fire Unit Truck (FUT), the Detachment Support Vehicle (DSV) and the Tracking Radar Tractor (TRT) to tow the 'Blindfire' flat-faced radar trailer.

What made the loading of the aircraft remarkable was the addition of the two Marconi DN 181 'Blindfire' radar units. The Blindfire tracking radar, supplied by BAE Systems Insyte, was a differential monopulse frequency agile radar, operating in F band providing fully automatic all-weather engagement to a range of 15km. This was the absolute latest radar tracking technology the British had to offer.

A team of eight men from 26 Squadron, RAF Regiment, climbed aboard the Hercules. They were the team responsible for training the Zambians on how to use their new weapons. These men were not to be 'stationed' in Zambia they were simply 'delivering' the system.

Just before 5pm, the Hercules taxied from the hardstanding to runway 24, waited for clearance and took off towards the southwest ... bound for Zambia.

The British Government were supplying their latest technology. In the right hands, the Rapier system would clear the sky of any Rhodesian aircraft approaching within 7km of Lusaka, or where ever else it might be placed, come rain or shine.

*

18,000ft above Norman Barr Safaris camp at Ndevu, South Luangwa National Park, Zambia

It was just before last light. Lieutenant Keith Wilson and his team of Selous Scouts sat silently in the bucking Dakota as it crossed the Zambian border at 10,000ft. They had crossed the northern border above Kanyemba, an outpost on the confluence of the Zambezi and Luangwa rivers where the borders of Rhodesia, Zambia and Mozambique meet. At 6,000ft, the temperature had dropped markedly. At 12,000ft, the air force dispatchers attached oxygen masks to each man. The flexible plastic tubes were attached to a line running the length of the aircraft, to oxygen bottles in a rack next to the cockpit door[34].

Wilson, Chiyeka, Ngwenya and Mundiya sat huddled against the side of the fuselage. Despite their extensive training on HALO jumping, the real thing was much more frightening. Wilson and Ngwenya had three operational HALO jumps under their belt, the others nil.

The bulk of their equipment was in the wooden crate next to the open cargo door. Each man carried an AK47 strapped to his side, khaki clothing, under an assortment of jerseys and overalls to keep out the freezing temperature. The air force despatcher crossed over to the men to recheck oxygen masks as the aircraft continued to climb through 15,000ft, showing the thumbs up to make sure each man was breathing normally.

As Ngwenya watched through the door the last rays of light shone into his face.

Wilson checked his watch and altimeter and signalled to the men … fifteen minutes to the drop zone. Tense nervousness … furtive glances left and right.

The plan was to exit the aircraft with enough light to see and manoeuvre in the air but dark enough when on the ground to hide their arrival.

 Cephas Ngwenya checked his altimeter, set to a negative height equivalent to the difference between the altitude of New Sarum air force base and the lower altitude of the drop zone. He had heard the more experienced jumpers discussing this bit of physics but it was lost on him. He fixed his eyes on the altitude that Wilson told him he <u>needed to open</u> the parachute, trying to picture it in his mind.

34   The Rhodesians did not have the HALO jumping equipment that would have included oxygen masks attached to an independent oxygen supply to support the soldier while waiting to exit and on the long way down.

The briefing Ngwenya and others had received had emphasised the need for pinpoint accuracy on the drop zone. This was mainly because of the rough terrain, and the extremely poor map coverage of the area. The most prominent navigational aid was the Luangwa River itself, that snaked southwards from central Zambia. A slight miscalculation and they would be in deep trouble. The drop zone was in a wide meander of the Luangwa River, swept clear by flooding. It showed up clearly on aerial photographs, one was strapped to the despatcher's leg. The benefit of this drop zone was that it was many kilometres away from any settlements, being in the heart of a national park.

'STANDBY', the Dispatcher shouted.

Ngwenya snapped out of his reverie and stood up with all of the others. They paired off. Wilson smiled, showing the thumbs up. All still had their oxygen masks attached. Ngwenya glanced down at his altimeter; 18,000ft ... *jump height!*

The dispatcher placed his headset on and spoke to the pilot. He needed to identify the jump-point himself; he was giving the pilot minor heading corrections while looking out the door. He seemed satisfied.

The men stood in the door behind the 'box'. The 'box', was a simple pinewood crate that contained radios, ammunition, explosives, extra water and rations for what was to be a potentially very long deployment into Zambia. The crate had been reinforced with nylon strapping. Three types of parachute were attached to the crate; spring-loaded pilot chutes, then a normal reserve chute would, in turn, drag out the main chute. The box had been invented by the Air Force and the SAS and used extensively by them. The system for opening was as simple as it was ingenious. Nylon string was sewn through safety fuse that was cut to the correct length for the period of free-fall. At the time of launch the safety fuse was lit with an electric igniter, once the safety fuse burnt through the nylon string the reserve chute was released to burst open. The spring-loaded pilot chutes would then pop open and drag out the main chute. A flashing red strobe light was attached to the top of the box so that it could be seen as it fell and to help find it after landing. All was very straightforward ...

The red light glowed at the door and the Selous Scouts stood up to begin the final equipment check. They had practiced jumping alongside each other, holding onto each other from the time of leaving the aircraft to the opening of the chutes. This had reduced the 'spread' at the landing site and in so doing, built up the confidence within the team. They would jump in twos, Ngwenya held Mundiya, Wilson held Chiyeka.

'Okay, let's go through this again,' called the dispatcher. 'Stand in the door, take three big breaths of oxygen, then when we shout GO, take a deep breath then jump. Hold your breath as long as possible, you should be able to breathe normally after about ten seconds ... You got it now?'

The men all nodded their understanding. Ngwenya played his instructions over in his mind ... *take a big gulp of oxygen and hold your breath ...*

The green light flashed, the dispatcher lit the safety fuse and he and his assistant launched the crate out the door, the four men following, leaping out into the unknown.

Ngwenya held Mundiya's arm tightly, his contorted face visible in the fast fading light. They raced after the spinning crate, the strobe light marking its path.

Seventy-three seconds after leaving the aircraft all four chutes opened, the box flew on to open at 2,500ft. Ngwenya checked his canopy was correctly developed. The feeling of relief was overwhelming. He looked around to see his teammates spread over the sky. Grabbing the control lines, he tracked in above and behind the other men who all seemed to be in control. The ground came up, he braced for the landing ... pulling on the control lines his speed stalled, then gently and in perfect control, he landed. He didn't even need to roll. Pulling in the parachute lines, Ngwenya looked around the sandy riverbed for the other men. The crate had hit the ground first, followed by Wilson and Chiyeka, Ngwenya landed about 30m away with Mundiya next to him.

It was completely quiet. The men crept carefully towards the crate. Wilson grouped the men into a tight huddle to make sure all was well and there were no injuries.

Unpacking the crate ran the risk of making noise, too much noise, so the plan was to wait until dark. This would also allow the group to check out their surroundings and to make sure they had not been detected. Together they dragged the crate through the soft sand into thick cover on the inside of the bend in the river.

Mundiya, responsible for the TR48, silently unpacked the radio and sent the code word for a successful insertion ... *Shatien*[35]. The Selous Scouts went to ground under a thick layer of scrub to wait ... their RV with their contact was set for the next morning.

---
35 Chilapalapa, bush, the bush.

*

A telephone rang in the office of Norman Barr Safaris, 5 Moobola Road, Numununga Industrial Area, Lusaka.

The voice asked, 'I am looking for a stuffed Leopard?'

'We only have a Honey Badger in stock.'

'Well your chickens have come home to roost.'

The phone went dead.

*

CIO HQ, Coghlan Buildings, Livingston Avenue, Salisbury City Centre

The telephone rang in the 10th floor office of Deputy Director John Sutcliffe, CIO. He was an early riser and made it his business to be in his office by 8am every morning. It was all about discipline and leadership. Sutcliffe led by example.

'Hello, Sutcliffe here.'

'John, Nigel Pennefather here.'

'My goodness Nigel, what gets you up so early?'

'We have a spot of bother, it appears that our wonderful political leaders have dispatched some rather nasty ordinance to Lusaka.'

'Are you talking about Rapier?'

'Yes ... the first lot's on its way.'

'Thank you Nigel ... I appreciate your help,' replied Sutcliffe, replacing the receiver.

Nigel Pennefather was the local MI6 representative based in Salisbury. The risk of Britain sending sophisticated missiles to Zambia had been identified for some time. MI6 were dead against it, particularly since they knew that by doing so the missile and radar technology would fall into the hands of the Soviets. The Cold War in Africa was being won by the Soviets and China hands down. Britain, the Commonwealth and the USA were relegated to minor players, hit up instead by African political dictators for financial aid, food shipments and the odd symbolic meeting where everyone could pat each other on the back ... but did nothing for their people.

MI6 were now reliant on the Rhodesians to neutralise the threat and, with a bit of luck, destroy the missiles before they could fall into the 'wrong hands'.

John Sutcliffe picked up the phone and dialled the number for his communications section, two floors below.

'Communications.'

'Bob, John here ... get a message to *Ben Nevis* ... I need him here in

Salisbury ASAP. Mark your message most urgent.'

The phone clicked on the other side without comment.

'Ben Nevis'[36] was the codename for the senior CIO agent in Lusaka. Sutcliffe smiled to himself, he loved the Scottish touch.

The code message was transmitted via telephone contacts in Johannesburg, then to Francistown in Botswana. In Francistown, the message was recoded and transmitted by way of flash radio signal to Lusaka on a fixed daily schedule that altered by ten minutes each day.

Inside a farm equipment shed 26km to the west of Lusaka, two men sat crouched over a radio receiver. The light for an incoming message blinked on and the man wearing the headphones wrote down the letters as they were received. The other man decoded it.

'You are invited to a party at Bright Lights, bring your own.'

Alan 'Jock' McLean, alias Ben Nevis, read the message he had decoded. He was being recalled to Salisbury, 'Bright Lights'. The fact that the invite said 'bring your own' meant immediate action required.

*

Soviet Monitoring Station, Soviet Embassy, Ridgeway, Lusaka

The Soviet Union had radio monitoring equipment in all their embassies in Africa. This was very powerful equipment that could pick up HF radio traffic in Rhodesia as well as transmissions from within Zambia. They also listened to traffic coming into and going out of the British and American embassies. Not all of it could be decoded but a reasonable proportion was. They also had telephone taps in Zambian State House and all the ZAPU sites in Lusaka, and a few other 'people of interest' including Joshua Nkomo and the other members of the ZAPU War Council.

Earlier that day they had picked up the confirmation that the Rapier missiles had been dispatched and their ETA in Lusaka.

The Soviets were aware of Rhodesian agents operating in Lusaka but had not been able to pinpoint the source of radio transmissions … they were however getting closer and closer.

The Soviet agent in charge of the monitoring station took down the message on one of the frequencies used for Ben Nevis and took it up to the Ambassador, Comrade Professor Vassily Solodovnikov

Solodovnikov read the message … *where and when is this party?*

---

36   Whisky distillery located at Lochy Bridge in Fort William and sits just at the base of Ben Nevis, Scotland's highest mountain, rising to 4,406 feet above sea level. A coastal distillery in the Western Highlands, Ben Nevis draws its water from the *Allt a'Mhuilinn* originating from two pools, *Coire Leis* and *Coire na'Ciste*.

5

Norman Barr Safaris camp at Ndevu, South Luangwa National Park, Zambia

An open game-viewing Land Rover negotiated the steep slope into the riverbed of the Luangwa River. It was early morning and the sun was just touching the eastern horizon producing another spectacular sunrise. The driver stopped, engaged diff-locks and the vehicle inched down, effortlessly climbing over the rough track into the riverbed.

A herd of Buffalo standing in the riverbed watched the vehicle's approach. They were used to the game viewing vehicles so there was no alarm or panic amongst the large animals.

The river cut a wide 80m path through the countryside with broad expanses of soft river sand on the inside of each meander. It was a harsh but magnificent country, deeply cut by streambeds with high surrounding hills. The severe, broken terrain and its shear remoteness made it unsuitable for farming. This, together with malaria and limited standing water, prevented any form of permanent settlement. It was an untouched, isolated part of Africa, where the wildlife still reigned supreme.

The only people living in the area were those that manned the few scattered game lodges and hunting camps. The war in neighbouring Rhodesia and the collapse of the Zambian economy meant that tourists were few and far between. The only people traversing the area on the rough, almost impassable, bush tracks were Zambian police and army patrols and the truckloads of ZIPRA cadres on their way to the Zambezi River 126km to the south.

At the bottom of the steep decent, the Land Rover turned onto the soft sand and stopped. The driver lit a cigarette and sat back, lifting his binoculars to study the herd of Buffalo. A Winchester Model 70 bolt-action rifle with a .358 Winchester chamber, sat in a cradle behind the driver. It did not have a telescopic sight.

A group of gregarious Redbilled Woodhoopoes cackled, *Haya, Haya Haya,* in an overhanging tree. Their call started slowly, building to a crescendo, as they fluttered excitedly from branch to branch.

In the thick bush under an eroded cut in the riverbank, some 200m in front of the Land Rover, a torch flashed three times. The driver responded with four flashes of the headlights.

'Good morning Mister Barr,' came a voice from behind the driver.

'Mister Wilson I presume,' replied the driver with a soft Scottish burr.

Lieutenant Keith Wilson walked around to the driver's door to shake the man's hand. The light was just good enough to see perfectly.

Norman Barr was a giant of a man with thick, greasy, unruly, red hair that hung below the collar of his hunting shirt. His hair merged with an equally red beard. Eyebrows joined in a thick forest above a large protruding nose. Deep green eyes peaked out through the hair.

Wilson proffered his hand. It disappeared into a giant mitt that seemed the size of a wicketkeeper glove. Barr's grip was beyond firm, Wilson could feel that the man was capable of crushing every bone in his hand with the slightest increase in pressure.

'We better be off, let's get your kit loaded,' said Barr, clearly not a man for chitchat or pleasantries, exactly like his mate Colonel Reid-Daly.

Wilson waved at his men, they came struggling across the thick sand dragging the heavy crate behind them.

A mature Cape Buffalo male may grow to 340cm in length and reach 700-900 kilograms in weight. Adult buffalo are extremely dark brown or black, with males typically darker. The body is barrel-shaped and the chest wide. The legs are stocky, the head massive, and the neck is short and thick. Apart from the majestic bulbous horns that curl up and inward, the most distinguishing character on the head are the large, droopy ears, fringed with long black hair.

Buffalo males take it as their responsibility to protect the herd. Older males will take the lead, backed up by bachelors of similar size and weight. This is a responsibility Buffalo bulls take very seriously indeed.

The Buffalo bull is described as having such an irascible disposition that he will attack his greatest enemy, man, without the slightest provocation. He is the only beast in the African bush that looks upon Man as owing him something … these animals have attitude … and they know how to use it.

While the stationary Land Rover sitting on the sand was acceptable, three men struggling through the sand dragging a crate was not. This was made worse by the herd being at their most vulnerable while drinking at the river. The intruders were between them and the protection of the thick bush beyond.

A large bull looked up from drinking as soon as he heard Wilson's softly spoken greeting. To the bull, Wilson standing next to the Land Rover effectively made him part of it. As the bull turned his head, the three men dragging the heavy crate broke cover.

The Buffalo bull snorted loudly to alert the herd, suddenly fifty pairs of deep black eyes were studying the interlopers.

A baby Buffalo gave out a distinctive plaintiff cry of distress.

That was enough to galvanise the big males into action.

Buffalo can run at 57km/hr over short distances, 100m is a short distance for a rampant Buffalo, even slowed slightly by soft sand.

The big male, followed by three juveniles, were the first out of the water. The leader was bellowing his warning, his giant head erect, nose in the air.

Ngwenya instantly saw the danger. He had his AK over his shoulder but it was designed for killing men, not Buffalo.

He dropped the crate and shouted 'Run,' at the other two.

The Buffalo bull had covered the first 25m before Norman Barr could react.

Buffalo do not mock charge … they finish what they start.

Ngwenya and the other two ran for their lives across the sand aiming for the steep-sided riverbank, covered in thick bush, tree roots and boulders.

'Fook,' muttered Barr, flicking the rifle out of is cradle, ramming a round into the chamber and aiming, all in a split second.

He fired, the Winchester bucking into his shoulder. The round flew high, the loud rifle crack adding to the panic amongst the animals.

'Foook!' he shouted in frustration.

Now the whole herd were on the move. There was no stopping them, they sensed danger, nothing was going to prevent them getting into the safety of the trees.

Barr bolted another round into the chamber, lifted the rifle, looked down the open iron sights, and fired again.

The 358 bullet hit the lead bull well back in the ribs, online for the heart and lungs. It was deflected by the ribcage, running up alongside it between the bone and the skin. It had not penetrated!

Thundering in pain, the Buffalo hesitated but did not falter.

Chiyeka was the first to reach the bank. Seeing an overhanging branch he leapt up swinging his legs hard, clamping them onto the branch. He twisted his body to get upright sitting astride the branch, his legs dangling each side. He screamed at Mundiya below him, leaning down to offer his hand.

Mundiya jumped, missing the hand.

The herd of Buffalo were now very close, charging for the protection of the bush, heads held high, bawling their distress.

Another rifle shot rang out … one of the lead animals stumbled and fell, squealing in agony, its forward momentum burying its nose into the soft sand.

Ngwenya jumped at the riverbank clawing at grass and tree roots, pulling himself up, kicking with his legs to get leverage. The sound of the charging herd was like nothing he had ever experienced before, loud thumping and bellowing, the stomach-churning thunder of hundreds of heavy hooves.

Mundiya jumped again, grabbing Chiyeka's hand, it held ... not tightly enough, slipping from the sweat. The hand came out.

'Mundiya!' screamed Chiyeka trying to urge his friend to try again.

Realising that it was too late, Mundiya pulled the AK47 into his hands, lifted it and aimed at the Buffalo bull, only metres away, at full unbridled stretch. He pulled the trigger, bullets sprayed at the animal ricocheting off its huge horns.

With sickening impact, the Buffalo was on him, horns flicking. Mundiya's body was lifted off the ground, thrown high, the rifle spinning clear.

Mundiya let out a plaintiff cry ... his body dumped back onto the ground, knocking him senseless.

Intent on destroying his victim, the Buffalo stood over the unconscious body, goring and tossing it with his formidable horns in vindictive fury, trampling it under his feet, crushing and mangling it with his knees and stripping off the skin with his rough and prickly tongue. The giant animal turned to run off, but his pain and distress forcing him to return again, with renewed appetite, as though his revenge upon the lifeless body might never be satiated.

Another rifle shot rang out. The Buffalo bull stood, turning to face his new enemy. Norman Barr had come running along the riverbank to get a closer shot. Bellowing again, the Buffalo threw up his majestic head, turning to charge at Barr, his eyes red with fury, the pain in his body excruciating, driving him onwards.

Barr knelt in the sand, aimed and fired again. Hit square in the chest, the Buffalo crumpled, the speed of his charge throwing his body forward, front legs collapsed ... his heart pierced ... legs kicking out in his death throws. There was one last bellow of defiance ... head thrashing ... the great animal died ...

The African bush returned to silence, the short, sharp, unspeakable violence already forgotten. The herd stood high on the riverbank, looking down at the body of their fallen comrade, heads held up, noses sniffing at the air.

Chiyeka looked down in stunned horror at the torn, crumpled

body of his friend. He jumped down from the branch, a sound of anguish came from the back of his throat. The shock and viciousness of Mundiya's death, the sheer terror of what he had experienced, made his body shake uncontrollably.

Chiyeka sank to his knees in the blood soaked sand, head bowed, '*Baba wethu osezulwini: Ibizo lakho alicwengiswe ...*[37]'

Wilson and Barr came running up. There was nothing anybody could do ... Mundiya was smashed almost beyond recognition.

Ngwenya joined them, shaking his head in disbelief. This was a man he had known for years ... trusted with his life ... braving the most frightening of battles, now lying dead from a Buffalo.

Barr fetched a blanket from the Land Rover and the Selous Scouts wrapped their friend carefully in it. There was a shovel in the back of the Land Rover that they used to bury Mundiya high above the high-water mark. They collected stones to make a cairn to help find the grave again later.

The Matabele conceive a person as made up of three aspects, the material and two spiritual beings. They believe that from birth to death, a person lives with a spirit, that looks after him and could bring good fortune or misfortune to him. This spirit was called *Idlozi* and a fine line of distinction existed between this spirit and the one that passed onto the ancestral world. The *Amadlozi* is the very powerful spirit that passes on to the next world.

As Mundiya had been killed by a Buffalo this was a potent omen. It meant that his spirit would likely enter into a buffalo as a form of reincarnation. They knew that they could not bury his body deep enough. It would very likely be dug up and eaten by Hyenas, spreading his bones over a wide area, some to be carried away by vultures. That was not a concern to Ngwenya and Chiyeka as Mundiya's ancestral spirit would already reside in the body of majestic Buffalo, a great representation of power and strength ... a fitting place for a brave warrior.

> *There's a highway of stars across the heavens*
> *There's a whispering song of the wind in the grass*
> *There's the rolling thunder across the Savannah*
> *A hope and a dream at the edge of the sky*
> *And your life is a story like the wind*
> *Your life is a story like the wind*

---

[37] Our Father, which art in heaven, Hallowed be thy Name ...

I'm searching for the spirit of the great heart to hold and stand by me
I'm searching for the spirit of the great heart under African skies
I'm searching for the spirit of the great heart,
I see the fire in your eyes
I'm searching for the spirit of the great heart that beats my name inside.[38]

*

Red Fox Hotel, Rhodesville Avenue, Greendale, Salisbury

'The Poms have sent Rapier missiles to Zambia,' said John Sutcliffe.

'Bloody hell, those things are deadly to low flying aircraft,' responded Alan 'Jock' McLean, alias Ben Nevis, secret agent and erstwhile Scania truck salesman.

The two men only ever met at the Red Fox Hotel, it was close to where Jock McLean lived before the CIO recruited him.

The only people in the world that knew Jock McLean was the spy codenamed Ben Nevis was John Sutcliffe, his boss Ken Flower the Head of CIO, and the head of CIO communications, Bob Brown. It was the most closely guarded secret in the entire intelligence community. There was no file, no information, no record of any description. The intelligence gathered by McLean, the missions he was sent on, were never written down, and if they were, they were so heavily sanitised by Sutcliffe as to be impossible to decipher.

McLean had been ripe for recruitment. He had been bored out of his mind since leaving 22 SAS. He had done a few jobs for The Firm, trained bodyguards in Kenya, attempted to assassinate the leader of Libya, Muammar Gaddafi and successfully assassinated three senior men in the IRA. He had applied for a job as head of security for a mine in Zambia that brought him out to Africa. Being a free agent, without a wife and kids, Jock could drift from country to country at will. At the time, he had very scanty knowledge of the war and politics in Rhodesia and frankly didn't much care.

The mine Jock was sent to had been close to the Zambian side of the Kariba hydroelectric dam. The only place to get a cold beer was at the horribly decrepit Leisure Bay Hotel … until they ran out, which was often. Jock McLean could abide a great deal of discomfort, but deprived of beer for too long, he became downright miserable. Fortunately, those were the days before the border was closed, so Jock

---

38   *Great Heart*, Johnny Clegg and Juluka.

and a mate from the mine travelled across the dam wall into Rhodesia.

The contrast was amazing. The Customs building was clean and newly painted, surrounded by carefully tended flowerbeds. The roads were free of potholes. The Customs officer pointed Jock and his mate in the direction of the Cutty Sark Hotel overlooking the lake and it was at that moment that he fell in love with Rhodesia.

They did not think that they would need foreign currency, it had not crossed their minds. With only Zambian Kwacha, and a skin full of beer, the whole thing was enormously embarrassing. Jock and his mate debated their problem in front of the perplexed barman, not sure of what to do next. Then the hotel manager stepped in. He offered to open them an account to be paid on their next visit. Jock could not believe that the man would trust them ... complete strangers. In addition, they were offered a room in the hotel and a slap up dinner. The Rhodesians were clearly another breed ...

During one of his many stays in Kariba, Jock met a man who said he worked at the tobacco auctions. After only the shortest of conversations, during which Jock told him he had been a policeman in Scotland, he was offered a job as head of security. After a few more idyllic days at Kariba, Jock returned to Zambia, resigned his job and moved to Rhodesia. The man had accepted Jock's story at face value, no thought of checking references or his background.

It was during a serious piss-up at the Salisbury Sports Club that Jock had been reacquainted with Jim Murray, a more junior operator from A Squadron, 22 SAS. Jim was a good 10 years younger than Jock. Jim told him that he worked in 'insurance.' In Rhodesia, Jock discovered, 'insurance' was the equivalent of 'oil company' in the UK.

Jock enjoyed the company of a fellow SAS operator and he and Jim would often meet for beers or a round of golf. On one such occasion, Jim had suggested that Jock meet a friend of his who had raised a business proposition. Jock, being carefree and happy-go-lucky had met with the 'friend' who turned out to be John Sutcliffe (CIO) ... and one thing lead to another.

The recruitment process to the CIO had been a revelation. Sutcliffe produced a file procured from MI6, covering Jock's entire military service with the Royal Engineers then the SAS, including the jobs he had done for The Firm.

Soldiers applying for 22 SAS selection needed to have served for three years with some other unit before they became eligible. Jock had joined the Engineers straight from school, as he could not see himself working in a distillery as his father had done his entire life. Jock had been a hopeless student, with interest only in disruption and playing practical jokes. He spent hours booby-trapping teachers class rooms, using fishing wire attached to drawers, doors, blackboard dusters, books and a myriad of other things, to spill water, flour, sugar, washing powder, or any other sticky substance that could create a mess. He had nearly burnt down the science lab with a wire attached to a Bunsen burner.

Jock was such a big strapping lad that corporal punishment issued by the headmaster with a heavy wooden cane had little effect.

Both Jock's father and grandfather had served with The Argyll and Sutherland Highlanders. The family were scandalised when Jock had stated he was joining the engineers to 'blow up things'. As it turned out he became very good at blowing up things and his commanding officer had suggested that he try SAS selection. He was a strong fit lad, with a bit of an attitude ... he had no idea what he was letting himself in for. In the end, his sheer determination not to be outdone was what got him through.

Sutcliffe's file on Jock was so comprehensive that he even had a copy of a charge sheet signed by the squadron commander where Jock had been disciplined for beating up three soldiers from the Parachute Regiment.

Jock McLean was a big man, with big determination, a big thirst, together with a big temper.

After a few meetings with Sutcliffe, Jock seized the chance for a return to the action and agreed to become a CIO agent to be posted to Lusaka in Zambia. It all seemed a wonderful adventure and Jock threw himself into the rigorous training that the CIO had arranged. He found himself to be horribly rusty after so many years out of 'the field' and found the physical demands taxing at first. The Rhodesians refreshed his weapons training on all the latest communist block equipment, including RPG7 rocket grenades, land mines, AP mines, explosives and small arms. He fired off thousands of rounds under Police Armaments Branch instruction at the Cleveland Rifle Range in Salisbury.

To bring his bushcraft skills back up to speed, he was placed with an experienced PATU stick in the Matusadona National Park on the southern edge of Lake Kariba in the Zambezi valley. While all this was going on, his cover story as a truck salesman had to be practiced and rehearsed relentlessly. He and Sutcliffe agreed that there was no point masquerading as a truck salesman working for Zambian dealer Southwood, if he knew nothing about trucks. His final instruction was in Johannesburg with a Scania dealership where he was given a two-week immersion course in all things Scania and all things trucks.

Through Jock's entire 6-month training, not one person asked him his name, or asked any questions of a personal nature. John Sutcliffe was the only person from the CIO he spoke to on any subject. Sutcliffe made all of the arrangements including transport and logistics. The final 'passing-out' ceremony was the presentation of three British passports, all with different names, including an exact copy of his passport. It was decided that he would travel on his own passport in Zambia as he had already travelled and worked there. The other passports were for … 'contingencies'.

'Jock, the first two loads of missiles and their support vehicles will be arriving sometime today. We think they will be taken to Mumbwa air force base where they will train the operators. We need to know where those missiles are positioned. If you have a chance to take them out … do so,' instructed Sutcliffe earnestly.

Jock nodded, there was not much else to be said on the subject … these missiles were a serious threat to Rhodesian external raids.

'On the next subject Jock, we are now convinced that more senior Cuban advisors have arrived in Zambia. We are thinking that they will be much more hands-on than the Soviets. We really need to know what they are up to … if you can snatch one, that would be excellent,' said Sutcliffe earnestly. He handed over an envelope with a few black and white photos of men with moustaches and sunglasses.

'Those were taken outside the Cuban Embassy.'

Jock knew that the CIO had other agents, in addition to himself, in Lusaka. They were, as he was, deeply buried. His safety and theirs depended on identities and mission information being compartmentalised on a strictly need to know basis.

'Hey Jock, brilliant effort on Mangena. The Zambians are convinced that he was assassinated by Mugabe's crowd. That magazine you left behind did the trick. The Cuban cigar box was a great touch, especially since the only person smoking that brand was the Cuban Ambassador himself!' laughed Sutcliffe. 'Our intercepts say that Kenny the Clown[39] has called the Ambassador in to explain himself! Good stuff Jock!'

Both men smiled, the mental picture was hilarious. Jock had broken into the Ambassador's car to steal the cigars, he still had a few left. He reached into his jacket pocket and passed a cigar over to Sutcliffe.

'Who Divides Wins,' quipped Jock, using one of his favourite expressions. It defined his mission perfectly.

---

39   Rhodesian slang, Kenneth Kaunda.

'Here is a list of your next targets.' Sutcliffe handed over another file. In it were two folders, they said ... Lookout Masuku (code 'Laurel') and Dumiso Dabengwa (code 'Hardy') ... Sutcliffe loved choosing code words.

Both men's attention was distracted as a magnificent strawberry blond woman walked into the bar. She sat down on a stool and ordered a beer, addressing the barman with a clear, polished, upper-class English accent.

*

Sarah Ann Burrell sat gazing distractedly into the mirror at the bar in the Red Fox Hotel. She could see her face between a row of *Famous Grouse* whisky bottles. Clearly, someone had managed to smuggle in a crate. With sanctions, Scotch whisky was well nigh impossible to get. As a result, it was extortionately expensive. Being a bit short of cash, Sarah could only look longingly at the golden liquid in front of her.

Sarah wasn't much of a beer drinker, but sometimes necessity required a few changes in likes and dislikes. The Rhodesian beer, Castle Pilsner, was cheap, of passable flavour, its saving grace being that it was strong. She lifted the glass and drained a quarter in one gulp.

The barman watched in fascination. Rhodesian woman knew how to drink but this one was in a class of her own. He had been serving her drinks for three days, plenty of drinks ... yet she showed no ill effects.

She lifted her fringe to look at the sticking plaster across her forehead. Still suffering from fearful headaches, the doctor had said that she had a bad concussion. There was bruising around the edges of the plaster that were turning a horrible yellow colour. The bullet had literally glanced across her forehead, another millimetre and it would have sliced off the front of her skull. She shivered at the thought of her own death. An inexplicable foreboding washed over her ... the feeling people describe as 'someone walking over their grave'.

The bar was cool and dark contrasting with the bright hot sunlight outside. A smell of spilt beer and stale cigarette smoke was strangely comforting. Sarah turned to see who else was in the bar. Two men were sitting at a table in the far corner, they smiled at her as she turned around.

She smiled back, lifted her glass and said 'Cheers!'

They both responded by lifting their glasses, returning ... 'Cheers'.

At thirty-five, Sarah had covered Vietnam, Congo, Algeria, Angola,

South West Africa and now Rhodesia. Sarah Burrell looked out of place in a war zone. The tall and willowy American, lanky with a sophisticated air, looked as if she would be more at home on the catwalk, than tramping through the hot dusty thornveld in khaki with notebook and camera in hand. In her youth she had indeed been a ramp model in New York.

Despite her stunning good looks, Sarah knew how to blend in. Her native broad Bronx New York accent was a door-opener everywhere except Rhodesia. Here, even the hint of a US accent aroused instant suspicion. Sarah smiled to herself, the local people were so deeply suspicious of Americans yet it was the British that were screwing them over. She could not believe how far she could get with a winning smile and her cultured and polished English accent that Julie Andrews would have been proud of. Sarah was as much actress as she was reporter.

A veteran journalist, Sarah was no stranger to counter-insurgency war zones. Rumour had it amongst the foreign press corps that in Vietnam she stole a march on rivals by securing flights on helicopters using means denied her male colleagues. The story that had done the rounds amongst the members of the press in Salisbury told of a former model and high-class prostitute in New York falling in love with a news photographer. She had followed him to Vietnam then picking up a camera, finding herself seduced by war and the men who fought it. It was a story that Sarah made no attempt to deny. She revelled in her reputation, it opened doors in all the right places.

With Sarah things were either black or white, she hated fence-sitting. This made her writing evocative and controversial. She was not above using wicked sarcasm as a weapon, nobody was exempt if she detected, what she would describe, as bull-shit.

Sarah Burrell stood out from the other foreign correspondents and photographers covering the bush war, partly because she didn't associate with them at their watering holes like the Quill Club in Salisbury. Burrell didn't hunt with the pack. She went her own way, preferring the company of soldiers to that of the press corps.

She had that unique, uncommon, female ability to cast a spell. Maybe it was her experience as a model, with men fawning all over her, or just her captivating looks, coupled with her supreme intellect. This meant that if she set her mind to it, no man could resist her.

In the past few days, Sarah had done her fair share of crying, attempting to drown her sorrow in the bottom of a beer bottle. She was not sure whether she had ever truly loved a man, but Jake Gallagher would have been close. They had worked on and off together, albeit for different news services, for more than a year. His soft West Virginian drawl and dark good looks had been what initially attracted her in a bar in Johannesburg. He was a gentle, quietly spoken man about her age. Jake was brave, never afraid to go to the very edge for a story. When he had convinced Newsweek to do a story on a Freedom Fighter camp in Zambia she went along, as she had done on most of his African assignments. Africa was a prime spot to work as a journalist, full of military dictators, one-party states, corruption, genocide and of course, her personal passion, war.

The Rhodesian attack on the terrorist base had been so unexpected. She and Jake had just finished interviewing the camp commander when the attack started. The sheer speed, force and brutality of the attack, the efficiency of the Rhodesian forces at killing the freedom fighters, had been confronting and terrifying.

She had written an obituary for Jake and sent it through to Newsweek. He was a highly respected journalist winning both story and photographic prizes, he was in a class all on his own. Her story for Associated Press had not yet been finished, she just couldn't get the right angle. The accepted protocol for the international press was labelling the terrorist bases as refugee camps. Sarah knew it was all bullshit. The camp at Kabanga Mission had been bristling with the latest Soviet weaponry. She resisted serving up the stories on Rhodesia with the spin demanded by the newspaper editors. The American imagination was fired by stories of subjugated, downtrodden black people, enslaved by a cruel white minority government, while passionately pursuing their freedom from oppression. As long as those black people were in Africa and not Detroit or Philadelphia that was. As Mark Twain said, 'Never let the truth stand in the way of a good story'.

While the Freedom Fighter story was bullshit, Sarah did not buy into the whole Rhodesian, fighting-for-survival-against-the-communist-hoards, thing either. To her they conjured images of a form of entry level Ku Klux Clan running some sort of demented bowls club ... *she had read that somewhere?* Outwardly, they were friendly, engaging and generous to a fault, but their attitude to their black population stank!

The Rhodesian leaders seemed to live in some sort of time-warp ... Ian Smith, the Prime Minister, was a kind of gentleman farmer, RAF pilot, colonial throwback, who couldn't read the tealeaves. He wore his stubbornness and intransigence as a badge of honour, while his country burned around him.

Sarah smiled to herself when she thought of the last meeting between the Rhodesian Minister of Foreign Affairs, P. K. Van der Byl, and the Foreign Press corps. He had brandished an UZI machine pistol throughout the interview, while giving an eloquent speech, in a posh English accent, on the failed British foreign policy in Africa.

That said it all ... they were all going down with the ship! In the Rhodesian situation, two 'wrongs' were desperately trying to make a 'right'.

Thoughts of Jake made tears prick at the corner of Sarah's eyes. She drained the rest of the glass and called the barman for another.

Sarah was convinced she knew Jake's killer. She had decided she was going to hunt down the man and expose him for the murderer that he was. There was a deep-seated feeling of hate and resentment building in her gut ... she was going to crucify him in a story to be spread around the world.

At first, she suspected the Rhodesian SAS, but then she remembered that some of the soldiers were black, the SAS did not recruit black troops. That pretty much left the RAR and the Selous Scouts. In her mind the man she was looking for was a Selous Scout ... she was convinced.

Keith ... where are you?

The gamble of presenting herself at the gates to the SAS HQ at Kabrit Barracks had not worked. Her not so subtle invitation to the SAS Captain hadn't worked either.

These people all know each other, even if this Keith wasn't SAS, he was probably an officer and known to them.

At the gates to the RLI barracks at Cranborne, they had been very helpful and obliging, she was told that they had four 'Keiths', but none of them were officers. One, Keith Bartlett, was a Warrant Officer but he was at the School of Infantry. That left the Selous Scouts.

She had driven out to Nkomo Barracks but the place was like Fort Knox, sprawled over a huge area. Finding someone was a needle in a haystack. She had put in a request for an interview with the Selous Scouts but had been flatly rejected.

Right now she was at a dead end and needed a drink ...

'Goodbye,' said one of the men sitting at the table.

She turned to look at him ... *my, my, you are a big unit!*

Smiling at him, 'Cheers' she said.

With a trained eye she took in the big man ... *forties ... obvious military or ex-military. Everybody in this country is military or ex-military.*

Both men nodded their heads as they left the pub. Sarah watched them go ... in a strange sort of way the big one seemed strangely familiar. She thought about it for a few seconds before returning to her beer ... downing it.

Crystal Gayle[40] was playing on the piped music into the bar ... Number 9 on the RBC, *Lyons Maid Hits of the Week*.

Sarah felt a sudden pang of homesickness ...

> *Why have you left the one you left me for?*
> *Has she heard, like me, that slammin door?*
> *Did you leave for good or just get bored?*
> *Why have you left the one you left me for?*

If the trail for this man Keith goes cold ... I might as well go back to Lusaka and finish my story ...

'Beer,' Sarah said to the barman pointing at her glass ... tapping her feet on the barstool.

> *Okay, come on in!*
> *You be my lover!*
> *Ill be your friend!*
> *You don't have to tell me, and I won't ask again!*
> *Why have you left the one you left me for?*
> *Has she heard, like me, that slammin door?*
> *Did you leave for good or just get bored?*

---

40 Crystal Gayle, *Why Have You Left The One You Left Me For* (1978), song written by Mark True, EMI Music Publishing.

6

170 nautical miles north of Lusaka International Airport

'Good day, Lusaka Approach, this is Danair 230, do you copy?' called the co-pilot. At 40, he was a veteran on Boeing 707s.

'Danair 230, Lusaka Approach, good morning,' replied the Air Traffic Controller at Lusaka International Airport.

'Lusaka, we request clearance to flight level one-one-zero, beacon Lima Whisky, track two-two-eight degrees, please confirm weather for landing.'

'Danair 230, you are cleared to flight level one-one-zero, wind two-eight-zero at five knots, visibility thirty kilometres, cloud three/eights at 600ft, QNH 1,021 millibars. Maintain your track.'

'Thank you Lusaka, Danair 230 out.'

Dan-Air Services Ltd owned the Boeing 707-321C, with British registration G-BEBQ, on charter to Zambian Airways. It was carrying freight from London Heathrow to Lusaka via Nairobi in Kenya. The crew had requested descent from their flight level of 31,000ft to 11,000ft. They could hear the air traffic controller talking to another aircraft 5 minutes ahead of them but on a different track.

*

Sergeant Ronnie Shikapwasha of the 2nd Battalion, Zambian Regiment, was immensely proud. He had been put in charge of a new missile that would protect his beloved country from the Rhodesians. Ronnie had been sent to England to be trained before on other missiles but now he had the latest equipment. The other ones were no good as they broke easily and they needed the wire … the wire was no good[41].

To be chosen for the new missile was a great honour. Not only that, the equipment came with three brand new Land Rovers that gave Ronnie complete freedom of movement. This promised enormous possibilities.

The British soldiers had helped Ronnie choose a site for the missiles. They assisted him to set up and make sure all the equipment was working.

Some other men had visited the site after the missiles had been installed. They were neatly dressed in suits and panama hats escorted by his commander, Captain Peter Chitengi. The men spoke to each other in a language that Ronnie did not recognize but they were very

---

41   Tiger Cat – wire-guided, ground-to-air missile.

friendly. The men walked around the launcher and the radar mounting, taking photographs and conducting a long animated conversation in their strange language.

One man had then spoken most urgently to Captain Chitengi.

After a long talk with the man, Captain Chitengi had taken Ronnie to one side. This was a very good talk because he gave Ronnie a pile of money in his hand ... in cash, One Thousand Kwatcha![42] *How!* ... *but that was a lot of money!*

All these men wanted was one of the missiles, after all, there were four on the launcher and another four in the truck. Ronnie thought that if it was okay with Captain Chitengi, then it was okay with him. He still had seven missiles left after all ... plus one thousand Kwatcha! *What a good day this was!*

The missile was heavy so Ronnie got his men to help carry the missile to the truck the men had brought. The men lay the missile on a mattress and wrapped it up very tightly indeed. They were so happy! They slapped Ronnie on the back and he could tell from their smiles they were thanking him. They even took out a crate of Chibuku beer to say thank you to Ronnie. What nice men, maybe the best white men he had ever met.

*

'Lusaka Approach, this is Danair 230, maintaining flight level one-one-zero, DME thirty-seven nautical miles, we request clearance to flight level seven-zero?'

'Danair 230, you are cleared to seven-zero, report when you have the runway in sight.'

'Seven –zero, report runway in sight, Danair 230.'

*

After the men had left, Sergeant Ronnie Shikapwasha had turned the missile system on. The launcher consisted of a large cylindrical unit carrying two missiles on each side, the surveillance 'Dagger' radar dish and identification friend or foe (IFF) system under a radome on top, the guidance computer, radar transmitter and receiver electronics at the bottom. There was a prominent parabolic antenna for sending guidance commands to the missiles on the front of the launcher.

Next to the missiles, on its own trailer, was the separate Blindfire tracking radar. Ronnie was sitting behind the third component, the optical tracker. Power to the three systems was supplied by two petrol

---

[42] About US$800.00.

driven generators. The loud clatter of the generators was the only sound.

It was a beautiful warm day, with only a few fluffy clouds. From his vantage point on top of a low hill, Ronnie could see for miles in all directions. He knew he had to be vigilant; the Rhodesians could attack at any time.

In the valley to the northeast, only 4.8km away, was a large training base for Zimbabwean Freedom Fighters. Ronnie was told he had to protect them as well as his capital 15km to the south.

Ronnie had watched aircraft pass overhead all morning. He was only 6km north of the eastern approach path into Lusaka International Airport. He knew the types of planes well as they passed high overhead ... he and his crew had a game guessing which country the planes come from. Ronnie had been taught to expect an air threat at low-altitude. The fast reaction time and high manoeuvrability of the Rapier made it a good weapon against Rhodesian Hawker Hunters and English Electric Canberras. The instructors from England had given him pictures of these jets so he knew what they looked like. He had not actually seen them in real life but he was confident he would recognise them if they came.

When the surveillance radar detected and acquired a target, the bearing data was downloaded to the tracking radar and the launcher, then automatically aligned to the target bearing. To allow the operator to monitor the Blindfire system when it was tracking the target, the optical tracker was slaved to the Blindfire radar.

Ronnie got a fright; the missiles suddenly spun around facing to the north. The 'Dagger' surveillance radar gave a buzz ... it had acquired a target. It said a range of 15km. Two lamps lit up on the Selector Engagement Zone (SEZ), a box containing 32 orange lamps arranged in a circle about the size of a car steering wheel. Ronnie looked into the TV screen on the optical tracker but could not see anything ... *it must be too far away.*

The surveillance radar automatically cued the Blindfire tracking radar and it immediately swung around to establish the target bearing, range and height. All three bits of equipment were now facing towards the north. Ronnie had been warned that the threat would probably come from the north, as that was where the freedom fighter base was.

The missile launcher made rapid adjustments as new tracking information was computed. The whole system seemed to vibrate in anticipation. It was as if the missiles were sniffing the air like deadly snakes flicking their tongues, testing the air for the presence of prey.

Ronnie jumped off his chair to look out into the horizon, sheltering his eyes against the sun. He called out to his men to look as well ... he cursed ... he had forgotten his binoculars. He glanced back at the TV screen ... there was still nothing on it.

The missiles locked-on, the buzzer sounded again, the target was now engaged for a radar tracked missile shot. The difference between the target and missile angles were instantly derived and automatically transmitted to the missile to guide it on to the target. It continued to shiver with tiny adjustments.

The English soldiers had switched off the IFF systems on the missiles to stop it 'alarming' whenever an aircraft flew over. This was because the software to detect civilian IFF systems had not been upgraded. Ronnie was told he had to make the decision to fire himself.

An aircraft came into view on the TV screen, Ronnie gave a huge sigh of relief when he saw it was a Zambian Airways Hawker Siddeley HS-748-263. *It had propellers, his enemy had jets.*

Ronnie reset the machine, but the radar carried on buzzing ... there was another target ...

*

'Lusaka Approach, Danair 230, airfield in sight, request visual approach,' called the co-pilot of the Boeing 707-321C, registration number G-BEBQ.

'Roger Danair 230 descend to flight level zero six, maintain heading two-two-eight degrees.'

There was a brief delay as the crew of the Danair flight finished their landing checklist.

'Flaps to 25 degrees,' called the Captain in control of the aircraft.

'Lusaka Approach, Danair 230, we will be turning downwind in one minute, we have the aircraft ahead of us in sight.'

'Danair 230, you are cleared to make visual approach, left base leg for runway one-zero. Report leaving flight level six zero.'

The crew of Danair 230, were tired, they had a sleepless night in the cheap hotel in Nairobi, they wanted to get onto the ground as soon as possible. The Captain increased the rate of decent.

'Lusaka Approach, Danair 230, we are through level six zero.'

'Danair 230, please contact Lusaka Tower on one-one-eight decimal one, good day to you.'

The co-pilot repeated his instructions and then twisted the dials to put the radio onto the new frequency for Lusaka Tower.

'Lusaka Tower this is Danair 230.'

'Danair 230, Lusaka Tower, good morning.'

'Lusaka Tower we are passing through flight level four-zero for visual approach, left base leg for runway one-zero.'

'Danair 230, turn finals on visual approach, runway one-zero.'

'Forty degree flaps,' called the Captain as he set the aircraft up for a landing. 'Undercarriage down and locked.'

*

At a QNH of 1,021 millibars, at an altitude of 6,000ft, the aircraft would have been at 2,200ft AGL at Lusaka. At 4,000ft on the altimeter, the Boeing 707 was only at 1,400ft above ground.

The Rapier missile radar did not know whether the target was hostile or not.

Ronnie Shikapwasha looked towards the incoming aircraft, it was low and it was coming directly towards him ... it was a jet, he could hear the engines.

The threat buzzer got louder.

The Rhodesians are coming ...

The engines of the jet were getting louder ... roaring ...

'The Rhodesians are coming,' screamed Ronnie and pressed the fire button.

The Rapier left the rail in a blinding flash ... the radar guided it towards the target at a speed in excess of Mach 2.5.

*

The crew of Danair 230 had no idea what hit them.

People on the ground saw a large portion of the aircraft structure separate in flight.

The right hand rear stabiliser and elevator were sheared off from the impact of the missile. The crew felt a solid thump travel through the airframe. The undamaged left hand elevator travelled to the fully up position, increasing the aircraft rate of pitch, nose down.

The natural reaction of the Captain was to pull the control column back.

There was no time at all.

The aircraft dived out of the sky at 130 knots, speed increasing, the angle of descent more acute every split second. It hit the ground at the vertical ...

A violent explosion followed, the impact sending a tremor through the ground that could be felt a mile away. Dust and debris were thrown high into the sky. The aircraft disintegrated, throwing pieces of airframe hundreds of metres from the point of impact. Fire spread, creating a fierce bushfire 3,600m from the threshold to runway One Zero. The pall of smoke could be seen for miles in all directions.

The debris field was covered with pieces of military equipment, radios, SLR rifles, ammunition, uniforms and webbing.

The controller in Lusaka Tower gave out a low moan ... he had watched the whole thing through his binoculars.

Sergeant Ronnie Shikapwasha, could not believe his eyes ... he screamed in fright and ran down the hill away from the missiles ...

*

Alan 'Jock' McLean stood on the top of the stairs pushed up against the side of the Zambian Airways HS-748-263. Looking out towards the west, he could see the burning crash site. He had just landed on a flight from Gaborone in Botswana.

Fire Engines were racing across the runway towards the crash.

'Shit!'

*

Luangwa River Bridge, Luangwa River, 210km east of Lusaka, Zambia

Lt Keith *Ikhanka* Wilson and his team of Sgt Cephas Ngwenya and Tpr Stanley Chiyeka, approached the 300m single-span suspension bridge over the Luangwa River with great trepidation. They were driving an old long-wheelbase Land Rover Series IIA lent to them by Norman Barr. The name Norman Barr Safaris was painted on the doors.

The trip south from Ndevu Ranch had been over ridiculously rough terrain and had taken hours. As the crow flies the distance to the Great East Road was only 39km but the actual distance through gorges and steep-sided hills was closer to 100km. Instead of taking the better road, in order to avoid army and police patrols, they took a rough unused bush track. The track was washed away in places, requiring the use of the winch to haul the vehicle through the gullies. In some cases they had to cut thick tree branches to help bridge the gaps. Bodies were aching from the relentless jarring and shaking from the Land Rover that had been built more as a form of torture than a means of transport.

Instead of trying to drive to Lusaka in the dark, they had decided to base up off the road and wait for morning. The three men were black and blue from bruises, and tempers were frayed. Sleep came easily after a meal of roasted Buffalo meat.

At first light, they climbed aboard the Land Rover and drove out onto the T4, the Great East Road to Lusaka.

The Zambian Army had built defences to protect all the major bridges from Rhodesian attack. The Luangwa Bridge was on the main arterial road between Zambia and Malawi on an extremely important trade route.

As the bridge came into view, Wilson changed down and slowed the vehicle so he had time to study the roadblock. On either end of the bridge, the Zambians had built a high sandbag zigzag, with a wooden boom and a machinegun nest covering the approach road. The Selous Scouts had left virtually all their equipment at Ndevu Ranch. All they carried were three AK47s, hidden at the bottom of a steel box, covered with layers of Buffalo meat. Explosives and detonators were hidden in a steel box welded to the underside of the Land Rover load tray. The TR48 radio was wrapped in plastic in the bottom of a large cool box full of ice and buffalo meat.

If they were compromised, they would have to try to overcome the guards on the roadblock and fight their way out.

The three men were dressed in khaki shorts and shirt with brushed leather 'veldskoens' and long socks. Each wore a floppy khaki hat with the Norman Barr logo looking every bit their part as game and hunting guides. A Winchester 270 bolt-action rifle in its canvas carry bag sat in a cradle behind the driver's seat. Wilson had a forged British passport in his pocket, while Ngwenya and Chiyeka had forged Green Zambian National Registration cards.

As they approached the boom across the road, flanked by sandbag walls, nobody could be seen. The place looked deserted. Wilson stopped the vehicle in front of the boom and hooted. There was still no movement.

'Hello,' shouted Wilson.

On the far side of the bridge, a man walked out into the road. He waved at them, his arm movement suggesting that they should come across the bridge.

A little perplexed, Wilson asked Chiyeka to jump out and open the boom. He did so and they drove through, continuing across the bridge to where the man was standing. Wilson pulled up, leaving the motor running.

Wilson smiled politely. The man was wearing dark green and brown Zambian Army camouflage uniform, similar to the British pattern. He had a British SLR slung over his shoulder and a webbing harness. He didn't appear to have anything in the pouches, although a water bottle was attached to the webbing belt.

'Where is Mister Barr?' asked the soldier, he clearly recognized the vehicle knowing that Norman Barr travelled the road frequently.

'He is sick with malaria, he asked us to drive these horns back to Lusaka for one of his hunting clients,' replied Wilson with his well-rehearsed story. The giant set of buffalo horns were conspicuous in the back of the open Land Rover.

'Ehhh,' replied the man nodding his head.

'Have you got identification?' asked the soldier, gesturing to the men in the back. They all took out their ID and Wilson passed the documents to the soldier. Ngwenya and Chiyeka did not say anything. They sat submissively avoiding the eyes of the soldier, knowing that the peasant population of Zambia were terrified of the Army and Police.

The soldier looked at the ID cards and Wilson's passport and handed them back.

'How long have you worked for Mister Barr?' asked the soldier, now making conversation.

'Only a month, I flew into the camp at Ndevu. This is my first drive to Lusaka,' replied Wilson, smiling broadly. He had to put on more of an English accent, to hide his 'Rhodesian'. The passport had stamps from all over Africa where hunting guides plied their trade, except Rhodesia of course.

'Ehhh,' nodded the man.

As they were talking, Wilson was scanning the surrounding area. There were no other soldiers to be seen. This man seemed to be the only one on duty. An old Second World War Bren gun was leaning on its bipod, on top of the sandbags.

'Have you got money?' asked the soldier after a pause.

'I have got meat,' replied Wilson gesturing to the steel trunk.

'Ehhh,' grunted the man, now more interested. He walked around to the back of the Land Rover and gestured towards the trunk. Ngwenya opened it, still careful not to meet the man's eye. He reached inside and pulled out a huge plastic bag of meat and handed it to the soldier.

'Shot yesterday,' quipped Wilson.

'Ehhh,' said the man, '... but I need money!' The weight of the bag of meat meant that the man had to hold it down next to his side.

Norman Barr had warned Wilson that this might happen, suggesting a range of tactics.

Still smiling, Wilson reached into his breast pocket and took out a few Zambian Kwatcha notes, handing them across.

'It is not enough,' said the man indignantly. 'I need more!'

'I haven't got any more,' replied Wilson starting to feel agitated, although still smiling disarmingly at the soldier. This was actually true. He had only a limited supply of money that he was going to need to support his mission.

'I don't believe it ...'

Wilson leaned forward and put his head on the steering wheel and sighed loudly. 'Please. I have no more money.'

'You can wait for my officer to come back, you can explain to him why you have no more money,' sneered the man.

Norman Barr made it his business to bribe the military hierarchy. This policy generally protected him and his people from harassment. As a new arrival, the soldier saw a weakness in Wilson, taking the opportunity to extort a bit more money.

'Please let me through ...' pleaded Wilson, sounding deeply distressed, keeping his head down on the steering wheel while his mind raced through the alternatives. They could sit around for ages waiting to get through the roadblock, plus the risk of a thorough search increased as the soldier looked for more money ... and found the weapons!

'Okay,' said Wilson, gesturing for the soldier to come closer as he fumbled in his pocket.

The man put out his hand.

In one fluid movement, Wilson, grabbed the outstretch hand with his left hand, yanked the man towards him, while his right hand armed with a hunting knife sliced backwards through the throat. The man stood looking at Wilson, his eyes wide with shock as blood burst through the savage cut flowing in a torrent down the front of his uniform. His lips moved but no sound came out.

Ngwenya was off the back of the Land Rover in a flash, catching the man before he fell. Then helped by Chiyeka he lifted him bodily into the back of the Land Rover. Blood spurting out with every heartbeat as the man gurgled in his own blood.

A pool of blood lay on the tarmac where the man had stood. Wilson opened the door and poured water over the blood to wash it away. Then taking sand from the side of the road, he rubbed it into the wet tarmac with his boot. The final touch was a bit of pee to make sure it looked like someone had taken a leak.

He then jumped back into the Land Rover and drove off as fast as he could. Ngwenya looked back as they climbed out of the river gorge, there was still nobody else anywhere to be seen.

Fuck! thought Wilson ... *so much for a successful clandestine infiltration ... one dead Selous Scout ... one dead Zambian Soldier.*

*

The 'Vatican', ZIPRA National Security and Order Offices (NSO), Latuba Road, Roma Township, Lusaka

The ZAPU-PF War Council was called to order. The great leader smiled at his leadership team. The meeting was being held at the National Security and Order offices (NSO) called the Vatican. The NSO was the ZAPU-PF counter-intelligence unit, secret police and enforcer. A holy place because no one but key personnel were allowed in.

The President of ZAPU-PF and the Chairman of the War Council, Comrade Joshua Mqabuko Nyongolo Nkomo, stood to his feet. In his sixties, Comrade Nkomo was an impressive man. He was a giant, both politically and physically, dominating the Zimbabwean freedom struggle for twenty years. He had suffered from obesity almost his entire adult life, impacting terribly on his health.

Nkomo known affectionately as *Umdala Wethu*, our old man, was driven by the struggle for freedom and the introduction of majority rule. He was born of missionary teachers in the arid Semokwe native reserve in southwest Matabeleland and educated in South Africa. It was when he was studying in South Africa that he met some of the influential leaders of the South African ANC (African National Congress) whose ideas influenced and sharpened his political career. It was during this time that he met Nelson Mandela and other regional nationalist leaders. He founded a number of small organisations, all banned by the British colonial authorities, before founding ZAPU in 1962. Nkomo spent ten and half years as a political prisoner at Gonakudzingwa, on the edge of the Gona-re-Zhou National Park in the far south of the country. On his release in 1974, Nkomo fled to Zambia to fight for Zimbabwean independence. He quickly moved back to the centre stage of the Zimbabwe liberation struggle, chanting his 'song', one-man one-vote.

Despite Nkomo's lengthy incarceration he understood the need for a negotiated settlement with the white Smith regime in Rhodesia. He was not consumed by hate of the white man in the same way as his erstwhile ally, Robert Mugabe of ZANU-PF. He was of the view that the British, the Commonwealth and the Americans would succeed in putting enough pressure on Smith to concede. The present internal settlement negotiations were not to Nkomo's liking and he refused to participate. All the while, his forces were growing, trained and equipped by his Soviet and East German brothers, for the invasion of Rhodesia if Smith failed to admit defeat. Time was on his side.

'Good morning Comrades,' said Nkomo softly.

'*Yee!*' replied his team in unison.

The five members of the War Council were not only brothers-in-arms but also tribal and religious brothers. They were all Matabele with warrior blood going back many generations, Zulu blood. In their veins flowed the blood of Lobengula, son of Mzilikazi the first King of the Matabele Tribe, all descendants of the Zulu Khumalo Dynasty. Mzilikazi had incurred the wrath of the powerful King of the Zulus, Shaka. He had been forced to flee his native land near the Black Mfolozi River in Zululand, South Africa, in 1821. Mzilikazi took his clan north, eventually settling in the area to become know as Matabeleland, north of the Limpopo River. He set about building his kingdom by subjugating the indigenous Shona tribe.

The War Council's ancestors had fought to free the Matabele Kingdom from white settlers who had occupied the land in 1890. They were present at the destruction of Alan Wilson's Shangani Patrol in 1893, then witnessing the final annihilation of the last of the Matabele army by maxim guns at Bembesi in the same year.

Now was the time for the final defeat of the white settlers ... the end of a seventy-year struggle for freedom!

Sitting around the table were the five permanent members of the War Council. On Nkomo's right, sat Party Commissar Samuel Munodawafa, Secretary for Defence Akim Ndlovu. On his left sat the nominated replacement Commander of ZIPRA, Lookout Masuku and next to him, the head of the National Security Organisation (NSO), Dumiso Dabengwa.

'Our first order of business is to confirm the appointment of our brother and comrade, Lookout Masuku, as Supreme Commander of our Revolutionary Army,' said Nkomo formally. 'May I have a show of hands?' Nkomo was a man for the occasion, a great believer in protocol and formality.

All the hands were raised.

'It is with great pleasure that I confirm your appointment Comrade Masuku,' stated Nkomo with a flourish of his arm. 'May you take us to a glorious victory.'

Masuku nodded his head in acceptance. He was a man of few words, preferring for his success to be measured by actions. He was a man of the people, the rank and file, the sons of peasant farmers and labourers.

'Next, Comrade Dabengwa, can you update us on the investigation into the death of our dear brother Alfred Mangena?' asked Nkomo.

Dumiso Dabengwa was a man possessed of a supreme intellect. The Rhodesians called him the 'Black Russian' because he had been trained by the Soviet KGB in Moscow and was fluent in Russian. Rumours that he carried the rank of Colonel in the KGB were rubbish, but Dabengwa revelled in the mystery that surrounded him.

Dumisa Dabengwa was Public Enemy Number 2 for the Rhodesians, second only to his boss, Joshua Nkomo.

Dabengwa had asked that the meeting be held in his offices. He suspected, correctly, that the Military HQ of ZIPRA, called The Rock, manned by Soviet, East German, and now Cuban advisors, was bugged.

In front of Dabengwa was a pile of manila folders, he picked up the one on top.

'The Zambian police report, so far, says that the explosive device was made of TNT. The explosive was in a Cuban cigar tin. It weighed about two kilograms, was attached with magnets and was detonated with a pull fuse. This meant the assassin had to be hiding in the yard to set off the bomb,' read Dabengwa from his notes.

'What do you think, Comrade?' asked Nkomo.

'The Zambians found an AK magazine with ZANLA scraped onto it. They believe unofficially that Mugabe's men killed Comrade Mangena. The Zambians are about to accuse Mugabe formally,' continued Dabengwa.

'Yes, but what is your opinion Comrade?' pressed Nkomo.

'It could be Rhodesians, they have agents in Lusaka and they have infiltrated the Zambian military ... they have also infiltrated OUR military!' said Dabengwa pointedly, looking around the table. 'It could be Mugabe ... he hates you *Umdala Wethu*, you are his major threat to power after victory comes. It could be the Zambians themselves, they are afraid of us ... but, this was a professional murder ... I think it was Rhodesian SAS, maybe Selous Scouts ... but definitely Rhodesians. They want us to think it was Mugabe.'

'So what should be our response,' asked Nkomo softly.

'*Umdala Wethu*, that is a political decision, we can blame the Rhodesians, or Mugabe or the Zambians. It depends on what outcome you seek.'

'I don't want to blame the Rhodesians ... there is a chance that they will side with us against Mugabe in negotiations. That is what President Kaunda has asked of me. That is also what the British have asked me,' replied Nkomo.

'What have the Soviets asked you, Comrade?' asked Dabengwa, the room became deathly silent, all eyes now on the Dear Leader. The question had massive implications. The whole freedom struggle was based on Soviet military and financial support.

Nkomo knew the enormity of the answer he was about to give. His face visibly paled with the burden on his shoulders.

'They want me to blame the Rhodesians. They want the war to escalate, they want a military victory for us ... then they want to crush Mugabe to prevent him taking power. That is what they have asked,' replied Nkomo, closing his eyes for a split second, as if he was saying a silent prayer.

'*Umdala Wethu,* what is your decision?' whispered Dabengwa, almost too afraid to ask.

'We will allow the Zambians to blame Mugabe ... we will say nothing ... we will mourn the death of our brother Mangena ... we will wait, like the great *M'fezi*[43] waits and strike when the time is right to blind our enemies,' replied Nkomo.

Comrade Joshua Nkomo knew he still had time to straddle the fence ... a foot in each camp.

---

43   Mozambique Spitting Cobra

7

Ridgeway Hotel, Independence Avenue, Lusaka

There was a loud, agitated knock on the door to room 215 of the Ridgeway Hotel. Flt-Lt. Adam Hamilton-Smyth, 26 Squadron RAF Regiment, had reached the short strokes so to speak. He decided to focus more on the matter at hand, choosing to ignore the insistent knocking.

The black prostitute that he had picked up in the hotel lobby seemed to be enjoying the experience as much as he was. She was moaning enthusiastically with each urgent thrust. Hamilton-Smyth was relishing his deployment to Zambia, there was an endless supply of sunshine, beer and sexual partners ... *so many women ... so little time!*

The phone on the bedside table began to ring, breaking his concentration.

'Blast!'

He extracted himself from a pair of surprisingly strong thighs and picked up the phone.

'Yes?'

'Sir, its Corporal Murphy, sorry to disturb you,' said the voice in a thick Irish accent.

'Be quick Murphy I am busy.'

'Well Sir ... some missiles have gone missing,' replied Murphy hesitantly.

'Whadayamean ... Missing?'

'Two missiles are missing from Rapier missile battery Bravo, Sir. I have just come back from checking on the team up there, Sir.'

'What the fuck do you mean Murphy?' screamed Hamilton-Smyth, his life flashing before his eyes.

'We went up there this morning Sir. One missile is missing off the rack and one is missing out the stores Land Rover.'

'Where are they? What did the Zambian people say? Speak to me man!'

'Well ... Sir ... it appears one missile was launched ... the other was ... taken away.'

Hamilton-Smyth leapt off the bed to stand, stark naked, next to the phone, his mind racing. He could not believe his ears now burning bright red as were his pudgy English cheeks.

'Where is the Zambian Sergeant Shik ... what ever his name is?'

'From what we can gather Sir,' Murphy paused, carefully choosing his words, 'It seems … he may have shot down a seven-o-seven, Sir. He ran away afterwards.'

Hamilton-Smyth, felt weak at the knees, he collapsed back onto the bed. It was unthinkable!

'Is there a *prooblem Dalling*?' asked the prostitute, seeing the shock on her client's flushed face.

*

Mazira[44] **Farm 26km west of Lusaka**

Alan Jock McLean, 'Ben Nevis', and Ian Southwood were preparing for another 'fishing' trip to Kariba. The latest radio message had given them the exact date and time for the next resupply of equipment from Rhodesia.

The equipment was delivered by SAS canoe across Kariba. The previous method of resupply had been in the false bottom of Ian's Scania truck, driven up from Botswana. The Zambian police and customs had started much more rigorous searches of vehicles entering Zambia from Botswana to clamp down on smuggling. There was a chronic shortage of foreign currency resulting in an explosion of smuggling operations, everything from food to washing machines and of course, weapons. The risk of compromising Ian's trucking and farming empire was too great.

Ian Southwood and his wife Patricia were born Zambians, becoming disenchanted with the oppressive and corrupt Kaunda regime. They had been recruited by the Rhodesian CIO to provide support for their agent Ben Nevis. In return for their services, their two teenage boys were at school at Hilton College in the Natal midlands of South Africa, and a nice little nest egg was building in their bank account in London. While they were being well rewarded for their services, the Southwoods found the adventure of being 'agents' exciting despite the enormous risk they were running. They knew that if they were caught they would be thrown in a Zambian jail never again to see the light of day. Nobody would be sent to save them.

The Southwoods trusted Jock McLean unreservedly. They knew that he was meticulous and careful and that the risk of being caught was relatively low. Ian, as an insurance policy, ensured that the local Zambian Police hierarchy had a constant supply of eggs from the three large chicken hatcheries on the farm. He also made generous donations to the police 'retirement fund'.

---

44   Eggs in Chewa/Nyanja, an official language and common *lingua franca* in Zambia.

A large arms cache, including foreign currency and radio equipment was held in an abandoned concrete underground water reservoir at the bottom of the farm. Ian had moved his farm onto centre-pivot irrigation, using underground water pumped directly over the fields. The water reservoir was now redundant and, in any event, too expensive to fix. A false bottom, cast in concrete was built under the reservoir creating a space four metres square and two metres high. The entrance to the underground bunker was via a short tunnel, concealed under the slab holding a borehole pump. The pipes to the pump could be disconnected, with the concrete slab it sat on, levered up using a steel pole on a set of hinges. Jock had set up a clever set of alarms to ensure that they would know if a farmworker or anyone else tampered with their set up. Ian kept a few feet of stagnant water in the reservoir as an extra precaution.

The large arms stockpile was part of the CIO plan to support future Rhodesian SAS operations in Zambia. It was a lot easier to smuggle people into the country, than people with weapons attached. Nobody in the SAS knew about Mazira Farm or Ben Nevis. The codeword for the arms cache used in the CIO/ SAS, communications was 'Funny Farm', a touch that appealed to Jock's sense of humour.

'Dinner's ready,' called Patricia Southwood. Dinner was served promptly at 6pm each evening.

The two men sat down at the dining room table as the maid placed a golden roasted chicken in front of Ian for carving. A plate of roast potatoes and vegetables was already on the table. Patricia Southwood thanked the maid for the meal and told her to knock off for the evening, she would clear up herself.

Ben Nevis Distillery draws its water from the stream, Allt a'Mhuilinn that originates from two pools, Coire Leis and Coire na'Ciste. Jock had chosen the names of these two pools as codewords for describing Ian and Patricia, shortened to CL and CNC respectively, in the NATO phonetic alphabet, Charlie Lima and Charlie November Charlie. Jock loved these small touches, a great believer in the significance of the stories behind things. It was his Scottish blood, the belief in tradition, his love of storytelling.

'You two boys out for the night?' asked Patricia, handing the potatoes to Jock.

'Just a short trip to see a customer,' replied Jock. The three of them used the word 'customer' to describe a target.

Before leaving for Kariba, Jock decided on a few days of reconnaissance of 'The Vatican', the ZIPRA NSO base, the home of

Comrade Dumiso Dabengwa.

It was necessary to use these code words around the house just in case the maid or the gardener was listening. The Zambian police had intimidated and recruited all the domestic servants of white people living in Zambia in the relentless search for spies.

'Yes, the customer has a big company, they need to replace their trucks ... could be a large sale,' added Ian with a smile. The word 'company' referred to a terrorist organisation. 'Sale' meant attack.

The three Rhodesian spies finished their meal with jovial chatter on domestic subjects including the latest news from the boys at Hilton. They had become very close, trusting each other implicitly ... all caught up in their shared great adventure.

At the end of the meal, Patricia stood up to clear the plates.

'Is this sale not too big for us? Will we need help from the Bank?' she asked.

'Bank' was code for Rhodesia.

'We need to establish how many they want to buy, if its too big a sale we will definitely need the Bank to help,' replied Jock. 'I have an appointment with the Bank in November.'

When they needed to use dates they used a month three ahead of the one they meant.

*

Arrivals Hall, Lusaka International Airport

Sarah Burrell stood in the queue of arrivals that had just got off the plane from Gaborone. As Zambia was a 'Frontline State', standing bravely against Apartheid South Africa and the rebel state of Rhodesia, she did not accept direct flights from Johannesburg or Salisbury. All passengers travelling to Lusaka had to travel through Gaborone in Botswana or Blantyre in Malawi.

The Immigration officials sat behind elevated wooden boxes, all sporting the same bored facial expressions perfected by customs and immigration officials the world over. The queue moved very slowly as the officials inspected each stamp in each passport seeking out the hated 'Rhodesia' stamp. The unfortunate souls that had such a devilish stamp were ushered off into interrogation rooms. Their luggage lay strewn over the arrivals hall as the police searched through each item.

Sarah had her US passport in her hand as well as her Press Card and her accreditation for Zambia. She always carried her documentation and identification in a zipped pouch on the inside of her flak jacket. It had come out with her when she was casevaced by the Rhodesians.

Her turn came and she stepped forward with a 'good morning' and a smile. She was wearing a pair of khaki slacks, a light cotton shirt unbuttoned at the top, probably one button too many. The official wearing his navy blue Immigration uniform gave her the once over ... his blank eyes slowly taking in each detail. The plastic nametag said 'Kayumba'. There was no reply to her greeting.

In compliance with African travel protocol, Sarah had slipped a US$20 bill between the pages of the passport. The official flicked through the pages and removed the bill, slipping it expertly under a pile of paper on his desk. Then, head bent over, he studied each page with both outstretched index fingers, carefully scrutinising the closely packed overlapping passport stamps.

There it was!

'You have been to Rhodesia!' exclaimed the man, pointing at the passport stamps.

'Yes, many times ... as you can see. I am a journalist.'

'Ehhh,' grunted the man. This was unfortunate as journalists were protected species, he couldn't harass her without consequences.

He counted five Zambian passport stamps. Looking a little agitated, the man went through the passport again, looking for the sixth.

'When did you *liv* Zambia the *last-e* time?'

'A week ago.'

'There is no stamp showing your *depatcha* ... where did you *liv* from?'

Something snapped in Sarah's brain, maybe it was all the bullshit!

'I left from Kabanga Mission on a helicopter after I was kidnapped by Rhodesians,' replied Sarah loudly.

The man's head shot up from the page as if he had been struck by an electrical charge. The statement had the same effect on the two officials on either side of him. There was a loud intake of breath from the other passengers still in the queue.

'*Whad* do you *min* ... *kiddenapped*?'

Everyone in the hall wanted to hear the answer including the cleaning lady standing behind the official with her mop and bucket. A policeman, in a light green uniform watching the luggage being unloaded by the baggage handlers, had heard the hated word 'Rhodesia'. He too was intrigued.

'I was kidnapped by Rhodesians attacking a refugee camp. I was wounded in the head, see,' replied Sarah loudly parting her fringe to show the angry red scar. Her voice carried to all the passengers in the queue.

Mr Kayumba realised that he had finally caught a Rhodesian spy! It was the first one! He could not believe his luck. His colleagues looked on with envy in their eyes. Spies were few and far between.

'Come with me,' demanded the official, getting up from his seat.

'No,' replied Sarah emphatically.

There was a collective intake of breath from the other passengers.

The man blinked in surprise. He looked at her as if he could not believe his ears. White people, especially white women, did not say 'no' to him.

Not to be defied, Mr Kayumba stretched down to grab Sarah by the arm. She swung out of the way.

'Leave me alone … I am not going to be interrogated by you. I am a member of the foreign press.'

The passengers in the queue gave Sarah a wide berth, not wanting to be sucked into the altercation.

Mr Kayumba waved at the policeman for help and the two men advanced on Sarah, both now more convinced than ever that she was a spy.

'All right … All right, you have rumbled me. I confess, I am married to a spy,' said Sarah, holding up her hands in submission, changing her accent instantly from New York to Oxford.

There was a murmur of consternation from the passengers and officials alike … *married to a spy!*

'*Whad* is your *rill nam*?' demanded Mr Kayumba with a degree of hesitation. Spies were potentially very dangerous.

All looked on, hanging on her answer.

'My name is Bond … Sarah Bond!' she replied proudly with her posh English accent, standing erect and straight-faced.

Passengers in the queue, mostly expatriate workers from the UK, started to giggle, one gave out a particularly loud, spontaneous guffaw.

Mr Kayumba glared at the passengers, confounded that these people saw such a serious situation as funny … he had a treacherous spy on his hands. This just made the passengers giggle more loudly … *pleased to meet you Mrs Bond.*

'*Shud* up!' shouted Mr Kayumba turning on the passengers, the policeman stood next to him in support.

The situation was rapidly spinning out of control. There was a growing audience including all the passengers waiting in the queues to get through immigration.

Sarah was on a roll, she wasn't ready to back off. This was bullshit and she was going on the offensive.

She ripped a US$50 bill out of her bag and waved it in front of Mr Kayumba like a mother waving a lolly in front of a recalcitrant child.

'Do you want more money? ... Here it is,' she called out, flicking the note into the air. The banknote fluttered through the air to fall gently onto the floor, its path followed wide-eyed by Mr Kayumba and the policeman.

This was too much for the passengers. The incongruity of the situation, this brazen woman going by the name of Mrs Sarah Bond was just too much. They dissolved into laughter. A woman had to sit on a chair her body shaking with laughter, tears running down her cheeks. The sound of laughter rang off the vaulted ceiling.

The ruckus brought the senior immigration man onto the scene. He came rushing forward followed by a posse of officials.

'What is the meaning of this?' the man shouted. He rounded on the laughing passengers, 'Be quiet!'

'*Dis wooman* is a spy,' said Mr Kayumba, pointing accusingly at Sarah, with one eye still on the US$50 note lying on the floor.

The senior man looked between Sarah and Mr Kayumba, trying to comprehend. The obvious confusion on his face added to the hilarity on the part of the passengers.

'I will come with you for torture and interrogation,' interjected Sarah loudly to the senior man, holding out her wrists as if to be handcuffed. As she did so she spun around so that the other passengers could see her wrists thrust together.

Each line Sarah delivered added waves of laughter with spontaneous applause, in the very best tradition of Monty Python.

The senior man ushered Sarah forward, waving the audience out of the way. Sarah bent down to sweep up the $50 bill, waved it about, and then with a flourish, tucked it into the chest pocket of the senior man. She turned to wink at the other passengers.

Mr Kayumba followed with the policeman and the rest of the official entourage as Mrs Bond was escorted to her interrogation. She received a standing ovation.

'Give my regards to Money-Penny,' someone called out.

Sarah waved back, just like a Rock Star.

> *Nobody does it better*
> *Makes me feel sad for the rest*
> *Nobody does it half as good as you*
> *Baby, you're the best*

*I wasn't lookin' but somehow you found me
It tried to hide from your love light
But like heaven above me
The spy who loved me
Is keepin' all my secrets safe tonight.*[45]

*

Office of The Minister of State, Foreign and Commonwealth Office, King Charles Street, City of Westminster, London

Philosophically, she remains Hobbesian: She expects the worst and is rarely disappointed. In moral matters, Britain has traditionally practiced a convenient form of ethical egoism, believing that what was good for Britain was best for the rest.
Henry A. Kissinger, U.S. National Security Adviser and Secretary of State, describing the British lack of morality[46].

Lord Baron Goronwy-Roberts of Caernarfon, Minister of State, Foreign and Commonwealth Office sat silently at his desk … all hell had broken loose.

'This is appalling,' said the Minister, his voice betraying his fear.

'Yes Minister,' replied the Permanent Under-secretary of State, Sir Charles Prior. Sir Charles was careful to keep his expression neutral, not giving anything away. Inside, he was seething with the stupidity of this minister and this government.

'We did warn you that this was possible. Placing sophisticated weapons in undertrained hands was very dangerous,' added Sir Charles gently, *you stupid bastard!*

'It's one of our own aircraft,' moaned the Minister. 'Four of our people are dead.'

'Yes … it is most unfortunate. The fact that it's one of our, British registered aircraft, may be a blessing. We can control the investigation,' said Sir Charles, his mind ticking off the options.

'Was it definitely one of our missiles?' asked the Minister for the umpteenth time as if simply by asking somehow, in some divine way,

---

45   *Nobody Does It Better*, Carly Simon (1977), composed by Marvin Hamlisch with a lyric by Carole Bayer Sager. The theme song from the James Bond film, *The Spy who Loved Me*.
46   For Thomas Hobbes (1588- 1679), men are nasty and brutish creatures, destined to fight continually among themselves, unless some greater power, the Leviathan, emerges to keep them in their place. In Hobbes's day, of course, this power was the British monarchy.

the facts would change.

'Yes Minister, it was.'

'What are we going to say? How can we explain this? The Prime Minister is livid. We have to find a solution,' pleaded the Minister, the anguish in his voice that of a condemned man. 'The Government is precarious as it is, we could lose a no-confidence motion.'

'Have you spoken to the Foreign Minister[47], Sir?' asked Sir Charles.

'Yes, yes ... he has announced all the usual things, promising Zambia a full investigation, assistance in any way possible and all that ... he is crowing of course, he voted against sending the missiles in Cabinet. Blast, what a confounded mess ... what are we going to do?'

Sir Charles could have laughed out loud, *what are 'we' going to do! There's no 'we' about it.*

The Minister sat defeated, visions of his being shamefully dismissed from the House of Lords flashed before his eyes. He would have to resign ... ministerial responsibility and all that guff. His pension would be in jeopardy ... pilloried in the press ... his reputation, his legacy, in tatters.

Praying for the intervention of political gods, he wrung his hands ... his face florid from the whisky he had been drinking, his mind consumed by panic.

Sir Charles remained silent for a moment enjoying watching his minister squirm ... *teach the supercilious bastard a lesson ...*

Despite his anger at this totally predictable turn of events, Sir Charles knew that it was his duty to find a solution, no matter what his personal feelings. Duty was everything ...

'Metal fatigue, Minister!' stated Sir Charles confidently.

'What do you mean?'

'It was a very old aeroplane, metal fatigue ... the wing simply fell off. Like the Comets[48] did, remember?' said Sir Charles triumphantly.

'Yee Gods, you've got it. Metal fatigue! That's it ... metal fatigue,' screeched the Minister leaping to his feet, pounding his desk with his fist. 'Can you pull it off Sir Charles?'

'Leave it all to me Minister ... just you remember ... stay on message, metal fatigue.'

The relief on the Minister's face was so powerful that it brought tears to his eyes ... his political career and reputation would remain intact ... the Government was saved. *He* had saved the Government!

---

47   David Owen.
48   De Havilland DH 106 Comet was the first production commercial jet airliner. A few tragic accidents were caused by metal fatigue forcing them to be withdrawn from service.

... Metal fatigue, beautiful bloody thing!

Sir Charles stood to leave the office; he could only take the Minister in small doses.

'Oh, by the way Sir,'

'Yes.'

'The Royal Air Force Regiment report that either the Zambians fired two missiles, or one is missing.'

'The bloody air force are always losing things. That's the least of our concerns,' said the Minister waving Sir Charles away.

The Minister turned towards the window of his office ... suddenly the miserably cold rainy weather took on a gorgeous aspect ... he shook his head at the brilliance of it all ... *metal fatigue ... thank you God for metal fatigue!*

*

Hotel Inter-continental, Haile Selassie Avenue, Lusaka

'Sarah, you can't carry on like this. These people will throw you into jail. They could do much worse,' urged Sam Porter, US Foreign Service Officer – Intelligence.

'You worry too much Sam. I know how to look after myself,' replied Sarah Burrell.

The couple were sitting on bar stools alongside the 'Long Bar' at the Hotel Inter-continental in Lusaka. Sarah had known Sam since Vietnam days. He had been a Captain in the Army Rangers, E 'Easy' Company, 75th Infantry Regiment (Ranger), a specialist in long-range patrol, scouting and reconnaissance.

Sam Porter smiled at her. They had struck up a close relationship in Vietnam, her bravery and determination was legend. Like most men meeting Sarah, he was, or at least had been, infatuated with her. Now married with kids he had moved on ... *but she was still a piece of work.*

Sarah smiled back, remembering a firefight she had been caught up in with the 9th Infantry Division in the Mekong Delta. They had sent Sam and his patrol to get her and a CBS TV camera crew out ... he was a seriously brave soldier ... *he wasn't too bad in the sack either.*

Sarah preferred the company of soldiers. The press corps were a bunch of lazy drunken slobs, most doing the barest minimum to get a story. Soldiers, combat soldiers at least, were straight forward, they said what was on their mind, they had an aura about them that Sarah loved, a sort of intangible presence that set them apart from other men.

Anticipating a problem at the airport, Sarah had telexed Sam before she left Rhodesia. He had been waiting in the Arrivals area when her plane got in. After a bit of earnest discussion, the Zambians eventually had to concede that 'Mrs Bond' wasn't a spy after all.

'What have you got planned?' asked Sam.

'Well, I want to finish my story on ZIPRA, but I really want to find the people that killed Jake. I am not going to let the bastards get away with it. When I have finished with them they will wish they had never been born!'

'You are dealing with some tough characters. You go after them … you may not come back. The Rhodesians are good, some of the missions they have pulled off here and in Mozambique are amazing, in many ways they are better than we were in Vietnam, with a hellova lot less support and equipment.'

'The fact remains that they are ruthless killers … too many innocent people are being killed. They behave as if Zambia is part of their own territory … although, who would want this shit-hole? These people really know how to fuck a country up.'

'You can't have that attitude around here Sarah, I may not always be around to get you out of the shit.'

'Can you get me an interview with one of the ZIPRA commanders?' asked Sarah, changing the subject.

'I can try … let me see what I can do. How are you planning to get around?'

'I have hired the driver Jake and I used before, Geoffrey Mwamba. He's got an old Landcruiser. He's harmless and he knows his way around, plus he's cheap. I'm a bit short of cash … I need a story.'

'I can lend you some money,' said Sam earnestly.

Sarah smiled at him; he was such a good man.

She touched his cheek with her hand, 'That's very sweet Sam. I'll be fine … you get me that interview, that's more than enough.'

'Evening Misses Bond,' called a man walking past, a broad smile on his face, having a good chuckle.

'Good evening,' replied Sarah, smiling and waving demurely.

*

State House, Independence Avenue, Lusaka

In the centre of Lusaka, only 2km from State House, is the original airport called Lusaka City Airport. After the building of Lusaka International Airport it became the centre of private aviation and was used by the Government for official flights.

A Dassault Mystère/Falcon 10 entered final for a visual approach for runway two six. Parked on the hardstand in front of the old terminal building were three Mercedes Benz limousines. Heavily armed men in khaki stood around the perimeter of the hardstanding. The aircraft touched down and taxied to a spot in front of where the cars were parked.

The door to the aircraft opened and dropped into place as the entry stairs. Six men in suits climbed out of the aircraft and were ushered into the waiting cars.

The cars raced off towards the exit gate in the direction of State House. The aircraft had British registration, with a tiny almost inconspicuous insignia on the nose. Under the logo read the word 'Lonrho'.

Lonrho was owned and controlled by a greedy, ruthless, arrogant, rampant capitalist. His name was Roland 'Tiny' Rowland, born Roland Walter Fuhrhop. As a boy, he was a member of the Hitler Youth. During the war, he was interned with Mosley's fascists on the Isle of Man. The first 30 years of his life were dominated and distorted by the simple fact that he was German.

As a businessman, Rowland had made selfishness a way of life, turning an ailing African mining company called Lonrho into an international giant by pillaging his way through the third world, bending rules, breaking opponents. Lonrho had operations in more than 40 countries in Africa, the Middle East and Europe, and profits that topped US$200 million. Its assets included newspapers, shipping lines, platinum, gold and copper mines, millions of acres of ranch and farm land, and hundreds of wholesale and retail trading firms.

Rowland funded all the black independence leaders, including a man he called a close friend, Joshua Nkomo. To cover his bases he also funded Robert Mugabe, and Bishop Abel Muzorewa. Most of his funding, however, went to Joshua Nkomo, with whom he had made an arrangement on mineral rights for when he came to power. In order to achieve this lofty goal, he was singularly focused on undermining the Patriotic Front alliance between Nkomo and Mugabe. In this sense, he was an ally of the Rhodesian government with whom he also had cordial relations, providing everything from oil shipments to 106mm recoilless rifles. He would feed the Rhodesians whatever intelligence he could muster to attack the Patriotic Front alliance and cast Mugabe in a poor light … even as far as killing Mugabe, an excellent outcome for him.

The motorcade from the airport swept into the driveway leading up to State House. An even larger security presence protected the perimeter.

As the cars pulled up in front of the main entrance, the six men got out, three had blankets pulled over their heads so that nobody could identify them. They were ushered into the building and led quickly to the private chambers of the President.

The door to the President's private meeting room was flung open and the smiling President stepped forward to welcome his visitor. Only one man entered the room, the others took up station outside the door.

'Welcome Prime Minister.'

'Thank you Mister President.'

President Kaunda turned to introduce his other guest.

'You have met the President of ZAPU, Joshua Nkomo?'

'Yes … many times.'

The big man stood up and offered his hand. The visitor stepped forward and shook the hand firmly.

'*Litshone njani Prime Minister, kunjani ukuphila?*'[49]

'*Ngiyaphila Joshua.*'[50]

'Our people are crying Prime Minister.'

'We are here to find a way to make it stop Joshua. We must find a way.'

'Let us begin Prime Minister,' said Nkomo gesturing to a chair.

The Prime Minister of Rhodesia, Ian Douglas Smith, took his seat opposite his military and political adversary … and hopefully, God willing, his ally for peace.

---

[49] siNdebele, Good evening Prime Minister, how are you?
[50] I am very well Joshua.

8

Soviet Monitoring Station, Soviet Embassy, Ridgeway, Lusaka

The Soviet Embassy in Lusaka did not only eavesdrop on their Cold War rivals. They also listened to the numerous telephone taps and bugging devices in various strategic places in Lusaka. This included enemy and friendly embassies and the Zambian government offices, most importantly State House.

On this evening Comrade Professor Vassily Solodovnikov, Soviet Ambassador to Zambia, and Comrade Colonel Lev Kononov, head of the Soviet advisory delegation to ZIPRA, were listening to an interesting conversation.

Also in the room packed with radio and communications equipment, was Comrade Lieutenant-Colonel Julio Ángel Casas, the chief Cuban advisor to ZIPRA.

A tape recorder, with a large reel of magnetic tape turning slowly, sat in the middle of a large table. An operator with headphones on provided a seamless translation of English into Russian into a microphone. None of the men needed a translation, they were all fluent in English. The tape would be sent back to Moscow.

All in the room listened in silence as the voices of Joshua Nkomo and Ian Smith came through on the loudspeaker. It was so clear that the men could have been inside the room. There were only two voices, clearly President Kaunda had left the room.

The conversation, in its second hour, had many ebbs and flows. Both men had displayed frustration and anger. There were accusations, recriminations and threats issued. The pervading impression of the two men was that there was begrudging respect between them. Both were careful not to overstep the mark, and none of the attacks were personal.

The subject had turned to Ian Smith's plan for an internal settlement[51], with elections to be held soon. An Interim Government was already in place that included black leaders in the Executive Council. A ceasefire had been called with amnesty offered to any terrorists who laid down their weapons. Nkomo's precondition was agreement to one-man-one-vote, complete majority rule. This was their principal area of

---

51 The so-called Internal Settlement was between the white Rhodesian Government and the leaders of Black political parties based inside Rhodesia, those that had not taken up arms. Smith was anxious to get Nkomo, who was based 'externally' to participate in the settlement as he would add to its legitimacy, and would gain the support of Britain and the UN.

disagreement, as Smith wanted seats reserved for whites in any new government … at least for 10 years or more.

The Prime Minister dropped the bombshell.

'Joshua, if you return to Rhodesia, you will be installed as interim leader. We will call an all-party conference. Mugabe can be included with our other leaders, but we must have a ceasefire.'

'That is very interesting Prime Minister, but as you know, many leaders, Fraser, Trudeau, Nyerere, Obasanjo, are all against any form of settlement with you. They have to be convinced you are serious.'

At the end of the third hour, the meeting came to an end. There was no formal agreement. Importantly, both had agreed to return to their leadership teams to discuss the proposals. The political settlement was still on the table. Both agreed that matters were urgent to prevent further bloodshed.

The tape went silent.

Professor Solodovnikov was the first to speak.

'Well it appears our friend Comrade Nkomo is serious about this settlement,' said Solodovnikov with concern in his voice.

'This will play into the hands of the British and Americans,' agreed Kononov.

'We have not come this far to allow the war and our ambitions to come to nothing. Emphatic military victory is what we need to solidify our position,' stated Solodovnikov as if giving a lecture at university. He was preaching to the converted.

Choosing to remain silent, this subject was outside the experience of Julio Casas. He was fluent in Russian so there was no need for translation.

'If we do not act quickly news of this meeting will leak out and others will assume the initiative,' agreed Kononov.

'We could change horses,' whispered Solodovnikov. 'Comrade Nkomo is weak, his tribe is too few to carry an election … surely he must know that.'

'Are you serious Comrade Ambassador? Switch our support to Mugabe?'

Both men studied each other across the table, the enormity of what the Ambassador was suggesting was way above their respective pay grades.

'No … Moscow would never agree. We need to derail this little re-approachment. It must be something decisive that will kill this initiative in its tracks,' said Solodovnikov. Changing the subject, he turned to Casas.

'How are your plans progressing Comrade Casas?'

Julio Casas was caught unprepared. He had been lost in his own thoughts.

'Ah ... Comrade Ambassador ...' he shuffled his papers. 'Three hundred Cuban soldiers are being transferred from Angola. They are being transported by cargo planes to Mumbwa, and then onto bases in the south of Zambia where the build up is taking place. They are all trained section, platoon and company commanders. Two hundred and fifty tanks are being unloaded at Luanda but they will take a long time, maybe six months to reach here. The DAAFAR[52] have sent a squadron, number 15 with twelve MiG-21MFs[53], also to Mumbwa,' replied Casas, reading from his file.

'Excellent Casas, you have moved very fast indeed. This will make all the difference,' smiled Solodovnikov. 'How is the reorganisation progressing? Are our brothers Masuku and Dabengwa co-operating?'

'I think I should answer that question, Ambassador,' interrupted Kononov. 'My people, and Colonel Casas of course, have reported to the ZAPU War Council providing a complete revision to the ZIPRA Order of Battle within Rhodesia, and its long term military objectives. This revision requires the development of a conventional ZIPRA Army while using its guerrilla forces to open the way for a full scale invasion of Rhodesia.'

'What resources will this require Lev Ivanovich?' asked Solodovnikov.

'The plan is based upon the training and equipping of at least five battalions of ZIPRA soldiers which will be task-organized following the model of Soviet Motorized Infantry Battalions. We estimate that this would be the minimum force required to defeat both the Rhodesian Security Forces and Mugabe's ZANLA terrorists ... afterwards,' replied Kononov.

'How long will this take?'

'We estimate at least a year Comrade Ambassador. Although, with this excellent Cuban support, it may be shorter,' smiled Kononov encouragingly at Casas.

'We need to move faster. We may have to bring forward Operation Zero Hour,' said the Ambassador gravely.

Operation Zero Hour was the code word for the full-scale conventional invasion of Rhodesia.

'First we need to kill all this talk of settlement!'

52　*Defensa Anti-Aérea y Fuerza Aérea Revolucionaria* - the Cuban Air Force
53　NATO codename, Fishbed J.

*

Alpha Bar, Chozi Road, Northmead Shopping Centre, Lusaka

Keith Wilson and his team of Cephas Ngwenya and Stanley Chiyeka had arrived in Lusaka without further incident. They had dumped the body of the Zambian Army guard after stripping his uniform and equipment, bound to come in handy in the future.

The Norman Barr Safari offices were in a small warehouse in Moobola Road in the Numununga industrial area. The warehouse was used as storage for supplies and equipment but included a taxidermy operation preserving game meat, hides, horns, heads, whole animals in some cases. The place had the stink of formaldehyde and other chemicals, coupled with the sickly smell of curing animal skins. A huge walk-in cold-room was where the buffalo meat was placed. Norman Barr supplemented his income with selling game meat, some poached when times were tough.

The Warehouse Manager did not ask any questions; in truth he said nothing to them at all, pointing them to a room on the mezzanine floor with bunk beds.

Wilson and his men had a chat about their plans and how best they could gather information. They agreed to start in places where tongues were at their loosest, the many bars and nightclubs scattered around the city. Wilson decided he would visit the 'white' expatriate hotel bars, while Ngwenya and Chiyeka the others. They had been furnished with a set of aerial photographs of Lusaka and some 1:50,000 maps but they were very old and out of date.

Wilson dropped Ngwenya and Chiyeka off at the Alpha Bar, Chozi Road, Northmead Shopping Centre. According to the intelligence reports, Alpha Bar offered the authentic African hooker-bar experience. It was a dump, plain and simple, full of working girls. The drinks were cheap, the music not bad, while the surrounding neighbourhood could be described as dodgy. Most importantly for the Selous Scouts, it was frequented by the members of the diplomatic corps looking for young and compliant girls at bargain basement prices.

Ngwenya and Chiyeka could freely admit to being 'Zimbabweans', as Lusaka was full of thousands of political refugees and freedom fighters. They were dressed as any young men out for the night, slacks and shirt with the confident swagger of boys who knew their way around. Ngwenya was not much of a drinker, a single beer would last him a whole evening, Chiyeka on the other hand was a party animal.

As expected, the bar was packed to capacity, typical for a busy

Friday night. The place was a hive of partygoers, locating a spot at the bar was as hard as finding a virgin amongst the heaving throng of dancing women. Alpha Bar was a mixture of scantily clad women, high heels, drunken men and underage girls. The lighting was subdued to the point of darkness, lit only by the spotlight aimed at the mirrored disco-ball in the centre of the ceiling. The dance floor was a throbbing mass, thumping away to Gloria Gaynor's, *I will Survive*[54].

> *Go on now, go, walk out the door, just turn around now*
> *'Cause you're not welcome anymore*
> *Weren't you the one, who tried to hurt me with goodbye?*
> *Did you think I'd crumble? Did you think I'd lay down and die?*

This was something very different for Ngwenya and Chiyeka, black people mixing freely with white people … drinking, dancing … at first it felt confronting. The men stood spellbound, scanning the room, standing close together as if for mutual protection.

> *Oh, no, not I, I will survive*
> *Oh, as long as I know how to love, I know I'll stay alive*
> *I've got all my life to live, I've got all my love to give*
> *And I'll survive, I will survive, hey, hey*

A young girl approached through the crowd, her steps were deliberate as if she was strutting a catwalk. Her eyes were focused on Chiyeka. When Chiyeka saw her coming there was a sudden intake of breath. She knew she was beautiful, revelling in the admiring eyes in the nightclub.

'You want to buy me a drink?' asked the young girl confidently in excellent English, standing square in front of Chiyeka, legs slightly apart, hands on hips.

She was a skinny girl, tall with a milk-chocolate smooth complexion. She had thick black hair tied in a ponytail. Her eyes reflected in the light of the spinning mirror-ball, bright and shining. She was the most beautiful woman Stanley Chiyeka had ever seen.

> *It took all the strength I had not to fall apart*
> *Kept trying hard to mend the pieces of my broken heart*
> *And I spent, oh, so many nights just feeling sorry for myself*
> *I used to cry but now I hold my head up high …*

---

54   Writers: Dino Fekaris, Frederick J Perren; Copyright: Lyrics © Universal Music Publishing Group.

Chiyeka glanced at Ngwenya for direction. Ngwenya nodded and took some Kwatcha out of his pocket passing it to Chiyeka.

'Beer,' the woman said before Chiyeka could ask.

'What is your name?' asked Ngwenya.

'Cindy. What's yours and your good looking friend?'

'I am Cephas he is Stanley.'

'You two are not from Lusaka,' she smiled knowingly.

It was obvious from Ngwenya's accent that they were from Zimbabwe. Chiyeka returned with three bottles of the local Rhino Lager.

'No we are freedom fighters from Zimbabwe,' replied Ngwenya using his cover story.

'You looking for a good time? If you have been in the bush you have not had a woman in a long time?' asked Cindy, looking demurely at Chiyeka. She lifted the beer bottle and took a deep swig of beer, her eyes remained fixed on Chiyeka. She wiped her mouth alluringly with the back of her hand, smiling up at him in a way that made her intentions clear.

'Maybe,' replied Chiyeka, glancing at Ngwenya, unsure of how he should be playing this.

'I prefer *Muzungus*[55], they pay better, but for you I can make an exception. You got money?' asked Cindy, still studying Chiyeka's face.

'You know many whitemen?' asked Ngwenya.

'Many, we have plenty of new ones coming. Some I have met are from Russia, but they don't pay, and they want to hit. The best are from England they pay plenty and are easy to please.'

'You have met Russians?'

'You ask many questions. Have you got money?'

'I am looking for a Russian, I met him when I was at the camp, Mboroma.'

'You have been to Mboroma?' asked Cindy incredulously, the surprise was clear on her face. Mboroma had a fearsome reputation as a detention camp and re-education centre. It was notorious even amongst the local Zambian population. The Selous Scouts had identified the location of the Mboroma base. It was on the list slated for attack, it was reported to house Rhodesian prisoners of war, ZIPRA deserters and kidnapped school children refusing to join the 'armed struggle'.

'Yes, we were both guards there, but now we are at Freedom Camp. It is much better, so close to Lusaka,' replied Ngwenya watching her

---

55   Zambian slang, white people, in this case white men.

eyes closely for signs of recognition.

Cindy finished her beer before Ngwenya had a sip of his. He gestured Chiyeka to get her another.

'Ah ... Freedom Camp, I have met people from there. There are many soldiers.'

The existence of the build up at this new camp, called Freedom Camp, had been reported to the Selous Scouts. Nobody yet knew exactly where it was. Ngwenya could not believe his luck, that this chance meeting was yielding so much information.

Chiyeka returned with another beer. Cindy took it, lifted it and sucked out another huge slug, her throat moving effortlessly as she swallowed.

'You have been there?' Ngwenya held his breath, waiting for her answer.

'No ... but my friend Lucy has. They pay good money for women to go, but there are too many ... its too dangerous. Some women have been beaten.'

'I have not heard of this. Are you sure we are talking about the same place?'

'Yes, it is the camp off Chikumbi Road to the north.'

'I will report this. We cannot have stories like this. Our mission is honourable. We seek our freedom like the people of Zambia!' stated Ngwenya indignantly; his heart almost skipped a beat.

'Chiyeka why don't you dance with this girl,' said Ngwenya giving his friend a nudge on the shoulder. 'Here,' he added, passing some more Kwatcha to Cindy ... you teach my friend to dance.'

Cindy took the money, stuffed it into her bra, then with a broad smile on her face, she pulled the excited Chiyeka onto the dance floor. The mass of closely packed, sweating humanity, were dancing, arms above their heads, swaying to the loud booming disco beat, Donna Summer, *I feel Love*[56].

> *Ooh*
> *It's so good, it's so good*
> *It's so good, it's so good*
> *It's so good*
> *Ooh*
> *Heaven knows, heaven knows*
> *Heaven knows, heaven knows*

---

56 Donna Summer (1977), Songwriter(s): Pete Bellotte, Donna Summer, Andrea Remondini, Giorgio Moroder, Mauro Picotto, Sweet Summer Night Music, Warner Bros Music.

Heaven knows
Ooh
I feel love, I feel love
I feel love, I feel love
I feel love

Cephas Ngwenya watched the couple dancing, amused at how his friend was enjoying himself.

Looking around the room Ngwenya could not help but wonder whether Rhodesia would ever be a place where black and white people could dance and drink together in the same place … with the same freedom.

I feel love
I feel love
I feel love
I feel love

*

Hotel Inter-continental, Haile Selassie Avenue, Lusaka

After dropping his men off, Keith Wilson continued on to the Hotel Inter-continental. He drove slowly, being careful to observe any signs of police or army on the roads. In many ways, Lusaka wasn't very different to his hometown of Bulawayo. The main difference was the sheer number of people in the streets, the litter on the sides of the road and the potholes. The buildings looked very much the same, with many of the original colonial buildings still standing.

Wilson had a Soviet Tokarev, semi-automatic pistol, under the seat of the Land Rover. He had thought long and hard about bringing it, but decided in the end that it was better to be able to fight his way out of a problem than simply being arrested.

The Inter-continental and the Ridgeway Hotels were two of the very few places to go for a good meal. The country was in dire straights, with food and petrol shortages. Almost all consumer goods, from soap to cooking oil were in short supply, fresh meat was hard to get and expensive.

After pulling into the Hotel carpark, he strolled through the reception area looking for the bar. The hotel was remarkably busy with the dining room almost full. Wilson was dressed in slacks, shirt and sports jacket while his long curly hair, deep sideburns and trimmed beard fitted well with the fashion of the time.

He ordered a beer and sat down to see what the night might bring. Soft dinner music was being piped through the dining room, adding to a relaxed atmosphere with the pleasant aroma of cigarette smoke and the murmur of conversation. For a brief moment, Wilson was reminded of the Holiday Inn, or Southern Sun in Bulawayo.

His position, alone at the bar, attracted a string of prostitutes using the hotel as the source of a vibrant trade. He smiled, signalling his decline, they seemed relaxed at his rejection, moving smoothly on to the next target.

Raucous laughter came from a table in the dining room. Wilson asked the barman the way to the toilet. He took a circuitous route through the dining room. The table had eight people on it, six men and two women. They all had dark complexions, the two women, had long, jet-black hair with bright contrasting lipstick and eye shadow. They were not speaking English; at first he thought it might be Portuguese. Wilson knew the language from childhood holidays spent in Beira in Mozambique. Walking past at a steady pace he realised they were speaking Spanish.

Moving back to the bar, Wilson asked the barman for another beer. He gave him a tip, the universal method of getting a barman to enter into a conversation. The bar was empty except for a couple at the far end, a short fat white man, negotiating with a sultry slim black prostitute in a sequined dress. She appeared to be driving a hard bargain.

'Busy night?' opened Wilson, putting on his best Pom accent.

'Ehhh, Saturdays are more busy.'

'Good to see more foreign tourists,' said Wilson indicating with his head the table of Spanish speakers.

'They are not tourists!' spat the barman with clear distaste.

'They look like tourists.'

'Those people are from Cuba; they come in twice a week. They don't tip and they behave like they own the place,' replied the barman, the expression on his face said it all.

'Do you know what they are doing in Zambia?' asked Wilson chancing his arm.

'I don't know ... you see that short one with the black moustache ... the one with the cigar,' said the barman indicating the Cubans, his voice suddenly conspiratorial almost a whisper.

'Yes.'

'He raped one of the girls out the back of the hotel. The doorman told me that he has raped other girls ... he likes them young ... Pigs!'

spat the barman.

Wilson just nodded, studying his beer, careful not to turn around. He could see the people on the table in the mirror behind the bar. This was a serious stroke of luck. He finished his beer and ordered another. The barman went on to prepare drinks for the other guests in the dining room and others coming into the bar. Almost as if someone had rung a bell, the bar filled up with people. The soft evening music gave way to Abba's *Take a Chance on Me*[57].

> *If you change your mind, I'm the first in line*
> *Honey I'm still free*
> *Take a chance on me.*

A small dance floor at the end of the bar was immediately full of people.

Wilson watched as the Cubans finished their meal and moved into the bar. The leader was obvious, holding forth while the others hung on every word. Not believing his luck on the first night of his arrival in Lusaka, Wilson decided that this would be his target.

The party broke up and the Cubans walked to the entrance together. There was a general 'good night' and they went out into the car park. Wilson followed.

The target walked briskly across the car park and got into a light blue Peugeot 504.

Trying not to make it obvious, Wilson walked briskly to the Land Rover parked on the opposite side of the carpark.

The Peugeot was already reversing out. Cursing himself for not parking closer to the entrance, Wilson broke into a run.

There was a load moan from behind a large van at the end of the carpark. Wilson hesitated, but continued towards the Land Rover.

The Peugeot was already in the driveway.

Fuck!

A woman gave out a stifled scream.

Wilson looked towards the van but in the darkness he couldn't see anything. There was a distinctive sound of a fist belting a head.

With a slight squeal of tyres, the Peugeot turned into Haile Selassie Avenue, going north.

Realising that there was no hope of chasing the car, Wilson walked around the side of the van. It was difficult to see, but there seemed to be two people on the ground.

---

[57] Abba (1978). Songwriters: Ulvaeus, Bjoern K / Andersson, Benny

'Hey!' shouted Wilson.

The man turned his head; he had his hand over a woman's face. *Blond hair!*

With the distraction the man loosened his grip, the woman screamed.

The man was up in a flash taking a wild swing at Wilson.

Wilson ducked underneath it.

There was a glint of a knife in the man's right hand as he lunged forward.

Jumping out of the way, Wilson lashed out with his foot, catching the man on the shin. There was a loud grunt, but the man came on, swinging the knife out in front of him in a slashing motion. There was no doubt in Wilson's mind that he intended to kill. The man was committed.

Stepping back and crouching, Wilson prepared himself ... *distance is important.*

The man lunged again.

Wilson expertly sidestepped, pulling back with his shoulder, then struck at the man's knife arm as it came forward. The downward chop smashed into the forearm. He then stepped in towards his attacker, trapping the arm, while his free hand thrust hard into the man's throat, crushing his larynx against the spine.

The knife dropped to the ground as the man fell to his knees; hoarse gurgling came from his mouth as he tried to suck for air. His hands flew to his throat as his breathing became more laboured, slowly suffocating. Wilson grabbed the man's head, pulled it back and then twisted with the full force of his body, there was a loud crack as the neck snapped.

Turning back, Wilson saw the victim sitting with her back against the van. Even in the poor light he could see that she had long blond hair.

'Are you all right?' he asked gently, keeping to his stiff English accent. He stepped towards her.

'The bastard tried to rape me,' replied the woman, her American accent immediately recognisable. 'He very nearly succeeded! I need to brush up on my karate knife defence.'

Wilson bent down to help her up, lifting her up by the elbow. He saw her face in the light. Her arm was bleeding from a deep cut. She held it tightly against her body. Blood covered the front of her shirt and her pants. Her shirt was ripped open and her bra had been pulled off. As Wilson studied her face, he could see that her eye was swollen nearly shut from a hard punch and her lip was bleeding.

'You are in bad shape, that arm will need stitches,' said Wilson.

'Do I know you?' asked the woman.

'I don't think so. We need to get you to a doctor.'

'No, I don't need any trouble with the police. What are we going to do with him?' she asked pointing at the body.

Wilson contemplated making a run for it, the woman would survive, even though she had lost a lot of blood. The last thing he needed was the police.

'You are obviously military, that move you pulled was out of the text book ... British SAS?'

'No, I just got lucky.'

'Bullshit! You killed him easy as pie.'

'Look we cannot stand here talking ... he tried to rape you, report it to the police, say you hit him in the neck with a stick.'

This woman's voice is familiar.

'No, I can't handle an investigation in this God forsaken place ... the cops are useless, they could blame me for killing him ... no way.'

This sudden turn of events had Wilson on the wrong foot ... the urge to run was overwhelming.

'Fuck!' he hissed under his breath.

'I will put his body in my Land Rover,' decided Wilson.

He grabbed the man's shoulders, dragged him across the carpark to the Land Rover, then lifted the body over the tailgate into the back.

'Look, this cut isn't so bad. I'll be fine. You better vamoose,' said the woman. 'What's your name?'

'Keith ... Keith Brown, what's yours?'

Keith ...

The woman hesitated ... the voice was familiar!

'Sarah Burrell.'

Burrell!

The mutual recognition was instant.

'You were the bastard that killed Jake at Kabanga Mission!'

'What are you talking about? I saved your life ... what were you doing in a gook camp anyway?'

Keith and Sarah stood in the half-light staring at each other, trying to think of what to say next ...

'You are Rhodesian ... I can blow the whistle ... you killed Jake.'

'If you try that ... I will have to kill you!'

Sarah could see that he was deadly serious, his hands twitching by his side.

Keith Wilson was way out of his depth, the thought of killing this woman in a hotel car park was impossible … his mind raced through the options … *run!*

He made up his mind. Pushing her out of the way, he jumped into the Land Rover, hit the starter and pulled out of the parking.

'You bastard!' Sarah screamed.

Wilson wasn't hanging about. He smashed his foot onto the accelerator, racing out of the carpark, the realisation that he had been compromised, escape was the only option … the mission was only 48 hours old and already gone to shit!

9

Hotel Inter-continental, Haile Selassie Avenue, Lusaka

Sarah Burrell woke up with a splitting headache. She scrambled for the packet of Disprin on the bedside table, pushed three out of the foil and swallowed them with a drink of water.

Her arm was throbbing painfully, blood had seeped through the bandage all over the sheets.

'Shit!'

Too exhausted to move, she lay back looking at the ceiling. She had placed a call to her friend Sam Porter at the Embassy asking him to bring over more bandages and some disinfectant. He was horrified to hear of her attack ... she had left out the story of the dead man and the mysterious Rhodesian special forces soldier that had been around at just the right moment.

She and her driver, Godfrey, had taken an early evening drive around the city so that Sarah could get her bearings. When Godfrey had dropped her back at the hotel, the man had approached her about a potential news story. He had lured her towards the van and then attacked her. All he said was that he was sent by 'Mister Kayumba' to teach her a lesson.

Thank God ... for Keith ...

There was no doubt in her mind, that she would likely have been killed after being raped. The question on her mind was whether this Mister Kayumba would have another attempt if he found out that she was still alive and relatively unhurt. For the first time in many years, Sarah felt real fear. This was a circumstance outside of her control and she was defenceless. The only real option was to get out of the country ... quickly.

An equally pressing problem was that she needed a news story ... she needed it badly. *I can't ask Sam for protection, a) he wouldn't be able to give it, b) he will insist that I leave the country. There must be some other way ...*

Lifting her head to look in the mirror, she was shocked at what she saw. Her left eye was black and blue, her lip swollen, hair a knotted mess ... *I look like Frankenstein's wife!* As she lifted her leg to get out of bed, a sharp pain shot through her thigh. Both inner-thighs were horribly bruised from where the man had kicked her legs apart. They were so sore she could hardly stand up straight ... *fucking bastard ... fucking useless excuse for a country ...*

Her mind wandered to this Keith Brown. *That can't be his real name ...*

Her energy and enthusiasm for extracting revenge for Jake's death was dissipating. What was the point of vilifying the Rhodesian murderers in the international press for attacking a defenceless refugee camp? *Refugee camp ... bullshit, there were more Soviet weapons and equipment there than on the Ho Chi Min Trail! This Cuban angle is interesting ... Castro is an enemy of the USA ... people in the US may be interested in the Cuban intervention in Africa?*

The thought came to her that this Keith may come back to kill her ... she had threatened him with exposure ... he would be seriously concerned.

Why didn't he just kill me last night ... it would have been so easy?

A new plan was taking shape in Sarah's mind ... *Keith What was written on the side of his Land Rover? ... Norman Barr Safaris*

*

Norman Barr Safari Offices, 5 Moobola Road, Numununga Industrial Area, Lusaka

'Chiyeka has found a beautiful woman, *Ikhanka,*' said Cephas Ngwenya in siNdebele with a giggle. 'She taught him to dance, Zambian style.'

Stanley Chiyeka with his usual broad smile, shook his head, 'She was tooo beautiful *Ikhanka.*'

'She told us many things. I have written them down. The most important was the location of this Freedom Camp. I have looked on the map so it must be roughly here,' said Ngwenya, pointing to an area with his finger on the map laying open on the floor.

'We should check that out today ... maybe recce tonight,' replied Wilson, also in siNdebele.

'Chiyeka wants to go back to see his woman *Ikhanka* ... he has love on his mind,' laughed Ngwenya. 'But she wants money!'

Ngwenya was finding the situation funny, laughing and pointing at the grinning Chiyeka.

'I am sure I can get more information *Ikhanka.*'

'Yes, but I already know that information,' laughed Wilson. 'That *Skellum* will give you the weeping sickness.' Wilson pointed to his crotch.

The three men laughed together ... so easy and comfortable in each other's company.

There was a knock on the door.

Keith Wilson slipped his Tokarev pistol out from behind his back. Ngwenya and Chiyeka were instantly alert, up in a flash, weapons at the ready.

'Yes?'

The door opened and the diminutive Welshman with no conversation was standing in the doorway.

'There's a body in my cold-room, I take it that it belongs to you?' said the man with a deadpan face. He spoke as if he found dead bodies in his cold-room on a regular basis.

'Yes, sorry about that. He fell down and died and I had no place else to take him,' replied Wilson with the faintest smile.

'Well you can't leave him there, he will upset my workers.'

'Yes, I quite understand, what do you suggest?'

'Well we could put him through the meat mincing machine,' said the man without any hint of a smile, 'but that would definitely upset my workers.'

'Sounds like burial in a shallow grave might be the answer,' quipped Wilson.

'Yes ... but do it now. Go out on the Kafue River road. You'll see some hills on the left, there's dirt track on the 40km peg, take it for about one click, bury him there. I'll give you a bag of quicklime.'

'Thanks, we'll get on it straight away.'

The man turned to leave ...

'Oh, by the way, just be careful, there are a few other bodies buried there,' said the man offhandedly, turning to go back downstairs.

'Okay boys, lets go and dump our body. But before we do that let's debrief properly,' said Wilson to his men.

They had a detailed debrief about the events of the night before. There was much to do. They had the rough whereabouts of the Freedom Camp and they had a Cuban target. Wilson had been careful not to discuss his meeting with Sarah Burrell ... some things are better left unsaid.

Heavy footsteps sounded on the staircase coming up to their room.

The Welshman appeared again.

'There's a woman who looks like she has gone ten rounds with Smokin Joe Frazier outside. She wants to talk to Mister Brown ... I take it that's you?' said the Welshman still stony faced.

Ngwenya and Chiyeka looked at their boss quizzically. This subject had not come up in the debrief.

'Is she alone?' asked Wilson.

'She's got a driver with her. You haven't been compromised have you?' asked the Welshman, now a little uneasy. 'You didn't beat her up did you?'

'Fuck! No I didn't … it's a long story to do with the body in the cold-room,' whispered Wilson softly. 'Look, we could be in shit here. Cephas, you and Stanley take your AKs and cover the driveway. I will go out to meet her. If it is a trap we have no option but to shoot our way out.'

The Welshman visibly paled. 'Have you any idea how long it has taken Norman and I to build up this operation? You've been here for two days and you fuck it up!'

Something seemed to click in the Welshman's brain.

'Okay, we have a cellar that leads under the neighbouring building, that leads to a storm water drain, don't ask how we did that, that leads to a manhole cover in the street behind. Parked across the street is a white Datsun 1200, here are a set of keys. If the police are outside they will not have covered the whole block.'

The three Selous Scouts could hardly believe their ears, this bloke was well prepared … not your regular, common or garden variety, taxidermist.

They took the stairs down onto the factory floor two at a time. Ngwenya going left, Chiyeka right. A set of painted-over windows ran across most of the front of the building. Some were cracked open for ventilation.

The Welshman appeared with a short barrel pump-action shotgun, with extra rounds in bandoliers across both shoulders.

'SSG[58],' he said with the first hint of a smile.

Wilson slipped the Tokarev into his pants behind his back and pulled his shirt over it. Then he cracked opened the office door out into the car park. Scanning the carpark, Wilson could see the blond woman standing next to an old battered Toyota Landcruiser. A black man, her driver, was standing next to her.

'I can't see anyone other than the woman and her driver,' whispered Wilson to the Welshman behind him.

'Okay, go out nice and easy, call her to come to you. Stand next to the door, don't go more than a few feet forward. If it is a trap, the police will show themselves as soon as you go out. If there is a problem, I will take out the woman and driver. You duck back in and we head for the cellar. Got it?'

'Yes got it.'

---

58 SSG: small game. Buckshot, equivalent to American OO buckshot round. Deadly over short range with 6.9mm lead pellets, 5.2 pellets per 10g of lead. Not much spread over a short range, makes a big hole.

'Go.'

Wilson stepped out into the driveway, his eyes flicking left and right for any sign of army or police.

The woman watched him. It was clear to her that he was seriously skittish.

'I am alone,' she called out. Her left arm was in a sling.

'What are you doing here?' called Wilson, his right hand behind his back holding the pistol grip.

'Just need to have a chat,' she replied, holding her right hand away from her body, to show that she wasn't concealing anything.

'Godfrey, take the truck around the block,' said Sarah addressing the driver. The man went around to the driver's side, jumped in, and with a thick cloud of diesel smoke, drove out into the road.

The woman walked stiffly across the carpark towards Wilson, he could see that she was in pain. Her face was a mess.

'Hi, I'm Sarah,' she said with a faint smile, wincing at the pain of her split lip. She held out her hand to shake his.

There was a heat in her handshake, soft and delicate, but firm and confident. She let her hand linger in his for a spilt second.

'We have not met under the best of circumstances,' said Sarah softly with a hint of a smile. 'Forgive my hair, I couldn't get an appointment with the hairdresser.'

Keith could not help but return her smile, this woman was a whole different ball game.

'You look just fine, for a person taking ten rounds with Smokin Joe Frazier. Did you get some stitches for that arm?' grinned Wilson, repeating the Welshman's words. He was impressed with the toughness of this woman.

'No, the cut wasn't that deep, should be fine in a few days.'

'You can't come inside, we will have to talk here. What do you want?'

'I need a story. I can help you … if you can help me.'

'What do you mean?'

'I have got an appointment to interview a Mister Cephas Cele. He is the ZIPRA Commissar and member of the Revolutionary Council.'

'So?' Keith refused to be drawn.

'Well, I might be able to gather some information that you might find useful.'

'Where is the meeting?'

'Zimbabwe House in Lukoma Road. It's their headquarters apparently. Would that be helpful?'

She watched his face carefully, his recognition was obvious. She had been a journalist a long time, she knew what she was looking for.

'How do I know this isn't some sort of elaborate trap? Anyway, why would you want to help us after you accused us of killing your friend?' asked Keith, still trying to process the offer this woman was making. Colonel Reid-Daly wouldn't believe it if he told him.

'Well, I want to write a story about your war. You will give me an interview, anonymous of course, giving your point of view.'

'No way! Look, you better leave. I don't need your help.'

Sarah's gamble wasn't working. Keith wasn't buying her story. She realized that she needed to give a bit more.

'Okay, I can help you get close to the Cubans. They are our enemy as they are yours.'

'Carry on.'

She had his attention.

'I can try for an interview. I have Canadian accreditation. They talk to Canadians. I can get you inside their embassy.'

'I'm interested, but I am not giving any interviews and you cannot write anything about me or my men.'

'Agreed,' said Sarah. It was a start; she could work on the other stuff. 'I'll set it up and let you know. Should I come back here?'

'No, absolutely not, you are not to come back here again under any circumstances. If you do, you will likely be killed. I mean it, this is serious shit. You stay away!'

'Okay settle down, I get it, you meet me at the hotel, room 212.'

The Landcruiser came back down the street and stopped next to the carpark.

'You better go now. Don't take my warning lightly. Never come back here,' said Keith with as much venom as he could muster. The tough-guy image was never one of his strengths. She knew it.

Sarah hesitated.

'Look, there is one other thing.'

'What's that?'

'The guy who you killed was sent by a customs official, called Kayumba. He works at the airport. Let's just say we had a bit of a run in. I think he might have another crack at me. Do you think you could have a chat to him … to stop him.'

Keith could hardly believe his ears. This American journalist was asking him to 'hit' a Zambian customs official.

'Jesus! Is this how you treat all your boyfriends? You put out a contract on them! You are one seriously dangerous lady,' laughed

Keith.

'Will you do it?' she asked trying not to smile, it was too painful.

'We'll see what we can do. That's us, Rhodesian security forces, your friendly neighbourhood guns for hire!'

'You watch too many movies.'

'Here, take this.' Keith stepped towards her, slipped out the Tokarev pistol, and pushed it into her sling. 'If he comes back before we can 'speak' to him, blow his balls off.'

*

Eagles Rest Resort, banks of Lake Kariba, Siavonga, Zambia

Time had stood still for the village of Siavonga built on the banks of the giant Kariba dam. It had been built to accommodate workers during the building of the dam in the 1950s and nothing much had changed, other than the potholes and decay. Jock McLean knew it well from the days he worked on the mine nearby. He knew it well as he had little to do at the time other than to wonder around and explore.

The village had a police station, a few shoddy government buildings and a string of picturesque chalets built on the shoreline. A shop called Joe's Boat Hire lay empty and derelict. The place was a perfect reflection of Zambia, beautiful countryside superimposed with rot and degradation.

The Eagles Rest Resort was little more than a fisherman's camp, with chalets built in the trees overlooking the lake. It was at the base of a narrow isthmus, the shape of Malaya, that jutted out into the lake. The end of the isthmus was undeveloped thick virgin bush reachable via a narrow walking path that led from the resort.

Jock McLean and Ian Southwood had not worried about making a booking, during the week the place was usually completely empty. They took just over 2½ hours to cover the 160km from Lusaka. They pulled up in the car park in Ian's Datsun 1500 truck piled with fishing gear, sleeping bags and provisions. The heat struck in a solid wave after the relief of driving with the windows open. They strolled over to the reception office.

It was empty.

From previous visits, they knew that the place was run by a Zambian by the name of Phineas. He was the manager, gardener, cleaner, receptionist, handyman and gillie.

A bell sat on the reception desk that Jock gave a good smack. Nothing happened, so he gave it a repeated set of slaps to the tune of Flower of Scotland.

Phineas had trained himself to hear the bell even if he was on the far side of the resort. After the beginning of the second verse on the bell, he came trotting over.

'Meesta Basil, Meesta Ronnie, you didn't phone,' said Phineas apologetically.

'No Phineas, just a last minute plan to come fishing. How has the fishing been?'

'Not good, maybe some bream on the point. Tiger are not biting, even with Kapenta.'

'Just two nights Phineas,' said Jock handing over ten Kwacha, enough for two days accommodation.

Phineas passed across the register. In Zambia, the law required that all guests in hotels sign a police form and produce their passports for identification. These had to be verified by Phineas as correct. The police collected the forms sporadically, and in theory, they were sent to Lusaka to check against immigration information.

They had learned from previous visits that Phineas was illiterate.

'Take number one,' said Phineas passing over the key.

'Are there any other guests?'

'No, you are the only ones.'

Jock pushed the guest register back over to Phineas, who carefully placed his X against the names of Basil Fawlty and Ronnie Corbett.

The chalets were spartan with an old wooden dining room table with four chairs, a threadbare couch, two bedrooms each with thin mattresses over wire springs. The beds were the sort that the body sinks into, that squeak loudly with even the slightest movement. The place had the familiar smell of floor polish and thatched roof while housing a thriving colony of spiders. If there was one thing Phineas did well, it was to polish the floors, but little else.

The view from the chalet was world class, the contrast of the light blue of the cloudless sky against the deep blue of Lake Kariba, with a backdrop of rugged tree covered hills on the Rhodesian side. Rhodesia was just 3km away as the crow flies ... or as the canoe paddles. On the face of it, it was a haven, but almost completely devoid of birds and wildlife. The locals had eaten everything to stay alive. They were now reliant on using nets, explaining why the fishing was so poor.

The sun set in the most spectacular way as it does over Kariba. Phineas had knocked off by 8pm and the resort was deserted. It was a full moon, due to set at 3am, the time set for meeting the resupply.

While there may not have been birds or wildlife, every bug known to man flew against the mosquito screens on the windows and door.

The mosquitoes seemed to have discovered a hidden passageway into the chalet. More appeared to be on the inside than on the out. The two men felt as if they were being eaten alive.

Eventually Jock and Ian couldn't take it any longer and went outside into the darkness away from the light. They quietly made their way along the path to the end of the promontory. A slight breeze came up off the lake that took away the mosquitos and the intense heat.

Both men sat in silence, looking at the stars and the brightness of the moon reflecting off the water. It was so bright that a canoe out on the lake would have been clearly visible from the shore.

Just offshore, at about 350m, was a tiny island, that just pushed up above the high water mark when the dam was full, which it was. This island provided cover for the SAS approaching in their canoes from Mica Point on the Rhodesian side. It also provided a place for them to wait for the rendezvous time.

At exactly 3pm Jock took out his hooded torch and flashed three times in the direction of the island on a bearing of exactly 95 degrees on his luminous compass. Four clear flashes were returned, indicating that four canoes were on their way.

In only a few minutes the first two canoes arrived, staying just off the bank in the deeper water. With finger's crossed against crocodiles, Jock and Ian waded out. There was no sound whatsoever, the men in the back of each canoe passed over the equipment all tightly wrapped in canvas and hessian to avoid any noise. Without a single word spoken, they disappeared as quietly as they came, replaced immediately by two others. Jock and Ian took their time wading under the heavy weight of the equipment, trying to keep their footing on the rocky bottom.

The supply drop went perfectly and after four trips back to the Datsun truck they had all the equipment loaded and concealed under sacks of sunflower seeds. They spent the rest of the morning fishing off the bank, and, as expected, caught nothing. Deciding not to stay another night to be savaged by mosquitos, the two men packed up the vehicle for the drive back to Lusaka, planning to get back before last light.

The Siavonga road travels about 60km due north before it intersects the Chirundu road between the border with Rhodesia and Lusaka. As the border was closed, the road carried very little traffic. At the intersection there were a few run down stalls selling fruit and vegetables and at one time carved curios and other touristy trinkets.

As they turned onto the main road, travelling north, they were confronted by a Zambian Army roadblock. The roadblock consisted of a few stones placed across the road, with a wide shoulder down either side.

Ian was driving.

'Slow down, stop about 50 yards short,' said Jock. They had practiced roadblock drills. Normally a few Kwatcha or some food was enough to get through. Of course, two white men driving in a vehicle was the opportunity for some sport for the Zambians.

Ian came to a gentle stop well short of the first line of stones. He left the engine running.

One of the soldiers waved his arm, for them to come closer. Ian inched forward, making the man continue waving at him. This gave Jock the time to assess the number of men on the roadblock and how well they were armed. They had enough weapons for half an infantry platoon in the back, as well as enough explosives to blow up a small town.

'Okay, I count four on the roadblock, there are two sitting under a tree on the right,' whispered Jock.

'I can't see any stopper group behind us, but there may be one further along,' replied Ian.

Eventually Ian brought the vehicle to a halt. Two of the soldiers detached themselves from their comrades and approached, walking along the road.

'You get out of the car! Put your hands up!' shouted the shorter of the two men.

Jock opened the car door and climbed out, holding his hands in the air. Ian sat behind the wheel, his fingers gripping the steering wheel … his mind racing … if they found the weapons they were dead meat.

'We waant to setch the vi-hik-kul,' said the short soldier coming forward waving his SLR at Jock. As he got closer Jock could smell the stink of booze, it was all over him.

His mate stood back watching, slightly unsteady on his feet from a skin full. Jock could see Chibuku cartons all over the side of the road. These boys had been at it for some time.

The short man cocked his weapon loudly.

'Kneel down on the road, keep your hands up.'

Jock obliged, the rough surface of the road immediately biting into his bare knees. They were still wearing their fishing kit, shorts and shirt, floppy hat.

The man put the muzzle of the rifle against Jocks forehead and gave it a hard push.

'I wonder what white man's brains look like,' he giggled.

Jock kept perfectly still, looking up at the man. The muzzle was strangely cold against his skin.

Lifting his rifle away, the man strolled past Jock to look in the back of the truck. It was a pile of fishing gear, a cool box and sleeping bags.

'Got eh al-chol?'

'In the cool box, there are three beers ... you can have them.'

'Ehhh,' replied the man, flicking open the cool box and pulling out the beer bottles, holding the tops between the fingers of his right hand.

'What's in the sacks?'

'Sunflower seeds.'

'Why do you take sunflower seeds fishing?'

'I have a farm, we sell them to people,' interjected Ian, still behind the wheel.

'Ehhh!'

Clearly the soldier had no need of sunflower seeds.

He walked back and passed the beers to his smiling mate. The man turned and handed the beers to the other men standing behind the stones.

One of the soldiers called out, 'Have they got any money?'

Ian took some Kwatcha out of his shirt pocked and held it out the window. The short man walked around and grabbed it out of his hand, immediately sticking it into the pocket of his combat pants.

'You get out the car. Go kneel next to your friend,' said the soldier, opening the door.

Ian followed his instructions.

'White people stink,' sneered the soldier, prodding Jock in the chest with the SLR. 'Say that you are soorry you stink!'

The man was enjoying himself.

Jock and Ian duly apologised for stinking.

'Giv-e me your peppas.'

'They are on the dashboard,' replied Ian.

The man leaned in and lifted out the two passports with Ian's Zambian Registration Card. He studied them closely.

'Look under the sacks,' said the soldier, turning to his mate. The man walked around the back of the truck and undid the tale gate, letting it drop down loudly. He could be heard pulling at one of the sacks, allowing it to fall onto the tar.

'I have ninety-nine[59] Kwatcha in my pocket,' announced Jock

---

59 The "99" call was a policy of simultaneous retaliation by the British Lions during their 1974 tour of South Africa. The tour was marred by on-pitch violence, that the match officials did little to control. Lions' captain

loudly. Ian flashed a glance at him.

Jocks hands were still above his head, so the man had to lean down to reach the buttoned shirt pocket. As he did so, Jock dropped his hands, yanking the rifle out of the man's grip. In one fluid motion, he spun it around and shot the man through the chest. Rising to his feet, Jock spun around towards the man with a sack of sunflower seeds in his hands at the tailgate. He died with a bullet between the eyes.

Ian scrambled to his feet to run around the back to get the man's rifle.

Jock corrected his aim at the men behind the rocks in the middle of the road. The first man went down. Jock missed the second as he ran towards the trees. Jock followed him with the open sights, BANG … down he crumpled into the dust.

Ian had the other rifle cocked and opened up on the men under the tree. Bullets were now being sprayed towards the vehicle from the trees. Ian, behind the back of the truck, aimed carefully into the trees, trying to suppress the incoming fire.

Bullets zipped and cracked overhead, the windscreen smashed to pieces. Jock, standing in the open firing from the shoulder, went through a magazine, pumping rounds into the bush. As the magazine emptied, he ducked back behind the vehicle to get a replacement out of the man's webbing. They were sitting ducks in the middle of the road.

Ian raced around the front and jumped into the driver's seat.

'Jock, get in,' he screamed.

Instead of getting into the passenger seat, Jock, picked up their passports from where they had dropped, then jumped into the back, thumping on the roof.

'Go!'

Ian gunned the old Datsun. Foot flat on the accelerator the engine over revving as he slammed it from first into second on the column shift.

Jock was firing into the bush on the side of the road, trying to aim at the base of the trees. He watched dust kick up from his bullet strikes. A repeated clunking sound as more bullets hit the side of the vehicle burying themselves in the sacks of seeds.

Down the road they went, Ian swerving the truck left and right,

---

Willie John McBride therefore instigated a policy of 'one in, all in' - that is, when one Lion retaliated, all other Lions were expected to join in the melee or hit the nearest Springbok. By doing so, the referee would be unable to identify any single instigator and so would be left with the choice of sending off all or none of the team.

Jock holding on for dear life, holding his finger on the trigger as the second magazine emptied.

They raced away as fast as the old truck would go, leaving a steady stream of petrol dripping out the back from a bullet through the petrol tank.

After only 10km Ian pulled off the road. The petrol gauge was dropping precipitously. The vehicle was a mess, full of bullet holes. There was no way they would be able to get through the road block at the Kafue River bridge 40km further up the road. It was heavily guarded against Rhodesian attack.

They needed to make a plan … and quick.

*

Westlands Farm, ZIPRA Freedom Camp, 19.5km northeast of Lusaka

Comrade Lieutenant-Colonel Julio Ángel Casas, the chief Cuban advisor to ZIPRA, drove through the gates to the training camp called Freedom Camp. It was late afternoon and the last of the exercises of the day were being completed.

The camp was deliberately built close to Lusaka, as the view was that the Rhodesians would never risk a raid so close to a major city. It was about 2 hectares in extent, squashed between the Chikumbi Road and the main north/south railway line to Kabwe and the Copperbelt. Chikumbi railway siding was only 800m from the northern boundary of the camp. It was an area of intensive agriculture, mainly market gardening.

As Casas passed the gate in his Peugeot he could see the old address sign of the original owner, it said, 'O'Donovan – Westlands Farm'. The farm had been expropriated by the Zambian government and given to the freedom fighters.

The original farmhouse was converted to the camp administration building, housing the camp commander and a few senior staff. Hessian screens to keep out prying eyes surrounded the central compound. Lines of tents marked the accommodation for the occupants of the camp.

As Casas stopped his car next to the front entrance to the house a 60-strong fatigue party was forming up on the uneven dirt parade ground. Their job was to scour the surrounding farmland and bush for firewood in order to cook the evening meal.

Comrade Colonel Julio Casas was in a foul mood. There were things on his mind. The girl he had raped the night before had kneed him in the crotch afterwards. It throbbed painfully. Beating her to a pulp had not provided any satisfaction. He was frustrated and upset at the sudden change of events.

Shaking his head, Casas despaired at the amount of work that was required to knock this rabble into a disciplined fighting force. They were much worse than the Angolans he had worked with before. They seemed enthusiastic enough, but they lacked drive, a willingness to train hard. They just wanted to learn to shoot, that was all that interested them. Trying to explain the complexity of a mobile armoured brigade, that he was appointed to create, was beyond all except a very few. While Casas was fluent in English, as were many of the cadres, the words he used and his accent confused them. This made instruction slow and tedious. The whole thing was made worse by the fact that very few of the newly arrived Cuban instructors could speak English, making any but the most basic of instructions slow and painstaking.

The real cause of Casas' temper was his irritation at having to take instruction from the arrogant, pompous, supercilious prick that was Colonel Lev Kononov. The Soviets always acted superior but Kononov was a real arsehole. Casas had encountered this sort of Russian attitude while he was training in Moscow, but Kononov had succeeded in really getting under his skin. He had decided that he hated the man with a vengeance.

Kononov was old-school Soviet. He had been a partisan during the Second World War in the Crimea. *For some reason,* thought Casas, *this gave him some sort of superior knowledge of insurgency operations in Africa! He was old, at the end of the line, only a year from retirement.*

Casas had fought for three years against the South Africans in Angola. He was a hardened professional; he knew what it took to win. *This old bastard had no real experience of Africa!*

Just the thought of the injustice of his situation made Casas feel ill, but he was trapped, his mission was high profile, people in high places were watching ...

Dressed in his Cuban green battledress, Casas stepped out of his car and took a salute from the officer organising the fatigue party ... *that's a start,* thought Casas. He walked up the three steps onto the veranda of the old house and pushed the screen door open. The old dining room was now a meeting room and three men were already seated at the table. All three leapt to their feet as he entered. They saluted smartly and he waved his hand for them to sit down.

The men watched Casas' face closely; they could tell that he was in a dirty mood.

'We have been tasked with an important mission,' opened Casas.

The two men on his left were Cuban advisors Captains Juan Fernández Ruz and Eduardo García Vigoa. On his right was a ZIPRA Brigade Commissar, Comrade Elijah Bandama. The men all nodded without saying anything.

'How many of the Strela [60] launchers do we have here?' asked Casas.

'Two, Comrade Colonel,' answered Ruz.

'Do we know why they are misfiring?' asked Casas.

'I don't think they are, Colonel,' replied Ruz, an expert on the missile. 'I know our brothers in ZIPRA have fired four missiles at Rhodesian aircraft without success, but it is a delicate weapon, it needs careful handling.'

'But a 737 is a big aeroplane! How can they have missed?'

'You are referring to the two shots at South African Airways 737s out of Victoria Falls. Both missiles launched but failed to track. They were fired from the right position from behind according to the debriefing. I can only assume the seeker head was damaged,' replied Ruz. 'We have asked the Soviets to check the batch and they are adamant that there is nothing wrong with them.'

'We need to ensure a strike ... the leadership are demanding it,' said Casas, his frustration was palpable; his face was drawn up in a sneer.

'Do you have any suggestions Comrade Colonel?' asked Vigoa.

'I do,' replied Casas.

He spent the next two hours briefing the men on what he had in mind. All three were initially shocked at the ideas but once they had time to think about it they could see the merit ... it was a low risk proposal ... with potentially enormous benefit.

Casas called the meeting to an end and left the three men to work out some of the finer details.

Ruz had agreed to give a select team of men much more intensive training on the use of the Strela missile.

*

Floor of the House of Lords, Houses of Parliament, London

Lord Baron Goronwy-Roberts of Caernarfon, The Minister of State, Foreign and Commonwealth Office stood to his feet.

'With permission, Mr Speaker, I wish to make a Statement on

---

[60] The 9K32 "Strela-2" (Soviet 9K32 "Стрела-2"—*arrow*; NATO name SA-7 *Grail*) is a man-portable, shoulder-fired, low-altitude ground to air missile system with a high explosive warhead and passive infrared homing guidance.

Zambia.'

The Speaker nodded consent.

'Zambia faces severe economic difficulties arising from the low world price of copper and difficulties with her road and rail links to the sea. The Rhodesian raids deep inside Zambia have reinforced the Zambian Government's concern about their national security. I have just heard of a further raid today. We have agreed to provide military aid to improve Zambia's defensive capability. Some ground equipment and spares have already been supplied strictly for the use of the Zambian armed forces and police. More will follow after detailed consultations with the Zambians. We will also step up military training for Zambians in Britain. No British service personnel or aircraft will be stationed in Zambia.'

Lord Baron Goronwy-Roberts retook his seat.

Lord Peter Carrington[61] rose to respond, 'I do not think that there will be anybody in any quarter of the House who does not sympathise with the economic position in which Zambia finds itself, due largely to the economic recession in the world, and of course, as the noble Lord said, to the falling price of copper. However, I do not think that the Government can have been surprised at the concern shown by a great many people in this country about the shipment of British arms to Zambia, because it coincided with an escalation of the war, and without any explanation it appeared to be almost an intervention in it. I agree, it is very much better that arms purely for the defence of Zambia should come from Britain than from Cuba or from Russia, with all the military and political interference that that might bring. The fact remains that the timing of the Government's announcement has made us very suspicious. Like it or not, there are guerrilla camps in Zambia, some—at any rate, one—not very far from Lusaka.'

'Here, here,' said a grumble of Lords in agreement.

Lord Carrington continued, 'From these camps on Zambian soil guerrillas enter Rhodesia and kill Rhodesians, black and white. It is surely not very surprising that the Rhodesian forces attack these camps. Now the Government have sought to remain neutral in all this, but if British arms are to be used to defend these camps, that is taking sides, and I must ask the noble Lord whether he will give an assurance to the House that British arms will not be used for the defence of these guerrilla camps.'

Lord Hubert Gladwyn[62] stood to take up Lord Carrington's

---

61 Peter Alexander Rupert Carington, 6th Baron Carrington, British Conservative politician. He served as British Defence Secretary between 1970 and 1974.
62 Hubert Miles Gladwyn Jebb, 1st Baron Gladwyn, hereditary peer, became

argument.' It seems to me that, as I think the noble Lord, Lord Carrington, said, nobody can object to our granting economic assistance on a considerable scale to Zambia in her present unfortunate position. The fact is that President Kaunda is in a very weak position. He has hardly any effective force at his disposal, and he therefore cannot prevent the establishment of guerrilla bases in his country even if he wanted to do so. Anyhow, they are there. I suppose the intention is for the Government to provide for the military air defence of the capital, Lusaka, but not in any way to give military assistance to the rebels in the defence of their guerrilla bases. It is obvious that the guerrillas will obtain air support and assistance in the anti-aircraft defence of these bases from countries other than ours in the fairly near future. Missiles against low-flying aircraft and helicopters are very easy to install and cannot easily be detected, and there is every reason to suppose that the guerrillas will go in that direction. However, if they do we cannot do anything about it. So I would ask the Government to say that it is not their intention to do anything to help the guerrillas protect their bases, which they will defend anyhow, but that our support will be limited to the defence of the capital, Lusaka, which I believe the Queen is to visit in the near future.'

Lord Baron Goronwy-Roberts rose to reply to the two questions, 'My Lords, I am grateful to both noble Lords for their comments on the statement that I have just read and, in both cases, for putting, if I may say so without presumption, the right questions. As for the assurance which both noble Lords sought about the destination and the use of the ground equipment and spares, the arms that we seek to make available to our Commonwealth partner, Zambia, I can give that assurance. I myself am very confident, totally confident, that the President and the Government of Zambia will do everything in their power, and effectively so, to ensure that this assistance is used by the Government for Government purposes; namely, those purposes very tidily described by the noble Lord, Lord Gladwyn, as the defence of Zambia at a time of considerable difficulty for that country and in the defence of its capital.'

The House moved onto other subjects.

Lord Baron Goronwy-Roberts padded his forehead with his handkerchief, relieved that no questions were asked on the air crash in Lusaka.

That Sir Charles Prior has done a marvellous job on this metal fatigue business!

---

involved in politics as a member of the Liberal Party. He was Deputy Leader of the Liberals in the House of Lords and spokesman on foreign affairs and defence.

10

Cuban Embassy, Plot 5574 Magoye Road, Kalundu Township, Lusaka, Zambia

All criticism is opposition. All opposition is counter-revolutionary.
Comrade President Fidel Castro

'The reporter is here Comrade Colonel,' said Captain Jose Gomez, Jose Casas' *aide de camp*.

'Huhh,' grumbled Colonel Casas. This was just another irritation. The Ambassador had delegated a press interview because of the excuse of his superior English skills ... *bullshit, he didn't want to risk any fallout from a misstatement. These autocrats spend their lives covering their arses!*

Gomez quietly opened the door and ushered a woman into the office. Showing her to a chair, Gomez closed the door but remained standing in front of it.

'Good morning Colonel, my name is Sarah Burrell from Associated Press,' said Sarah, stepping forward with a smile. Her lip was less painful, but still swollen. She was wearing her standard African reporter's uniform of white shirt and khaki trousers. The fitting of the shirt would have been described as a bit too tight, with one button too many open at the neck. A camera bag hung over her shoulder and she carried a black leather-bound notepad in her hand.

'Good morning, Miss Burrell,' replied Casas in deeply accented English, taking in the blond hair and stunning body. The black eye and split lip were unexpected. He had her press credentials in front of him, a clever concoction of her past stories, she was noted as being from Ottawa Canada and not the US.

'You have an accident?' asked Casas pointing to her eye.

'Just walked into a door, you know how it is.'

Despite the damage to her face, Casas could see that she was a stunningly beautiful woman. His eyes were drawn back to the unbuttoned shirt and the movement beneath.

Speaking in Spanish, Casas said, 'You didn't tell me she was so beautiful Gomez.'

'Yes, Colonel she certainly is,' replied Gomez.

Sarah remained impassive.

'Maybe I should give her one, what a tight ass!'

'Yes Colonel.' Gomez was aware of his boss's proclivities. He spent a great deal of time cleaning up after him. Paying off women, taking them to hospital after being beaten up. The Colonel may have been a brave soldier but he was a depraved lout in every other respect. Gomez bit his lip, thinking of what the Colonel might do to this reporter if given half the chance.

Though the Colonel did prefer young black women who were in abundant supply. Still it beats working in the squalor and oppression of Havana hands down!

'Who is the man in the carpark?' asked Casas in English, looking out the window.

'He is my boyfriend, he is a local game guide, I asked him to drive me over,' replied Sarah.

The gate to the Cuban Embassy was made of heavy wrought-iron, supported by two substantial concrete pillars. There was an unarmed private security guard in a guardhouse next to the gate. He had allowed Wilson and Burrell into the embassy carpark after checking off their names on a list.

In the carpark outside, Keith Wilson stood leaning against Godfrey Mwamba's Landcruiser. He made a mental note of each detail. He was not allowed into the Embassy building, there were two very sturdy looking men in Safari suits at the entrance also unarmed but they were obviously military.

On the way from the front door to Casa's office Sarah had made special note of the layout. The building was a large split-level residence with all the offices of the senior officials in the front part overlooking Magoye Road. An annex had been built onto the back of the building, housing more offices and accommodation for the junior officials.

The Ambassador lived on the premises with his family, but Casas and a few other senior people lived in rental accommodation in the surrounding suburbs.

'So what can I do for you Miss Burrell?' asked Casas politely with a supercilious smile.

It always paid to be polite to the foreign press.

'Why are you in Zambia, Colonel?' enquired Sarah, not wishing to engage in any further niceties.

Casas launched into his prepared statement, 'We are here to support the freedom of the people of Africa from their colonial oppressors. The West underestimates Africa's march towards unity and development. The enemies of Africa have tried to silence the African struggle for freedom and economic development. We, and President Kaunda, denounced economic colonialism. The West have always wanted to be the owners of all the resources that Africa possess.'

'So what is Cuba's role? You are hardly an example of successful economic development?' asked Sarah pointedly.

There was a flash of surprise across Casas's face. This woman was starting to needle him after only one question.

'The West are trying to find new ways to dominate us, and they underestimate us.'

'Are you talking about Cuba or Africa Colonel?'

A little flustered, Casas carried on with his statement, 'The West cannot continue saying Africa cannot develop because what Africa needs is human capital. Africa needs technology as well, and instead of offering that technology, the West refuses it. Cuba has stepped in to help with human capital and technology. Thousands of Cubans now fight in Africa and more than 150,000 Cubans are in Africa at different moments and currently a lot more are still here offering services in different fields. Fidel Castro has said that all we are doing is settling the debt that we have with humanity.'

'Is the technology you refer to weapons, Colonel? How does that help economic development?'

'You cannot have economic development when the people are in chains. We are here to ensure freedom of all oppressed people,' stated Casas, raising his voice. This woman was starting to upset him. He was not used to a woman asking him questions ... women were strictly for fucking ...

'What about the oppression of your own people Colonel?'

Casas leapt to his feet, glaring at Sarah, his eyes aflame.

'Cubans that serve in Africa are the descendants of thousands of slaves that were brought to Cuba. We can say that we are the same. We must deliver freedom and development to these people, by any ... any means possible ... we will sweep the colonial oppressors into the sea!'

Casas's arm was outstretched towards the distant 'sea'. He slammed his fist into his hand for emphasis with each 'any', making a loud slap.

'What is your comment on the murder of missionaries in Rhodesia by the freedom fighters, Colonel?'

'It is lies, lies ... the missionaries were killed by Selous Scouts and blamed on the brave freedom fighters ... it is obvious!'

'Are you going to invade Rhodesia, Colonel?'

'It is enough!' shouted Casas, his face was flushed with indignation. 'How dare you come here to ask these questions! This is a war ... we are here to win it ... what ever it takes!'

'Are you working with the KGB, Colonel?'

'Get out … get out,' screamed Casas, spittle flying from his mouth … his pent up frustration getting the better of him. He came around the edge of his desk. Sarah remained seated, unfazed by his outburst.

'Tell me about the political prisoners in Cuba, Colonel? Are there political prisoners here in Zambia?'

Casas grabbed the arm of the chair, thrusting his face within an inch of hers. She could smell the stink of stale cigar smoke.

His extreme agitation clicked him back into Spanish. 'I should teach you a lesson you would never forget you white bitch! Get out of my office!' He made to grab at Sarah's wrist.

'Okay Miss Burrell!' stepped in Jose Gomez. He gently tapped her on the shoulder. 'The interview is over. The Colonel is a very busy man with much on his mind.'

'Get this cow out of my office,' screamed Casas at Gomez still in Spanish.

Sarah stood up, her face unmoved by the violent outburst, she had succeeded in her mission. This was going to make interesting reading back home … *maybe the New York Times will run with it?*

'*Adiós y gracias Coronel*[63],' smiled Sarah in perfectly accented Spanish, sweeping out of the office, nodding politely at Casas as she left.

*

Railway Bridge, Banks of the Kafue River, 48km south of Lusaka

Jock McLean and Ian Southwood had abandoned the Datsun truck on a bush track ten kilometres short of the road bridge over the Kafue River. They had loaded as much weaponry that they could carry into backpacks and made off on foot through the bush towards the river. They had rigged the Datsun with enough explosive to blow up a small country, having removed the number plates and any other form of identification including the name of the trucking business on the doors.

Jock had also laid a few POMZ-2M AP mines on the edge of the track leading to the vehicle and two sets of boosted Soviet TM46 anti-tank mines on the approach road. The explosives in the truck were rigged to explode on a 4hour timer.

After carefully anti-tracking the two men had painstakingly made their way to the river in the cover of darkness.

The sound of the truck exploding carried easily to them through the still night.

---

63   Goodbye and thank you Colonel.

At first light, they moved close enough to observe the railway bridge over the Kafue River less than a kilometre south of the village of Kafue on the far bank. Any thought of crossing the road bridge was impossible. News of the attack on the roadblock would have reached the defenders of the bridge and two white men trying to cross … *well it didn't need a rocket scientist to figure out how that would go.*

The railway bridge, for some reason, wasn't defended anywhere near as well as the road bridge. Jock figured maybe a platoon, with even numbers on either side. The bridge was 430m long, a single track, steel lattice over concrete piers sunk into the riverbed. As far as he could see, the guards simply sat on the side of the track. They hadn't built a machinegun nest, or dug slit trenches. A few tents had been erected near the side of the track to protect the soldiers from the heavy summer rainstorms.

The railway line came up from Livingston, opposite the Victoria Falls, to Lusaka. The nearest siding on the line south of the Kafue River was at Mazabuka about 44km away. The railway line travelled virtually dead straight from Mazabuka to the Kafue on a gentle downward slope into the river's flood plain.

Jock and Ian decided to observe the bridge guard's routine before making a decision on what to do. The Kafue River was well over 400m wide in most places and full of crocodiles, so swimming was an absolute last resort. Getting to the river was also a challenge as a wide 600m swampy marsh followed the course of the riverbank. The railway line had been built up out of the marsh on the approach to the bridge. The only way onto the bridge was along the railway line.

As the day passed, they watched two goods trains, pulled by Garratt 20th Class 4-8-2 + 2-8-4 steam locomotives, travelling to the north and only one travelling to the south. They crossed the bridge at low speed but did not stop. The guards lolled about chatting; there was no sense of security or patrolling the approaches to the bridge.

The Kafue station on the other side was an important stop for the old steam trains to take on water.

As night began to fall, the two men discussed their options.

'Well, we can sneak across the railway line, walk into Kafue and call Patricia to fetch us,' suggested Ian Southwood with a smile.

'Two honky's that haven't had a bath, carrying RPG-7s and AKs, are likely to attract a bit of attention. The car breakdown argument also doesn't hold up well either,' replied Jock. 'No, I think we are going to have to catch a train to Lusaka.'

'You mean run along the railway line and jump on the train?'

'Pretty much, but while we are here we might as well create a bit of havoc,' laughed Jock, hatching a plot.

An enormous far off explosion carried to where the two men were hiding.

'Sounds like the Zambians have hit our tin. That should keep them occupied for a while,' quipped Ian.

An old Zambian Bedford RL with ten men on the back had missed the first boosted landmine but struck the second with the front right wheel. The unprotected cab was ripped off the front of the vehicle killing the driver and his passenger, the ten men on the back were hurled into the air injuring all of them seriously. Four died at the scene. Rescuers in a Land Rover sent to help, struck the first landmine smashing the vehicle almost beyond recognition, killing all six people on board. Five disorientated soldiers, were killed by POMZ AP mines as they stumbled about in the dust and destruction.

Despite all the landmine explosions and the subsequent manhunt, the Zambians did not seek to boost the protective force for the railway bridge over the Kafue River. A sweep line was set up from the site of the landmine explosions, travelling out in a huge circle.

While Jock and Ian sat on the side of the railway line planning their escape the first line of searchers were less than 4km behind them. They were not following spoor, but instead searching houses, villages, rocky outcrops, anything that could hide the fugitives.

As the sun went down Jock and Ian started to build a pile of rocks and wooden poles onto the railway line. The wood they got from a nearby abandoned cattle kraal. They chose a point where the track began a slight incline before the long downhill towards the bridge. After about 2hours they had an impressive obstruction, better looking than effective. A train would have been able to plough through it without any problem whatsoever.

Just before midnight, a train could be heard approaching from the direction of Mazabuka. It was not travelling fast, less than 15km/hr. Ian and Jock crouched in thick bush next to the track and waited.

Slowly the old puffing steam train approached, the giant headlight on the front visible long before the train arrived. The sound of the deep huffing and wheezing of the engine filled the night. The driver saw the obstruction on the tracks from over 300m and slammed on his brakes. The Rhodesian SAS had been blowing up trains in Zambia and the train's crew were thrown into panic. Sparks flew off the steel rails as the wheels locked. The train only had ten empty bulk trucks and a guard's van but it was still too heavy to prevent the train slamming through the flimsy obstruction. The wooden logs were thrown to the side of the track by the cowcatcher with a loud crunch.

Eventually the train stopped with a spitting hiss as the brakes were released. Jock and Ian could hear the driver and his stoker, shouting at each other, they had both jumped off the train and run off into the bush, expecting to be either blown up or shot in an ambush. The guard was shining his torch out of the rear carriage, not game to come into the open.

Jock and Ian took the opportunity to come out of the bush, scramble up the steep embankment. Jock had set an explosive charge against the track with a one-hour timer and clicked it on. Once again, they left a 'ZANLA' marked AK magazine next to the track, then climbed a ladder on the side of one of the empty trucks and dropped down into it.

They could hear the chattering of the driver, stoker and guard as they shouted at each other in the dark. Once they realised that they were not to going to be ambushed they settled down. Their voices dropped as they discussed what to do next.

Jock checked his watch; it had been twenty minutes since the timer had been set.

Come on, get on with it!

Eventually after half an hour, the driver and stoker climbed back aboard and the train restarted for the short trip across the bridge to Kafue.

Jock and Ian sat in the darkness as the train chugged away. The open truck they were in clouded up in thick stinking coal smoke, making them cough and splutter. It was torture, both convinced they would suffocate long before they got any where near Lusaka.

'We can't stay in here,' hissed Jock.

This was a classic case of a well-laid plan being undone by unforeseen circumstance. Jock was already thinking through options. He climbed up the ladder on the inside of the truck to see how close the bridge was. The headlight on the train picked up the steel girders on the approach to the bridge. A cooking fire was burning 15m from the side of the track surrounded by Zambian soldiers having a drink-up.

'Can you throw a cricket ball?' asked Jock over the sound of the train.

'I wasn't too bad in my day,' replied Ian, used to Jock's sometimes obtuse questioning.

'Well grab M962s out of the bag, pass me one, on my call, throw as hard as you can.'

The train slowed as it approached the threshold to the bridge, Jock held a grenade in his hand ready to pull the pin with his teeth like Audie Murphy. The note from the wheels changed as the engine crossed onto the steel bridge, the driver gave a loud blast on the whistle.

Holding on to the ladder with one hand, Jock waited for the right moment.

'Okay Ian, one ... two ... three ... Go!'

Jock pulled the pin and hurled the grenade as hard as he could towards the cooking fire. Ian, from inside the truck, threw his first grenade out over the top into the night ... any cricketer would have been proud. The grenades sailed out into the darkness landing right next to the cooking fire. Ian followed with a second grenade ...

Three thudding explosions carried over the noise of the train.

A war broke out at the bridge. Heavy machinegun fire sprayed tracer high into the air as the imaginary Rhodesian bombers flew overhead. The gunfire grew in intensity as the Zambians shot at ghostly Rhodesian soldiers, their own people and cattle grazing in the nearby field.

Jock watched in awe as the battle raged, they had completely underestimated the number of Zambian troops, there must have been hundreds. Fire was joined from the Kafue side of the bridge as the soldiers there broke into panic ... *the Rhodesians were attacking!*

Tracer was now being swopped from both sides of the river; a 82mm mortar was brought into action ... it looked like the final scene to the film, *Bridge Over the River Kwai*[64]. The driver of the train opened the throttle, spinning the giant steel wheels as they bit for traction. Bullet strikes were now hitting the sides of the railway trucks, spitting sparks from whining ricochets.

Jock was in his element screaming into the dark as the battle raged on. His blood was up, 'Pass me the RPG,' he screamed at Ian.

The train was nearly over the bridge, the driver, hanging on the whistle in a continuous throaty roar. As the truck they were in passed over the end of the bridge, Jock punched out an RPG projectile into the midst of the Zambians hiding next to the track. The HE round exploded in a blinding flash. For the Zambians, the sound of the gunfight, the train and the whistle there was no way of knowing where the rocket came from.

Jock was really enjoying himself, calling Ian to pass him another

---

64   *The Bridge on the River Kwai*, a 1957 British-American WWII film directed by David Lean.

round.

The railway siding in Kafue was only 900m from the bridge. The driver was racing to get into the town; he continued to pump the train whistle as if it were deflecting bullets.

Jock watched as the train entered the station. There were only a few floodlights mainly next to the huge water tower used for replenishing the steam engines. His mind was already thinking through the options. Sitting in the back of the suffocating truck all the way to Lusaka was a problem as was what they would do when they got there. Two white men climbing down off an empty railway truck, even if they were unarmed, was always going to raise suspicion.

'Ian we're at the station, I think this is our stop,' called Jock lifting the RPG-7 towards the huge water tank, silhouetted against the floodlights. The rocket gave a loud crack as it ignited and punched into the water tank easily driving a hole through the steel skin, exploding inside the full tank setting up a violent shockwave. The lid blew off.

The two men were up and over the side of the truck as quickly as they could, jumping down next to the track. There was a commotion from the driver and his fireman as a wave of water spewed out of the water tank drenching everything in its path.

'We need to make a call,' whispered Jock as they dashed between the lines of empty carriages in the siding.

'Maybe the station will have a phone?'

'Good idea!'

The Kafue station building is a single story building built in the 1950s, with a single platform. The Station Master's office was on one end identified by the painted label. There was nobody about as the citizens kept their heads down while their security forces continued the battle at Kafue Bridge against the ethereal Rhodesian invaders.

As they trotted down the passage, Ian lifted the receiver on the payphone on the off chance that it was working, it wasn't.

The Station Master's office was locked, and protected by a thick steel security door. The windows were also barred.

'I was hoping we could do this quietly,' sighed Jock.

'We need a diversion,' suggested Ian.

'Okay, I will set a charge on the door, you go to the edge of the building and shoot the steam engine with an RPG. Wait for me … on my call. Happy?'

'Happy.'

Jock went to work with a lump of plastic, a det and a fuse of cortex. Ian walked to the edge of the building and took careful aim at the steam engine 150m away. Once he had lit the fuse, Jock joined Ian next to the building, 'any second now.'

Jock tapped Ian on the shoulder and the RPG fired, the projectile streaking across in a split second, impacting the centre of the firebox. The train seemed to rear up with the power of the explosion and the release of superheated steam. The steel parted throwing burning coal and jagged metal outwards, incinerating the driver and fireman, setting a nearby line of old wooded carriages alight.

The door to the Station Master's office blew off, hanging by only one hinge. The inside of the office was dark but Ian felt on the desk for the phone ... picked it up and with the light of a pencil torch dialled home.

It was late ... the phone rang and rang. Ian felt a knot in his stomach ... *had anything happened to Pat!*

Come on!

'Hello, Mazira Farm.'

Thank God!

'Hello Patricia, I am sorry to be phoning so late. I can't talk for long but you and Ian are invited to a party at our place in Sunningdale on the 11th, please come early.[65]'

'Yes, thank you, can I bring anything?[66]'

'You can bring half a dozen beers, we look forward to seeing you. Good night.[67]'

Ian replaced the receiver, 'Right all set. Let's get going.'

The war to the south had died down ... the loud thud of the timed fuse on the railway line carried through the night. A three-metre chunk of rail had been blown out of the track. This would derail a goods train coming up from Livingstone later that morning.

Jock was delighted with his two days work, two trains, two Zambian vehicles and dead and wounded soldiers, mostly shot by their own people.

*

Lukanga Swamp, 137km northwest of Lusaka

Captain Juan Fernández Ruz, Cuban Revolutionary Army, needed

---

65   By using Patricia's full name and not the usual 'Pat' he was sending a distress signal. Sunningdale is a posh neighbourhood in Lusaka, but was also code for Kafue. Come early meant early morning, the next day! Different day numbers meant different things – the 11th was 'tomorrow'.
66   Pat was asking where?
67   Ian is saying 6km on the Lusaka side of Kafue.

to find a way of helping his trainees understand the capability of the Strela-2M[68] missile. Practical instruction using fast, low flying aircraft was essential. They had practiced watching slow moving commercial airliners fly into Lusaka International Airport, but that was not sufficient.

Ruz had contacted his friend Captain Alberto Ley Rivas, the commander of the Cuban MIG-21 squadron that had just arrived in Zambia. They had discussed the options and decided that it would be best to practice with the Zambian J6s (MIG-19) just in case anything went wrong. The MIG-19 was the first supersonic fighter of the Soviet-bloc, manufactured under license in China as the Shenyang J6, with a top speed of over Mach 1.3 (760knots) at altitude.

Assembled on a dirt road, 2km to the north of Lukanga Swamp, was the small ZIPRA team of Strela missile trainees. The swamp was a large inland basin that filled with runoff in the rainy season. It was a good choice as it was dead flat and aircraft could be seen approaching from a long distance. Captain Ruz had arranged for the Zambian pilots to fly over the swamp at various speeds at different heights as a training exercise. He did not tell them that the exercise involved heat-seeking missiles. It would have made them nervous.

Ruz led the six men carrying three launchers with missiles attached up a low hill due north of the swamp with an excellent view of the horizon in all directions. A vast expanse of green vegetation stretched out into the distance.

Ruz had trained the ZIPRA cadres on aircraft identification, showing the aircraft used by the Zambian Air Force, the new Cuban MIG-21s, the Rhodesian Hunters and Canberras as well as the South African Impalas, similar to the Zambian Aeromacchi MB326GBs, Mirage IIIs and F1s. It was a lot to remember and difficult to apply in practice when a fast moving jet is approaching at low level.

Ruz checked his watch, only a few minutes before the jets arrived.

Three Zambian J6s had taken off and were already speeding across the countryside at 1,000ft AGL in a loose V-formation. They took only 8 minutes to reach Lukanga Swamp from their base at Mumbwa. They made an impressive sight in dark green and brown camouflage livery while the noise from their engines was deafening, scattering terrified livestock on the way.

Ruz warned his trainees to get ready; the first man lifted the missile onto his shoulder.

All was perfectly quiet.

---

68   NATO reporting name SA-7b, SAM7, ground-to-air heat-seeking missile.

The reaction time measured from the carrying position, with protective covers on, to missile launch was trained to be 13 seconds. Ruz's trainees had yet to achieve this result. It was possible, but required considerable training and skill that these men did not yet have. With the launcher on the shoulder, covers removed and sights extended, reaction time from fire command to launch reduced to 6–10 seconds depending greatly on target difficulty and the shooter's skill.

Travelling at 430knots, well below maximum speed, the J6s covered 1km every 4 seconds.

The missile launcher system consisted of a green missile launch tube containing the missile, a grip stock and a cylindrical thermal battery. The Strela has a slant range of about 4.2 km, a ceiling of 2,300m, and a speed of about 500m/second, Mach 1.75. The missile is a tail-chase system; its effectiveness, therefore, depends on its ability to lock onto the engine heat source at the rear of low-flying aircraft.

Ruz had warned his trainees to keep their fingers away from the firing triggers once the missile acquired a target; they were just to get the buzz of a target acquisition. They had practiced this before with slow flying airliners.

Placing his hand on the man's shoulder to steady him, Ruz watched the seconds tick by on his watch.

There was no warning for the young ZIPRA cadre. The three J6s passed overhead before the sound flooded over him with a thunderous roar.

The cadre spun around, tracking the aircraft with the iron sights on the launch tube, gently applying half-trigger. He pressed the trigger again; the missile registered the infrared signature, a green light flashed through the sight and the buzzer sounded.

The aircraft were skimming away over the swamp leaving grey exhaust smoke with a throbbing booming sound behind them. It could have been nervous excitement or the need to make a good impression, the young cadre hit the trigger again … just what he had been warned not to do.

The missile locked on, producing a steady buzzing noise and a red light flashed in the sight mechanism. The on-board power supply was activated and the throw-out motor ignited. The throw-out motor fired the missile out of the launcher at 32m/second, rotating the missile at the same time at 20revs/sec. The cadre continued to hold the launcher on the target. After 0.3 seconds the rocket motor ignited. The heat from the blast buffeted the men standing next to him as the missile climbed away, beginning its deadly flight.

The missile's un-cooled, lead sulphide, passive infrared seeker head can detect infrared radiation at below 2.8µm in wavelength; the rapidly departing J6s were producing a lot of heat in this band. The missile left a distinctive cloud of white smoke as it streaked through the sky at Mach 1.75, marking the path to the target making minute corrections to its flight.

There was no warning for the pilot of the J6, just a loud BANG as the missile impacted, throwing shrapnel into the engine and tailplane, causing the engine to flame out. There was no time to recover or eject, the aircraft dived into the swamp at a speed over 370knots disappearing completely from sight as it embedded itself deep in the mud. There was a muffled explosion and a plume of black smoke ... then nothing.

The ZIPRA cadres stood in complete shock, mumbling to themselves in siNdebele. Captain Juan Ruz stood riveted, his eyes fixed on the spot where the aircraft had ploughed into the swamp. His mind was trying to take in what had just happened. Making a decision, he screamed at the cadres to pack up their equipment then ran headlong down the hill his trainees in tow. They jumped onto the vehicle and drove off in the direction of Lusaka.

All the men with him were sworn to secrecy ... *this batch of missiles does work!*

*

Freedom Camp, Westlands Farm, Chikumbi Road, 19km north of Lusaka

The Zambian government went into paroxysms of blame and recriminations about the attacks on the train and Kafue Bridge. The Rhodesians were accused of the senseless act of terrorism. The *Times of Zambia* called for the declaration of a State of Emergency. President Kenneth Kaunda brought the Zambian military to full alert, but what worried him most was the fact that ZIPRA and their new Cuban allies now outnumbered his own military and were better trained and equipped. One of his new J6s had been reported missing in suspicious circumstances.

Kaunda had effectively lost control of his own country.

All the evidence pointed to ZANLA for the attacks on the trains, but there were two white saboteurs in their midst, attacking targets indiscriminately. Roadblocks were set up on all the major roads and all white males were being searched and interrogated.

Keith Wilson knew he needed to work fast on the information concerning Freedom Camp. He had managed to transmit a coded message to Selous Scout HQ on the whereabouts of the camp and his instructions from Colonel Reid-Daly were clear ... reconnaissance as a precursor to a strike. He did not know who had blown up the trains and killed the Zambian soldiers, but in Wilson's mind, it was almost certainly the SAS stirring the pot.

The mood in Lusaka had noticeably changed. While before Wilson was largely ignored, now the locals stared at him where ever he went. There was a feeling of foreboding and fear. From being just another white man, he like all the others, was viewed with intense suspicion and hostility. His operational effectiveness was now a serious concern. Travelling around at night was highly risky.

The three men agreed that Wilson would work the Cuban angle, while Ngwenya and Chiyeka would do the reconnaissance.

Wilson drove Ngwenya and Chiyeka out on the Great North Road an hour before last light. They drove until reaching the Chikumbi Road intersection at the 13km peg. They had not passed through a roadblock although fully expecting to do so. Wilson turned onto the dirt road towards Chikumbi siding and drove for a further 2km.

There were agricultural smallholdings on both sides of the road with very little natural bush. On an empty stretch of road, Wilson slowed and the two Selous Scouts jumped off the back of the Land Rover and stepped into a patch of long grass. Wilson continued for another kilometre before turning around and following his same route back to the main road. He did not see anyone at all.

Ngwenya and Chiyeka lay down in the long grass and waited for nightfall. The only person they saw was on old man on a squeaking bicycle, riding towards the north. Once it was dark, the two men stepped out onto the road, Ngwenya set his compass on a bearing of 49 degrees and they began the 5km walk to a spot believed to be just south of the camp. Pinpointing the exact location of the training camp was what they were there to find out.

The going was slightly downhill but otherwise flat open countryside. The sound of singing was their first hint that the camp must be close. They found a rocky outcrop, and listened. Numerous cooking fires were in an area to their north and the sound of singing was unmistakeable. *Chimurenga* revolutionary songs were very familiar to the two Selous Scouts, hearing them many times before on pseudo-ops.

Deciding that this was a golden opportunity, the two men hid their packs in a hole in a termite mound and walked down the hill towards the camp. A rusted three-strand barbed wire fence marked the boundary. They stopped and knelt down. Fences could be patrolled, while the sound of crossing them can alert a guard some distance away. A train could be heard in the distance slowly approaching from the south. The main north-south railway line to the Copper Belt marked the eastern boundary of the camp.

As the noisy train chugged past, they carefully slid through underneath the bottom strand of the fence and walked towards the singing. They noticed almost immediately that a network of slit trenches had been dug along the boundary, connected by well-worn paths. The trenches themselves were shallow, with little attempt at overhead protection. Mostly overgrown with grass, fields of fire had not been cleared for some time. The surrounding grassland grew to over waist height.

Ngwenya led the way along a path towards the railway line. They moved carefully and silently, making sure not to stand on anything that would make a noise. The quarter moon picked up the white sand of the path perfectly, making walking along it much easier. When reaching what must have been the corner of the property next to the railway line, they found what was supposed to be a bunker for a machinegun nest. It was empty except for a mat of weeds, roofed in with a roughly thatched four-posted structure. There were no weapons, certainly no machineguns, and the trenches showed no signs of recent occupation. The place seemed completely undefended, indicating that the occupants of the camp believed that they were safe from attack.

Turning towards the north along a path parallel to the railway line, the two men made their way towards the sound of the singing. The ZIPRA cadres had gathered together on a large dirt football field near the original farmhouse buildings. A huge bonfire was set in the middle of the field with the men sitting in rows circling it. Nobody was carrying rifles or weapons of any sort.

Ngwenya and Chiyeka were ignored as they joined the circle of men, sitting down amongst them. The voices pulsated in a gyrating rhythm, some men were on their feet, dancing in wild abandon. The words were the classic revolutionary theme of throwing the settlers out of their homeland, after taking all their possessions and slitting their throats.

The leader of the song stood next to the fire. He held his hand in the air and the voices died away. Three men made their way through the seated crowd towards the fire. A murmur of anticipation went up from the ZIPRA cadres.

As the light of the fire illuminated their faces, Ngwenya recognised them immediately, Party Commissar, Samuel Munodawafa, Commander of ZIPRA, Lookout Masuku, and the head of the ZIPRA National Security Organisation, Dumiso Dabengwa. These were faces that were imprinted on Ngwenya's brain, all on the Selous Scout hit-list. It crossed his mind that if he had an AK in his hands at that very moment, he could wipe out the most powerful of the ZIPRA leadership. He and his fellow Selous Scouts had studied these men for years, to the point that he felt he was on first name terms.

Samuel Munodawafa stood forward.

'Comrades we are here to welcome our new commander of our revolutionary army, Comrade General Lookout Masuku,' called out Munodawafa in a clear penetrating voice.

There was a hush from the men as they waited to hear the words of their new leader, the man to take them into battle, to lead them triumphantly back into Zimbabwe to take back the riches they deserved.

A rumble of sound came from the men, a deep-throated repetitive chant, 'jee'a ... jee'a ... JEE'A ... JEE'A.'

Lookout Masuku waved both his arms above his head in recognition of the impi war cry, last heard in battle at Bembezi in 1893. All that was missing was a thudding of knobkerries against hide-covered shields.

Both Ngwenya and Chiyeka found themselves caught up in the chanting. This was part of their heritage as part of the Matabele nation. These men surrounding them were all blood brothers ... yet now mortal enemies.

Masuku began his speech in a soft but clear voice, 'Comrades it is a great honour to lead you into battle ... ' He seemed short in stature from where Ngwenya was sitting, but his voice built in vibrancy and authority, as he launched into a long diatribe exalting the importance of their future in the freedom struggle. Ngwenya could hear every word as clearly as if the man was standing next to him.

Masuku did not see himself as a terrorist. He was a freedom fighter in a legitimate struggle against an oppressive and illegal regime. He knew that power was based on a combination of personal strength and controlled brutality. Masuku, as with Nikita Mangena before him, sought to rule his forces by fear. They needed to fear him more than the enemy. This same principle applied to the local rural population of Zimbabwe, but absolute power needed to be tempered with humility and respect.

Masuku warned, 'only if you treat the population with respect do you find it easier to fight the enemy. We are fighting for the liberation of these people. If we kill them, who are we going to rule?' The rural population needed to understand that ZIPRA was embodiment of power. No opposition was to be tolerated and unstinting support was demanded. Masuku's orders were also clear regarding informers. He ordered that all informers were to be summarily executed. 'An informer is more dangerous than someone who is carrying a gun,' he said.

If Alfred Nikita Mangena had erred in his leadership, it was in the area of military aggression. He interpreted his orders as being simply to subdue and control the Matabeleland area. He was to build up his forces through continued infiltration and to recruit from the rural population, to be sent back over the border to be trained. He had built up a considerable supply of arms and ammunition, housed in a network of arms caches. This was all in readiness for the eventual political capitulation of the illegitimate Rhodesian regime at the hands of the British.

Masuku and the ZAPU political leadership now changed their strategy, it was time to take the battle to the enemy. He exalted his forces …

'The real battles are to come when our glorious leader, Joshua Nkomo, through us, his military instrument, is to take control of the country to make sure that Mugabe and the Shonas did not assume power.'

The soldiers burst into spontaneous applause and loud chanting … they all hated Mugabe and the Shonas, mortal enemies for over a hundred years.

Lookout Masuku finished his speech to wild applause and singing … the men chanted their readiness for battle … for victory.

'JEE'A … JEE'A.'

After further speeches by the Political Commissars talking about the communist creed, the meeting broke up and the men were sent back to their tents. Ngwenya and Chiyeka walked back to the boundary fence, crossed it, and climbed back up the low hill to wait for morning.

Despite being dressed as pseudos, the Scouts still needed to climb the hill without leaving any telltale spoor. They did not know whether ZIPRA in the camp sent out patrols to look for unwelcome visitors. It was vital that they entered the OP position without being detected. This required careful anti-tracking techniques with each man climbing into the hill from a different angle.

From first light, the two Selous Scouts began their carefully planned observation of Freedom camp.

The Selous Scouts had turned observation into an art form. One person at a time manned the OP concealed in a heavily camouflaged lookout. Each man kept a careful log of all that he saw, noting vehicles arriving and leaving, the routine followed by the soldiers in the camp and the people living on the surrounding farms. The senior cadres issuing orders each got a name based on their clothing and routine. At times, depending on the wind, it was possible to hear the soldiers talking to each other. There was a great deal of marching and drilling but very few weapons were in evidence.

Each OP had a 'base' where the off-duty team members could sleep or eat. This was where they kept their food and equipment. There was no cooking of meals or boiling of water for tea, cooking smells and gas can be smelt a long way off. All possible sources of sound were also carefully considered, opening food cans, scraping of spoons, checking of weapons, cleaning weapons and the like. Talking was in hushed tones and only when totally necessary. Most communication was done with hand signals.

Ngwenya and Chiyeka were only carrying Tokarev pistols. They took turns on the OP at two-hour intervals.

From his initial observation, Ngwenya concluded that the camp was organised into three sections. The first was based around the original colonial style farmhouse, with the parade ground and flagpole. Ngwenya estimated it was about 1,300m from their OP. Next to the farmhouse was a neat line of tents amongst a stand of gum trees. This, he believed, was the HQ element. A gravel track led from the farmhouse to Chikumbi Road. The only form of defence he noted were two, twin-mounted DShKM 12.7mm anti-aircraft machineguns, in emplacements north and south of the farmhouse. Both were left unmanned.

The other two sections of the camp were housed in tents in separate areas of thick bush. These housed the trainees. With his binoculars, Ngwenya could count the number of long-drop latrines that helped him to assess the number of men in the camp. He saw no women or children in the camp, only loud boisterous youths of military age, for ZIPRA, 14 years or older. All wore a mishmash of Soviet and East German uniforms, grey trousers, green forage shirts, and webbing belts and boots that were either black with side straps, like the Rhodesian pattern, or British style ankle boots with a bright shiny stud on each side. A few wore East German reisfleck combat jackets, and a number wore wide-brimmed khaki floppy hats.

Two guards, though sometimes only one, were on duty at the truck-cab guardroom at the gate. There was a surprising number of vehicles visiting the camp; mainly civilian vehicles but also a few GAZ-66 Soviet built trucks. Four GAZ-66s were drawn up next to the farmhouse in a makeshift MT yard, with two new looking UAZ-469 Soviet jeep-type vehicles.

Ngwenya made careful note of the blue Peugeot 504 that Keith Wilson had seen at the Cuban Embassy and in the Inter-continental Hotel carpark. The driver of the Peugeot was the 'head honcho', as Wilson described him. There were only three other Cubans picked up on the first day of the OP, Ngwenya gave them names, *Ilizwi* for his high squeaky voice that easily carried to the OP, *Ihembe* for his yellow shirt, *Ndebvu* for his thick black beard. Based on their initial observations, Ngwenya and Chiyeka estimated that the camp housed between 800 and 1,000 cadres.

As the afternoon wore on Ngwenya took on his shift in the OP, scanning and noting down the activity below. He added to the sketch plan of the camp he had drawn in his notebook. His mind passed to thinking of his wife and son back on his small farm near Tjolotjo north of Bulawayo. Tjolotjo was the village in the centre of Nata Tribal Trust Land. His family had lived in the Nata region for many generations. His clan had been part of the Zulu invasion of southern Matabeleland by Mzilikazi in 1838. All of his ancestors had been warriors; they fought the Shona tribes, Kalanga, the Shangaan, the white man and each other. It was a natural thing that Ngwenya had become a policeman; his father had spent thirty years in the BSAP before a ZIPRA landmine killed him.

At 5pm exactly a large party of cadres were paraded on the soccer field then dismissed to look for firewood. Half the group went to the north, while the other half made their way directly towards the small hill that Ngwenya and Chiyeka were hiding in. The hill was thickly wooded, so it was an obvious choice. From what he could see, only one cadre in the work party was armed with an AK. As the men slowly approached, Ngwenya crawled back through the bush to where Chiyeka was sleeping.

Deciding that discretion was the better part of valour, the two men shouldered their backpacks and made off towards the railway line that was lined with thick vegetation on both sides. They were careful to brush away their spoor and left no sign of where the OP had been situated.

They walked out of the thick undergrowth onto a well-trodden path leading to the railway line. To anybody watching they would have looked no different to ZIPRA trainees from the camp.

As they approached the embankment of the railway line, a man stepped out of the bush carrying an AK ... but without a magazine attached.

He saw them and said in siNdebele, '*Litshone njani,* good evening, Comrades.'

'*Salibonani,* hello' Ngwenya said in a shocked reply. The cadre looked very young, no more than seventeen years old.

'Where are you going?' the cadre asked.

'We are going to look for women,' Ngwenya responded.

The man laughed, 'These Zambian women won't let you fuck them without a fight.'

'Ehh, but we are two,' replied Ngwenya smiling back at the man indicating Chiyeka behind him.

'Do you have permission to leave the camp?' asked the cadre, still smiling. It appeared that the camp instructors had set well-concealed sentries. Ngwenya and Chiyeka had not picked them up from the OP.

'Are you alone Comrade?' asked Ngwenya, trying to buy some time.

The man looked at him in surprise, it was a strange question. His facial expression changed to one of suspicion.

Ngwenya reacted in an instant, his training kicking in with a shot of adrenaline. He chopped down on the back of the cadre's neck with vicious force, at the same time grabbing his mouth to avoid any sound. The young man collapsed in his arms. Chiyeka lifted the man's legs as they carried him into the bush next to the embankment.

If you want to know something, why not ask the person directly? Ngwenya had not yet considered this possibility.

The two men worked quickly, tying a gag around the cadre's mouth and securing his legs with electrical cable carried in their backpacks. The man awoke with a start, his head spinning from side to side as he tried to come to terms with his position. His eyes focussed on the two men leaning over him, the look of abject terror was unmistakeable as he screamed silently into the gag, urinating and defecating into his trousers.

Ngwenya held his finger to his lips for the cadre to be quiet.

'We are not going to hurt you Comrade,' whispered Ngwenya in siNdebele, with his mouth next to the man's ear. '

Chiyeka had recovered the AK. It had only one round in the chamber, the cadre had no other equipment and his pockets were empty. It seemed the instructors in the Freedom Camp had little confidence in their recruits.

Voices carried to where they were hiding as the work party arrived to collect firewood. The sounds of laughter and loud conversation got closer. Once again, Ngwenya held his finger to his lips to make sure the man made no noise. To add extra emphasis, he slipped his hunting knife out of the sheath strapped to his calf and held it next to the man's throat.

The work party were breaking off low hanging branches with loud cracks as the wood gave way. From what Ngwenya could hear, they were throwing the wood into a pile to be lashed together in bundles to make it easier to carry. It was possible to hear every word they said.

As soldiers do, they were complaining about the food, the accommodation, the instructors and the discipline. The lack of women in the camp was also a topic of conversation as was the restriction on alcohol. Standard army recruit stuff ...

Ngwenya and Chiyeka both lay down in the long grass next to their captive, with Tokarev pistols in their hands ... if discovered, they would shoot their way out.

Pushing his knife hard against the skin of his captive's neck, Ngwenya hissed into his ear.

'Be very quiet Comrade ...'

Still the voices got closer, the men seemed to be approaching along the path used by Ngwenya and Chiyeka earlier.

'Zinyeza!' someone shouted.

'Zinyeza where are you, you lazy bastard?'

They were calling Ngwenya's captive. He pushed his knife deeper, splitting the skin.

A debate followed as the men in the work party discussed what had happened to Zinyeza.

'He has snivelled back to camp,' said one.

'He has gone to the village to see his girlfriend,' said another. It was all friendly banter, it appeared that Zinyeza was notoriously unreliable and therefore nobody was particularly concerned.

No serious search was suggested and the men continued down the path.

Ngwenya held his breath as the men walked past in single file, the dust from their boots filling his nose. He did not look up, keeping his face buried in the grass ...

There was a call and the file stopped. A man was speaking loudly to the others, telling them to walk down next to the railway line where the bush was thicker.

A man was standing on the path only a few metres from where the Selous Scouts were hiding. Ngwenya twisted his head slowly to look at Chiyeka, his eyes said it all, he was preparing to lunge up if the man came any closer. Ngwenya blinked purposefully, to confirm he had the same idea in mind.

Someone began to pee in the grass not far away. Loud jovial conversion carried on as the men swapped stories. Another man started to piss, this time much closer; Ngwenya could smell the nauseating odour. His mind raced as he tried to assimilate all the options ... *get up and run, shoot it out, stay still, try to bluff my way through pretending to be a ZIPRA cadre. ... the only option is to stay still and hope they pass by, if they find us, we will take out as many as possible.*

Someone shouted instructions and the men started to move off. A boot appeared right next to Ngwenya's head. He could smell the man's perspiration. His body tensed ready to spring, his stomach cramped in anticipation. The boot moved away, as quickly as they had arrived, the noise of the men faded away. Ngwenya continued to lie perfectly still. Bathed in sweat, he could feel it pooling in the small of his back. The nervous tension made his whole body ache. He tried to bring his breathing back under control, his heart still pounding in his chest.

They lay still for nearly half an hour before Ngwenya signalled to Chiyeka to get up. Carefully and silently, they got to their feet, staying crouched over to peak out above the grass. Doing a 360-degree check, there was nobody about. The path was well worn so it was highly likely that a local farm worker or villager would pass by, they still had to be very careful.

The plan set with Wilson was a two night OP, with a pick up at the same place on Chikumbi Road at 3pm the next day. Ngwenya signalled to Chiyeka, to help him, and together they hoisted the young cadre onto Ngwenya's shoulder. With Chiyeka leading the way, they hurried back to their OP position in the thick undergrowth on the hill.

It was time to find out some information ... from the horse's mouth so to speak.

11

Hotel Inter-continental, Haile Selassie Avenue, Lusaka

Keith Wilson returned to the Norman Barr Safari's warehouse, took a shower, trimmed his beard, and headed back to see Sarah Burrell at the Hotel Inter-continental.

Wilson found himself in unfamiliar territory. He had cut a deal with Sarah that got him into the Cuban Embassy compound … his boss Colonel Reid-Daly wouldn't believe it if he told him … nobody would believe it.

This woman had an effect on him that was beyond his experience, way beyond his experience. It could be said … she was out of his league. Just the sight of her, the smell of her hair was captivating, it sent a chill down his spine with an unequivocal signal to his crotch that seemed to take on a mind of its own.

The whole situation was surreal, he was in the middle of an incredibly dangerous mission, and yet he had no fear, no nervousness or anticipation. She seemed to make the whole thing seem possible … a kind of stability … it was almost as if she had taken command of his mission.

Sarah had lined up the Cuban that Wilson had decided should be the 'target' for the snatch. She was actively helping him plan the operation. The clarity and breadth of her thought process was as good as, or better, than most of the senior officers he had met. Keith Wilson was faced with the reality, that in terms of planning in an urban environment, this girl was way better than he was … light-years better. His training provided for a sense of subtlety in pseudo operations, the infiltration of terrorist gangs where his knowledge of Matabele culture, language skills and bushcraft were of paramount importance. In an urban environment, the level of subtlety was completely different. On the one hand, it was possible to be bold and aggressive, but on the other, the level of planning had to be much more considered. The options were much greater and more complex.

Keith Wilson decided that he was seriously enjoying himself.

He waited in the hotel bar for Sarah, nursing a beer and watching the passing parade. The usual string of prostitutes were waiting for suitable clients; wealthy, well dressed, members of the Zambian Government entertained foreign guests; and expatriate workers were transiting to and from the Copper Belt.

Reunited by Peaches and Herbs[69] was playing softly in the background.

> *I was a fool to ever leave your side*
> *Me minus you is such a lonely ride*
> *The breakup we had has made me lonesome and sad*
> *I realize I love you 'cause I want you bad, hey, hey*

Wilson had got to know the barman quite well, helped by generous tips in US dollars. Reuben was a well-informed fund of information, happy with Wilson's story that he was a big game hunter and safari guide. He knew the regulars from the Chinese, Soviet and Cuban Embassies frequenting the hotel. As importantly, Reuben knew the Zambian police informers and undercover agents hanging around the major hotels looking for the dreaded Rhodesians! Wilson had his ID checked at least three times a night ... he was getting used to it ... his cover was now second nature. Norman Barr Safaris was a well-known operation and clearly Norman's sponsorship of the local police force paid dividends.

There was a tap on his shoulder, Wilson turned around.

'How does a girl get a drink around here?'

Standing in front of him was Sarah wearing a very tight, sleeveless, black pantsuit, with a high collar and a deep V-neck that plunged tantalisingly low. Her hair was tied back and she wore dark eye make-up that accentuated her deep green eyes and disguised her recovering black eye. Her arms were lightly tanned, clearly responding well to the hot African sun. He caught a whiff of perfume mixed with shampoo.

Wilson slipped off the barstool, to stand in front of her. She was virtually his height in the low sandals she was wearing. His eyes took in everything, drawn to the delicate movement beneath ...

She leaned forward and kissed him on the cheek, lingering for a split second ... her touch sending that signal ... it flashed an electrical current through his body ...

'Reuben, beer for the lady,' called Wilson, staring into her eyes, now fixed on him as if she was reading his mind. A tight knot settled in his stomach.

She didn't need to have much of an imagination regarding her impact on Wilson ... Sarah was an operator, she knew exactly what she was doing ... enjoying herself.

---

69   Written by Dino Fekaris and Freddie Perren, R&B vocal duo Peaches & Herb. Released from their 1978 album, *2 Hot.*

Lover, lover, this is solid love
And you're exactly what I'm dreamin' of
All through the day
And all through the night
I'll give you all the love I have with all my might, hey, hey

'Hey Lover, you ready to catch yourself a Cuban?' she smiled mischievously, her full lips covered in a dark red/brown lipstick. Her split lip was almost healed.

Wilson glanced left and right to see if anyone had heard her, 'Jesus, Sarah, be careful.'

She threw her head back and laughed, a throaty, uninhibited laugh, while her eyes danced in his.

'You blush really brightly, Wilson,' said Sarah, still giggling. She had taken to calling him Wilson, instead of Keith.

Reuben returned with the drinks, he could not help but smile. He knew … he'd seen it a thousand times before. He retired to a discreet distance, as more guests entered the bar.

Wilson could only grin back at her. She had him in a kind of vice, squeezing him to the point where his mind went blank.

'I think I've got a plan on how to snatch your Cuban,' whispered Sarah, leaning forward again close to his ear, her breast brushing his arm.

The electrical current hit again … this time at higher voltage.

'We can't talk about that here,' hissed Wilson, struggling to remain in control.

'Why not, nobody can hear.'

'Are we still going to recce the Cuban's house tonight, I thought that was what we agreed?' asked Wilson, trying to get down to business.

'Yes, of course, but let me tell you my plan first,' insisted Sarah, she had never felt more alive in her life … *what a story this is going to make!*

She outlined her thoughts on a plan that Wilson listened to without asking any questions, taking in all the details. It was as good a plan as any; it was Sarah's role in it that had him worried.

'Sarah, this is not your war. This is way too dangerous, these people are ruthless. If you get caught, it doesn't bear thinking about. No, I am sorry, you can't do it.'

'It's my choice … I want to do it. These Cuban's shouldn't be here, they shouldn't be in Africa with their sick, twisted, ideology. They are a bunch of thugs … we need to teach them a lesson,' replied Sarah with real venom in her voice, her whole demeanour changed. She was instantly all business, ready to execute her mission.

Finishing their beers they walked through the hotel lobby towards the carpark.

Wilson took the driver's seat while Sarah did a quick check around the carpark for signs of surveillance.

Driving out of the carpark, Wilson turned east on Haile Selassie Avenue. Not having an address for Comrade Colonel Julio Ángel Casas, their plan was to follow him home after work.

Wilson was familiar with the route to the Cuban Embassy in Magoye Road, only 4.5km away. The traffic was light, no military or police were anywhere to be seen. Driving slowly past the embassy entrance, they could see that Casas's Peugeot was still parked inside. The sentry at the gate was in the guardhouse and the gates pulled closed and locked. All the lights were on in the front part of the embassy.

Driving on a few kilometres, Wilson executed a neat U-turn and drove back towards the embassy. He pulled off the road 300m from the gate at the intersection of Luanginga Road, turned off the lights and switched off the engine. None of the streetlights were working and the security light at the gate to the embassy was the only light in the street.

Neither Wilson nor Sarah noticed the red Fiat 127, parked further to the south where the road bent towards the intersection with Msanzara Road. The occupants of the Fiat, Jock McLean and Ian Southwood, had watched the Landcruiser pass by, but because of the bend in the road, could not see that it too was watching the embassy entrance.

McLean and Southwood had been at the embassy for an hour, recording all of the comings and goings, taking careful note of the people arriving and leaving the embassy, vehicle descriptions and registration numbers. They already had a pretty good list compiled by Patricia Southwood during her observation of the embassy while they were creating havoc on the road back from Kariba.

Jock had an RPG-7 wrapped in a canvas bag in the boot and was seriously considering shooting two rounds into the embassy. He hated going out on reconnaissance without spreading a bit of 'alarm and despondency' afterwards. His instructions were to make a snatch, so putting the embassy and its staff on high alert would just make the snatch more difficult. From what they had seen, there were three likely candidates in Cuban military uniform. One was the bloke with the blue Peugeot 504.

A Zambian police Land Rover turned south onto Magoye Road from Lukanga Road. They were on their regular night patrol of the network of embassy houses in that part of Lusaka. The headlights picking up two people sitting in the Landcruiser parked on the side of the road.

'Fuck,' exclaimed Wilson as the Land Rover drove past; the two policemen in the front seat clearly very interested in them. Sarah grabbed Wilson by the collar, pulled him towards her and kissed him full on the lips, then wrapping her arms around his neck in a tight grip. She held him in a vice, whispering through her lips.

'Take it easy,' she whispered, sticking her tongue into his mouth.

Wilson's heart beat in his chest, trying to decide what to do, difficult while in a passionate embrace with a super model's tongue in his mouth. Electricity was now flowing in all directions …

Sarah was enjoying herself, '… breathe, you are going to suffocate,' she giggled.

The Land Rover slowed down as the policemen debated whether they should check on the vehicle. In the dark, it was not possible to see the faces of the occupants.

The policemen had been instructed to stop and search any vehicles parked near foreign embassies at night. Deciding to check, they stopped and reversed back towards where Wilson and Sarah were parked.

Wilson turned on the headlights.

The two policemen got out of the Land Rover, holding their hands up in front of their eyes against the Landcruiser's bright headlights. Both had pistols at their side.

'Turn off the headlights,' shouted one of the policemen.

'Be cool, it'll be fine,' whispered Sarah still kissing Wilson passionately.

One of the policemen came round to the driver's side window and banged hard on it with a torch. Wilson wound down the window.

'What can I do for you officer?' asked Wilson.

'What are you doing here?' asked the policeman pointing the torch into Wilson's face, flicking it in Sarah's direction lingering on the top part of the pantsuit.

'We are making out officer,' stated Sarah in her best New York accent. 'Look officer, I am a married woman and this is my boyfriend. Please, nobody can know about this.'

'Ehhh,' grunted the policeman unimpressed. 'Let me see your ID.'

His partner had gone around to the back of the vehicle and was checking inside with his torch.

'I've got money officer, please leave us alone,' said Sarah, now visibly upset, beginning to cry. She was fiddling in her handbag, putting on a perfect performance of a woman in distress.

'You, get out the car,' ordered the policeman pointing at Wilson.

This was an escalation. Wilson summed up his options.

Wilson hesitated, fumbling for the door latch. The policeman's face was only inches away as he leaned over, panning up and down Sarah's body with the torch.

Lifting his arm, Wilson smashed his elbow into the policeman's face, the nose exploding in blood. The man let out a scream of shock as the pain shot into his brain. Leaning hard on the car door, Wilson heaved it open, crashing into the policeman, knocking him off balance. Wilson kicked hard at the man's crotch, sinking his boot with all the power he could muster. The man's brain exploded in agony, as he collapsed onto the ground with a deep-throated groan.

The other policeman grabbed his revolver out of the holster and ran around the side of the vehicle. Wilson crouched down, then launched himself at the man's waist in a rugby tackle, knocking the pistol from his hand.

As the two men hit the rock hard ground, an RPG-7 projectile impacted the front door of the Cuban Embassy. The heavy door, with steel bracing, exploded inwards in a thudding explosion killing both guards on the inside. A second RPG round entered one of the front windows. It flew across the room, through a steel filing cabinet to explode against the wall beyond. The wall disintegrated into thousands of razor sharp slivers of brick, killing an embassy official in the open plan office beyond.

The two explosions lit up the night, distracting Wilson for a split second. The policeman scrambled to his feet, and escaped into the dark.

'Jesus!' exclaimed Wilson in disbelief ... *somebody was attacking the Cuban Embassy!*

Climbing back into the Landcruiser, Wilson gunned the engine, spinning the tyres on the loose gravel until they bit into the tar accelerating down Magoye Road past the burning embassy. They narrowly missed the Fiat 127, now beginning a sharp U-turn across the road, getting a brief glimpse of the two men in Afro wigs in the front seat.

Who the fuck are those people?

Wilson was shaking from the adrenaline; he could feel the sweat running down his back. Sarah seemed relaxed.

'Did you get a look at those two guys in that red car back there?'

asked Wilson, slowing the Landcruiser down to a more respectable speed.

'No I didn't but they were definitely honkies,' replied Sarah. 'I saw the one in the driver's seat clearly ... he was a honky for sure.'

'Who the hell are they?'

'It's obvious,' replied Sarah, '... you are not the only game in town!'

Wilson glanced at her, she was smiling at him, relaxed as you please.

'That policeman back there, definitely made Godfrey Mwamba's Landcruiser,' said Sarah, 'we are going to have to dump it.'

As they drove slowly back to the hotel, Sarah slid across the bench seat. She took Wilson's arm and rested her head on his shoulder.

Keith Wilson felt as if his body was about to explode ...

*

Jock McLean and Ian Southwood drove slowly through the streets of Lusaka towards the M9, back to the farm off Mumbwa Road.

'Did you see the people in that Landcruiser?' asked Jock.

'Not very well, it was definitely a white bloke and a white chick,' replied Ian.

'Have we seen that Landcruiser before anywhere?'

'No, I don't think so. It seems bloody strange that they drove past us, then after we hit the embassy they come racing back, like we gave them a fright or something.'

'Yee, bloody strange.'

'You reckon they were also watching the embassy?'

'Maybe, it seems too much like a coincidence.'

'If they were, what are the chances that they are CIO from Bright Lights?'

'Bloody good chance! I am going to have to ask. Did you dump that Mushala stuff?' asked Jock.

'Yes, I left it at the side of the road,' replied Ian slowing at a stop street. Ian had left a Mushala propaganda poster on the side of the road.

'That should give the bastards something to think about,' laughed Jock.

Jock and Ian alternated with 'evidence' left at scenes of their activity. The two main choices were Robert Mugabe's ZANLA, usually 'ZANLA' scratched rifle magazines, pieces of Chinese uniform and the other was posters of Adamson Mushala. Mushala had been running a Zambian opposition insurgency from his headquarters, deep in the

Mulumbwanashika Forest in the far North-Western Province. His group were violently opposed to Kenneth Kaunda's UNIP party and his one-party state. It was a low level rebellion but it was enough to make Mushala and his group public enemy number one in the mind of Kaunda and his cronies.

Sirens could be heard blaring in the distance.

*

Hotel Inter-continental, Haile Selassie Avenue, Lusaka

Wilson dropped Sarah back at the hotel and drove back to the Norman Barr warehouse. His mind was churning with the delayed shock of the attack on the two Zambian policemen and the ramifications of being identified ... *the beard has to go!*

What was more disturbing was the fact that someone had attacked the Cuban Embassy ... *it had to be SAS!*

Keith Wilson felt exposed and vulnerable, the feeling of uncertainty caused by a lack of control over events.

How can they send me to snatch a Cuban official and then shoot up the embassy in the middle of my mission? Something is seriously wrong!

Wilson was already composing the radio message back to Andre Rabie Barracks in his mind.

Sarah, despite her outward bravado, was feeling shaken after the events at the Cuban Embassy.

These Rhodesians are crazy ... sending two separate teams on the same mission!

There was no doubt in her mind that the RPG attack was by Rhodesian military. She had seen them hunched down in the front seat of the Fiat, their faces white as a sheet, wearing identical black woolly wigs, *for God's sake!*

Still ... Wilson handled himself like a pro, taking on those two policemen. He's a serious operator ...

Just the thought of seeing Wilson in action was exciting. He awakened a primeval instinct deep within her. While he was unspeakably dangerous, he was equally vulnerable and inept. She was having fun playing with him, he was like a gentle puppy dog mixed with Rottweiler ... the instinct to kill ever present. It was the contradiction between his old world manners, gentleness and politeness, and his ability to kill in an instant that was intoxicating. Wilson's predictable innocence was addictive.

The thought of him made her smile as she took the lift up to her room.

I'm going to have to cut and colour my hair …

She turned the key in the door and pushed it open. Stepping inside, she felt for the light switch on the wall.

A hand came out of the dark chopping down viciously on her wrist. Before she could scream, another clamped over her mouth. She could feel the strength in the arm holding her head back … the stale stink of nervous sweat, cigarette smoke and alcohol. Kicking out backwards with her feet she tried to hit his shins. The man bent her back further at the same time pushing her forward into the room.

Summoning up all her strength, Sarah dropped her weight forcing the man to grip tighter to hold onto her. She kicked up with both legs driving hard, at the same time thrusting her head back viciously. Her head caught her assailant on the nose. He let out a loud grunt in pain, loosening his grip slightly. Sarah twisted, spinning her whole body off the ground. The power of the leverage pulling her head out of the man's grip as she fell to the floor. The man stood silhouetted in the light from the passage outside. Disorientated, he staggered back, holding his bleeding nose.

Sarah let out a scream worthy of any horror movie, rushing forward throwing her shoulder into the man's solar plexus like a linebacker in her beloved American Football. Driving him into the passage, there was a loud groan as the air was driven from his lungs. She kept up her momentum, her legs pumping, driving him backwards, ramming him with full force into the far wall.

Winded, her assailant swung his arms to try and push her away, catching her with a glancing blow on the side of the head. As Sarah fell back, the man turned and ran towards the fire escape.

Pulling herself back to her feet, Sarah stood chest heaving from the shock and exertion. Her pantsuit top had been torn off the shoulder.

Doors opened along the passage, heads popped out to see what was going on.

Sarah held up her hand, still out of breath, 'It's okay … just a little disagreement with my boyfriend,' she said with a weak smile.

There was a rumble of muffled voices as doors closed again.

Sarah stepped back into her room, closed the door and set the latch. She was still panting, trying to regain her breath. With a shaking hand she poured a glass of water gulping it down, trying to regain control. Her whole body began to shiver as shock set in, water spilling from the glass.

Collapsing on the bed, Sarah began to cry, trembling as she brought her knees up to her chest … the man was wearing the uniform of the

Zambian Immigration and Customs Service.

*

Freedom Camp, Westlands Farm, Chikumbi Road, 19km north of Lusaka

'Now Comrade Zinyeza, I am going to ask you some questions and I want you to answer truthfully,' instructed Sgt Cephas Ngwenya, Selous Scout. He spoke very softly, each word pronounced deliberately in his native siNdebele.

Stanley Chiyeka was on OP shift while Ngwenya was interrogating their capture in the admin area.

The admin area was in thick bush between large granite boulders. Thorny vines and acacia trees created a solid intertwined barrier of vegetation with the only way into the hideout by crawling on the stomach.

The sun had only just risen so it was still cold from the night before.

Ngwenya had his notebook in his hand ready to write down the information he was given.

'Comrade, please make sure you tell the truth or I will hurt you very badly,' emphasised Ngwenya, smiling to soften the serious threat he was giving. Zinyeza nodded his understanding, his eyes wide with fright. 'Now I am going to remove the cloth around your mouth, do not make any noise, do you understand?' The man nodded, he understood.

The man was still tightly bound hand and foot, his hands uncomfortable behind his back. As Ngwenya slowly removing the gag, the man seemed to relax slightly, breathing more easily.

'Where are you from, Comrade?' asked Ngwenya. Always better to start with an innocuous question.

'I am from Nkai.'

'I know it well, I am from Tjolotjo,' smiled Ngwenya trying to put the man at ease.

'How long have you been with ZIPRA comrade?'

Ngwenya was always careful to use the word 'comrade' when he addressed captives; it was a sign of respect, but also showed camaraderie and understanding. He could see that it was confusing, that a black man was speaking to them in their own language, but fighting on the other side.

'One year.'

'Who is the commander of your camp?'

'Comrade ZIPRA Brigade Commissar, Elijah Bandama.'

'There are some men speaking a strange language from over the ocean, where are they from Comrade?'

'They say they are from Cuba, but I don't know where that is. Some can speak a little English. Before, we had white men from Russia, they have gone, I don't know where.'

'What have you been trained to do Comrade?'

'I have been trained to shoot the bazooka[70] at aeroplanes. They said that I am to be sent to Rhodesia in two days to shoot down aeroplanes.'

'What is this bazooka?'

'It is a spear that shoots across the sky with white smoke, but very, very fast. It chases the heat from the engines of the aeroplane and explodes. I have seen it work. It is not the same as the bazooka on the hill behind us which is much bigger.'

'The hill behind us, what are you talking about?'

The man's eyes flicked side to side, as he nodded with his head. Ngwenya lifted the young man to his feet.

' ... Which hill do you mean?'

The man turned towards the south and indicated with his head a low hill 3.5km to the southwest. 'That one, it goes by the name of Mungule, there is a big bazooka on that hill.'

Ngwenya could hardly believe his ears. They had been briefed on ground-to-air missiles; he had seen pictures of them.

Sitting the man down on a rock, Ngwenya continued, 'What can you tell me of this bazooka?'

'The Zambians have this bazooka, they made us go to the top of that hill and dig trenches and make the ground flat for the bazooka which is on a trailer. There are four on the trailer and they have other machines that make the bazooka work. When we were digging the holes, I saw white men in uniform speaking English. The Zambians told me they were from England.'

The man was speaking so fast that Ngwenya was having difficulty getting all the information down. The detail was beyond what he had expected.

'Tell me about the bazooka you have trained on?'

'It is like an RPG, but bigger, and the spear is much bigger, it fits in the front and is fired from a launcher on the shoulder the same as a RPG. It is heavy to carry.'

'Does the bazooka have a name Comrade?'

'The Cubans just call it *Flecha*[71].'

'How many are there Comrade?'

---

[70] The use of the word 'bazooka' was a generic reference to any form of rocket powered weapon, including the RPG-7 and SAM-7 (Strela2M).

[71] Spanish - arrow

'In the camp there are three launchers and nine spears. Each team must carry a launcher and three spears.'

'Did they tell you where you are going in two days, Comrade?'

'No,' lied the man, feeling more relaxed with the questioning; it seemed to be making Ngwenya happy.

'Who is the most senior man of the Cubans?'

'His name is Colonel Casas.'

Ngwenya continued to ask questions of the cadre, Zinyeza. He was careful to ask the same questions in different ways to make sure the answers were consistent. The information was staggering, the names of all the Cubans, the weapons, the number of trainees, names of the all ZIPRA officers and their respective positions. The presence of ground-to-air missile batteries needed careful attention.

Stanley Chiyeka, in the OP position, had not seen much difference from the activity of the previous day. A red car came down the road towards the camp. He had not seen it before. He refocused the binoculars to see if he could make out the occupants.

Turning into the main gate, the red car drove past the sentry in the old lorry cab. The man came running out, chasing after the red car as it continued on its way, throwing up a cloud of dust behind it. Just as this was happening, the familiar blue Peugeot appeared, also turning into the gate.

As Chiyeka watched, the red car stopped next to the farmhouse building. Two white men got out. They were both wearing khaki clothing as expected of farmers. Soldiers surrounded them shouting abuse and waving their arms threateningly.

The Peugeot stopped next to the red car and the Cuban soldier he had seen before got out. The Cuban waved his hands in the air in a very angry fashion, pointing at the two men.

After much shouting and gesticulation, the men jumped back into the red car, and it reversed down the road at great speed chased by the cadres. The car spun around, narrowly missing the gate guard jumping into the bush out of the way. The red car skidded out the gates, back onto Chikumbi Road, and raced off in a thick cloud of dust back towards Lusaka.

Chiyeka wrote down what he had seen, checked his watch, 2:30, time to pack up to RV with *Ikhanka*.

Keith Wilson had decided to do a little more reconnaissance of his own before picking up his men. He had driven the Norman Barr Land Rover out onto the Great North Road looking for signs of army transport trucks. He had left Godfrey Mwamba's Landcruiser with the

Welshman, now out the back of the warehouse, giving it a new paint job with a new set of number plates and engine numbers. Wilson had wanted to blow the vehicle up but the Welshman would have none of it. A Landcruiser was an extremely valuable vehicle. In Zambia, many vehicles had ground off engine and chassis numbers as most had been stolen from South Africa and Botswana and smuggled into Zambia. If the police were worried about ground off engine numbers, there would be virtually no vehicles on the road in Zambia.

Wilson could hardly believe his eyes, coming towards him, going like a bat out of hell, was the same red Fiat 127 from the night before, with the same two blokes in it, just without their Afro wigs. He thought of turning around to follow, but the Land Rover was way too slow for a car chase.

Those two blokes are everywhere! They have to be Rhodesians!

After gathering his thoughts, he drove on for 20km before turning back towards Chikumbi Road. As he slowed next to the RV point, Ngwenya and Chiyeka appeared out of the bush and jumped on the back of the Land Rover. He pulled a U-turn back towards the main road. Ngwenya slipped into the passenger seat.

'I have plenty of news for you, Cephas,' smiled Wilson.

'You can't have more than me *Ikhanka*. Where is the *mandebvu*[72]?' replied Ngwenya returning the smile, pointing at Wilson's shaved face. He was happy to see his boss.

'It is a long story.'

As they drove passed the hill called Mungule, Ngwenya pointed, 'There is a bazooka on the top of that hill.'

Wilson turned to look at Ngwenya, he knew him not to be a man prone to exaggeration.

'Yes *Ikhanka*, there is a British bazooka on top of that hill!'

Fuck me gently … thought Wilson … *its all happening at once* …

Back at the OP occupied by Ngwenya and Chiyeka, the young ZIPRA cadre lay quietly in death, his throat slit open, a pool of blood soaking into the soft soil …

---

72 Beard

12

Carpark, Lusaka International Airport

Keith Wilson, Cephas Ngwenya and Stanley Chiyeka were parked under one of the three large shade trees in the airport carpark. It had been a hot day so being able to sit under the tree had been a relief. They were parked on the extreme northern end of the carpark that was mostly empty.

Wilson had been shocked to see the state that Sarah was in when he had briefly visited her in the early morning. She had been crying, her eyes were puffy and swollen. The thought that Sarah was in danger was enough for Wilson; it was time to do something about it.

To pass the time they had watched the aircraft coming and going, practicing aircraft ID. Only one military aircraft, a Royal Air Force C-130, had landed. Wilson pointed it out to his two men, they had never seen one before.

An airport police patrol had stopped to talk to them. The police were happy with the story that they worked for Norman Barr and were waiting for a hunting party from Germany to land.

From time to time, Wilson lifted his binoculars to check the car they were watching, an old grey Peugeot 404. He checked his watch.

'Our man should be knocking off any minute,' said Wilson.

'We have everything ready,' replied Ngwenya sitting in the back of the open Land Rover with Chiyeka.

'Good.'

A Zambian Airways HS748 came into land, the noise of its engines tremendously loud as it went into reverse thrust.

A group of men in uniform came out of the airport building. They stopped to talk in the carpark; there was some laughter that carried to where the Selous Scouts were sitting.

Wilson turned on the engine.

One man walked towards the grey 404, unlocked it and got in.

'Game time,' called Wilson.

The 404 drove slowly across the carpark and out onto the airport road back towards Lusaka. Wilson followed at a discreet distance.

Keeping at a respectable slow speed, the 404 turned onto the Great East Road then a further 4km before turning right at the Chongwe roundabout. Wilson accelerated a little to get closer. It was knocking off time across the city so there was plenty of other traffic.

The car entered Mutendere Township. This was the target's short cut to his home in Chilenji South. He then turned east into Alick Nkhata Road on the southern boundary of Helen Kaunda Township.

Approaching a stop sign, Wilson pulled much closer, to within 25m of the grey 404. As the 404 slowed to a stop, Wilson pulled up next to the driver's side window.

'Are you Mr Kayumba?' called Ngwenya to the man.

With a surprised look on his face, the man turned his head.

'Yes.'

Less than a few feet away, Ngwenya tossed a 1kg slab of plastic, with a five second fuse attached, onto the back seat.

'See you in hell!' shouted Ngwenya in siNdebele, as Wilson gunned the Land Rover across the intersection, forcing pedestrians to jump out the way.

The bomb went off with an enormous deep THUD. The Peugeot exploded in a white hot flash, turning it into a million pieces of shrapnel spreading out at supersonic speed. Wilson could feel the heat of the explosion on his back as he raced away.

The rolling destruction killed people crowded at the intersection, turning over a nearby lorry. A bicycle sailed up through the air, spinning like a top. A street vendor with a vegetable stand next to the road disappeared in a thick cloud of smoke and dust, shredded vegetables sprayed into a fine mist.

The shell of the Peugeot was burning fiercely, melting the tar. The car had no doors, bonnet or boot. All were turned into spinning missiles. Mr Kayumba's body was vapourised, only his badly melted plastic nametag survived.

Wilson drove on slowly to the Intercontinental Hotel. He parked in the carpark and asked his two men to wait for him. He walked through the lobby and nodded to the barman as he passed. Knocking twice on the door to Sarah's room, he waited a few seconds and knocked twice again. He heard the latch being pulled back, and the door opened. Sarah stood back, the Tokarev pistol in her hand.

'Mr Kayumba has gone to meet his ancestors,' said Wilson softly.

'Thank God,' sighed Sarah, her face showing the signs of crying, her eyes still red and puffy. 'Thank you Wilson ... I need to get some sleep now, I had a tough night.'

'No problem. I understand.'

Sarah stepped forward.

'Hold me Wilson,' whispered Sarah putting her face into his chest. He could feel her shivering. Not sure what to do, he put his arms around her, hugging her tightly. Her arms lifted around his neck, pulling him tightly.

The feeling of being so close to her was overwhelming. Nothing in his life had ever felt so right … There was a tangible heat from her body, he could feel it against his chest.

'Its okay, you're safe now. I won't let anything happen to you,' breathed Wilson close to her ear. The faint smell of her shampoo filled his senses. A wave of absolute commitment, of responsibility, washed over him. A sensation ran through his body, almost a physical reaction, a consciousness that he was to protect this woman come what may.

She released him, tears running down her cheeks, 'Thank you Wilson,' she whispered. Her usual composure had deserted her. There was a tremor in her voice that Wilson had not heard before. The sensation to keep her safe, to comfort her, was the most powerful emotion he had ever felt.

They stood holding each other in the tight embrace. To Wilson it felt like an eternity, but really only a few seconds.

She released her grip, kissing him lightly on the lips. Standing back, she stretched out, brushing the hair from his forehead. Her touch was delicate as gentle rain.

'Get some rest Wilson,' she whispered.

The door closed with a soft click.

Wilson lingered for a moment, he leaned forward to rest his head against the closed door. His mind was a jumble of conflicting emotions … this mission was taking on monumental proportions that he was having difficulty coming to terms with.

> *The night is coming and the starling flew for days*
> *I'd stay home at night all the time*
> *I'd go anywhere, anywhere*
> *Ask me and I'm there because I care*
> *Sara, you're the poet in my heart*
> *Never change, never stop*
> *And now it's gone*
> *It doesn't matter what for*
> *When you build your house*
> *I'll come by*
> *Drowning in the sea of love*[73]

---

[73] *Sara*, Stevie Nicks, lyrics © Sony/ATV Music Publishing LLC. Fleetwood Mac album 'That's enough for me'.

*

Independence Avenue, Lusaka

We heard the sound of guns. We ran into houses to hide. Our friends were being shot. We heard others calling: 'Come and see your friends are dead.' We ran up and down; we saw people shout, some dying. The guns the soldiers used started from ground level and then rose to treetops. Chickens died, goats died, and trees lost their leaves. We ran up and down. Old people were crying. There was confusion. We kept saying, 'God, what has happened?'"

David M Gordon quoting Mercy Mfula an eyewitness to the massacre of Lumpa Church Members by UNIP Militia 1964[74].

Towards the western end of Independence Avenue, branching off Cairo Road at its southern roundabout, stands the Freedom Statue. The sculpture, of a man with arms raised clutching broken chains, symbolises the struggle for freedom from colonial rule and is dedicated to the victims of the struggle for independence. The statue, by British sculptor James Butler was erected in 1974 during celebrations of the 10th Anniversary of independence from Great Britain.

Ian Southwood and Jock McLean parked across the road under a tree. It had been dark for two hours and traffic was light.

Ian, born a Zambian, looked at the Freedom Statue as a sick joke. 'Freedom' in Zambia was illusionary. Lusaka Central Prison housed Christian missionaries arrested for bringing Bibles into the country. Ian and Patricia had been part of a local support group of Christians trying to get them released. Ian had only been able to visit the people in prison once and the stories were horrific. They had been beaten with rifle butts, prodded with bayonets, stripped of their clothes and incarcerated in cells covered in human filth. Blindfolded, barefoot and in chains, they sang Gospel hymns as they were paraded through the streets of Lusaka. They were finally confined with a thousand other prisoners, most of whom had never been brought to trial. Some had been in there for as long as 8 years without a trial or legal hearing.

The conditions in the Zambian socialist 'rehabilitation centre' were

---

74 *Rebellion or Massacre?* David M Gordon, quoting a personal account of the massacre of the Lumpa adherents by the United National Independence Party (UNIP) militia is perhaps the darkest chapter in the story of the regime of Kenneth Kaunda. Kaunda demonstrated a pathological hatred against The Lumpa Church of Alice Lenshina. Her church had steadfastly refused to accept the Kaunda regime. Lenshina was captured and jailed without trial until her death in custody in 1978.

unbelievably degrading; no running water, no toilets, no bathing facilities or showers. The entire prison was one big, stinking, disease ridden pit. The missionaries were sharing their cells with the leaders of Kaunda's political opposition, Godfrey Miyanda and Frederick Chiluba.

Ian shook his head in disgust.

Jock had prepared a length of Cordtex[75] detonating cord attached to an electrical blasting cap.

The Freedom Statue stands off Independence Avenue, under a large tree in the grounds of the National Museum. The museum grounds and the statue itself were in darkness all the bulbs in the security lights had gone.

Ian started the Fiat and drove down the road, executed a U-turn, then turned off the main road into the deserted museum carpark. He parked within a few metres of the double-life size statue on top of an 8ft concrete plinth. With Ian's help Jock climbed up onto the plinth and wrapped the Cordtex around the right arm a half dozen times. He then dropped back to the ground and ran the electrical cable back to the car where he connected the electrical initiator.

Ian started the car, Jock twisted the initiator and the statue's right arm was neatly amputated at the elbow.

Both men could not help laughing hysterically at the disfigured statue, now more representative of the state of Zambia ... broken.

Adamson Mushala was about to be blamed for another piece of wonton destruction.

*

Zimbabwe House, Lukoma Road, Lusaka

It was common for the ZIPRA leadership team to meet at the ZAPU HQ called Zimbabwe House in the evening. Present at the meeting was General Lookout Masuku, ZIPRA Commissar Dumiso Dabengwa and ZIPRA Brigade Commissar, Elijah Bandama. The meeting had been called to discuss the relationship with their allies, the Soviets and Cubans, and targeting for the forces infiltrating Rhodesia. The ZAPU leader Joshua Nkomo could not attend as he had been summoned yet again to a meeting with the Zambian President.

---

[75] Cordtex is a type of detonating cord generally used in mining. It uses an explosive core of pentaerythritol tetranitrate (PETN) which is inside its plastic coating. It is commonly the thickness of electrical extension cord and 'burns' at 2 km per second.

The Zambians had whipped themselves into a frenzy of blame and recriminations as the relentless attacks on military and civilian targets escalated. Kenneth Kaunda was beside himself, as control of his country seemed to be slipping from his grasp. There was a sense of panic in the ruling elite, fingers were being pointed at him and he was powerless to respond. Joshua Nkomo was summonsed at all hours of the day and night to discuss the latest attacks, taking every opportunity to lay the blame at the door of Robert Mugabe's ZANU, Adamson Mushala, or the Rhodesians in that order. Evidence found by the Zambian police pointed squarely at Mugabe and his Chinese backers.

Kaunda was desperate … he needed the war with the Rhodesians to stop. While he disliked Ian Smith intensely, he needed a result out of the latest set of meetings. Intense pressure was being brought to bear on Nkomo to settle with Smith by Kaunda, the British Government, the USA and the Commonwealth governments (outside of the Mugabe backers; Nigeria, Tanzania, Australia and Canada).

The political machinations continued in the background while the soldiers prosecuting the war progressed as best they could.

Zimbabwe House was hardly an impressive building. It was little more than a dilapidated old colonial style 1920s house. The building was on the corner of Conakry Road and Lukoma Road. Behind the complex was a disused sanitary lane that led to the Great North Road. An 8ft brick wall surrounded the whole property except for an unfinished section on the southern boundary.

The old house had a corrugated iron roof and was desperately in need of repairs and a coat of paint. Many of the glass windows were broken, cracked or missing. Drying clothing and makeshift curtains made from hessian hung in front of the windows. There were a few prefab outbuildings that housed staff personnel. Two Soviet GAZ trucks were parked in the dusty unkempt yard, plus an assortment of civilian vehicles in various stages of disrepair. A few sat on blocks with their wheels removed. Two Land Rovers were parked at the front door. The compound was not heavily defended, with five cadres dressed in civilian clothes lounging on the veranda.

The room used for meetings was the original dining room that looked much worse for wear. A faded picture of *Umdala Wethu,* Joshua Nkomo, hung on the wall. The 'boardroom' table was really two trestle tables made out of interior doors removed from their hinges and pushed together. Each of the senior ZIPRA men had lever-arched files in front of them.

'We should begin, Comrades,' said Dumiso Dabengwa, the self-appointed chairman of meetings pertaining to strategy. His boss Lookout Masuku was a quieter man, new to the job, not given to asserting himself.

Taking their seats, it was clear that the three military men were comfortable in each other's company. There was a friendly, cooperative atmosphere free of pompous posturing that was often the case when ZAPU 'politicians' were present. They were all from the Matabele tribe, compounding their strong bond of friendship and respect.

'We should begin with the missiles. Comrade Bandama, what have you achieved?' asked Dabengwa.

'Thank you Comrade Dabengwa. We now have three teams trained on the new SAM-7 missiles. The Cubans have done a good job, and the men are ready … it is a pity the Zambians were used for target practice,' smiled Bandama. The news of the accidental shooting of the J6 had filtered through to the leadership.

The men laughed, they had small regard for the Zambian military that they saw as useless amateurs. There was no concern about the J6 accident whatsoever … *there was a war on, these things happen.*

'What are we going to do with these missiles?' asked Masuku, the $64,000 question.

There was silence around the table … they had been given a game-changing weapon that could wreak havoc amongst the enemy, removing air superiority.

'That depends on our strategy,' replied Dabengwa. 'If we want to destroy morale amongst the Settlers, then we should shoot down civilian airliners. If we want to reach agreement with the Smith Regime then we should either do nothing or focus on military aircraft.'

'If we do nothing we will be seen as weak by our Soviet and Cuban allies, and that pig Mugabe,' said Masuku, his distaste clear on his sneering face. 'We are coming under pressure from the KGB, Comrade Solodovnikov and Comrade Colonel Lev Kononov, to be more aggressive. They tell me we are losing the initiative while Mugabe is pushing thousands of fighters into Zimbabwe from Mozambique.'

'I agree, they want us to escalate our activities, they want a grand attack from us across the Zambezi, Operation Zero Hour,' nodded Dabengwa. 'But what about these missiles?'

'*Umdala Wethu* is talking to Smith, we know this. I have no taste for killing civilians unless it is unavoidable in extreme circumstances,' said Masuku emphatically. 'How can we rule Zimbabwe if we have committed atrocities? Our people have made mistakes, and they will be punished when the time comes ... but our policy can only be the freedom of our country and our people by military means. I did not agree with my predecessor Comrade Mangena who sanctioned the attacks on the Boer airliners[76] at Victoria Falls. If we had succeeded, the Boer would be camped in Lusaka now, in the same way that he was in Luanda in 1975. The Boer has immense power and will use it if he is provoked. That is a battle for others.'

The other two men nodded their agreement.

'*Umdala Wethu* would agree with me, we must only shoot down military aircraft!' ordered Masuku, looking closely at his comrades. 'The men trained on these missiles must be sent to Zimbabwe, but their orders must be clear. No attacks on civilians! Is that clear Comrades?'

'Yes General' said Dabengwa and Bandama in unison.

'Now let us turn to Operation Zero Hour ... Comrade Bandama, tell me of our latest tally of troops and equipment ...'

The meeting continued for another two hours as the three senior ZIPRA soldiers discussed the build up and training of their forces.

*

Selous Scout HQ, Andre Rabie Barracks, Inkomo Barracks, 40km northwest of Salisbury

Military Intelligence was a misnomer in the Rhodesian Army for, apart from the good work of a few dedicated territorial officers at Joint Operational Centre levels, they rarely produced anything of value for war planners to work on.
Lt. Col. Ron Reid-Daly, OC Selous Scouts[77]

The Boss, Colonel Ron Reid-Daly sat in his small operations room with his head of intelligence Major Rob Warner. This room was off the main Operations Room accessed through a hidden door at the back. This smaller room accommodated all the maps and details of external operations. Very few personnel had access to this room that Reid-Daly used as a second office.

In front of them were the latest set of situation reports sent through by Keith Wilson and his team in Lusaka. A map of Lusaka and a set of aerial photographs were open on the table, marked up with the various places that Wilson and his team had investigated. A detailed

---

76 Black nationalists throughout Africa referred to the Apartheid regime in South Africa colloquially as the 'Boer', Afrikaans for farmer. The terms so used was intended to be derogatory. Masuku is referring to South African Airways.
77 *Pamwe Chete – The Legend of the Selous Scouts*, Ron Reid-Daly at 365.

reconnaissance report described the so-called 'Freedom Camp' north of Lusaka. This was all news to the Selous Scouts as it would have been to COMOPS. The existence of at least three other training camps around Lusaka was also reported but Wilson had not yet pinpointed their location.

The report on the attack Wilson had witnessed on the Cuban Embassy was startling and concerning. So too, was the report on the number and level of training on the Soviet SAM-7 Strela missiles. The news reports coming out of Britain of the dispatch of missiles, had been confirmed by Wilson in a report of a Rapier site within a few kilometres of Freedom Camp. There were bound to be others ... they needed to be identified urgently or Rhodesian aircraft were going to start falling out of the sky over Zambia.

'We are going to have to take this Cuban Embassy report to the CIO Sir. It was bound to be their people,' said Rob Warner.

'Yes, but I hate talking to the bastards. They can't be trusted. Still, we need to get to the bottom of it, we can't have Wilson and his team taken out by our own people! I will have a little heart-to-heart with John Sutcliffe,' replied Reid-Daly.

'Wilson's doing an amazing job, who would have thought a country boy from Matabeleland could turn into a super-spy,' laughed Warner.

'Just goes to show what I have always said, let the people who know what they are doing get on with the job! Fortune favours the brave! The useless bastards at COMOPS need to get out of the way,' spat Reid-Daly, venting his frustration at the desk-jockeys at COMOPS.

'Good news that Wilson has identified a Cuban for his snatch ... are you going to give him the green light to execute?' asked Warner.

'Yes ... send confirmation immediately ... snatch the Cuban,' replied Reid-Daly, never one to delay an obvious action. He laughed, 'I am looking forward to dropping off our Cuban at CIO HQ ... their faces will be something!'

Reid-Daly finished his briefing with his intelligence officer and returned to his office.

'Sue, please get John Sutcliffe of the CIO on the phone,' said Reid-Daly to his secretary Sue Croukamp.

It was only a few moments before the phone buzzed on his desk.

'Is that you John?' said Reid-Daly dispensing with pleasantries.

'Yes Colonel, what can I do for you?' asked Sutcliffe, he had very few dealings with Reid-Daly. He disliked the man intensely as a stuck up Sergeant-Major promoted beyond his competence. His mind was racing, as he knew Military Countre-Intelligence were tapping the

Colonel's phone. His department had supplied the equipment.

'I need to meet with you rather urgently, how does the Meikles Hotel sound, at 6:30?'

'Yes ... that would be fine,' replied Sutcliffe, not wishing to get into conversation on the phone.

'Good, your round, your budget's bigger than mine!'

This important meeting was fated to never take place ...

*

Lake Kariba inlet, 3.5km east of Sanyati Gorge

A Zambian Police patrol boat crossed Kariba Dam. The boat had departed Siavonga at last light carrying six ZIPRA freedom fighters. They had covered the 32km (bearing 162°) in a little over 3 hours, stopping at predetermined intervals to ensure that they had not been seen by any roving Rhodesian boat patrols. The lake was dead flat without a hint of breeze.

Entering the bay just east of the deep Sanyati Gorge, the driver had the V8 inboard engine barely ticking over. As they closed on the bank, the distinctive scrape of submerged trees on the aluminium hull sounded like the beating of drums in the deathly quiet.

It was impossible to see the bank in the pitch darkness; just the gentle lapping of the boats wake hitting the shore. The boat had a shallow draft but the men would still have to wade the last few metres to the bank. They were in a narrow gap between the Matusadona National Park and the Charara Controlled Hunting Area. This meant that the terrorists could bump into anything from a Hippo to a pride of lions, not to mention the giant Nile crocodiles that flourished in the lake.

As the driver felt the nose of the boat touch ground, he cut the engine. Cuban Captains Juan Fernández Ruz and Eduardo García Vigoa whispered a few final instructions to their young trainees. Then, with hushed encouragement, the ZIPRA cadres slipped over the side and waded ashore. They went slowly and carefully so as not to make any noise. Each carried his AK47 with a RPG rocket projectile on his back. The man in the lead carried the Strela2M (SAM-7) launcher cradled in his arms.

As the leader of the band reached solid ground he checked his luminous watch. They had ten hours to cover the 28km hike to their target area in the Whamira Hills on the Zambezi escarpment.

Theirs was to be the most important mission of the war – this had been explained to them by Brigade Commissar, Elijah Bandama and his Cuban advisors.

13

Section of Rhodesian Hawker Hunter fighter-bombers in support of External raid over Maamba Zambia

Dolphin 1:	Red Leader, Dolphin One … do you copy.
Red Section:	Dolphin One, Red Leader, Go.
Dolphin 1:	You are being tracked by Low Blow[78] radar, bearing two-zero-one, range six thousand. Unidentified radar, bearing one-six-eight, range seven thousand.
Red Section:	Fuck … (a hissing sound of static) Roger copied … we will maintain route to target …

Red Section was flying air support for an external attack on a terrorist base near the mining village of Maamba in Zambia. The Hawker Hunters had been lit up by a 'low blow' radar used to control Soviet SAM-3[79] surface to air missiles. There was another radar signal they could not identify. The Hunter pilot was talking to an air controller aboard Dolphin 1, a Rhodesian Air Force DC-3 'Warthog'. The old DC-3 was loaded with radio and radar monitoring equipment that was flying a racetrack pattern along the Zambezi border.

Dolphin 1:	Red Leader, Dolphin one … is advised two Zambian Farmers[80] are airborne from Mumbwa.
Red Section:	Copied … any other happy news?
Dolphin 1:	We will scramble Yellow Section to intercept.
Red Section:	Copied … target in two minutes.

Rhodesian radar could pick up the launch of the two Zambian Chinese built J-6 fighters from the Mumbwa air base 100km to the west of Lusaka, 275km north of the Rhodesian target in Zambia. The

---

78   SNR-125 'Low Blow' 250 kW I/D-band tracking, fire control and guidance radar (range 40km).
79   The Isayev S-125 *Neva/Pechora* (Soviet: C-125, NATO reporting name, SA-3 *Goa*), speed Mach 3 – 3.5, radio command guidance, range 35km, intercept between 100m and 18km.
80   Chinese Shenyang J-6, Chinese copy of the Soviet MIG19PM, single seat supersonic jet fighter. The J-6 has a maximum speed at altitude of 1,540 km/h, Mach 1.45. Service ceiling 17,900m (58,700 ft). Combat radius with two drop tanks about 640km. Powerplant is two Liming Wopen-6A (Tumansky R-9) turbojet engines.

Hunters were a good 270knots slower than the J-6 that had a faster rate of climb, a higher service ceiling, and, probably, more agile. They were a major threat, but that had not yet been tested. Dolphin 1 was scrambling two Hawker Hunters from Flyde air base near Hartley, carrying South African V3Bs, copies of the US AIM-9 Sidewinder J air-to-air heat-seeking missiles, to ward off the Zambians if they attacked. The V3Bs evened up the score … a little.

They would find out in a little over 20 minutes.

Standing on the canvas covered dispersal point at Flyde were the two Hawker Hunters of Yellow Section. Sitting on camp chairs next to the aircraft were Flight Lieutenant Mike Lamb and Air Lieutenant Nigel Nelson. In addition to the V3Bs, each Hunter had four 30mm Aden cannons and a pair of 1,200 litre drop tanks. There had been numerous call-outs during the morning proving to be nothing at all, so when the hot line started ringing there was very little reaction. This time the call wasn't to go on cockpit standby as before, but rather to scramble immediately.

The letter home Mike Lamb was writing went flying as he scrambled to get into the cockpit. In a matter of minutes the two jets were screaming down the runway thumping through the hot 40°C air rising off the glistening-mirage.

'Dolphin One, Yellow Leader. We are airborne, three-zero-nine, sixteen hundred feet, speed four hundred knots. Please advise,' called Mike Lamb the section leader.

The Hunter Section were flying northwest towards the Zambian border, planning to cross over Lake Kariba towards the target area 27km across the border. After take-off they remained at low level bumping through the hot turbulent air mass. It was their intention to remain at low level for as long as possible to avoid being detected by the Zambian radar.

'Yellow Leader, maintain your course and speed … standby,' replied the controller in the Warthog.

The Zambian J6s had turned to the south, travelling very low and very fast.

Yellow Section coming in from Flyde accelerated into Zambia over Lake Kariba still at low level.

'Yellow Leader … Dolphin One.'

'Yellow Leader Go.' Lamb was pressed tightly into his seat as his aircraft accelerated under 60% combat power. His voice was slightly strained as he sucked in short gulps of oxygen between the violent jolts on the airframe.

'Roger pitch up to flight level two-zero-zero.'

Lamb and Nelson pulled back on the stick and pushed the throttles forward calling for full power. They soared into the cloudless blue sky as avenging angels. Levelling off at 20,000ft, they listened to the mission controller sounding like a horse racing commentator, with all the instructions he was giving the pilots to intercept the target. The controller's excitement was clear in his voice; no Rhodesian pilots had successfully intercepted Zambian J6s.

'Yellow Leader, drop your tanks, come right to three-five-six.'

The instruction to drop tanks struck Lamb and Nelson like a thunderbolt. This command was a shock to the Rhodesians as they never threw their drop tanks away as there weren't any replacements. This was no training sortie. It was serious. The adrenaline was flowing. On the Air Controller's radar screen the aircraft became a 'merged plot'. This meant that they and the enemy were all in the same piece of sky. The Hunters still hadn't spotted their enemy.

A green/brown camouflaged J6 flashed 10,000ft below Yellow Section.

Lamb banked his Hunter into a tight left turn, followed by his wingman.

The second J6 appeared.

'Bogeys nine' o'clock low,' called Lamb as he buried the stick into his stomach pulling positive G in the turn. The J6's were doing Mach 1.2 (485knots), going like hell, the turn was so wide Lamb almost lost sight of them.

At this point Lamb's mind went blank. For nearly ten years he had trained for this one moment, intercepting an enemy aircraft. He scanned the sky ahead of his Hunter trying to spot the J6's as they sped away. A wave of frustration flowed over him as he cursed a missed opportunity. He felt no fear from being in a vastly outclassed obsolete aircraft.

Blinking through the sweat pouring into his eyes, Lamb saw a J6 coming head on towards him from his one o'clock position. Still turning towards him Lamb flicked the trigger safety over to the cannon position.

The J6 was going to fly through his gunsights ... *squeeze off a few rounds!* The excitement exploded in his brain ...

A bright flash lit up underneath the wing of the J6.

An incredibly fast telephone pole came hurtling towards Lamb, trailing a solid white smoke trail. The PL-5[81] missile was

---

81   PL-2/PL-5 (Chinese versions of Soviet K-13 (NATO AA-2 'Atoll') air-to-air missiles.

corkscrewing violently, a swirling circular smoke trail stringing out behind it.

In his training he was taught to break towards the missile. This could or should create a tracking problem for the missile and cause it to overshoot … possibly.

Faced with reality Lamb found it took a lot of willpower to turn towards something he knew was trying to kill him. Still, he kept breaking towards the incoming missile … his heart was pounding, his hands slick inside his flying gloves.

The PL-5 flashed over his right wing, a thudding shock wave struck the airframe as it disappeared behind him.

He thought it had missed completely until he heard a dull thud and felt a light bump on the aircraft. Immediately scanning all the gauges he could not see any indication of damage. Looking up from the instrument panel, the second J6 flew over his canopy. His twisted his neck violently, flicking into a tight turn, pumping right rudder, pulling the stick back into his gut … G coming on … the J6 disappeared ahead of him.

Jesus those things are fast …

'Yellow Two, I may have been hit,' called Lamb.

'I can't see smoke or damage,' replied Nelson, 4km behind the flight leader. 'The bogeys have gapped it to the north.'

Lamb rolled the aircraft onto its back and headed for the ground. The whole fight had lasted no more than 60 seconds from the time the Hunters pitched up to 20,000ft until they turned for home.

It was then that Lamb got a fright. He had not retarded the throttle, now rushing at the ground in a vertical dive. When he pulled the stick into his stomach to recover from the dive all that happened was the aircraft changed attitude but not direction. The momentum was so great the aircraft carried on descending.

'Yellow Two, I have a problem … the aircraft is not responding.'

Nelson could see his leader screaming toward the blue waters of Lake Kariba.

'Eject … Eject,' called Nelson seeing the danger.

Eject … flashed into Lamb's brain … it was unthinkable the country had so few aircraft with no hope of replacements … he had to recover …

Lamb fought the heavy jet, thumping left and right rudder as if to unjam the controls.

Eject …

Just when Lamb thought that this was the end, the aircraft bottomed out just above the water. He had to make a decision whether to fly towards Kariba or Victoria Falls towards the west. Kariba was fractionally closer, 150km … 16 minutes at 300knots.

Nelson made the decision for him … 'Yellow Leader … Kariba, do you copy?'

'Kariba copied.' Lamb banked towards the northeast.

A radar warning audio buzzed in his helmet, from his 6 o'clock, from behind. Enemy radar was tracking him. Was it the Zambian SAM-3 anti-aircraft batteries or was it the J6?

'Yellow Two, is someone behind me?' called Lamb craning his neck.

Nelson scanned the sky but could not see anything. He was flying 2km behind and slightly above.

'I can't see anything behind you, get as low as you can, increase speed,' called Nelson scanning the sky.

Lamb was so low he was raising a cloud of water spay behind him. The radio alt read 50' and the speed approximate 400knots. At this stage Lamb was beginning to think that he'd over-reacted and that he might not have been hit.

Had I got out of the fight too early?

The aircraft was performing as if there was nothing wrong with it. No vibrations and no handling difficulties.

Oh well, tomorrow I'll be back.

Five minutes later, less than halfway to Kariba, the first warning light flashed on.

EP pump failure![82]

Instinct took over, his first reaction was to call his wingman and tell him he had a failure.

'Yellow Two, I have an EP pump warning.'

Nelson pulled out his emergency checklist, and started reading the failure procedures for Lamb.

All the necessary switches had been set.

While Nelson was reading the EP pump failure, Lamb got the second failure, *right hand fuel pump failure.* This is not too serious under normal operating conditions as the engine can gravity feed. While Nelson was reading the fuel pump failure procedure and Lamb was confirming that they were done, another light on the warning panel appeared.

Hydraulic system failure.

---

82 Engine driven hydraulic pump failure.

With a sudden violent vibration, the controls became sluggish and heavy ... *only 600ft above the water* ...

'Jesus Christ what's that?' screamed Lamb as another jet passed less than 200ft above his canopy ...

*

Captain Alberto Ley Rivas, the commander of the Cuban 15 Squadron DAAFAR, pushed the throttle forward on his MIG-21. His mission required split second timing. He had not expected to see two Rhodesian Hawker Hunters at low level over Kariba. His MIG was flying at just over 600knots sweeping over the Hunters as if they were going backwards ... luckily for them, they were not part of his mission. Beneath his wings were two Soviet Atoll AA-2C infrared heat-seeking missiles.

Rivas scanned his cockpit instruments and checked his mission profile strapped to his left leg. He clicked the transmit button on his radio.

'Jaguar, Hawk Two, do you copy?' he said in Spanish.

'Hawk Two, you are fives,' replied a clear voice, so clear that the man could have been sitting in the cockpit.

'I am three minutes from the target.'

'Standby ... target is not in play ... standby.'

Rivas cursed below his breath and retarded the throttles to slow his speed ... *what is going on ... the target is late?*

*

Comrade Lieutenant-Colonel Julio Ángel Casas stood on a high promontory near the village of Siavonga on the Zambian side of Lake Kariba, approximately 20km due east of Kariba Airport. Behind him was a quad-mounted missile battery called the Rapier system. The alert alarm on the 'Blindfire' flat-faced radar was silent.

Casas glanced at his watch, 5:00pm exactly, near the end of another beautiful hot clear day in Africa. It was perfectly still, not a hint of breeze. The silence was broken only by the hushed conversation of the Cuban crew on the Rapier system. They had learned to use the system very quickly, helped by the Zambian owners.

Twisting his head, Casas thought he heard the sound he was waiting for. Straining his senses he shook his head ... *mind playing tricks*. Before the sound he was waiting for could carry to him, the missile alert system buzzed loudly.

'Contact' called the Cuban NCO on the launch controls. 'Bearing eight-six degrees, 15km.'

Casas lifted the handpiece on the HF radio.

'Hawk Two, Jaguar, target is in play, I say again, target is in play.'

A distant voice responded immediately, 'Copied, target is in play.' The radio went dead.

The sound of turbine engines at full power carried on the faint easterly breeze.

'Bearing nine-six degrees, range is ten kilometres, Comrade Colonel,' called the NCO.

Casas lifted his powerful binoculars and could see an aircraft in the distance climbing in a banking left hand turn.

'Fire!' shouted Casas.

The Rapier missile shook on its rail for a split second before ejecting in a blinding flash. The radar directed the missile to the target at a speed in excess of Mach 2.5.

There was a bright flash as the Rapier self-destructed at the limit of its range, well short of its target.

The first part of the hoax had been set!

*

Captain Alberto Ley Rivas thrust the throttles through the gate and engaged afterburners accelerating the MIG-21 back to 650knots. The nitrogen cooled, heat-seeking AA-2C missile heads sniffed the air for a distant heat signature. There was no sound in his headset, the missile was not picking up a target.

The target continued its banking left hand turn towards the south, slowly increasing speed and height.

Rivas knew, within a 6km radius where the target should appear. He adjusted his heading to the south.

The missile gave a soft growl in his headset.

The growl grew louder.

Rivas caressed the firing trigger. He knew he needed to be behind his target for the missile to be certain to track.

Rivas' target appeared in the fading afternoon light, the sun glinted off the silver fuselage.

The insistent growl in his helmet was demanding a shot.

He pulled the trigger, immediately banking hard right, diving away towards the cool blue water of the lake.

Behind the departing MIG, the large four-engined aircraft crossed over the shoreline of the lake, 7,000ft above the bone-dry bush below.

There was a great orange flash as the proximity fuse ignited the missile's explosive head below the number three engine. Shrapnel travelling at supersonic speed entered the wing, engine and fuselage. The starboard wing dropped and the aircraft veered to the right. All electrical and mechanical control to the engines had been severed. Fire spread across the wing as the aircraft momentarily stopped the uncontrolled turn, plunging towards the ground.

Miraculously the pilot managed to pull the aircraft out of the dive. Levelling out, he managed to get the aircraft under control but still descending at incredible speed. As he watched, the altimeter unwound, he looked left and right at the rugged terrain below, looking for a place to put down. All that could be seen was the rugged broken country on the edge of the escarpment. The aircraft flew on, keeping on the same track towards Salisbury ... now impossible.

Both pilots searching the ground below.

There was a calmness in the cockpit despite the deadly peril.

The pilot called the crew to prepare for a crash landing. Responding with incredible grace, the cabin crew called for the passengers to assume the brace position. Nobody panicked, a few burst into tears. Those on the starboard side watched in horror as the wing burned in front of the windows.

Aiming at a clearing, the pilot tried to drop the flaps, only the port side responded. The aircraft struck the highest trees, snapping through them easily. It was wings level when it struck the ground. The starboard wing hit a giant Msasa tree with tremendous force, tearing it from the fuselage. The nose pitched up as the enormous force bounced it back into the air, the impact causing the tail to shear off. The aircraft slid on, tearing up trees, throwing up a thick cloud of fine dust, striking a 2m deep ditch, ploughing into the far bank, then disintegrating, spinning debris flying in all directions.

The full fuel tanks exploded, engulfing the main section of the fuselage in a deadly fireball. The flames blew out in a firestorm igniting the surrounding bush, throwing choking smoke high into the still afternoon air.

Passengers and crew, still strapped to their seats, lay sprawled in the wake of the wreckage as the fire spread towards them ...

With their deaths, died the future for the tiny landlocked country in the middle of Southern Africa, nothing could ever be the same ... all its people victims of the worst possible depravity ... the hoax had been sprung!

*

On the high hills of the escarpment over looking the banks of Kariba, only 17km from the crash site, a small group of ZIPRA freedom fighters watched in awe as the smoke from the fires caused by the air crash lifted into the sky. The aircraft had passed directly over their position but was already on fire before they could launch their SAM-7 missile. They had been well briefed and trained to attack the aircraft that travelled on a fixed schedule, (5:05pm) like clockwork, not altering its flight path by more than a few hundred metres.

There was some consternation that the aircraft had been shot before they could make their own attack. The men muttered their frustration, debating what must have happened.

To their north, way in the distance, they could see two Rhodesian Hawker Hunters preparing to land at Kariba airport.

The ZIPRA leader led his men down the hill travelling towards the west, away from the crash site. He knew he only had one night to get away before the Rhodesians came looking.

*

Rhodesian Combined Operations HQ, Milton Buildings, Jameson Avenue, Salisbury

There were no volcanic-like eruptions emanating from the Milton Buildings powerhouse ... Everything just bumbled on, more or less as it always had ... no one made any brilliant and far-reaching strategic decisions ... and no one at all was sacked for their unsatisfactory part in the day-to-day running of the war ... and no bright lads were plucked up from below, hurriedly laden with rank and given carte blanche to get on with it ...

Lt. Col. Ron Reid-Daly, OC Selous Scouts[83]

The briefing room at COMOPS HQ in Salisbury sat in stunned silence. The only sound was the ceiling fan that spun at half power, making a faint grinding sound like a dog with a bone. Nobody dared speak.

Outside in the passage the sound of shoes on the highly polished parquet flooring carried through the open door.

A door slammed.

Telephones rang in the neighbouring room, the urgency of the ring

---

[83] *Selous Scouts Top Secret War*, Lt.Col. Ron Reid Daly, Galago (1982) at 274

sent a shiver down the spine … *more bad news.*

Fast paced footsteps approached the door and an air force Group Captain entered the room.

'As you were,' he called waving his hand as the men braced up. He carried a small manila folder in his hand and a roll of maps. Moving to the head of the table he sat down, removing his cap to place it in front of him.

Still nobody spoke.

Opening the folder, Group Captain Norman Walsh, the 2IC of COMOPS, began to read.

'An Air Rhodesia Viscount, VP-WAS, flight RH 825 has crashed after take-off from Kariba Airport. This took place at approximately 5:20pm last evening. The total number of passengers and crew on board numbered fifty eight, eighteen survived the crash including two air hostesses.'

Norman Walsh swallowed hard, taking a brief moment to look into the expectant faces of the other men in uniform in the room.

'It appears that ten of the survivors were subsequently shot … and bayoneted to death by terrorists, the other eight have been recovered to Andrew Fleming. All those deceased are burned beyond recognition, only the tail section of the aircraft remains in any way intact.'

'Jesus …' exclaimed one of the men softly.

Walsh cleared his throat.

'Gentlemen, it is unclear at this time what caused the accident, these are old aircraft even though expertly maintained. Clearly there was some sort of catastrophic failure, but the pilot managed to get it down in a field with directional control, and reduced speed. The aircraft may have made it if not for a deep donga in its path that caused it to cartwheel and disintegrate.'

'What are we going to do?' asked Major Rob Warner of the Selous Scouts.

'We need to get to the bottom of this quickly, in the meantime cool heads must prevail,' replied Walsh.

'Our people are sifting through the wreckage and recovering the bodies. Post mortems will be done on those that were shot,' said Chief Superintendent Jim Winston, BSAP Special Branch – Terrorist Desk.

'The wire services are reporting some interesting stories already,' added John Sutcliffe, Deputy Director Branch II CIO.

'We should put that out of our minds until we know for sure. Then we will act accordingly,' replied Walsh in his usual measured fashion. He then sat forward in his chair, placing his clasped hands on the desk in from of him. Speaking softly but with deep intent he added, '... but I will tell you this Gentlemen, if this aircraft has been shot down then we will rain hell down on these people in a manner hitherto unimaginable!'

*

Foreign and Commonwealth Office, King Charles Street, City of Westminster, London

The Foreign Office expressed its shock at the incident [the Viscount disaster] but said it had no independent evidence of what had happened or who was responsible. 'Yet again there has been a horrible and tragic incident in Rhodesia involving innocent civilians. We deplore the whole incident which, once more, underlines the need to bring this disastrous war to an end by negotiation and achieve independence and majority rule for Zimbabwe.'
Foreign Office Statement – September 1978

Lord Baron Goronwy-Roberts of Caernarfon, The Minister of State, Foreign and Commonwealth Office, Deputy Leader of the House of Lords, was feeling all of his 65 years. This Rhodesia business would not go away. It was two days since the news of the Viscount disaster. It irked him beyond measure.

Why won't this fool Smith chuck in the towel ... can't he see its all over!

Goronwy-Roberts had been called to the office of the Foreign Minister Dr David Owen to discuss the Rhodesian situation ... *for the hundredth time. Bloody nuisance!*

There was a knock on the door and, without waiting for an invitation, Sir Charles Prior, Permanent Under-secretary of State walked in.

'Yes?' asked Goronwy-Roberts distractedly.

'Worrying news, I am afraid, Minister,' replied Sir Charles in his flippant way, as if he took joy in providing the means to upset his boss.

Goronwy-Roberts did not reply, merely gesturing tiredly to a chair in front of his enormous desk.

'It seems Minister,' began Sir Charles earnestly, his eyes fixed on those of Goronwy-Roberts, '... that the Air Rhodesia Viscount may have been shot down by one of our Rapier missiles.'

'What!' shouted the Minister leaping to his feet. His hands were visibly shaking but not from the bottle of *Glenfiddich* in his desk drawer.

'A missile battery has been found abandoned on the shores of Lake Kariba, close to the flight path for aircraft departing Kariba Airport,' said Sir Charles mildly, always amused by his ability to engender panic in his minister at the drop of a hat.

'You have got to be joking!' spluttered Goronwy-Roberts. His face was as pale as the blotting paper on his desk pad.

'I am afraid not Minister. It appears that the battery mysteriously removed itself from its site to the east of the Lusaka International Airport, and reappeared on the sunny shores of Lake Kariba, minus one missile from the bank of four. It was discovered by a group of visiting German big-game hunters and reported to the Zambian police. The Germans took a few photos and have given them to *Stern* magazine.'

Sir Charles was making every effort not to be seen to be enjoying himself. He never ceased to be amazed by the politician's inability to appreciate the unintended consequences of his actions. Their ignorance was staggering, matched only by their bravado.

'Can we put a lid on this?' asked Goronwy-Roberts quietly, his face now changed to a florid red colour, the lines on his face deeply creased, his lips quivering.

'I am afraid not Minister. There are reports in the Sarasota Herald-Tribune, the New York Times and the Washington Post that the aircraft was brought down by one of our Rapier missiles, they quote eye witnesses,' said Sir Charles. He placed a set of telegrams on the Minister's desk from the British Embassy in Washington.

'My God, we are done for!' groaned Goronwy-Roberts, collapsing back into his chair, his face now in his hands. 'What are we going to do?'

'There's more, Minister. The newspapers quote intelligence sources in the UK and Rhodesia confirming that the aircraft was brought down by Zambian troops using our Rapier missile.'

'We must deny everything! Deny! Deny! What proof do they have? A missing missile is not enough!' cried Goronwy-Roberts. 'We need somebody to blame.'

'The Rhodesian Government have been remarkably controlled, but I would imagine that if this news is true, they will scream blue murder. One wonders how they will retaliate, as retaliate they will,' added Sir Charles, now quite enjoying himself as he heaped more pressure onto his Minister.

'I will have to resign, so will the Foreign Minister ... the Prime Minister will demand it.'

There was a pregnant pause as Sir Charles studied his minister intently, taking pleasure in his discomfort ... *so well deserved ... sending* missiles to Zambia ... two civilian aircraft shot down ... what an infernal joke!

Goronwy-Roberts stood up from his desk, turned towards the window and stood looking out of it. His shoulders hunched over dejectedly ... like a condemned man soon for the gallows.

Sir Charles sat and watched as the politician twisted in the wind.

'Maybe all is not lost as yet Minister,' whispered Sir Charles, ready now to throw the lifeline to a man close to drowning.

The Minister turned. 'Yes, what is it, what do you have?' squeaked Goronwy-Roberts looking down at Sir Charles, his eyes pleading for salvation.

'We can get the ZIPRA guerrillas to take the blame. It is known that they have been trained and supplied with Soviet shoulder launched anti-aircraft missiles.' The lifeline was now in the air, descending towards the desperate drowning man.

'Yes, Yes!'

'What self-respecting terrorist, or should I say Freedom Fighter, would not take this opportunity to claim a masterful blow against a racist, oppressive regime that kills its own people indiscriminately at home and in neighbouring countries?' asked Sir Charles rhetorically.

'Yes indeed!'

'Comrade Joshua Nkomo is the obvious choice, his forces are based in Zambia, they are trained by Soviets, Cubans and East Germans, they have the weapons, and they have the means to deliver them!'

'You are a bloody genius Sir Charles! That's it. Blame it on the terr ... Freedom Fighters. How will we get them to admit it? We need a confession!' demanded Goronwy-Roberts now animated, pacing left and right. Victory and deliverance were again at hand, a close run thing.

'Leave it to me Minister, leave it to me,' replied Sir Charles, smiling broadly, marvelling at the rank gullibility of a man with such an obvious lack of intelligence - a political animal, led easily to and from the slaughter.

> *The shooting down of the civil airliner and the massacre of survivors has just occurred. Did the Prime Minister protest to President Kaunda about the ghastly barbarities which are mounted from camps in his country?*
> *Did the Prime Minister take the opportunity of protesting to President Kaunda about what Lord Goronwy-Roberts in another place has referred to as the sickening technique of abduction, which has put 100,000 Rhodesian children in terrorist camps in Zambia?*

Sir Ronald Bell, House of Commons member for Beaconsfield, questioning the Prime Minister James Callaghan. The Prime Minister's answer was simply 'No'.

*

BBC Interview with Joshua Nkomo

'We brought that aircraft down, but it is not true that we killed any survivors.' Mr Nkomo said. 'The Rhodesians have been ferrying military personnel and equipment in Viscounts and we had no reason to believe that this was anything different. The Rhodesians should know this is a military zone.'
Joshua Nkomo BBC Interview in Lusaka

'Why is shooting down an Air Rhodesia plane not terrorism?' asked the BBC interviewer.

'You British are confused, what is this business of a terrorist? If we wanted to shoot down Rhodesian planes we could bring them down every day! The people who are terrorists are those people led by Ian Smith!' chortled Joshua Nkomo to the applause of the audience gathered to listen.

The short interview ended with spontaneous applause and Nkomo smiled and waved as he returned to his office at ZAPU Headquarters.

Dumiso Dabengwa followed his leader into the office and closed the door behind him.

'This is truly a disaster Comrade,' said Nkomo softly. 'Could this be our people?'

'*Umdala Wethu*, we have trained cadres in Rhodesia with the SAM-7. It is possible,' replied Dabengwa earnestly.

'How can we be sure?'

'We will not know for many weeks, we have no way of contacting our brothers in the country.'

'The Rhodesians are sure to come after me and all our leadership, Comrade.'

'The British have promised us protection if we accepted responsibility immediately,' said Dabengwa. 'I had a call from their Foreign Office in London.'

'I don't trust them, how can we trust any of these lying white men?'

'We have their aid money, that is something. They have promised you support against Mugabe when the time comes.'

'I still don't trust them! We are going to have to raise our security even greater, disguise our movements, never be in one place for any length of time ... this is now our burden. Smith will certainly break off our talks, the whites will want revenge ... I fear many innocent cadres will die because of this.'

All Dabengwa could do was nod his agreement. His mind was racing to assimilate all the possibilities. ZIPRA had drawn a line in the sand, they had thrown down the gauntlet, there would be no going back. They would now be forced to fight the Rhodesians to the death. The military invasion planned by the Soviets and Cubans was now their only alternative.

Peace talks were off the table!

*

Park Lane Hotel, Salisbury

Nigel Pennefather, the local MI6 representative in Rhodesia, disguised as an employee of BP, made his way through the lobby of the Park Lane Hotel. He was dressed in a cream coloured safari suit with shorts and long khaki socks, a green BP logo embroidered on the shirt pocket. He blended in perfectly with his long dark hair and thick sideburns. It was a hot day outside and his soft English complexion was flushed red. His trained eye scanned the people in the lobby and the nearby bar looking for his contact.

John Sutcliffe, Deputy Director Branch II CIO, waved from a booth in the corner of the bar.

Pennefather walked across the room with a smile as would any person seeing an old friend. Sutcliffe stood up and the two men shook hands. With a flick of his wrist Sutcliffe called across a hovering waiter, dressed neatly in a starched white uniform with a red fez.

'Gin and tonic please' asked Pennefather.

'Pilsner for me,' said Sutcliffe and the waiter departed.

There was no one else within earshot.

'What the fuck have you people done Nigel?' demanded Sutcliffe.

'I know it looks bad, but we well may have been responsible, or at least it was our missile shot by the Zambians. I have no idea how the missile battery got to Kariba. The RAF Regiment had them under their control. It is a terrible business.'

'That's an understatement. The government from the PM down is baying for blood, plenty of it. Heads are going to roll. Plans are being drawn as we speak,' said Sutcliffe, the look on his face showing that he meant business.

'Look, Nkomo has accepted responsibility. We need to agree that all enquiries lead to him and his ZIPRA cronies. We need to blame a Soviet Strela SAM-7 shot from the shoreline of Kariba,' replied Pennefather calmly. His short speech came across as well rehearsed, as if he was reading a communiqué.

'The PM and the cabinet like the idea of a Rapier, it fits everyone's opinion of you lying and deceitful Poms. That prick David Owen should rot in hell,' said Sutcliffe, raising his voice.

'Steady on old fruit, there is a bigger game in play. I have been authorised to offer you a deal,' said Pennefather leaning forward conspiratorially.

The conversation stopped as the waiter delivered the drinks. Pennefather took a deep slug of the gin and tonic before continuing.

'If you ensure that the investigation points to a Strela missile, we will help with your reprisals,' whispered Pennefather.

Sutcliffe could hardly believe his ears. He took a sip of beer, automatically making a scan of the room to ensure that no one else was close enough to hear.

'Carry on,' replied Sutcliffe guardedly. The British Government was a nest of the most deadly and unpredictable vipers on earth.

'We will ensure that all the Rapiers left in Zambia are disabled. In addition, we will provide detailed intelligence on the ZIPRA bases you want to hit in Zambia. We can arrange diversionary activity if needs be. We will release spare parts for your Hunters through your intermediaries, but not the Canberras. You may attack terrorist bases without comment from us. You may do as you please ... all except killing Joshua Nkomo,' listed Pennefather as if reading the news on the BBC.

'Nkomo is public enemy number one. The PM and COMOPS want him dead. The whole country wants him dead,' stated Sutcliffe forcefully.

'He may be an innocent bystander despite his boasting in the TV interview. He has no way of knowing for sure if his people brought down the Viscount, frankly neither do we.'

'I will have to push this up the line. Give me 24 hours,' replied Sutcliffe downing his beer and getting up to leave. He could hardly believe his ears. The Poms were clearly rattled.

*

Soviet Embassy, Ridgeway, Lusaka

Ambassador Comrade Professor Vassily Solodovnikov was overjoyed. He could hardly believe how perfectly the plan had been executed. All was falling into place. Comrade Colonel Lev Kononov, head of the Soviet advisory delegation to ZIPRA sat opposite the Ambassador, next to him was Comrade Lieutenant-Colonel Julio Ángel Casas, the chief Cuban advisor to ZIPRA.

'Well done Comrade Casas, I congratulate you on a brilliant mission,' said Solodovnikov in English, smiling broadly.

'Thank you Comrade Ambassador,' replied Casas solemnly, always wary around the Soviets.

'We have the British who think it was them, we have ZIPRA who think it was them, and we have the Zambians who think it was them … brilliant,' laughed Kononov.

'Who cares who it was, the fact is that Comrade Nkomo is now back in our court. He is caught between a rock and a hard place to use an English expression,' smiled Solodovnikov.

'My pilot assures me that it was his missile that made the strike. He said he saw the Rapier self-destruct well short of the target,' said Casas to ensure that credit was being given to the Cubans.

'Yes, Yes Colonel, we understand, full credit will go to the Cuban Revolutionary forces. I have already prepared my signal to go to your military high command in Havana,' lied Solodovnikov. He had no intention of drawing any attention to this magnificent act of deception.

'Now we can go with full confidence into our planning for the invasion of Rhodesia, Operation Zero Hour. Any thought of internal settlement is doomed to failure, and any hope of agreement between Smith and Nkomo is dead. Comrade Nkomo's military triumph will be our triumph, another pawn for the glorious Soviet Union and her ally Cuba!' stated Solodovnikov expansively, his unbridled joy, patent upon his face.

The chess moves had been made, the tactics had been executed, the Soviets had called 'Check?' The question remained as to whether the game being played for Rhodesia was 'Checkmate!'

14

Hotel Inter-continental, Haile Selassie Avenue, Lusaka

Sarah Burrell had the Times of Zambia in front of her on the breakfast table. The headline confirmed that the Rhodesian Ministry of Transport had announced that their investigation showed that the Viscount called *Hunyani* had been shot down by a Soviet made Strela missile. The article repeated Comrade Nkomo's claim of responsibility for the shooting down, but not for the death of the survivors. He blamed the Selous Scouts.

President Kaunda of Zambia had expressed regret at the loss of life but emphasised that the struggle for freedom in Zimbabwe must continue. President Kaunda's announcement was the only one made by a head of state anywhere in the world. The Governments of the United Kingdom, the United States, Australia, Canada, and the whole Commonwealth, were sickeningly silent. There was no press release from the office of the Secretary General of the United Nations. Only one churchman outside of Rhodesia expressed regret, Archbishop Desmond Tutu of the Anglican Church of South Africa. All others, from the Pope down remained silently indifferent. To the rest of the World it was as if nothing had happened at all.

Keith Wilson entered the dining room and made his way over to Sarah's table. His face was drawn, there was no welcoming smile, just the look of a man under immense pressure.

'This is bullshit,' said Sarah pointing at the newspaper.

'This is bullshit in a million different ways,' replied Wilson, sitting down opposite her.

She studied his face, now clean-shaven, his hair cut shorter. The boyish purity of spirit was replaced with a steely determination.

'Nkomo is dead,' hissed Wilson. 'I will do it myself, I don't need to wait, the order will surely come.' He was seething with anger, his voice cracked with emotion.

'Have you received any orders?' asked Sarah, overstepping the mark as always.

This brought a hint of a smile to Wilson's face.

'You never give up do you?'

'Well, are we still going to snatch a Cuban?'

'Those are still my orders, we need to do it tonight. He comes here to dinner on Thursdays, we will get him tonight on his way home.'

'What do you need from me?' asked Sarah, unable to contain her excitement.

'Come on Sarah, you know how dangerous this is. You will stay here until the job is done. That's final!'

Sarah sat back in her chair and smiled at him, the smile she knew had a powerful effect on him. She watched his face as it softened, his gruff attempt at denying her melting.

'We shall see,' she said, leaning forward to pat his hand.

It was all he could do not to jump at her touch ... she exuded a tangible power drawing him to her. Her mere presence set a vice clamping across his chest, making it difficult to breathe.

He smiled back into her eyes. She made everything seem possible.

*

Selous Scout HQ, Andre Rabie Barracks, Inkomo Barracks, 40km northwest of Salisbury

Colonel Ron Reid-Daly, like every other unit commander in the Rhodesian Army, was stunned by the developing events. While they had talked about the enemy shooting down airliners, it was now a reality. It was still impossible to believe. Their worst fears had materialised.

The shock of the event was rapidly giving way to anger, a white-hot anger that demanded revenge. The Government had declared Martial Law over one-fifth of the country, COMOPS had been ordered to mount external raids on all known targets. A maximum effort was called for.

Ian Smith spoke to the nation on television where he announced 'steps to liquidate the internal workings of those organisations associated with terrorists.' Within three days 200 arrests had been reported. Military courts were empowered to impose the death penalty on terrorists and people aiding and recruiting them. Nkomo's chief representative in Rhodesia, Josiah Chinamano left by air for London. His wife Ruth was already there.

At a press conference in Salisbury, Smith called Joshua Nkomo a 'monster', and said, 'I sincerely hope that I do not have any truck with that gentleman – I think he has put himself out of court.'

Robert Mugabe and Joshua Nkomo were summonsed to Cuba for talks with Fidel Castro, where greater military support was to be discussed.

The life of Joshua Nkomo now played on the mind of Colonel Reid-Daly. He had the means to make a powerful contribution. His head of intelligence, Major Rob Warner, entered the Operations Room carrying a signal.

'Cat Stevens reports that he is making the snatch of the Cuban tonight. He requests uplift by helicopter at last light tomorrow at Point 126,' said Warner.

'Good, we need our Cuban more than ever,' replied the Colonel. 'Where do we stand on Nkomo?'

'I have put a proposal before COMOPS to take him out. They are considering it. The SAS are not too happy; they claim that such a mission is their turf,' replied Warner.

'They don't know anything about our man Cat Stevens and we should not enlighten them. I also don't want the CIO to know. We will present our Cuban to them and say nothing about how we got him,' said the Colonel forcefully.

'The CIO know we have reconnaissance operatives in Zambia. They organised the passports, papers and ID documents.'

'Yes, but they are not aware of the breadth of our plans. We just have to hope that our people don't bump into their people again,' replied the Colonel. 'You should go on the helicopter, see Wilson and tell him to expect instructions for a hit on Nkomo.'

'Yes Boss,' replied Warner. He turned and walked purposefully from the room.

*

Zimbabwe House, Lukoma Road, Lusaka

Ian 'Coire Leis' Southwood and Jock 'Ben Nevis' McLean sat in the parked VW Beatle on Conakry Road, facing south towards Zimbabwe House, on the corner of Lukoma Road. It had been dark for three hours with no movement on the road. The house itself was obscured by the high wall built since their first attack on Zimbabwe House a year before.

The ZIPRA leadership team usually met at Zimbabwe House in the evening but no vehicles had arrived or departed in the past few hours. McLean's orders from Bright Lights were simple; inflict ZIPRA casualties, the more the merrier.

It never ceased to amaze Jock that, despite the repeated attack on ZAPU/ZIPRA installations, they were never effectively guarded. He was once again in his dark blue overalls, Afro wig and face-veil. Only his eyes were not obscured. It was always hot in his disguise and he was sweating profusely.

Ian started the VW, drove south down Conakry Road, over the intersection with Lukoma Road, continued for two blocks, then left onto Sheki Sheki Road. At the intersection with the Great North Road he turned left again, northwards towards Lukoma Road, making a full 360 of the target. There were no police cars or military vehicles to be seen.

Turning back onto Lukoma Road, Ian slowed down to allow Jock to jump out. They both checked the surroundings carefully before Jock exited, expertly diving into the long grass on the verge. He carried a backpack with two makeshift claymore mines made from five-litre oil cans packed with high explosive, ball bearings and an assortment of nuts, bolts and nails scrounged from Ian's workshop on the farm. An AK47 hung on his shoulder with a pouch with four spare magazines on his waist.

Ian had his own AK47 with a RPG-7 under a blanket on the back seat. He carried on down Lukoma Road to wait for the evening's game to kick-off.

Jock jumped over the three-strand fence on the eastern neighbour's property and made towards the wall surrounding Zimbabwe House. A shallow drainage ditch followed the length of the wall. It was topped with a single strand of barbed wire.

Squatting down next to the wall, Jock stopped to re-gather his breath and check that he had not been seen.

After ten minutes of silent observation, with deep steady breathing, Jock tossed a 30-pound breaking strain fishing line up over the strand of barbed wire. It was rigged with a fishing hook that he gently pulled until the slack was taken up. Jock attached the bunker bomb leaving it hanging flush against the wall, about a metre off the ground. He inserted two detonators and set the timer for 30 minutes. Crouching low, Jock pushed through the grass and weeds until he reached the half-completed wall on the southern boundary. Here the wall was only a metre high, abutted by outbuildings. This explained why the wall had not been completed. The corrugated iron outbuildings had been built since his last attack. They were being used for accommodation as Jock could hear animated conversation coming from inside. The occupants seemed to be enjoying themselves, speaking loudly with continuous outbursts of laughter.

Jock set another bunker bomb between the wall and the corrugated iron outbuilding, setting the timer to detonate roughly five minutes after the first bunker bomb.

After positioning his mines, Jock rechecked his watch. He took a moment to control his breathing, then moved to the second phase of the plan. Dropping two ZANLA marked AK magazines next to the wall to help with the subterfuge, he moved back along the boundary wall towards Lukoma Road where the main entrance to the compound was situated. There he waited … checking his watch instinctively every few minutes.

With fifteen minutes to go before the detonation of the first bunker bomb, Jock slipped the AK off his shoulder and approached the main gate.

A clear, starlit sky above, perfectly quiet, not a breath of wind … Jock's heartbeat accelerated.

The presence of the sentry on the gate was revealed by a slow and measured snore. It was the slumber of the deeply contented.

The double gate was made of wrought iron, chained closed with a large padlock. He felt in his pouch for a chunk of plastic explosive that he squeezed onto the lock and stuck a detonator into it with a pre-cut length of cortex. Lighting the fuse he retired to the edge of the wall. As he waited the few seconds he removed a grenade from his pouch.

The gate blew inwards with a loud thud. The one side slammed against the door to the guardhouse trapping the man inside. Coming abruptly awake, his face and eyes covered in dust, the guard was unable to see the grenade slip in under his feet.

Jock had the AK in his hands walking purposely forward towards the old colonial house. The tin roof of the guardhouse blew off behind him as the guard was reduced to a bloody pulp.

Once on the veranda in front of the house, Jock pumped rounds into each unprotected window. A man came out through the front door to be cut down where he stood.

Jock was starting to enjoy himself. He changed magazines then walked around the side of the house towards the outbuildings. An RPD opened up in the dark, the green tracer rounds spraying high into the sky, as if the attack was coming from winged predators. Jock could hear men shouting and screaming from inside the buildings. The RPD was joined by AKs as the men in the outbuildings, on opposite sides of the compound, began shooting at each other. The corrugated iron provided no protection for those inside.

The crossfire forced Jock to duck back towards the main house. He skirted the front, making for the gate. All hell was breaking loose behind him as the ZIPRA cadres shot at anything that moved. After less than half a minute, Jock was back in Lukoma Road with Ian gunning the VW towards him. The door flung open as Ian approached and Jock leapt in.

'Fucking beautiful,' he screamed, adrenaline flooding his system, irrationally contemplating going back in.

Turning south onto the Great North Road, Ian slowed to a more reasonable speed, not wanting to give the impression of fugitive bank robbers.

Back in the ZAPU/ZIPRA compound, the firing died down. After a few minutes the men ventured out of the buildings. They collected in small groups, all talking at once, trying to fathom what had just happened.

The bunker bomb detonated, turning the concrete wall into a million jagged pieces of shrapnel. The men standing next to it were scythed down, covering them in chunks of concrete and thick white dust. The few shocked survivors shrank back from the gaping hole in the wall, to be cut down minutes later by the second bomb. Sheets of corrugated iron spinning like power-saw blades cut through the air, slicing men in half, amputating heads and limbs.

It was a scene of absolute carnage. Blood soaked bodies lay strewn across the ground, dust lifted into a thick choking cloud above the compound. The night filled with the screams of wounded men with the most ghastly injuries.

Miraculously, no members of the senior ZIPRA command were injured. Only one member, Party Commissar Samuel Munodawafa, was in residence at the time. He stood disconsolate in the devastated courtyard. As he surveyed the scene a cold shiver ran down his spine ... *this is just the beginning ... the Rhodesians were coming ...*

ZIPRA had indeed unleashed the whirlwind.

*

Hotel Inter-continental, Haile Selassie Avenue, Lusaka

Keith Wilson, Cephas Ngwenya and Stanley Chiyeka sat under the stars in the Norman Barr Land Rover in the carpark of the Hotel Inter-continental. All three were dressed neatly in slacks and sports jacket as to be expected of three young men out on the town. Both Ngwenya and Chiyeka had commented that they could hardly recognise Wilson without his beard. Ngwenya had observed with a smile that it made Wilson look like a seventeen year-old. Wilson's clean-shaven face made Ngwenya feel a little uncomfortable. After years of working together, it seemed strange and unnerving. He looked forward to the end of the mission so that Wilson could grow it back again.

Wilson had briefed his men on the location and layout of their target's house in the tree-lined Joseph Mwilwa Road, in the salubrious suburb of Maluba. The house was only 2km from the hotel as the crow flies. They knew their target shared the house with one other member of the Cuban embassy delegation but it was unclear whether there were any weapons in the house.

Earlier in the day, Wilson had taken his team for a drive through the suburb, noting the various route options that the target could take on his short drive home. They also noted the best escape route back to the Norman Barr warehouse in Numununga, just over 3km away. They decided that the best weapons for the night were their Tokarev pistols. Each man carried two spare magazines in their jacket pockets.

To complete the preparation, Wilson had taken his team inside the hotel for a drink. They sipped on Coca-Cola until the Cubans arrived for dinner. Chiyeka had been encouraged to chat up one of the many prostitutes patrolling the bar to complete the scene. Wilson marvelled at how comfortable his men were with their newfound confidence as undercover agents. They demonstrated not an ounce of nervousness, happy to discuss their cover as escaped Zimbabwean freedom fighters. Wilson made a point of introducing his men to Reuben the barman. There was nothing strange about the young English big-game hunter befriending Zimbabwean Freedom Fighters.

Unsure of exactly how to inform his men of the help he was getting from Sarah Burrell, Wilson kept it brief, explaining that she had used her press pass to gain access to the Cuban compound thereby helping identify the most senior Cuban military advisor. Ngwenya and Chiyeka had seemed happy with that explanation.

The blue Peugeot 504 driven by Colonel Julio Ángel Casas drove into the carpark and parked near the entrance. Wilson and his team had a clear view of the vehicle as its only occupant climbed out, locked the door and walked up the stairs into the hotel lobby. Once Casas had sat down for dinner, the three Selous Scouts slipped back out to their Land Rover to wait. They took turns strolling around the carpark, observing Haile Selassie Avenue to make sure no Zambian police or military were lurking in the shadows.

Way in the distance the sound of sirens carried on the evening breeze. Wilson did not give them a second thought.

As planned, Ngwenya and Chiyeka jumped off the Land Rover and went back into the hotel. They took up their positions on two comfortable lounge chairs in the bar, ordered Cokes from Reuben and waited. Chiyeka, a man born for the stage, set about chatting up a pretty young prostitute sitting on a nearby barstool.

The Cuban dinner party had all arrived promptly. Casas was in an obviously buoyant mood. The laughter from his table carried easily to the bar. Ngwenya studied the group closely, memorising their faces. There were four men and two women, all talking in Spanish. The whisky flowed freely as the sons and daughters of the revolution indulged themselves.

Casas got up to go to the toilet, slightly uneasy on his feet, the 18-year old single malt scotch taking effect. Ngwenya watched him closely, summing up how much effort it would need to subdue him. While Casas was short, he was thickset, likely too powerful for Ngwenya to take down on his own. Relying on stealth rather than brute force, Ngwenya would have been happier to slit the man's throat in the toilet and be done with it.

The Cuban dinner came to an abrupt end when Casas stood up, held his glass out in a toast and dismissed his underlings to their beds. It was clear to Ngwenya that what had brought the party to such a precipitous end was the arrival of a particularly attractive girl in the bar. Casas clearly had a keen eye, not as drunk as he made out. As soon as he had said his goodbyes to his staff, Casas entered the bar and made a beeline towards the woman seated at the bar.

Ngwenya signalled to Chiyeka to disentangle himself from the prostitute he had been talking to. Chiyeka walked out through the lobby into the carpark to warn Wilson that the dinner was over and Casas was now negotiating with a prostitute. It was only a few minutes before he would be ready to leave. Taking his place in the passenger seat of the Land Rover he and Wilson waited. They could see directly into the hotel lobby from the carpark.

Casas had negotiated his position in quick time, entering the lobby with the girl on his arm. Ngwenya was only a few metres behind him.

'Good evening Colonel', said a tall woman dressed in a black full-length evening dress.

Casas stopped and turned towards the person speaking to him. From the expression on his face he did not recognise her at first.

'Fuck!' hissed Wilson, when he saw Sarah enter the lobby.

Not sure what to do, Wilson sat tight, watching …

'You remember me Colonel, Sarah Burrell, Associated Press, you gave me an interview,' said Sarah brightly.

Casas blinked, turned to look around the lobby to see if anyone else was watching. Ngwenya stopped to look at a bookstand. He had recognised Sarah immediately.

'Leave me alone,' spat Casas, not impressed with the interruption to his plans.

'I am sorry our interview went badly Colonel, I was hoping that I might buy you a drink ... to apologise,' said Sarah politely. The smile on her face was unrelenting.

'I ... I don't want to talk to you, I don't want a drink, leave me alone!' snarled Casas, not impressed in the slightest.

Snapping into fluent Spanish, Sarah replied, '*No preferiría a una mujer real*? Would you not prefer a real woman Colonel?'

Casas could hardly believe his ears. His face flushed with anger. He rounded on Sarah, venom in his eyes. The discussion drew the attention of the doorman, and the people behind the reception desk.

'*Vete a la mierda?* Fuck off, who do you think you are?'

'How can a brave son of the revolution consort with prostitutes? Why is it that he must pay for a woman?' smiled Sarah, still in Spanish, not missing a beat.

The whisky, the circumstances, the sheer bravado of this brazen woman was too much for Casas, he lashed out with the flat of his hand aiming at her face.

Sarah stepped back out the way, Casas's hand missing her by a few inches.

'Fuck!' whispered Wilson again from the Land Rover. Jumping out of the seat, ready to run into the hotel.

'Stop!' shouted the doorman stepping forward.

Sarah backed away with feigned surprise, her hands held to her face. The prostitute was equally shocked, letting out a plaintive squeal.

Casas stood in stunned disbelief; all eyes in the lobby were on him.

'I think it's time you went home Sir,' said the doorman politely.

Grunting loudly, Casas grabbed for the girl's arm, but she backed away, no longer interested in the deal he had offered.

'Come here you bitch!' shouted Casas in English, not to be denied.

The girl turned and ran back towards the bar.

'Please Sir, its time for you to go home,' said the doorman more loudly.

'Looks like you're in for a lonely night, Colonel,' called Sarah as the doorman ushered Casas towards the entrance. If looks could kill, Sarah Burrell would have died a horrible death that instant.

Ngwenya, unsure of what had actually been said, brushed passed the doorman as Casas was escorted down the stairs to his car. He walked briskly across the carpark towards the Land Rover.

'Is that the woman who has been helping you *Ikhanka?*' asked Ngwenya as he jumped into the back of the Land Rover.

'Yes it is,' replied Wilson, not sure what else to say. He started the Land Rover, revving the engine, getting ready to depart.

'I don't think she likes the Cuban,' added Ngwenya with a laugh. 'The Cuban definitely does not like her.'

Casas reversed the Peugeot out of the parking space; tyres squealed as he gunned the engine towards the exit. Casas was a very unhappy man.

Wilson followed as closely as he could as Casas accelerated down the road to the north. Casas turned off at the spot that Wilson considered most likely and continued to drive fast through the suburbs. Confident that Casas was on his way home, Wilson backed off on the speed. The Land Rover was no match for the Peugeot in any event.

The headlights of the Land Rover picked up Casas as he bent over fiddling with the lock on the security gate to his house. Wilson pulled the Land Rover across the road to stop behind the Peugeot. Casas stood up from the gate lock, shielding his eyes from the bright headlights. Wilson, Chiyeka and Ngwenya were out of the Land Rover in an instant, coming down the side of Peugeot at a sprint.

Realising that he was in trouble, Casas reached inside his blazer for his pistol. Before he could withdraw his hand, the three Selous Scouts were on him. Wilson punched him hard in the mouth, while Ngwenya and Chiyeka went for his arms. As expected, Casas was enormously powerful. Unaffected by Wilson's punch, he swung around with the men on his arms giving out a loud roar of anger. Holding a smelly sack from the warehouse in one hand, Wilson tried to get it over Casas's head. The man swung his head violently from side to side making it impossible to get the sack over.

The scuffle drew the attention of someone inside the house. A light came on in one of the bedrooms. The front door opened and a man stood silhouetted against the light. He had a rifle in his hands. Three other men joined him.

Casas bellowed out for help in Spanish, bringing the men running towards the gate. Wilson, realising that he was fast losing the initiative, smashed Casas in the face with his pistol. This slowed Casas considerably, his knees buckled slightly. It was enough to get the sack over his head and drag him towards the Land Rover. Wilson smashed him again hard on the back of the head.

The men reached the gate, shouting loudly in Spanish, rifles in their hands, trying to aim into the bright headlights. One let off a warning shot. The sound reverberated in the still night. Ngwenya lifted his pistol and fired back, with a loud groan one of the men crumpled to the ground.

The Cubans on the other side of the locked gate opened fire in earnest. Blinded by the headlights, they blazed away into the dark. The Peugeot effectively blocked their line of fire with bullets sailing high over its roof.

Wilson and Chiyeka hauled the dazed Casas into the back of the Land Rover. Ngwenya crouched behind the Peugeot returning fire. Another of the Cubans gave out a squeal as Ngwenya hit him in the leg.

Back in the driver's seat, Wilson shouted for his men to get in. He gunned the engine as he slapped it into reverse, the tires spinning in the gravel. Chiyeka leapt into the back, landing on top of Casas. As the Land Rover gathered pace, Ngwenya dived full length into the back, smashing into Chiyeka, his pistol flying off into the dark.

Racing down the road, Wilson made their escape in the direction of the Norman Barr warehouse. Sirens were already blaring in the distance.

The good citizens of Lusaka were having a very noisy, interrupted night.

Unbeknown to Wilson, the attack on the ZAPU offices had disturbed a hornet's nest with Zambian police and military setting up roadblocks on every arterial road across the city.

Wilson turned left on the Great East Road towards the industrial area. As they crossed over the railway line, ahead of them was a large traffic circle at the intersection with Cairo Road. It was crawling with police and army. Army trucks blocked all entrances to the traffic circle. Cars were being searched at the side of the road.

'Fuck,' said Wilson under his breath.

Casas had stopped squirming. Both Chiyeka and Ngwenya were holding him down with their boots. Blood was seeping through the sack probably caused by the repeated smacks from Chiyeka's pistol to keep him quiet.

Wilson slowed the Land Rover. Two cars ahead of him stopped on the side of the road. Soldiers in uniform pulled the drivers from their seats and began ransacking the vehicles. Luggage lay strewn along the side of the road. Wilson noted factory buildings and warehouses down both sides of the road. Their only escape was down the reserve next to the railway line. There was no way they were going to bluff their way through the roadblock.

'Hold on tight' shouted Wilson, as he pulled a hard right turn across the road, bounced over a drainage ditch then down the steep slope towards the railway line.

The Zambian Police at the roadblock immediately opened fire as the Land Rover disappeared off the side of the road. A Zambian army Unimog gave chase, the Land Rover break lights providing something to shoot at.

Wilson turned off the headlights losing sight of the rough track. Bouncing hard as they hit a drainage ditch, Chiyeka and Ngwenya were thrown painfully against the side of the Land Rover. Chiyeka's pistol was dislodged from his hand to clatter loudly onto the steel tray. Miraculously the Land Rover did not stall, Wilson slammed it into reverse and pulled back out of the ditch, driving back at it at an angle, taking them safely over.

Fire from the Zambians intensified, a machine gun was mounted above the cab of the chasing truck. Green tracer whistled overhead disappearing into the night. The rough track made careful aim impossible.

The dirt track led to Chisango Road. Wilson pulled left off the railway reserve onto the road and gunned the Land Rover towards the east. The Great North Road appeared ahead, blocked by lines of military vehicles. Soldiers were everywhere.

Wilson aimed at a gap between two of the trucks. The Zambian Unimog pulled onto the road behind them, its headlights on bright.

Nervous soldiers, having heard the approaching gunfight, opened fire on the Unimog. Rifle flashes blinked left and right as Wilson reached the gap. A man stepped out with a raised rifle. Wilson hit him square with the centre of the bonnet, throwing his body clear. Now they were in amongst the Zambian troops milling about in the road. The Unimog behind burst into flames. At full speed, with an enormous crunch it ploughed into the line of trucks blocking the road. The fire quickly spread, ammunition and fuel tanks exploded. Men, engulfed in flames, rolled in the roadway, gunfire filled the night, the acrid stench of burning rubber clogged the air.

Driving straight through the intersection Wilson weaved left and right trying to avoid Zambian soldiers running about in panic. They were shooting in all directions, unsure of who or what was the enemy.

The gunfire and explosions had brought people out into the street. Wilson put his headlights back on, immediately picking up people lining the road on both sides. All were looking towards the east at the fire and explosions that had spread to neighbouring buildings.

A young child ran across the road in front of Wilson forcing him to swerve. At the speed he was travelling he lost control. The Land Rover careened across the road, ploughed through a group of onlookers trying to leap out of the way, then smashed into a wire fence. Wilson was thrown hard against the steering wheel breaking his nose and cracking a rib, knocking all the wind out of him. Ngwenya and Chiyeka were thrown out of the back into the road. The unconscious Casas remained lying in the back of the Land Rover.

People in the crowd screamed in shock. They ran towards the Land Rover thinking it belonged to the police. The people helped Chiyeka and Ngwenya to their feet, both men covered in cuts and bruises. A man approached the Land Rover gently lifting Wilson's head from where it lay against the steering wheel. When he saw it was a white man he let go, shouted out in alarm, pointing at Wilson as if he was some sort of monster ...

The mood of the crowd changed instantly. They dragged Wilson from behind the steering wheel, letting his body fall to the ground. Ngwenya shouted at them to stop. Still very groggy, he and Chiyeka pushed the crowd standing over Wilson away. Ngwenya leaned across the driver's seat to grab Wilson's pistol that had fallen onto the bench seat.

'Stop!' Ngwenya shouted repeatedly, waving the pistol at the crowd.

Wilson gave a load groan as he started to regain consciousness.

More people joined the crowd. They were baying for Wilson to be given to them. Pushing forward, some grabbed for Wilson's arms to drag him away.

A police vehicle was approaching from the scene of the fire. The people, arms waving, turned to run into the road to stop it. There was shouting, screaming and pointing towards the Land Rover.

With Ngwenya's help Wilson pulled himself to his feet. Blood covered the front of his shirt, his chest ached and he was struggling to regain his breath. He was breathing in short sharp sucks. Every time he inhaled, it was as if a knife pushing into his chest.

'Cephas,' whispered Wilson. 'Start the Land Rover ... quickly.'

Without hesitating Ngwenya slid behind the wheel, pushed the gear stick into neutral and pressed the starter. The engine came to life immediately.

'Give me the pistol,' called Wilson taking it from Ngwenya. 'Get in Chiyeka,' he ordered.

The crowd, realising that these men were trying to escape, pressed in. One grabbed at Wilson's arm, pulling him. A pain shot through Wilson's chest making him wince painfully. The man pulled again. Wilson waved the pistol at him, he tried to shout but no sound would come from his throat. Not dissuaded, the man pushed forward shouting, yanking hard on Wilson's arm. In desperate agony Wilson shot him in the thigh.

The gunshot had the effect of startling the crowd, while the wounded man screamed in pain, rolling in the dust.

'Go,' shouted Wilson with all the strength he could muster.

Ngwenya shoved the Land Rover into reverse and pulled away from the fence, the bumper had snagged some of the wire mesh pulling it with it. This had the momentary effect of forcing the crowd to pull back from the side of the Land Rover.

'Get in *Ikhanka*,' shouted Ngwenya.

'Go Cephas … Go man!'

Wilson lifted the pistol and shot a round towards the police car. The crowd hesitated giving Wilson a wider berth. Wilson could see police were running towards the Land Rover.

Wilson lifted the pistol, taking careful aim. He fired … a policeman sprawled in the road, his weapon skidding across the tar.

Ngwenya had the Land Rover back on the road.

'Get in … please *Ikhanka*!' shouted Ngwenya.

The police were now shooting indiscriminately at anything that moved. Screaming in terror, the crowd scattering in all directions, many falling to the guns fired by the police.

Wilson staggered after the panicked crowd, firing the pistol into the air, adding to the confusion. Ngwenya watched Wilson hobbling away into the dark; there was nothing he could do. He shoved the Land Rover into first gear and raced off down the road with their valuable captive.

Once Ngwenya had made his escape, Wilson slowed to a painful shuffle keeping in the shadows of the surrounding buildings. The pain in his chest was excruciating. It seemed to be getting worse, as if a sharp stick was being pushed into his lungs.

The crowd had now dispersed, while the policemen could be seen carrying their wounded comrade towards their vehicle. Bodies lay in the road, those people wounded by the police, lay moaning for help.

Still in the shadows of the buildings, slowly, painfully, Wilson moved west down Chisango Road. He approached Luanshya Road in the heart of the Namununga industrial area. Drawing on the last of his reserves, each breath was now pure agony, he stopped briefly to assess his next move. The Norman Barr warehouse was less than a kilometre away …

A black veil came down over Wilson's eyes. He slid down against a fence post, the pain was just too much … *just a short rest … time to recover.*

Keith Wilson passed out ... slumped in the dust next to the road.

15

Norman Barr Safari Offices, 5 Moobola Road, Numununga Industrial Area, Lusaka

Cephas Ngwenya and Stanley Chiyeka had not slept a wink. They had spent the remaining hours of the night walking the surrounding streets near the warehouse hoping to find Wilson. Casas, still with the sack over his head, was tied up in the cold room. They had wrapped him in a blanket so he didn't die, but frankly Ngwenya didn't care if he did. His only concern was for Wilson.

To complete their mission the Cuban colonel had to be delivered to the RV at last light that evening. The RV point for helicopter uplift of their captive was about 32km south east of Kafue Bridge on the road to Chirundu.

The two Selous Scouts were making tea when they heard a step at the door. Both men reached for their AKs. Someone knocked.

Ngwenya stood up and opened the door his rifle at the ready.

'Mister Brown here?' asked the short Welshman with a smirk.

'No,' replied Ngwenya not sure what to say.

'You have another body in the cold room, this one's still alive, get it out!'

Ngwenya opened the door completely, to look at the Welshman, not sure what he could or couldn't say. What he did know was that he needed help.

'Mister Brown was left behind after we snatched that man downstairs. The captive has to be delivered tonight,' said Ngwenya slowly.

'Is Mister Brown dead?' asked the Welshman matter-of-factly.

'No, but he was injured when we crashed the Land Rover.'

'I saw that ... you have all but ripped off the front bumper ... '

Ngwenya didn't answer ... he was lost in his own thoughts.

The telephone began to ring in the office downstairs. The Welshman took the stairs two at time to pick up the phone. Ngwenya and Chiyeka could hear him answer the phone. The only words the man used on the phone were 'Yes ... Yes ... I understand.'

The phone call finished and the man came back up the stairs.

'It seems Mister Brown has been picked up by the Zambian Police. I have been ordered to get you out of town. They will break him and he will then lead them to this place,' spat the Welshman. 'All of us are now in serious danger.'

'We cannot leave. We must get Mister Brown back,' replied

Ngwenya.

'I am not going to argue with you … I don't give a fuck about your Mister Brown or you for that matter … but I do care about me and Mr Barr,' stated the Welshman leaving no doubt about his resolve. 'Pack your shit and get ready, you leave in ten minutes.'

*

Mazira, alias Funny Farm 26km west of Lusaka

Only a few minutes after the phone call placed to the Norman Barr warehouse in Lusaka the phone began to ring at Mazira Farm. Patricia Southwood was in the kitchen while Jock and Ian were in the tool shed across the yard.

'Hello, Mazira Farm,' she answered.

'This is the insurance company speaking.'

'Yes,' Patricia's heart leapt into her throat.

'Your premiums have not been paid. Please pay them immediately. Is that clear?'

'Yes,' replied Patricia already feeling bilious. The phone clicked on the other side.

She replaced the receiver as if it was a piece of Ming China.

'Beauty!' she called the maid.

'Yes Madam.'

'I have to go to the shed to speak to Mister Southwood. Please watch the chicken in the oven.'

Before the maid could answer Patricia was out the back door, walking as fast as she could to the tool shed, fighting back tears all the way.

'Jesus,' was all Jock could say when Patricia burst into the farm office.

Ian looked at his watch.

'They will be calling in ten minutes, we better fire up the big means,' he said referring to their HF radio.

The message Patricia had been given was the most serious alarm call they could be sent from Rhodesia. It meant that they were to break their scheduled radio calls to take an immediate most urgent message … this included the potential of shutting down their operation and implementing the plan for their escape.

Patricia burst into tears. Ian held her in his arms stroking her hair.

'Settle down Pat. I am sure it will be fine. We haven't been compromised. It'll be something else,' he said unconvincingly.

*

Lusaka Central Prison, Paul Banda Road, Lusaka

Keith Wilson was unsure of whether he was in a dark room or he was blindfolded. His body seemed to be strangely distanced from him, he was tied up in a foetal position on a wooden surface. He was aware of his hands and legs, yet he felt paralysed. It was stifling hot while the air was rancid with the stale stink of hundreds of human bodies.

The pain in his chest was excruciating, he could taste blood in his mouth ... unable to move. A dizzy spell hit him ... he coughed. The pain was as a knife twisting in his chest, making his eyes water. His head seemed to be restrained in some way. He was unable to move it from side to side.

Head spinning from nausea, he threw up. Vomit stuck in his throat, choking him. It was either cough or die drowning in his vomit. He spat and coughed at the same time, the pain in his chest making him cry out in agony. Chest heaving from the effort, he closed his eyes to regain control. Each breath was a short sharp suck ... it was all he could manage.

He became aware of light out the corner of his eye, then the sound of scraping footsteps. He spat again, trying to clear his throat.

A sheet was lifted off his face, bright light streamed painfully into his eyes, forcing him to shut them tightly.

'Meesta Brown?' said a distant voice.

Wilson couldn't tilt his head to see who was talking.

'Meesta Brown, are you awake?'

'Yes,' croaked Wilson, wanting to throw up again.

'I am Inspector R. K. Kabamba of the Zambian Police. We want to ask you some questions.'

The voice seemed friendly enough.

Wilson was aware of other people in the room. He could hear their breathing.

'I am in great pain. I cannot answer questions now. I need medical assistance,' croaked Wilson, keeping his eyes shut, playing for time as he tried to get his mind to focus.

'You will get all the help you need once you answer a few simple questions,' said the Inspector kindly.

Wilson chose to remain silent. Blood was still trickling down the back of his throat causing an irritation making him want to cough.

'I must sit up, my throat is blocked and I can't breathe.'

Someone loosened the bindings on his wrists that had him

strapped to the table. Rough hands pulled him upright. The sudden compression of his chest as he sat up caused a stabbing pain, making him wince painfully.

Opening his eyes slowly Wilson counted four men in the room with him. Two policemen in uniform while the other two men were in suits.

'Where am I?' asked Wilson.

'That is no concern of yours, Meesta Brown,' said the Inspector smiling down at him. 'Now, you work for Meesta Norman Barr?'

'Yes.'

'You are British?'

'Yes.'

'Why did you run away from the road block?'

'I was drunk and did not want to spend the night in a Zambian jail.'

'That is enough!' said the taller of the two men in suits. He spoke loudly in deeply accented English. Stepping forward to address Wilson, 'You are Lieutenant Keith Wilson of the Rhodesian Selous Scouts and you have kidnapped a man of great importance to us.'

The tall man held up a piece of paper, thrusting it into Wilson's face. It was a grainy picture of him in his camouflage uniform on parade at Andre Rabie Barracks.

'That's bullshit, I demand to see a lawyer,' replied Wilson defiantly.

'Where you are going there are no lawyers,' replied the Police Inspector, still smiling politely.

'This is a terrible mistake,' moaned Wilson, shaking his head from side to side. 'I don't know what you are talking about.'

The Police Inspector poked Wilson in the chest with his forefinger, making him cry out in pain.

'I am pleased that we have passed on from your alias as Mister Brown so quickly. Now Lieutenant Wilson, you will answer the questions put to you by His Excellency Comrade Vassily Solodovnikov, the Soviet Ambassador to Zambia,' stated the Inspector still maintaining his friendly tone.

'Where is Colonel Casas, Lieutenant?' asked Solodovnikov.

Wilson's mind was racing, they seemed to have him stone cold. *How did they get my photograph? How do they know I have Casas?* He was staggered that they had a photograph of him ... it meant they had photos of everyone!

'Come now Lieutenant, you don't want to make this any more painful. Where is Colonel Casas?' added Comrade Colonel Lev Kononov, the other Russian in the room.

'I am sorry, I don't know what you are talking about,' replied Wilson shaking his head, putting on his best imitation of confusion. His mind was reliving the defence against interrogation course taught to him by the Selous Scouts. The best he could hope for was to hold out for twelve hours, that should give Ngwenya enough time to get Casas to the RV point for uplift. 'I need to rest. My chest is very painful. I think I have broken a rib.'

'You will have plenty of time to rest Lieutenant. If you do not answer truthfully, a broken rib will be the least of your concerns,' whispered Solodovnikov menacingly, a grim smile stretched across his face.

*

Hotel Inter-continental, Haile Selassie Avenue, Lusaka

Cephas Ngwenya and Stanley Chiyeka had cleared their kit out of the Norman Barr warehouse as instructed by the Welshman. Casas was carried out to the Land Rover shivering violently and mumbling incoherently. They had lifted the blood soaked sack to take a look at his face. It was a purple pulpy mess with one eye swollen shut, blood still seeping from his nose.

Chiyeka had suggested that they just slit the man's throat and dump him on the side of the road. This suggestion had great appeal as they were in grave danger, with a better chance of survival without a captive Cuban colonel in their Land Rover.

Ngwenya had decided that the mission was no longer important. Making the RV to deliver the captive was secondary importance. Their first task was to establish where Wilson was being held. In Ngwenya's mind there was no way that Wilson was being left behind to die in a Zambian jail.

The Welshman had left the warehouse after packing the repainted Landcruiser with files and an assortment of hunting rifles and his shotgun. He had waited for Ngwenya and Chiyeka to pack their kit, together with the tightly bound Casas, into the Land Rover and locked the warehouse behind them. They were given clear instructions never to return.

Ngwenya and Chiyeka had discussed their options. Attacking a jail or a heavily guarded building with only two of them was suicide. They were confident they could ambush a small convoy of vehicles but that required careful planning and good intelligence. There was no time for any of that, Wilson only had a few hours left before he broke under interrogation or died. To find Wilson, Ngwenya knew he needed help. The only person he could think of was the white woman at the hotel that Wilson said had helped him before. He did not know her name or anything about her. They both agreed that enlisting the help of the mystery white woman was the only option.

The two men sat waiting in the carpark of the Hotel Intercontinental. The sun had been up for only half an hour so there were very few people about. The drive across town from the warehouse had been uneventful as the police roadblocks had been taken down. Only a few army trucks were seen parked on the side of the road.

'Just go and ask the people at reception to call her Cephas,' said Chiyeka helpfully.

'I don't know her name ... she is American, I heard her speak,' replied Ngwenya, thinking hard. He glanced at his watch, time was of the essence. *Wilson would be tortured and killed, they will break him first ... No help would be coming from Rhodesia.*

'What can I say?' asked Ngwenya.

'Just say you are the driver and your boss told you to fetch a white woman from the hotel and drive her where she wants to go. Say she wanted to see some wild animals. You are dressed like a guide,' suggested Chiyeka.

It seemed plausible.

Ngwenya slipped out of the driver's seat just as Casas gave out a muffled groan. He went around the back of the Land Rover and lifted the sack. Casas was awake but still shivering with a gag tied around his mouth.

'You, you!' demanded Ngwenya, pointing into Casas's face.

Casas blinked, looking up into Ngwenya's cold black eyes.

'You be quiet or we will beat you more or kill you. Do you understand?' said Ngwenya viciously. He meant every word.

Ngwenya pulled the sack back down over Casas's face and walked across the carpark. Striding purposefully up the stairs into the hotel lobby, he made directly to the reception desk. A young woman was on duty.

'I am here to pick up an American woman,' asked Ngwenya with the thickest accent he could muster, pronouncing each word deliberately to give the impression of a man with a very poor command of English.

'What is her name?' replied the girl politely.

'My boss told me, but I can't remember English names. She is tall with long hair,' replied Ngwenya, now very uncomfortable, he could feel sweat running down his back despite the cool morning.

'We have a Sarah Burrell, she is an American reporter,' said the woman helpfully.

'Yes, that is it,' replied Ngwenya nodding and smiling with relief.

The girl picked up the phone to call Sarah's room. It was answered almost immediately.

'I have a man here to fetch you,' said the receptionist.

Ngwenya could not hear the answer on the phone, but he could see the face of the receptionist change to one of suspicion.

'She says she is not expecting anyone,' said the girl looking into Ngwenya's face. 'Have you got the right hotel?'

Panic rose in Ngwenya's gut, all his instincts were telling him to run.

'Yes, I am sure it is right ... tell her Wilson sent me.'

Ngwenya could hear the phone click down on the other side.

'She is coming down, wait over there,' directed the girl, pointing to a sofa in the lobby.

Sweat covered Ngwenya's brow. He was having difficulty coming to terms with the desperate situation they were in. He had no idea what he was going to say to the woman. There was no way of knowing whether she would help. She may betray them to the authorities. There was no plan, just a vague idea of attacking the place that Wilson was being held and freeing him. He knew in his heart that if the situation were reversed, Wilson would not leave him behind ... even if he died trying. These were the thoughts that now occupied Ngwenya's mind.

I will try to free Wilson or die trying.

The woman entered the lobby, her blond hair tied up in a ponytail. She was wearing khaki slacks and a white shirt. She walked straight towards where Ngwenya was sitting. A large leather sling bag sat across her shoulder, while a camera hung from a strap around her neck.

Standing up, Ngwenya's mind went blank. Talking to white women was not part of his experience.

'You're with Wilson?' asked the woman softly, putting out her hand.

Ngwenya took it gently as if he was afraid it would break. The strength in her handshake came as a shock. There was a power in her that Ngwenya had not expected.

'Yes ... we have a problem,' whispered Ngwenya, glancing furtively around the lobby.

Sarah could see he was nervous and agitated. Sweat was beading on his forehead and on his upper lip.

'Would you prefer to talk outside?' she asked with a smile.

'Yes ... please.'

They walked outside into the bright sunlight. Ngwenya indicated a large tree in the carpark. He waved for Chiyeka to join them.

'What has happened?' asked Sarah, deep concern in her voice. 'Did you snatch the Cuban?'

'Yes, he is in the Land Rover,' replied Ngwenya pointing across the carpark. 'They have captured Wilson.'

'My God ...' Sarah felt a wave of dread pass over her, making her feel lightheaded.

'There was a roadblock, we tried to escape but we crashed the Land Rover. Wilson created a diversion so that Chiyeka and I could get away with the captive,' replied Ngwenya, speaking slowly as if talking to a young child.

'Jesus ...'

Ngwenya could see the concern in her eyes, it was clear to him that she and Wilson had a deeper connection. What that connection was there was no way of knowing. He had no experience of the ways of white women. He had been a district policeman, then a Selous Scout. He had spoken to only a handful of white woman in his whole life. This was the first white woman who had offered to shake his hand.

Ngwenya studied the woman's face as he waited for her to speak again.

'Do you know where they are holding him?' asked Sarah gently.

'We know nothing except that he has been caught. ... Wilson stayed behind to make sure we got away with the Cuban,' repeated Ngwenya as if convincing himself that the nightmare was true.

The consequence of those few simple words were clear to her ... he sacrificed himself for his men.

'What can I do to help?' asked Sarah, her mind trying to come to terms with the appalling reality that Wilson was either already dead or being tortured ... likely to be dead in only a few more hours.

'We think that there can only be a few places,' said Ngwenya glancing at Chiyeka who nodded his agreement. 'It can be at the police headquarters, the army Arakan Barracks, the Central Prison or the Kamwala Remand Prison. They will all be well guarded.'

These were places that Wilson and his team had reconnoitred over the past few weeks.

'My God ... ' said Sarah again. The reality of the situation flooded in on her. 'They will be interrogating him.'

'He will only last a few hours of torture, but he will not tell them about us ... or you ... he will die first,' said Ngwenya. The simplicity of his words left no doubt in Sarah's mind that he was right.

Sarah felt tears prick at her eyes. *He will die first.* Her feelings for Wilson were complex ... a strange, haunting, fascination ... his brutal, violent proficiency, coupled with a perfect clarity of innocence. There was an evocative magnetism about him, drawing her in, driving her to want more of him. It was a set of emotions she had never experienced before ... a hypnotic animal attraction that had aroused her in an inexplicably primal way.

Her eyes moved from Ngwenya's to Chiyeka's. Both held her stare with the same conviction. In her heart she felt a deep bond with these men, moved by their abiding loyalty and their belief that she could help them. She shook her head, snapping back into reality.

'Well we better get on then. No time to lose. You need to drive past each of these places. I can go in and ask some questions,' stated Sarah confidently, now all business.

Chiyeka smiled at her, giving Ngwenya a playful punch on the arm. There was a relief felt by all three of them, they were together, the future uncertain but they were together.

The three of them walked back across the carpark to the Land Rover.

'My name is Sarah.'

'I am Cephas, this is Stanley,' replied Ngwenya, the offer of her first name prompted him to give theirs. It seemed to cement their joint resolve.

'Can I see the Cuban?' asked Sarah.

Ngwenya lifted the sack to reveal Casas' bruised face, still smeared with dried blood. Casas recognised her instantly, blinking wildly his body twisting from side to side.

'Well Colonel, it seems that you are in a spot of bother,' said Sarah putting on her cultured English accent.

The flicker of an idea crossed her mind ... Colonel Casas may be useful yet.

*

Selous Scout HQ, Andre Rabie Barracks, Inkomo Barracks, 40km northwest of Salisbury

The phone was ringing in Colonel Reid-Daly's office. His secretary picked it up and immediately put it through to the Colonel who had just arrived to start his day.

'Reid-Daly.'

'John Sutcliffe here Colonel,' said Deputy Director John Sutcliffe,

Branch II, CIO.

'What can I do for you?' The venom in Reid-Daly's voice was unmistakeable.

'Your man Wilson has been picked up by the Zambians.'

There was shocked silence ... a sudden intake of breath.

'When did this happen?'

'Our agents close to the Zambian police reported that he was picked up early this morning. They have him at Lusaka Central Prison. Serious business,' said Sutcliffe.

'Fuck!'

'We don't have much time Colonel ... they will break him.'

'Can we mount a raid to get him out? I can have people ready in a few hours.'

'I don't think we have time. Plus the air force has been given the green light for Operation Gatling to take out the terrorist base at Westlands Farm amongst others. They are going in tomorrow at first light.'

'I can't leave my man there ... we must get him out. Can you help?'

'The Zambians have locked down the whole city. They are literally going house to house searching every white expatriate and every white owned premises. They have roadblocks on every major road into the city. Any white person in the streets is being stopped and searched. Our people cannot move in the city Colonel.'

Sutcliffe was silent on what or who had caused the uproar. The Colonel was equally silent on the fact that his men may have a high-ranking Cuban captive ... and he was due for uplift that very evening ...

'Did they get the whole team or just Wilson?' asked Reid-Daly.

'They only got Wilson from what we can gather.'

'I need to think about this ... '

The Colonel put down the phone. His man was in mortal danger ... he may already be dead.

'Did we get a sitrep from Cat Stevens?' he called his secretary.

'No Colonel, they have missed this morning's schedule.'

'Get me Major Warner ... do it now!'

16

Mazira, **alias Funny Farm 26km west of Lusaka**

Jock McLean and Ian Southwood had a large hand-written foolscap page in front of them. They had decoded the 'most urgent' message just received from their handlers in Salisbury.

Ian had checked the coding twice to make sure they had everything.

Their instructions were to conduct another reconnaissance of Westlands Farm to make sure that it was occupied and gauge the number of terrorists in the camp. They were also told that a Rhodesian agent had been picked up by the Zambians and was being held at Lusaka Central Prison. They were to establish his status … alive or dead and his exact whereabouts in the prison. All travel inside the city was to stop until the police reaction had died down. The most shocking part of the message was that they could expect a police search of their farm at any minute. The police and army were searching all white owned farms within the Lusaka area.

'What are we going to do?' asked Ian Southwood. 'We can't drive through the city to get to Westlands Farm. How can we get close to Central Prison?'

'The first part is to drive the long way round using farm roads and tracks to circle the city from the north, that way we can approach the camp from Chikumbi Siding,' replied Jock.

They carefully packed up the radio and lowered it into its concealed hiding place below the floor, then pushed the heavy wooden workbench over the concrete hatch, replacing all the tins of old paint, grease and oil.

As they walked out into the sun Ian saw a cloud of dust on the approach road to the farmhouse.

'We've got company Jock. You better make yourself scarce,' said Ian pointing at the dust in the distance. Without a backward glance, Jock took his AK and a small pack then moved off into the surrounding mielie fields.

The sound of vehicles carried to Ian as he walked slowly back to the house. Two dark blue Land Rovers followed by six heavy army trucks pulled up a few hundred metres from the farmhouse.

Patricia ran out the back door to meet Ian.

'What do you think they want?' she asked, alarm in her voice.

'Its got to do with the job we did last night and a few other things. They are not onto us, they are searching all the farms. Look, we have discussed this many times, they will likely be after Jock and I. They will probably leave you alone. No one knows about the radio in the shed and the weapons are under the old reservoir.'

'What if they have been tipped off?' asked Patricia, tears in her eyes.

'They won't find anything. Don't worry. Try to stay calm.'

'Oh my God,' said Patricia her face in a bright red flush. She held her hand to her mouth in fright. 'What about the Tokarev pistol, its in my handbag?'

Ian was momentarily stunned. They had all decided that Patricia should carry a pistol because of the dangers of driving the country roads on her own. It came straight out of the arms cache. The cover story was that they had bought it off a Zimbabwean Freedom Fighter for 5 Kwacha, the going rate.

Patricia dashed back into the house, grabbed the pistol out of her handbag and buried it in a large tin of bread flower in the kitchen.

'Do you think the staff have said anything?' asked Patricia, coming back to the kitchen door.

The heavily armed soldiers and police were climbing out of the their vehicles and assembling in a loose echelon.

'No, I don't think so. Jock and I have set tamper devices on all the hiding places. We would know if someone had tried to open them.'

'What will happen if they do find the stuff?' asked Patricia dreading the answer.

'They will torture me then hang me,' said Ian bluntly.

The Southwoods watched as the soldiers went about surrounding the farmhouse. Machine guns were positioned covering each corner of the house. It certainly looked more serious than a routine search.

As they watched, a Land Rover came forward to park next to the back door. A tall black police officer, with obvious senior rank, climbed out.

'You are mister Southwood?' he asked with a very proper English accent, having been trained by Scotland Yard.

'Yes,' replied Ian politely.

'We are searching for illegal weapons. Do you have any?' asked the policeman pointedly. His whole demeanour suggested that he knew that weapons were concealed on the farm.

'I have an old twelve bore shot gun I use for shooting snakes,' said Ian innocently.

'We are looking for weapons of war Mister Southwood, weapons from Rhodesia.'

'We have no such thing. You are welcome to search,' replied Ian waving his arm expansively.

The policeman smirked, 'We will Mister Southwood, we will.'

The couple were both body searched where they stood, then made to sit at the kitchen table as a troop of policemen entered the house.

There was no subtlety in the search, draws were tipped open, cupboards flung aside, the contents strewn on the floor. A man opened the tin of flour looked inside and put it back on the shelf. They went from room to room; until the destruction of the inside of the house was complete, even to the extent of knifing open the upholstered furniture and mattresses.

A ladder was called for and a man went up through the manhole cover into the ceiling. There was a loud yelp as he triggered a large rattrap that Ian had set. He came down with the trap still attached to his finger.

The search then focussed on the tool shed and the other outbuildings. There were old cars that Ian used for spares, tractors, scrap metal, bags of maize, piles of empty sacks and racks of farm tools and implements. Nothing was found.

The soldiers formed into a sweep line then systematically covered the farm, prodding the ground with their bayonets looking for freshly dug soil. The sweepline ended at the bottom of the ploughed fields, next to the old abandoned reservoir.

A soldier, helped by his comrades, scaled the wall to look down at the shallow pool of water at the bottom. It was a hot day so the soldiers were showing signs of fatigue. Some stopped to drink from their water bottles while others sought the shade of the few trees surrounding the reservoir. One sat down on the pipework attached to the rusting pump. The overall enthusiasm for the search was rapidly fading. As more soldiers returned from the surrounding fields they sat down in the shade of the wall of the reservoir, laughing and joking with one another.

The man sitting on the pipe attached to the borehole pump, twisted around to speak to a friend. As he did so the pipe moved with him. There was a loud click as the trigger release of the trapdoor sprung open. The man gave out a yelp as he leapt to his feet as if hit by an electrical shock. He called out in alarm, pointing to the concrete plinth the pump was sitting on, now a few inches clear of the ground.

Crowding around the pump, the soldiers debated what this meant. A sergeant came marching over to demand what the fuss was about. He took one look at the plinth and the pipe and ordered three of his men to lift the protruding pipe. The counter-weighted trapdoor lifted up very easily, sitting up vertically on its hinges. The sergeant gingerly leaned over to look down the hole. He could see a ladder leading to the tunnel below. The men shouted in excitement, jumping up and down, one even shot his rifle into the air.

Hesitant at first, the sergeant called for a torch, handed to him by one of his soldiers. Pointing the torch down the hole, he waved it from side to side to make sure there weren't any booby traps or snakes. He then carefully climbed down the six-foot ladder into the cool dampness below ground. As he crouched down he focused the torch down the low tunnel, illuminating the canvas tarpaulin covering the arms cache. He let out a triumphant shout. Unable to control his excitement he bent down to make his way down the low tunnel.

Thirty kilograms of plastic explosive detonated. The power of the explosion tore through the bottom of the reservoir, lifting it into the air before crashing back to the ground. Those sitting with their backs to the wall were crushed as it collapsed on top of them. The water in the bottom shot upwards in a giant fountain. Chunks of brick and reinforcing sprayed outwards, cutting down the soldiers standing around the pump. The violent explosion tore into the men. Limbs were severed, spewing blood and gore outwards in a gushing sheet.

Ian Southwood heard the powerful explosion. He knew instantly what it was … his stomach turned … it was all over …

*

Lusaka Central Prison, Paul Banda Road, Lusaka

Lusaka Central Prison was less than two minutes drive from Sarah's hotel down Nationalist Road. It was the obvious place to begin their search for Wilson.

Sarah sat in the passenger seat next to Ngwenya with Chiyeka in the back. His boots planted firmly on Casas's face. Sarah had a New York Yankees baseball cap pulled low over her face with a pair of large sunglasses. She had her camera ready on her lap.

Driving slowly so as not to attract attention, Ngwenya pulled left into Paul Banda Road. The sides of the road were lined with street vendors selling everything from transistor radios to live chickens and goats. As they drove past the entrance to the prison, Sarah clicked off a few shots in quick succession. It was a typical colonial designed building reminiscent of the Her Majesty's Prisons in England. Huge green double doors blocked the high vaulted entrance. The outside wall averaged 15m high, higher at the maximum-security section where it was topped with barbed wire. The roof was flat and made of reinforced concrete with floodlights on each corner.

'Pull over to the side of the road, quickly, under that tree,' urged Sarah, pointing where she wanted Ngwenya to go. She clicked off more photos.

'You see that black Mercedes Benz?' called Sarah pointing across the road.

'Yes,' replied Ngwenya, not sure of the importance.

'That belongs to an embassy. Can you see the little stubs for the nation flags?'

'Yes I see it.'

'That means someone from an embassy is visiting the prison. All we need to do is wait to see who it is.' Sarah clicked a few more photos, zooming in on the car.

An army truck was parked next to the prison and a few soldiers in camouflaged uniforms could be seen patrolling the perimeter.

A side door next to the large double doors opened and two men in suits emerged.

'Bull's-eye!' exclaimed Sarah.

Ngwenya could feel the excitement in her voice. As they watched, the two men walked towards the car. The driver jumped out to open the door for them.

As Sarah zoomed in on the faces of the men, what she saw made her suck in a breath.

'What is it?' asked Ngwenya, alarmed at her reaction.

Casas moaned softly, clearly overhearing the conversation.

Chiyeka stomped down hard.

'If I am not mistaken that is the Soviet Ambassador to Zambia and local KGB enforcer, Vassily Solodovnikov … and his tame Rottweiler, Colonel Lev Kononov. I think we can be sure that Wilson is in this prison.'

Before Ngwenya could stop her, Sarah was out the Land Rover and hurrying across the road towards the Mercedes Benz. One of the men climbed into the Mercedes as the driver shut the door behind him then ran around to the other side to help the second man.

The driver returned to open his door. Sarah reached him as he touched the door handle.

'Excuse me,' she said. 'I am looking for the Lusaka Prison. Is that it over there?'

The driver was shocked at the interruption. He was a big man in a dark suit with a military bearing. Not replying to her question, he sought to move the woman out of the way. Sarah pushed between him and the car door, preventing him opening it. She leaned hard against it so as not to be easily dislodged.

She matched the man in height, looking defiantly into his eyes. 'You look Russian. Are you Russian?' asked Sarah, flashing the camera in his face clicking off a photograph.

'Get out of my way!' he demanded loudly with a guttural East European accent.

One of the back doors to the Mercedes opened and a tall man got out.

'What is the meaning of this?' he demanded.

'My goodness, Ambassador Solodovnikov, what a surprise,' squealed Sarah delightedly with a melting smile.

'Do I know you?' asked Solodovnikov.

'We met only briefly at the Canadian Embassy. I am Sarah Burrell with Associated Press. I am doing a story on prisons in the third world. That must be a subject you know a lot about?' said Sarah mischievously, still with her dazzling smile.

'I don't know what you are talking about,' grumbled Solodovnikov. 'Now please leave us to get on with our business.'

'You visiting a friend in prison Mister Ambassador?' asked Sarah disarmingly.

'That is enough! Anatoly drive on!' shouted Solodovnikov climbing back into the backseat.

Before Solodovnikov could pull the door closed, Sarah wedged her body in the way. The driver came towards her, fists clenched, the look of great violence on his face.

'I interviewed a friend of yours Ambassador, what was his name now ... a Cuban. What was it ... I interview so many people ... Casas ... Lieutenant-Colonel Julio Ángel Casas. That's it!'

Solodovnikov literally leapt back out of the car. So did Kononov out the other side. The three men crowded in on Sarah.

'What do you know of this man?' demanded Solodovnikov, now extremely agitated.

Watching from across the road, Ngwenya and Chiyeka saw the altercation. When all three men advanced on Sarah, Ngwenya started the engine, slammed it into gear, then pulled a u-turn across the road. Pulling up behind the Mercedes.

The three Russians were taken off guard, the driver whipped a pistol from his shoulder holster and aimed it in the direction of the Land Rover.

'Don't worry about them, they are my guides,' shouted Sarah.

Ngwenya felt for his Tokarev pistol under the seat.

Sarah did not break stride. 'How is Colonel Casas? Not a very nice man I think. Training freedom fighters isn't he?'

'We have nothing to say to you!' shouted Solodovnikov.

The heated exchange had attracted some of the prison guards, who were making their way across the entrance carpark. Ngwenya looked at Chiyeka, things were rapidly getting out of hand. Casas let out a deep groan. Chiyeka pretended a coughing fit while stamping his feet.

Realising the escalating danger, Sarah changed tack.

'Nice to see you Mister Ambassador, I must go now,' smiled Sarah. 'We must have a drink some time, to talk about our mutual friend Colonel Casas. I hope he remains well.'

With that Sarah jumped back into the Land Rover, Ngwenya slammed it into gear, racing out the dirt carpark, leaving a cloud of dust behind them.

Solodovnikov and Kononov watched the departing Land Rover in disbelief

'She was sending us a message Lev. She knows where Casas is being held. I am sure of it,' said Solodovnikov.

'Should we get the Zambian police to pick her up?' asked Kononov.

'She is part of the Press Corps. Arresting reporters is never a good idea. No, we will wait for her next move.'

*

As the black Mercedes Benz pulled out of the prison grounds two blue police Land Rovers raced up to the gates of the prison. They hooted loudly. The gates opened and they drove in. In the back of the second vehicle lay Ian Southwood, blindfolded, bound and gagged, bleeding from a deep gash on the back of his head from being pistol-whipped.

*

Selous Scout HQ, Andre Rabie Barracks, Inkomo Barracks, 40km northwest of Salisbury

Colonel Ron Reid-Daly and Major Rob Warner had spent two hours debating options for extracting their team in Zambia. Reid-Daly had also called Frank Patch, the Director of the Rhodesian Prison Service to establish whether anyone knew the layout of the Zambian Central Prison. Patch had dispatched one of his retired prison officers, Ross Jackson, under police escort to the Selous Scouts HQ. He had with him a roll of old blueprints of the prison. Jackson had been a prison officer in Lusaka during Federation days.

As soon as he arrived on the base Jackson, a man well into his sixties, was ushered into the Operations Room where the Colonel, Rob Warner and another officer were waiting.

Reid-Daly perfunctorily greeted the retired prison officer, before immediately getting down to business.

'Where would the Zambians hold a prisoner detained for serious security offences?' asked the Colonel gruffly.

Jackson looked around the room in amazement; he had been gardening in his vegetable patch at his home in Highlands when two police Peugeot 404 B-cars had arrived. They didn't even give him time to change. He was still dressed in his gardening shirt and shorts, his old torn floppy hat held in his hands.

'Well, I would say almost certainly at Lusaka Central Prison,' said the older man thoughtfully. Impressed at being in such auspicious company. 'I worked at the prison between 1958 and 1964 ... those were the days ... we ran the place like a well oiled machine.'

Warner unrolled the blue prints on the map table holding the corners down with souvenir AK magazines.

'Does this ring a bell?' Warner asked Jackson.

The man got to his feet, unfolded his glasses and studied the plans. He twisted them around with the main entrance at the bottom of the page. Then, slowly at first, he began to point out the names and functions of each of the buildings. Warner carefully wrote each description onto the blue prints. Warner also produced a more recent aerial photograph of the prison. The layout had not changed much except for a few additional outbuildings in the prison compound.

'Can you give us an idea of the daily routine at the prison?' asked Warner, once all the buildings and rooms had been identified.

'Things may have changed of course, but prisons change their routine very rarely,' replied Jackson. 'It was a long time ago ... you are testing my memory ... we locked up at 5 o'clock at night and by 6 o'clock the night routine had started. The key to the main gate was retained by the night duty officer who sleeps in the prison here,' explained Jackson pointing to a room just off the main courtyard, next to the entrance.

'Carry on,' urged Reid-Daly trying to chivvy the man along.

'After the cells were locked up, the keys were put in a safe in the administration office ... or was it the superintendent's office,' Jackson faltered, trying hard to remember. 'No, I think it was the superintendent's office. The night duty officer did not have a key to the safe, that was always kept by a day duty officer ... for obvious reasons.'

'What about prison guards?' asked Warner.

'Well ... one on the main gate, inside of course, two always on the maximum security cells, here and here,' pointed Jackson. Warner marked the spots with a red NeoMagic felt-tipped pen. 'A prison NCO and two guards walk beats in the prison at night. On the walls four guards armed with shotguns. A guard, also with a shotgun, is locked in the watchtower. The two alarm sirens are in the watchtower, one operated by electricity the other with a manual crank handle.'

There was a knock on the door.

'Yes?' shouted Reid-Daly impatiently.

'Urgent call for you Colonel,' said his secretary.

'Put it through here,' replied Reid-Daly, walking towards the phone on a desk in the corner. The phone rang once, Reid-Daly lifted the receiver, it was John Sutcliffe from the CIO.

'Hold on for a second John ... Mister Jackson, thank you very much for your help today. I don't have to tell you that what has been discussed is top secret.' The Colonel waved for Jackson to be ushered out of the room.

'Yes John?'

'We are now in the same boat, one of my people has been picked up. We think he is being held at Lusaka Central as well,' replied Sutcliffe.

'So what do you have in mind?' asked Reid-Daly.

'Well the air force tell me that you have a Cheetah going out on a clandestine operation tonight ... the word is to Lusaka ... We may have to use it for an attack on the prison instead of what you had planned,' stated Sutcliffe.

Reid-Daly hesitated, it never failed to amaze him that the CIO had fingers in every pie. He was now caught in a quandary ... it was time to come clean.

'John, my people have snatched a senior Cuban official. We believe that they still have him. We are due to pick them up at last light this evening at a pre-arranged RV south of Lusaka.'

There was silence on the other side of the line. Sutcliffe was contemplating throwing a tantrum and seeking the Colonel's instant cashiering, court martial ... *he was a bloody menace!*

'Well it seems we have to kill three birds with one stone instead of just two,' replied Sutcliffe resignedly. 'Are your men up to this type of mission or should we call in the SAS?'

'Bullshit ... we will deal with this. I have a team standing by. We will need two helicopters plus a bit of heavy air support if the shit hits the fan,' replied Reid-Daly ... never keen on deferring to the SAS.

'Air support is going to be a problem ... the Blue Jobs are going after Westlands Farm tomorrow morning,' added Sutcliffe. 'The Cheetahs can be released because no ground forces are being used in the attack, it is a pure air operation.'

'Well, we will just have to make do. I will phone you back in an hour or two to update you on the plan.'

Reid-Daly replaced the receiver.

'I am the only officer that can do this job Boss. I am here, I am briefed and I have a team of eight ready to go. There is no time left to brief anyone else,' urged Rob Warner.

The thought of losing one of his best, if not his very best officer, in what was a virtual suicide mission gave Reid-Daly pause for thought. He looked into the eyes of his most trusted man, seeing the fierce determination written there.

'Carry on ...'

*

Mazira, alias Funny Farm, 26km west of Lusaka

Jock Mclean, sat next to the radio that he had rigged up in the tool shed opposite the farmhouse. He had stayed hidden in the mielie fields, easily avoiding the half-hearted search by the Zambian soldiers. He had watched Ian being carted away after the booby-trapped arms cache had killed the best part of a platoon of Zambian soldiers. The Zambians had left the farm after they had caught their man. No one was keen to stay behind in case more booby-traps lay hidden.

Patricia was left helplessly crying in the courtyard as the police and army vehicles pulled out. She was unaware that Jock had crept out of the bush to make his urgent radio report.

Jock knew they would be back, and this time, would raze the farm to the ground. After using Patricia as a shield against other booby traps, she would also be arrested. Two soldiers had been left at the farm gate to prevent anyone entering or leaving. He estimated only an hour or two at most before the return of the Zambian troops.

Wrapping an AK in a sack together with an RPG and three projectiles, Jock had packed the VW Beetle with whatever ammunition and explosives he had left. The vehicle was hidden from view behind the shed. He was determined to try to get Ian out of jail ... no matter what. If he didn't try, Ian was done for.

The radio blinked as the final message came through from Bright

Lights. He wrote down the code as quickly as he could, then sent the flash acknowledgement.

Jock read the decoded message twice. There was no doubt that he was surprised the CIO had reacted so quickly. The rescue mission was set for next morning, the exact time still uncertain. He was to lend 'support', then execute his own exit plan to fly back to the UK and wait for further instructions.

The instructions regarding his 'support' were absent. Jock interpreted this as 'diversion'. Instructions with reference to Patricia were to get her out.

Instead of putting the radio back into its hiding place, Jock packed it up together with the other kit into the back of the VW. He had a stash of US dollars for emergencies, he folded these into his button up shirt pocket.

As he looked out the shed window, Jock could see Patricia standing at the back door. The staff had all run away for fear of being interrogated by the police. She was completely alone. He made up his mind.

Using the side of the building as cover Jock dashed across the short distance to the side of the house. Lifting himself up, he climbed in through an open window. Uncertain as to whether the Zambians had left a guard in the house, Jock had his Tokarev pistol at the ready. He edged his way down the passage towards the kitchen and dining room. The highly polished parquet flooring added to the risk that his rubber-soled boots would squeak.

As he pushed his head around the corner to look into the lounge, Patricia walked into the room. She saw him, her hands flying to her mouth, her eyes wide with fright, then pointing towards the lounge.

Jock held his finger to his lips, indicating for her to go back into the kitchen. Bending down he lifted his khaki trousers to extract his hunting knife from a scabbard strapped to his calf.

The guard was sitting in an easy chair his rifle across his lap, looking out of the front door over the fields beyond.

'Would you like a cup of tea?' called Patricia from the kitchen.

Jock's heart missed a beat as she called out, reassessing his plan.

Patricia came back into the room and asked the man again. He thanked her politely and accepted the offer.

In a few moments Patricia was back carrying a tray with a teapot and teacup on it.

'I will put it on the veranda if you like,' she said, her voice steady and unhurried.

The man got up from where he was sitting and followed Patricia towards the front door.

Jock moved with lightning speed. He came across the room as a raging bull. The man had absolutely no chance. Jock took him in the small of his back, throwing in his powerful shoulder, driving him forwards into the doorframe at tremendous force. The impact was vicious, smashing the man's face hard into the unyielding steel doorframe. The breath forced out of his lungs, he released the rifle to clatter to the floor.

Before the man had any chance of recovery, Jock yanked his head back, exposed his throat, then sliced it open to the bone. Blood spurted forward over the wall and onto the veranda. Patricia dropped the tray with a loud crash, in total shock at the swiftness and finality of Jock's violence. Dragging the man onto the veranda to bleed out, Jock waved for Patricia to come out of the house.

Patricia was visibly shaking, her arms folded in front of her.

'Pat, we have to get out of here now, you must come with me,' said Jock urgently. Tilting his head towards the dead man on the veranda he continued, 'that has put paid to any thought of you staying.'

Patricia was crying now. Deep sobs wracked her chest, tears running down her cheeks unable to speak. Her whole life had come crashing down. All she and Ian had worked for had come to an end. They always knew there were risks, but the sudden realisation of a catastrophic disaster was something different.

'Pat, I received a signal, the Rhodesians are coming for Ian tomorrow. I have been told to execute the exit plan, you must come with me. We need to go now Pat,' said Jock as gently but forcefully as he could.

She looked up at him, her eyes swollen red from crying.

'I have my emergency bag packed. I have my false passports ... I was going to shoot the guard with the Tokarev. I couldn't, my hands were shaking so much ... I was so worried about Ian ... I couldn't think what to do,' stuttered Patricia. 'I didn't know what had happened to you Jock ... it has been terrifying ... I just can't think anymore.'

'Its okay Pat, get your things, come with me. I have the Volksie packed out the back of the shed.'

She gathered her things from a concealed compartment under the bath and they made their way out of the kitchen door. She retrieved the Tokarev from the flour container, wiped it off and stuck it into her handbag.

Jock carried Patricia's bag to the VW and they both got in.

'Pat, when we get to the gate, we will have to kill the two guards.

Don't worry, I will handle it. You must have your pistol ready just in case.'

She nodded, taking out the Tokarev and placing it in her lap. Jock had a folding butt AKM across his knees.

Jock started the engine and they made their way slowly towards the main gate. The guards were lounging out of the hot sun under a large tree at the side of the road. Surprised to see the VW approaching they scrambled to their feet and stood out in the road.

'Bend down Pat,' instructed Jock.

Stopping the VW forty metres short of where the soldiers were standing, Jock stuck his head out the window.

'I am from Livingston Farm, next door, I am looking for Mister Southwood, do you know where he is?'

One of the soldiers waved for the VW to come closer. Jock stayed where he was, his foot just above the accelerator.

The soldiers lifted their rifles, using them to wave Jock forward. Jock inched ahead slowly, the VW in first gear.

The soldiers were now calling out waving at him impatiently. The one on the left came marching down the road waving his AK expansively, shouting at the top of his voice.

Jock hit the accelerator. The wheels spun slightly in the soft sand, but the old VW jumped forward. Aiming the nose directly at the soldier, Jock lifted the AKM with his free hand. The soldier tried to jump out the way, but was too slow. Jock hit him square with the front of the bonnet, his head thrown forward to smash hard against the windscreen, his rifle flying free. Swerving further to the left, in one motion, Jock lifted the AKM and shot the other soldier in the chest.

His foot flat on the accelerator, Jock raced past the dead man towards the main Lusaka / Mumbwa Road. They had no sooner pulled out onto the tar road, than a convoy of army trucks approached, all turned off the main road in the direction of Mazira Farm.

For the first time in his life Jock Mclean did not have a clear picture in his mind of what his next move was to be …

17

Lusaka Central Prison, Paul Banda Road, Lusaka

After Keith Wilson's brief initial questioning, the two Russians had left. Wilson's shoes had been removed, he was stripped naked and cavity searched. Handcuffs were clamped on so hard behind his back that the blood couldn't flow. Two Zambian soldiers with AKs, bayonets fixed, frog marched him naked down a dark, dirty corridor; then through a heavy steel door and a barred gate to be thrown into the darkness of a stinking concrete cell. The door slammed behind him with the loud sickening sound of the key in the padlock.

He could hear shouting in the corridor outside with the loud echoing of more doors being banged shut. As he looked around him, Wilson could see the walls of the gloomy cell were smeared with human filth. The oppressive smell was nauseating. Each laboured breath seemed to assault his senses.

Light came through a small barred recessed window high up on one wall. Hoards of insects were there, feasting on the excrement. Cockroaches crawled over his feet while mosquitos attacked in swarms. With his hands so tightly bound behind him he was defenceless as his skin was turned into a mass of angry red bumps and bites.

Still breathing in short sharp gulps to ease the pain in his chest, Wilson closed his eyes. The sound of mosquitos buzzed in his ears, that infuriating sound, made worse by knowing they could bite him with impunity. He tried to recall his training, *calm yourself mentally and concentrate on surviving.*

A picture of Sarah swam into his mind, *cling to something positive … fix it in your mind … think of Sarah.* Eyes tightly shut he began to methodically build a picture of the internal layout of the jail, making a mental note of the passages he had seen. The faint bustle of street noise filtered in from outside.

How long will I have to wait?

A scream broke the silence, an urgent desperate scream, muffled by the thick walls … a blood-curdling sound. The voice was calling out to stop, begging for mercy… then fading away. Someone was shouting abuse in the local language.

Wilson was not a man given to fear. He handled fear on his own terms but in that moment he felt fear, it crept up his spine as if struck by a jet of ice-cold water. Sweat poured down his face into his eyes making them burn with irritation … still the infernal buzzing …

relentless biting, as if he was being eaten alive.

A sound of a heavy door opening carried into the cell, hobnailed boots beat on the concrete floor. The key was thrust in the door to the cell, then flung open. Two armed guards stepped forward then grabbed him by the arms. Out in the passage, Wilson could see two neatly dressed policemen and more soldiers. Another naked white man, bent over double with a sack over his head, was being pushed down the passage at the end of a round, pig-sticker AK bayonet. Each thrust opened another puncture wound that spurted blood as the man squealed in pain. Blood ran down his torso streaking over his legs leaving bloody footprints behind him. The man was pushed past Wilson into the cell he had just left.

Held between the two soldiers, Wilson was manhandled down the corridor into a much larger room. A single wooden government-issue chair and two desks, set a metre apart, were the only furniture. Three bare light bulbs hung from the vaulted ceiling, their milky light reflected off the pools of dried blood on the concrete floor. Bloody handprints and dirty smears covered the walls, all pervaded by the same oppressive stink of tightly packed human bodies. The murmur of hundreds of voices carried through the high-set windows from the exercise yard outside.

A steel meat hook hung from the ceiling on a heavy chain attached to a pulley. The two soldiers tied a wire cable to his ankles. Pulling down the meat hook, they slipped it through the cable binding Wilson's feet. Both soldiers then hung on the pulley, yanking Wilson's feet out from under him, throwing him hard onto the concrete floor. The pain in his chest thrust as a red-hot poker, taking his breath away … the pain was so intense, his chest so tight, that he could not cry out.

Hanging with his head two feet off the floor, Wilson closed his eyes as tightly as he could … *Sarah*.

The smiling policeman in immaculate uniform walked into the room, taking a seat at one of the tables. All Wilson could see were his highly polished shoes. The man introduced himself again as Inspector R. K. Kabamba of the Zambian Police, but added 'Special Branch'.

The interrogation began predictably at first, the policeman asked a number of questions about the Selous Scouts. Wilson denied all knowledge sticking to his cover story.

'Meesta Wilson,' said Inspector Kabamba, 'you must understand that to withhold vital information from us is fruitless. You are alone, nobody will come for you, if you tell us what we want to know then you will not suffer any more pain.'

'I am in great pain already,' whispered Wilson with all the breath he could muster. 'I must have medical assistance.'

Blood from his bleeding ankles trickled done his legs, over his torso to drip off his chin. Hanging upside down Wilson's head felt about to burst, incessant pounding in his ears.

'You MUST have nothing Meesta Wilson. You have killed many people here in Zambia … innocent people … why should we show you any mercy?'

Kabamba signalled to the soldiers to place a large bucket of foul water below Wilson's head. They both returned to the ropes attached to the pulleys lowering his head into it. As his head submerged, someone hit Wilson in the small of the back with a heavy iron rod. The effect was to open his mouth, sucking a gulp of foetid water up into his mouth. His lungs contracted trying to suck more air, instead water rushed up into his throat. In a desperate thrust with his head, Wilson tried to knock over the bucket of water but it merely slipped backwards and forwards on the slippery floor.

Wilson began to wheeze, the pressure in his head building to dangerous levels, he could feel his brain shutting down close to blacking out.

His head came clear of the bucket, water poured out of his mouth and throat, he coughed convulsively spitting and vomiting simultaneously. The effect of near-drowning put Wilson's body into a spasm, he began to shake uncontrollably. Pain in his head felt like it would split open, now far worse than his chest.

Waiting for Wilson to recover, Inspector Kabamba spoke casually to the two soldiers, making a joke in the local Tonga language. One of the guards pissed into the bucket.

'Are you ready to talk to me now Meesta Wilson?' asked Kabamba, 'this can go on all day.'

Wilson's mind was already screaming to make it stop; he needed to buy some time.

'My people have the Cuban Colonel, he is still in Lusaka, they will kill him unless you release me,' wheezed Wilson.

'So, you have the Cuban? Well that is a good start. Where is he being held?'

'I will only tell the Russians, bring them here and I will tell them.'

'No you will tell me.'

Kabamba signalled the two guards and Wilson's head was again dropped into the bucket. This time he held his breath and braced for the strike with the iron rod. It came harder this time, Wilson could feel the nerves in his legs and arms tingle from the impact on his spine.

He knew then that Inspector Kabamba could not afford to kill him. Not yet ...

Sarah ...

*

Jock Mclean and Patricia Southwood, drove slowly down Paul Banda Road outside Lusaka Central Prison. Jock was familiar with the prison as he and Ian had it as one of their optional spreading-shit-and-derision targets. They had once held visions of releasing the hundreds of political prisoners kept there.

It was late afternoon, with the shadows thrown by the tree-lined street beginning to lengthen. As they drove past, a black Mercedes Benz with darkened windows pulled up outside the huge green double doors of the main gate.

'Ian is getting some important visitors,' commented Jock to Patricia.

She remained silent, huddled in the passenger seat, so traumatised that she could not speak.

From Jock's previous reconnaissance he knew that prison staff and their families occupied most of the houses in the neighbouring streets. On the south side of the prison were cultivated fields used for growing fruit and vegetables for the inmates and the prison staff. Some of the fields lay fallow, providing a perfect LZ for helicopters. *That would be the point when the attack will go in.* The problem was that the main gate was on the north side, giving the attackers at least 200m of open ground exposed to the machine gun and searchlight in the watchtower. He and Ian had previously discussed how much explosive was needed to blow through the perimeter walls. In their estimation it was much more than two men could carry.

On the eastern side of the main prison buildings was a 3,000sqm walled courtyard used for exercise. As the prison was so full, the courtyard also housed prisoners, living in the open, exposed to the elements. It was possible, they had thought, to get a helicopter into the courtyard but it would have been exposed to the armed guards in the main watchtower and the watchtowers on the corners of the exercise yard.

If Jock was going to create a diversion it had to be on the north side of the prison to draw attention away from the LZ.

'Lets go and get some tea at the Ridgeway,' said Jock to Patricia. 'Don't worry, only a few more hours. We'll get him out.'

*

'We are going to have to trade this Cuban for Wilson's release,' said Sarah Burrell to Cephas Ngwenya.

Ngwenya sat silently behind the wheel of the Land Rover, parked under a tree in Independence Avenue. He was way out of his depth, a bush fighter and saboteur, comfortable in the role of infiltrating enemy gangs, not the cloak and dagger of a spy. He had relied on Wilson's lead, happy to follow his instructions, but he was now filled with uncertainty. This white woman was beyond his comprehension.

The plan was always to deliver the Cuban to the RV point with the helicopters to be uplifted back to Rhodesia.

Nodding his understanding, Ngwenya was unsure of what he could contribute to such a scheme ... *Wilson trusted this woman.* Delivering the Cuban to the RV meant certain death for Wilson.

We can always get another Cuban ...

Sarah was deep in thought, her mind racing through the options as she sat in the passenger seat. Chiyeka sat silently in the back alone with his thoughts, but equally determined to try to free his leader. Casas was silent after being rammed by Chiyeka's fist every time he moaned.

The thought crossed Sarah's mind that she could go to the American Embassy, kick up a fuss, accuse the Russians of kidnapping, send a story to New York exposing the Cubans and Soviets in Zambia. There was no time for any of that; they would kill Wilson without any hesitation ... no, she had to do this on her own.

'We have to get the Russians to agree to get Wilson delivered to their embassy. We can make the exchange outside the gates ... then you can escape with him into the bush, try to get back across the border,' whispered Sarah, working through the options in her mind.

'What would stop them telling the Zambians, we would never get out of Lusaka alive?' replied Ngwenya. 'Maybe we should go to a place well outside of the city, where we can be sure that no soldiers are waiting.'

Sarah nodded, turning to look at Ngwenya. He was like nobody she had ever met, quietly spoken, a silent and determined killer and yet there was a contradictory gentleness and compassion about him. His devotion to Wilson was obvious, but he was no fanatic. His respect and loyalty was personal, not borne out of some military discipline or *esprit de corps*. In many ways Cephas Ngwenya was not military at all, just a man doing his personal duty for those he respected and trusted. He did not contemplate the broader political picture. To him it was pure loyalty and dedication to a man he had come to love as a friend … as a brother … caught up in all the ambiguities of war.

While they had never discussed it in any meaningful way, Ngwenya knew that Stanley Chiyeka felt exactly the same way that he did. They had to make every effort to get Wilson out before the Zambians killed him … or die trying.

'So what do you suggest?' asked Sarah earnestly.

'We must get to the south of the Kafue River, from there we can walk to the Zambezi.' This would be 83km over some of the most rugged terrain in Zambia.

'Okay, so we tell the Russians that we will meet them on the other side of the Kafue River,' agreed Sarah.

'To the south of the River, only a short way, is the intersection with the road to Mazabuka … that is where we must meet the Russians,' said Ngwenya, it was an area he knew well from previous missions to Zambia. There were good vantage points where they could detect any attempt by the Russians or Zambians to ambush them.

'Right, so we are decided. Drive me to the Soviet Embassy so I can inform them of the plan, ' replied Sarah, flashing her smile.

The two Selous Scouts merely nodded their heads in agreement, Ngwenya pulled out onto the road for the short drive to the embassy.

Lusaka Central Prison and surrounding streets

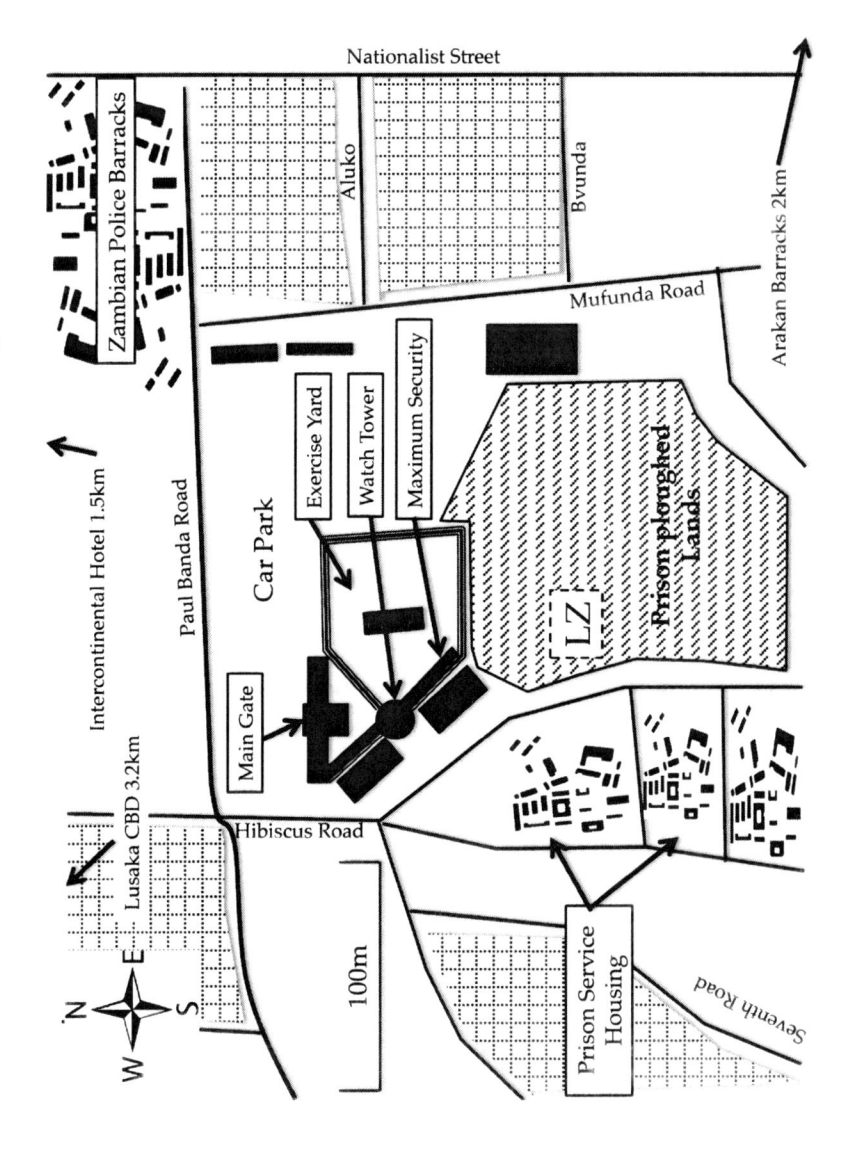

*

Soviet Embassy, Pandit Nehru Road, Ridgeway, Lusaka

Inspector Kabamba of the Zambian Special Branch had placed his call to the Soviet Embassy informing them that his captive had confessed to holding the missing Cuban Colonel.

Comrade Ambassador Vassily Solodovnikov and Colonel Lev Kononov sat in the Ambassador's office contemplating their next move. They knew that the loss of Comrade Lieutenant-Colonel Julio Ángel Casas to the Rhodesians would set back plans for the invasion of Rhodesia and would require a detailed tactical review. The delay could cost the liberation struggle another year. They were not particularly concerned about whether Colonel Casas remained alive, what they wanted to avoid was him having the chance to speak. Forcing the Rhodesian infiltrators to kill him was one of their preferred options ... as long as Casas never faces interrogation.

The phone rang on the Ambassador's desk. Solodovnikov picked it up.

'*Da?*'

He listened for a brief moment.

'Escort her to my office.' He turned to Kononov, 'It appears we have an unexpected visitor. The American reporter.'

There was a gentle knock on the door and Sarah Burrell was waved into the office. Her unkempt long hair hung dankly from beneath the baseball cap. Her white short-sleeved shirt was creased with perspiration marks under the arms. Her face showed no signs of makeup and she looked tired.

There were no pleasantries exchanged on either side.

'You have one of my people?' asked Solodovnikov softly.

'Yes.'

'Where is he?'

'I want Keith Wilson to be released.'

'I have no power over the Zambian authorities.'

'Bullshit ... you own the Zambian authorities.'

Vassily Solodovnikov could not help himself, he smiled at this woman's temerity. Sarah held him in a defiant, unflinching gaze.

'You are playing a dangerous game for a newspaper reporter.' A slightly sinister edge had entered Solodovnikov's voice.

'Look, I have your Cuban Colonel. If you want him back, you give me Keith Wilson and safe passage to the border.'

'You overestimate my influence Miss Burrell,' smiled Solodovnikov, now quite enamoured with the sheer determination of this woman. He was quite certain, that if needs be, she would kill Casas herself. There was no doubt about that in his mind. He detected that Wilson meant a great deal to her, making her much more dangerous.

Sarah stepped forward to within only a few feet of where Solodovnikov stood next to his desk. Kononov made to get up but the Ambassador waved for him to stay seated.

She lifted the baseball cap off her head, brushing her hair away from her face with her free hand. She fixed him with a deeply focused gaze as if a lioness stalking prey.

'Let me be clear Mr Ambassador. We will pump your Cuban for every bit of information on your activities here in Africa until he has no blood left in his body. His body will then be delivered to your gate in pieces big enough to fit in a shopping bag. We will then write this up in a series of articles in the New York Times that will expose you for what you really are, a communist thug exploiting the people of Africa to your own ends … your personal reputation will be destroyed to such an extent that you will be recalled to Moscow in disgrace, your career will be over. The choice is yours … Comrade.'

Sarah spat the word 'comrade' at Solodovnikov with such venom that it was made to sound the worst possible insult.

Solodovnikov's face clouded in anger, he was unaccustomed to threats, especially delivered by a woman. He was visibly shaking with anger, his fists clenched tightly at his sides, his lower lip quivered as he struggled to regain his composure. Kononov got to his feet, uncertainty flashed across his face as he realised that his boss was about to attack this woman physically.

'How dare you speak to the Ambassador like that,' bellowed the old Colonel, trying to create a distraction.

Solodovnikov lifted his arm towards Kononov, showing that he was attempting to regain control, bowing his head slightly as he re-gathered his thoughts.

Sarah did not flinch, preparing to defend herself.

'Where do you want to meet to make the exchange?' asked Solodovnikov, his voice in a cracked whisper.

'The intersection with Mazabuka road south of the Kafue River Bridge … seven am tomorrow.'

'So be it,' replied Solodovnikov, his head still bowed.

'Make sure you come alone in one of your diplomatic cars, no soldiers and no police.'

'Yes,' hissed the Ambassador.

Sarah turned towards the door.

'Miss Burrell,' called Solodovnikov.

She stopped to face him.

'My advice to you … after this is all over, is to go back to your homeland and never return. I am not a man given to idle threats, but if our paths cross again the outcome for you will be of the worst possible kind.'

'Fuck You!' yelled Sarah back at him, her face pure defiance. She opened the door to the office, walked out, then slammed it shut behind her, so hard that the umbrella hanging on the back fell to the tiled floor with a clatter.

The two men watched her go … dumbfounded.

18

Selous Scout Training Base, Wafa Wafa Kariba

The camp, known as Wafa Wafa, takes its name from the Shona words *Wafa Wasara,* loosely translated meaning 'those who die, die - those who stay behind, stay behind[84]'. As depicted by its name, it was dry and hostile with dangerous animals including lions, elephants, buffalo, leopards, crocodiles and hippos while poisonous snakes infested the surrounding bush. The area where the Selous Scouts were trained was about an hour's drive, on very rough dirt roads, south of Kariba. It consisted of a collection of grass-roofed huts, an assault course and very little else. A few blackened rocks designated the dining room. Most food was consumed raw.

This was the place that struck fear and dread in the hearts of those recruits chosen to go through the selection course. Only 15% ever survived to wear the distinctive brown beret with silver osprey badge.

Parked on the dusty rifle range twelve hundred metres due east of the camp were two Cheetah helicopters[85]. The three-man crews and the eight Selous Scouts chosen for the mission stood under a tree next to the rifle range. The sun was low on the westerly horizon giving them only a few more minutes for the final briefing.

Major Rob Warner had assembled his assault team with the helicopter aircrew in a semi-circle in front of him. Warner was briefing the team on two missions, the first being the uplift of the Cuban captive at the predetermined LZ south of Lusaka, while the second was the rescue mission for Keith Wilson in Lusaka Central Prison. The short distance for Plan A meant the helicopters could return to refuel before embarking on Plan B.

Each member of the team had an aerial photograph of the Plan A LZ located in abandoned fields only a few hundred metres north of

---

84 Also 'I am Dead, I am Dead. Danger, Danger'.
85 The story of how Rhodesia got the 11 Bells is interesting. One unsubstantiated account claims that they were a gift from the Israelis. The story goes that the Selous Scouts had captured a CT that had been trained in Libya. The CT claimed one of his instructors was Jamal Al-Gashey one of the infamous Black September terrorist leaders who master minded the murders of the Israeli Olympic team in Munich in 1976. This information was then relayed to the Israelis who sent their agents to Rhodesia. Under interrogation the CT was able to give them the location of the terror training camp in Libya and a detailed layout of the camp. Within 24 hours the Israelis had launched a covert operation into Libya using submarine launched special forces. The Israelis however missed the target by 10 minutes. As a sign of good faith they gave Rhodesia the Hueys by way of thanks.

the Lusaka - Chirundu Road. The pilots and co-pilots of the Cheetahs had maps marked with the route in and out of Zambia.

The distance from Wafa Wafa to the LZ was 46.4 nautical miles (85.9km) as the crow flies. Estimated flying time was thirty minutes give or take a few seconds. The route was north along the Zambezi River then west following the main road to the LZ. As Rob Warner described it, 'just around the corner.'

Plan A was simple: fly along the main road to Lusaka at 1,000ft AGL soon after last light. Locate the LZ, wait for the signal from the ground, land, collect the package and then back to Rhodesia. Only one helicopter was to land while the other provided cover in case any Zambian military vehicles appeared on the road. Both had twin-mounted .303 Brownings at the left hand door.

Rob Warner finished his briefing then asked for questions. There weren't any.

The Selous Scout team were indistinguishable, the bearded white soldiers were covered in thick camo-cream, all wore Rhodesian camo uniforms, Soviet issue webbing, kidney pouches and light pack. This was a fast in and fast out operation. All carried AKs except the gunners in each stick carrying RPD machineguns.

Warner suggested a quick brew of tea before take off. He then asked his signaller on the 'big-means' to inform Andre Rabie Barracks that all was in order and on schedule.

Just as the sun hit the horizon, with its magnificent reds oranges and purples reflecting off the deep blue of the Kariba waters, the helicopters took off. They headed out over the lake in line astern then turned right onto a bearing of 355°.

The pilot in the right hand seat of the lead Cheetah, Air Lieutenant Peter McNeil, blinked his eyes to adjust his night vision. The co-pilot, Air Sub Lt 'Dicky' Bird sat impassively next to him with a map open on his lap. Sam Jacobs, the choppertech, requested to test his guns. McNeil agreed; the fuselage vibrated as .303 tracer punched out into the fading light.

Only a thin arc of retreating light on the horizon appeared in front of him. To the East, on the right, the horizon was already dark. Flying at 80 knots he did not waste time climbing to their planned altitude for night flying. He held the helicopter steady at 1,000ft AGL using a map on his lap and dead reckoning navigation. McNeil always felt a little strange reflecting on the use of the words 'dead reckoning'. He figured it got that name because if you reckoned wrong, you would be dead.

'Red One, Red Leader do you copy?' McNeil called the pilot in the number two Cheetah.

'Red One copied,'

'Roger, 5 minutes to the turn.'

The lead helicopter had a single red running light on the top of the rear vertical fin and rudder.

The helicopters were flying north along the Zambezi River gorge towards their turning point at the bridge at Chirundu. McNeil reflected on how rare it was to fly at night. Flying time and heading; *when the time runs out, start looking around and hope you are somewhere close to where you wanted to be.* Even scarier, he did not have the luxury of accurately plotting the heading and distance. There was no information about winds, so no way to factor in wind drift corrections, or to confirm an accurate ground speed. In the end he just looked at his map and guessed, estimated a heading and counted grid squares. The Rhodesian pilots counted on being lucky while flying at night.

McNeil blinked again, fighting the butterflies in his stomach, trained to ignore the disorientation he was feeling. *Trust your instruments. The instruments do not lie to you. Your 'seat of the pants' sensations will.*

As darkness fell, colours quickly faded into shades of grey. Steep valleys broke the terrain they were flying over with hills rising to over 1,000m. The LZ was perilously close to a range of hills at 200m above the ground.

McNeil banked tightly to turn onto heading 271° as they flew over the brightly lit bridge at Chirundu. He squinted into the distance trying to pick up landmarks, still inbound at 1,000ft AGL. A car's headlights on the road below gave him reassurance. The trees below were an unbroken sea of black. There was no clearly discernable horizon just a fuzzy band that transitioned from the blackness of the ground to something a little less black for the sky. There was no moon. Only a few of the brightest stars were visible in the hazy sky above.

A north-south river was a waypoint, with a smaller tributary running east-west. The surface of the water was smooth as a mirror. He could just barely distinguish the textural difference between the treetops and the rivers. His destination was due west from the confluence of the rivers, 6km away.

McNeil dialled in the radio frequency for the Selous Scout call-sign at the LZ, and hit the intercom. Warner, wearing a set of earphones, was sitting on the bench seat immediately behind him.

'Sierra Two Zero, this is Red Leader, do you copy?'

The radio hissed loudly in his helmet earpiece.

'Sierra Two Zero, this is Red Leader, do you copy?'

There was no reply on the radio as Red Leader called again. They had anticipated that the men on the ground may not be able to make radio contact.

McNeil stuck to the south side of the road at 70 knots, still at 1,000ft AGL. He knew the road below was far from straight, twisting and turning through the broken hills. McNeil slowed down to 50 knots. All eyes in the helicopter scanned the bush for the light of a green flare.

A platoon of Zambian military had stopped on the side of the road to buy beer from a street vendor in a roadside village. The sound of the approaching helicopter carried easily on the early evening breeze. They knew that the approaching helicopters were not Zambian as theirs were all unserviceable.

Red tracer lifted from the side of the road. Warner saw it coming. He stretched to tap the pilot on the helmet to warn him. Samuel Jacobs, the choppertech facing the opposite side, was unsighted. McNeil turned to look at Warner, pointing towards the ground. The first tracer rounds cracked past the helicopter. More tracer lifted into the sky … rising slowly at first, then shot past in streaks of light.

The rounds hitting the side of the fuselage sounded like banging with a hammer. Dicky Bird, in the left hand seat, slumped over as a round entered the fuselage below his feet directly into his unprotected chest.

McNeil rolled the helicopter over on its side, sucked the cyclic into his stomach to spin the helicopter on her axis, pulling lots of pitch to stay out of the hillside. The helicopter came around in a 5g left hand turn, blade bounce, thrashing at the air.

He glanced to his left, Bird was hanging in his harness … 'Dicky?'

There was no answer.

A 12.7mm round severed the tail boom at the synchronized elevator. This caused the aircraft to lose balance and to nose down. As they were at low-level, McNeil used what flight control he had left to aim towards the road. Running out of altitude and flight control, the aircraft nose and underside hit an unseen hut in a village at the side of the road. The straw roof and mud walls reduced the impact. Skids crumpled as the aircraft crashed through the hut, impacting the ground hard with the engine still at full power, the blades ripping round and round throwing choking dust and debris into the cabin.

McNeil was thrown violently against his harness but managed to hit the kill switch for the engine. Those in the back were tossed about against the roof of the helicopter; some thrown out into the ruins of the hut. One died instantly from a broken neck. Sam Jacobs' face had been smashed against his guns knocking him senseless with blood pumping from his face, nose and ears.

The Zambian troops screamed with excitement as they saw the helicopter go down. They rushed across the road in the direction of the crash, some 1,000m away.

The second Cheetah pulled into a tight orbit above the crash, the door gunner firing towards the muzzle flashes from the Zambian SLRs.

The pilot in Red 1 knew he needed to get his men on the ground. He pulled pitch as he descended toward the treetops. The helicopter nosed over and dropped down towards the village. Red 1 couldn't see an LZ, so applied power to pick up airspeed to go back around. Clattering in orbit, he came in from a different direction, aiming at the centre of the village clearing where there appeared to be room.

WHOP, WHOP … WHOP

Terrified Zambian villagers rushed out of their huts running into the surrounding bush. Woman and children screamed in horror as the helicopter descended towards them, the worst possible nightmare. Tracer from the attacking Zambian troops cracked overhead.

Red 1 flared as he saw the LZ, it was really tight. Just before he touched ground he screamed at the Choppertech to clear the tail rotor. The Choppertech stuck his head out signalling with a thumb's up that the tail rotor was clear.

There was a WHAP-WHAP, WHAP-WHAP WHAP-WHAP at about 500 beats per minute as the main rotors struck the tops of mud huts and surrounding trees.

Red 1 tried to hover, difficult in the dark with a full load of troops and fuel, whacking at the tree branches sending splinters flying off in all directions. He pulled power to stay in the hover, the noise of the main rotor warning in his headset was picking up. As soon as rpm got out of the green range, a loud horn started booming in his ears.

The pilot waved at the Selous Scouts in the back to jump, still 6ft in the air. They responded instantly, leaping out into the darkness. Red 1 was able to recover rpm, the warning light went off, and the power came back. He pulled power and come straight up out of the village above the trees. After clearing the trees, he did a right pedal turn to bring back rpm.

Dumping the nose, Red 1 went screeching back down the valley towards the approaching Zambians. He side-slipped to allow his gunner's Brownings to bear. The fuselage vibrated as the gunner hung on the triggers, tracer rounds throwing up dust in front of the approaching Zambians.

On the ground the Selous Scouts ran forward to protect the downed helicopter. Flames were flickering from where the straw roof had been ignited by the red-hot turbine engine.

Peter McNeil cracked his harness open and pushed open the side door. Those Selous Scouts in the back that were still in one piece were pulling the injured out, dragging them away from the helicopter.

'Get them well away,' screamed McNeil, knowing how big the fireball was going to be when the fuel tanks ignited. He ran back to help Dicky still hanging in his seat. He pulled open the left hand door and leaned in to release the harness. His hands came away slick with blood. Slipping his arm behind Dicky's back, he pulled. Dicky slumped over but his left leg was trapped in the wreckage. Rob Warner appeared by his side. Both tried to drag him free. It was no good, the leg was firmly jammed in the fuselage.

Warner put his fingers to Dicky's neck. He could not feel a pulse.

The flames caught hold, leaping into the air.

'There's nothing we can do,' screamed Warner, seeing the blood all over the co-pilot's flight suit. He pulled McNeil away. Smoke filled the air, spreading as the flames took hold. The Cheetah seemed to sigh as the hydraulic fluid began to hiss, then the whole aircraft exploded into a convulsive fireball. The wave of superheated flame blew out over the surrounding huts, turning the whole village into a raging inferno.

The Selous Scouts dragged their injured men into the bush on the edge of the village. Zambian troops could be seen skirmishing forward in the light of the burning village. They were engaged by machinegun suppression fire as Warner summed up the position.

Three men were seriously injured, unable to walk because of severe back or neck injuries. Two were dead. Both Dicky Bird and Sam Jacobs died in the burning helicopter, nobody could save them.

Realising that there was no chance of getting Red 1 back into the village with the Zambians shooting at them, Warner made a decision. The men gathered round.

'Okay, listen to me. We are going to skirmish forward using covering fire.'

He indicated where he wanted the gunners to position themselves and explained what he wanted to the others with hand signals. There was a collective nodding of heads.

The fire from the Zambians had stopped. They had clustered on the edge of the village nearest the road. Warner could see them through the raging fire.

The two Selous Scout gunners ran off through the bush to the left to get in position. Warner heard two clicks on his A76 radio when they were ready. He pressed his own handpiece with two rapid clicks and the machineguns opened up.

Using the burning huts as cover, the Selous Scouts dashed forward.

Caught in the cross fire, the Zambians broke and ran back towards the road. Out in the open the gunners picked them off one at a time. Bodies lay twitching in the dust as the Selous Scout skirmish line passed over them, each body taking a few extra rounds to make sure.

Orbiting above the village, Red 1 watched the short sharp battle play out. The door gunner picked off a few runners that made it to the road. Firing into the two Zambian army vehicles parked next to the road, one burst into flames igniting overhanging trees.

It was all over in a few minutes. The surviving Zambian troops disappeared into the bush. Warner called in the helicopter and it landed gently in the middle of the road now illuminated by the raging bush fire. Loading their dead and injured the Selous Scouts climbed back into the helicopter. Warner was the last in, making sure that he checked off each man carefully. The charred remains of Dicky Bird and Sam Jacobs were left behind.

The Cheetah lifted back into the night heading back towards Kariba. The mission was a costly failure. Their ability to mount the raid on the Lusaka Central Prison now severely compromised.

*

Soviet Embassy, Pandit Nehru Road, Ridgeway Lusaka

Sarah Burrell and her two-man Selous Scout team of Cephas Ngwenya and Stanley Chiyeka had no intention of driving to the planned RV point with the Soviets south of Kafue. They planned something different.

To make sure that the Soviets were playing ball, they decided to watch the Embassy to see whether Keith Wilson was fetched from the prison. Surrounding the embassy on two sides was open ground with long grass and trees. The locals used the empty ground as places for a drink up as the area was littered with empty Chibuku cartons.

Ngwenya and Chiyeka found a spot in amongst the trees where they could get a good view of the entrance to the embassy. Sarah stayed with the hapless Casas and the Land Rover in the carpark of the Intercontinental Hotel, only one block away.

Parked under a tree on the eastern boundary of the carpark, Sarah decided to do a little interrogation of her own. She pulled the sack off Casas's head. She was shocked by what she saw. His face was swollen so much that his eyes were virtually closed. It was a purple pulpy mess with cracked bleeding lips from the repeated kicking and punching by Chiyeka to keep him quiet. Dried blood matted his hair and the whole front of his dinner suit was covered in blood. Blood still seeped into his moustache, clogged with spittle and mucus. He was unrecognisable from the cocky, arrogant prick she had first met during her interview at the Cuban Embassy.

'Well Colonel, the situation has changed somewhat wouldn't you say?' observed Sarah.

The eyes blinked but it appeared that Casas could not hear her.

'Come on Colonel let's have a little talk.'

Sarah twisted the top off a water bottle and held it to Casas's lips. He coughed as blood splattered out of his throat.

Sarah sat back in surprise. Casas was in a really bad way. He made no sound, even his breathing was barely discernable. He lay flat on his back with his hands tied behind him, his feet tied tightly together to the support for one of the rear bench seats. She poured more water into his mouth and watched him swallow. Casas probably had brain damage. He was virtually unconscious and could not speak.

It struck her at that moment that this was likely to be the condition that Keith Wilson would be in if they did recover him. It was too awful to contemplate.

Sarah pulled the sack back over Casas's head. She closed her eyes and said a silent prayer for Wilson. Praying that he would survive ...

Come back to me Wilson ...

19

Mana Pools airstrip, Zambezi Valley, 87km Northeast of Kariba

The closest point to Lusaka in Rhodesia was a poor dilapidated dirt airstrip on the Zambezi River at Mana Pools north of Kariba. Four Rhodesian Alouette III K-car gunships had positioned to this airstrip in preparation for their raid on the ZIPRA training camp called Freedom (FC) Camp (Westlands Farm) north of Lusaka. The airstrip was secured by a platoon from 2 Independent Company (RAR) based at Kariba who had trucked in Avtur for refuelling.

The mission to Westlands Farm would take 36 minutes flying time with full fuel load and ammo for the 20mm cannon. That left 20minutes maximum time over the target before being forced to refuel. A K-car could get through a lot of 20mm rounds in 20 minutes ... more than enough time. An external support base for refuelling and rearming the helicopters had been set up deep in the Zambian bush east of Lusaka. The helicopters were tasked to support raids planned on two other known terrorist bases on the same day.

The leader of the K-car section for the attack, quaintly called Pink Leader, was Sqn Ldr Graham Cronshaw. A radio message came through to him at 8pm in the evening that he would have unexpected visitors.

The sound of the approaching Cheetah flying at 2,000ft was heard well ahead of its arrival. Those on the ground at Mana Pools popped two flares to show the pilot where to land and the Cheetah put down precisely between them. Cronshaw knew Flt Lt Peter McNeil well from his time on 7 Squadron but was surprised to see him with his load of Selous Scouts including Major Ron Warner.

'To what do we owe this unexpected pleasure?' asked Cronshaw with his characteristic smile.

McNeil introduced Rob Warner and replied, 'Well Sir, we lost my aircraft in Zambia this evening on an extraction mission. Dicky Bird and Sam Jacobs didn't make it.'

Both men were well known in the Squadron. Cronshaw nodded but made no comment; there was nothing to say ... *good men died.*

'I have another mission in the morning, it's a bit hush-hush but we may need some support from you if we get into trouble,' continued McNeil, pleased that his Skipper hadn't made any remark about the two lost airmen. There would be plenty of time for that ... when the mission was over.

Cronshaw looked at Warner and McNeil knowing it was pointless asking for more information. The Air Force knew the importance of mission secrecy, strictly need-to-know basis. McNeil was equally in the dark as to Cronshaw's mission.

'We have to fly to Lusaka tomorrow morning to deliver a few important messages,' replied Cronshaw with little expression on his face. 'I am not sure what I can do to help.'

'Well Sir, as luck would have it, we are also going to Lusaka tomorrow. We have to pick up a package. Our problem is we are down to one aircraft and we will not have anyone to help secure our LZ. We were hoping you may be able to help,' said McNeil with a faint smile, knowing his Skipper would move heaven and earth to help.

'You can imagine we need all the aircraft we can get for our mission … but as it happens I have a reserve K-car. We have all our aircraft serviceable so you can use it. You remember Shorty Korff?'

Cronshaw turned to a group of pilots sitting around a glowing campfire, 'Shorty!' Air Lt Shorty Korff walked over carrying a mug of hot tea.

'Shorty, you have been called up off the bench for tomorrow's game. I will leave you with Peter McNeil here to brief you in. The less I know about your escapade the better.'

'Thank you Sir,' said McNeil with a smile.

Warner stood to thank Cronshaw as the Squadron Leader got up to finish his dinner. Cronshaw shook his hand, 'All in a day's work Mister Warner. Your friendly neighbourhood air force.'

Cronshaw turned to Shorty Korff.

'By the way Shorty, you make sure that McNeil here knows all our comms frequencies for tomorrow in case we need to communicate. Should be a busy day over Lusaka. Good night gentlemen.'

McNeil's replacement choppertech was busy refuelling the Cheetah and cleaning the twin Brownings. He was new to the squadron, going by the name of 'Jimmy' Moorcroft. Jimmy, because he could play a mean guitar in the tradition of Jimmy Hendricks. McNeil had not met him before.

McNeil knew Shorty Korff well, they had been on the same basic flight training course at Thornhill. McNeil's co-pilot was also a new man to the squadron, Arthur Mills. Korff, Mills and McNeil sat down to plan their route into Lusaka. McNeil explained the mission, handed over aerial photographs and maps. Shorty could not believe his ears.

Attacking a Zambian jail in early morning light! This would be one for the books!

*

Soviet Embassy, Pandit Nehru Road, Ridgeway Lusaka

'What do you think?' asked Sarah Burrell.

'Nobody has left the Embassy, in fact there has been no movement at all,' replied Cephas Ngwenya.

It was 3am, surprisingly cold for early summer. Sarah had walked back through the bush every hour or so since they had set up the OP on the Soviet Embassy.

'I think the bastards have decided to call our bluff,' said Sarah, frustration in her voice.

Ngwenya and Chiyeka nodded, not sure what to say. This woman was an enigma to them, but they remained happy to follow her lead to get Wilson back.

'The Cuban Colonel is either sleeping or unconscious. I can't tell for sure but I think that the beating you gave him has caused permanent damage,' added Sarah.

'Eh,' was all Ngwenya replied. He had long since stopped caring about what happened to the Cuban.

The three slipped back into silence. Each consumed by their own thoughts, trying to come to terms with what the next day would bring.

Sarah could not help but be impressed by the dedication of the two black Selous Scouts. They had very little to say, speaking only when questioned. They had a brooding power about them, a confidence that was hard to describe. They seemed to have no regard for their own safety, focused instead on the task at hand. The dedication of the two black soldiers was something Sarah had never considered in her press coverage. It was a contradiction, difficult to define. It was all too easy to characterise the war as a black v white, colonial v freedom fighter conflict. She was having great difficulty considering how she would report her experience. *The whole thing was a massive contradiction.*

The sound of an engine carried across the bush.

'Finally,' whispered Sarah.

A set of headlights appeared at the gate and the guard pushed the gate open.

Sarah was up on her feet followed by the two men, running back to where she had parked the Land Rover.

'They must be driving to the prison. Wait for them to leave; we don't want them to know they are being followed,' called Sarah as she jumped into the passenger seat.

Ngwenya gave it a few seconds, then started the Land Rover and drove out of the bush towards Nationalist Road on the way to the prison.

*

Lusaka Central Prison, Paul Banda Road, Lusaka

The Soviet Mercedes staff car was parked in front of the green gates to the prison. The whole front of the building was illuminated with powerful security lighting. The lights were on in the main watchtower and the guard could be seen standing next to the mounted machine gun. The characteristic magazine showed it to be an old Second World War Bren gun.

The surrounding streets were completely empty. There were no cars on the road at all. Cephas Ngwenya felt very exposed as they drove slowly past the prison entrance. Sarah slid down to hide as had Chiyeka in the back. He drove another hundred metres down the road before pulling in under the tree they had parked under the day before. The deep shade from the starlight made the Land Rover virtually invisible.

They did not notice a blue VW Beetle parked on the south side of the prison compound next to the open cultivated fields.

Sarah glanced at her watch ... 5:30am. It would be light in less than an hour.

Inside the prison Inspector Kabamba had greeted Comrade Ambassador Vassily Solodovnikov and Colonel Lev Kononov. He had been keeping them informed throughout the night of his progress with the interrogation of Keith Wilson and Ian Southwood. He had established in his own mind that, while the two men were definitely Rhodesian spies, they did not know each other. This in itself was very interesting.

Both the captives had given incriminating information, but Kabamba had not been able to get names of the senior Zambian officials acting as Rhodesian informers. He was convinced that the Rhodesians had agents in high places within the Zambian government. Kabamba was running out of time with Wilson, as he knew that he was to be exchanged for the kidnapped Cuban Colonel.

Kabamba led the two Soviets down the passage to the interrogation room. Both men were familiar with interrogation so they were not shocked to see the state Wilson was in. Kabamba had passed a metal bar between Wilson's tied hands and legs and hung him between the two tables. He had been beaten by the two guards with a police baton that lay on the table covered in blood. They had mostly beaten the lower back, his feet and hands. Kabamba had ripped out a fingernail with a set of pliers.

'Lieutenant Wilson, can you hear me?' asked Vassily Solodovnikov.

Wilson's arched body was hanging below the steel bar, his head lolling forward. The angle had stretched his chest backwards. That strangely had provided relief from the agonising pain in his chest. His feet and hands were swollen and blue from the beating and the lack of circulation.

Wilson made no response.

'Untie him please,' asked Solodovnikov, turning to Kabamba. The Inspector nodded to the guards to pull open the knots at Wilson's hands and feet, then lifted him up into the chair. His matted black curly hair hung over his face, his hands and feet burning painfully as the blood rushed back. The pain in his feet was so bad that the pressure of having them resting on the floor made him wince. His hands sat upright on his knees without any feeling in them whatsoever. The finger with the missing fingernail was dripping blood on the floor.

'Lieutenant Wilson, I have a few very important questions that I need answers to,' asked Solodovnikov.

Wilson remained silent, his eyes clamped shut, trying desperately to get a picture of Sarah back into his mind. In the past hours he had promised himself that if he survived this ordeal he would follow her to the ends of the Earth. It seemed that nothing else mattered ... just Sarah. She was now everything in his world.

'I need the names and locations of the other spies in Zambia and I need to know which of the freedom fighter leaders are Rhodesian agents. You must answer me Lieutenant Wilson!' asked Solodovnikov keeping his voice steady.

Wilson shook his head slowly from side to side indicating he did not know the answer.

'My people will kill the Cuban Colonel,' croaked Wilson.

'We don't care about the death of one Cuban Colonel, there are many more from where he came from. I need this information Lieutenant, or I am afraid, this night will be the last for you on this earth.'

'Piss off,' was all Wilson could manage.

Solodovnikov turned to Inspector Kabamba.

'You may kill him in your own time Inspector.'

In his cell a few down from the interrogation room, Ian Southwood sat in silence, his head between his knees. Mercifully he was no longer bound. He was shaking his hands gently up and down to stimulate the circulation. Both his eyes were swollen shut and he had pins and needles in his feet from the repeated beating on his lower back. The puncture wounds from the pigsticker bayonet were seeping pus and infection was setting in. Despite the bitter cold of early morning, he felt sweat running down his face as his body temperature began to climb as the infection took hold.

Southwood tried to picture his family in his mind but nothing would stick. A feeling of complete hopelessness had taken over his tortured mind. He dreaded the sound of footsteps at the cell door portending the beginning of another round of interrogation.

He prayed that if this was to be his end, that it come quickly.

20

Mumbwa, Zambian Air Base 100km west of Lusaka

Captain Alberto Ley Rivas and his wingman Lieutenant Jorge Neto were on cockpit standby in their Zambian Air Force F6s. They were parked in hessian-covered pens on the hardstanding next to the control tower. The sun was just coming up over the eastern horizon. The average high temperature for the month had been 31°C, but Rivas had been told to expect another hot day at 35°C.

This was the most dangerous time as the Rhodesians almost always attacked in the early morning.

The Zambian pilots were taking too long to master the quirky complexities of the F6 at the limits of its flight envelope. Rivas, under instructions from the Soviet advisory mission in Zambia, had taken to flying operational missions in the F6s. They were not allowed to commit their own MIG-21s to battle. He and his fellow Cuban pilots relished the prospect of taking on South African Mirages and Rhodesian Hawker Hunters, easily out-turned, if not out-run, in air combat – the F6 was equal to the task.

The F6 sported audaciously swept-back wings that, at 55 degrees, were considered the right answer to drag rise during high-speed flight, but were also problematic at low speeds due to the lower lift-generating ability of their wings. Two powerful afterburning turbojet engines gave it a respectable status of a transonic fighter, with a top speed of Mach 1.3. A set of three hard-hitting 30-mm cannon and two first-generation PL-2 heat-seeking missiles completed the weapons suite supplied to Zambia.

The F6 was considered 'disposable' by the Chinese, as they were intended to be operated for only 100 flight hours (or approximately 100 sorties) before being overhauled. This fact was a concern to Rivas as the Zambians had not kept accurate records of flying hours on engines and airframe.

Rivas could hear the conversation between Mumbwa tower and Lusaka tower where the only radar coverage for the country was positioned. Lusaka tower managed both military and civilian traffic with both military and civilian controllers. In addition to the control tower radio traffic, Rivas was tuned to the Soviet radio monitoring station based at their embassy in Lusaka. The Soviets monitored Rhodesian radio traffic as an indicator of a pending attack on training bases in Zambia. This was primarily to protect their own military advisors as well as the newly arrived Cubans.

The Soviet air traffic controller came up on the radio. He voice spoke English with an unmistakable Russian accent, referring to Rivas' section by their Zambian call-sign, Falcon 1 and 2.

'Falcon One, we are picking up a high level of radio traffic in sectors 1 and 2, standby for immediate take-off.'

Sectors 1 and 2 were designated by the Soviets as New Sarum and Thornhill air bases. The radio monitoring station was sometimes augmented by satellite surveillance, but that was not the case this morning.

Rivas signalled to his wingman, watching as he waved his hand to confirm that he had heard the message.

'Falcon Section, scramble ... scramble,' called the controller in Mumbwa Tower.

*

Rhodesian airspace 94km east of Kariba

A strike force of two Rhodesian Canberras, called Green Section, had taken off from New Sarum air base in Salisbury turning towards the north. As the aircraft approached the border, they began their descent from 4,500ft AGL to 1,600ft AGL to get under the Zambian radar. The radar had, however, picked them up soon after take-off and had been plotting their course towards the border.

Two Rhodesian Hawker Hunters, Blue Section, were flying on a course to rendezvous with the Canberras just before they crossed the Zambezi River into Zambia. To the south another section of Hunters, White Section, were flying over Lake Kariba at low level on their way to the Zambian air force base at Mumbwa.

The radar operators at Lusaka tower had sent out the warning to the Zambian military, including the three Rapier missile batteries positioned east, west and south of Lusaka International airport. A section of F6s had been scrambled from Mumbwa.

Once the Canberras dropped below 1,600ft AGL they disappeared off the radar scope, but the Zambians knew a strike was in-bound. The Zambians were also tracking the slow moving Rhodesian Command Dakota, call-sign Dolphin 3, that was flying along the border over Lake Kariba. This was also a telltale sign of an attack in progress.

Green Leader Canberra Section

Navigator: Start descending from this road.

Pilot Green Leader:	Okay. Do you want me to maintain the same speed or do you want me to reduce to 250kts?
Navigator:	No, maintain the speed. We'll have to increase it to maintain 300.
Pilot:	Okay
Pilot	Green Section, Green descending.
Navigator	Go right four degrees ...
Pilot:	Altimeter setting QNH 1019 is set now, 4,500 feet, 310kts.
Navigator	Zero-zero-five (flying virtually due north)
Pilot	Zero-zero-five. Ja.
Pilot:	Green (talking to the other Canberra). Right, let's tighten it up a bit now.
Navigator:	Coming up to one minute out. We're on track and we're on time. Get your speed up.

Green Section was one minute out from their rendezvous with a section of two Hawker Hunters (Blue Section)

Blue Leader:	Green, what's your level?
Green Leader:	Roger, we're at 1,600 feet.
Pilot Green Leader:	290kts coming up.
Navigator:	290kts.
Blue Leader:	Got you visual.

The Hunters dropped down into loose echelon formation with the Canberras.

Pilot Green Leader: Okay. We're coming up to the stream now.

The Canberras and Hunters crossed over the Zambezi River, flying at 290kts (537km/hr). The excitement in the voices of the aircrew was building ... taking shorter breaths ... concentrating hard ...

Navigator:	Zero-zero-six.
Pilot Green Leader:	Zero-zero-six we've got. We're crossing the stream now.
Blue Leader:	Check.
Pilot Green Leader:	Well done JR! (Blue Leader Hunter)

*

Zambian airspace 35km southeast of Lusaka

*That he which hath no stomach to this fight,
Let him depart; his passport shall be made,
And crowns for convoy put into his purse;
We would not die in that man's company
That fears his fellowship to die with us.*[86]
Henry V in Act IV

All the helicopters at Mana Pools took off together, set course for Lusaka, skimming over the Zambezi only a few hundred feet above the trees. They were flying in a loose formation stretched out behind Pink Leader, the lead K-car heading for Freedom Camp at Westlands Farm.

Air Lt. Peter McNeil was the pilot of the last helicopter in the line following his top cover, the K-car flown by Shorty Korff.

Sitting behind McNeil's seat was Rob Warner with his headset on. He had reduced the raiding party to six as they were anticipating passengers on the way back.

McNeil swivelled his head to glance at his choppertech, Jimmy Moorcroft. Moorcroft lifted his gloved hand with a thumbs up.

Checking his watch, McNeil counted off the minutes to when they would part company with Pink Section. He had never been to Lusaka before so he was not familiar with the landmarks. Shorty Korff, up ahead, had a much more detailed understanding of the terrain because of his previous missions. The briefing had been ridiculously short on detail; there had just not been enough time for preparation. McNeil had visions of circling the Lusaka CBD looking for the prison amongst the jumble of buildings.

The co-pilot Mills had a map open on his lap as he followed the route to the city. It was not difficult as the main road was about 2km over his left shoulder.

'Two minutes to the roll-out,' called Mills on the intercom holding up two fingers.

McNeil turned his head and nodded. Oxygen masks, sunglasses and helmet obscured all the faces of the aircrew. Nobody was talking, all deep in concentration.

'Okay. We're on track, on time,' called McNeil on the intercom.

---

[86] The St. Crispin's Day speech is a famous speech from William Shakespeare's play Henry V in Act IV Scene iii 18–67.

'It's about thirty seconds before Pink Section leave us,' replied Mills.

McNeil strained his eyes to try and pick out the first suburbs of the city. All he could see was an endless expanse of bushland stretched in front of them, the treetops catching the early morning sunlight.

'Sierra Section, good hunting,' called Sqn Ldr Graham Cronshaw as his K-cars peeled off to the right, heading northwards to their target.

McNeil applied more power to close with Korff's K-car, just to his left, slightly behind.

The K-car door gunner waved.

'I have the city visual, five minutes to target,' called Korff.

'Come down a bit,' replied McNeil, calling for the helicopters to drop to 300ft.

The first houses shot past beneath their clattering blades, people on the ground were looking up, some waved.

The widely spaced houses of smallholdings with centre pivot irrigation gave way to densely packed buildings.

'Heading three-five-three, come back to eighty-five knots,' called Korff.

Mills had a black and white aerial photo on his knee, glancing between it and what he could see on the ground.

Straining his eyes, McNeil looked out in front of the helicopter for Arakan Barracks, their turning point to the target. There was traffic on the roads below, the glint of the sun off their windscreens.

'Come left to three-zero-two,' called Korff. The sprawling military base appeared beneath them, unmistakeable with parade grounds, barrack rooms and MT yards.

The two helicopters banked to the left over a parade ground full of Zambian soldiers. A few looked up.

'Hospital coming up on the left,' called Korff.

'Can anybody see the prison?' called McNeil. 'It must be on the right of our track.'

All the buildings below looked the same. The hospital was easy to pick up with the smokestacks of the boiler room. They could not see the prison.

'We must have missed it, bank left,' called Korff as he threw his helicopter into a tight turn.

Fuck!

'What's that?' shouted Moorcroft pointing out below them. 'I think I see it, sort of triangular shaped.'

'Yes ... that's it,' called Mills, holding up the aerial photograph.

'The LZs to the south, in those open fields.'

'Roger Sierra Leader, the target is below us, your LZ is just to the south of that watch tower, copied?' called Korff.

'Copied'.

McNeil started a tight turning descent towards the charred remains of a burnt out field. The helicopter shuddered, as he brought it to a hover about 20ft above the ground. A quick glance at the power gauge, 99%! His eyes focused on the prison wall as a fixed visual reference about 150m in front of him.

The full load of fuel, ammo and people was almost too heavy. McNeil barely had enough power to maintain the hover. As the helicopter descended he felt the ground cushion kick in.

He called on the intercom, 'Sierra Two, get ready to debus.'

McNeil felt a tap on his helmet as Warner confirmed he was ready.

Bullet strikes on the scorched dust, leapt in front of the exposed canopy. The prison guard in the watchtower had opened up with the Bren gun.

Bullets entered through the perspex, whipping and cracking wildly. *Fuck!*

*

Mumbwa, Zambian Air Base 100km west of Lusaka

Captain Alberto Ley Rivas and his wingman Lieutenant Jorge Neto started their F6s and within two minutes, were taxiing out for take-off.

'Hunters eleven o'clock,' called Neto seeing two Hawker Hunters (White Section) pull up for an attack.

Rivas strained his neck to see what Neto was taking about but could not see anything.

Panicking that they had been caught on the ground at the wrong time, Neto decided on a hasty take-off and pushed up the throttles to execute a sharp turn on to the runway. Unfortunately, use of excessive power caused him to veer off into the soft mud on the side of the runway. Stuck in the mud, he became an unwitting spectator as the Hunters screeched overhead at no more than a few hundred feet.

The thunder of the Hunter engines carried easily through Riva's canopy.

Rivas pulled onto the runway, as he lined up, he saw the lead Hunter bank tightly to the left, the sound of its engines still beating in his chest. Sweat prickled on his forehead, his hands slick inside his gloves. He shoved the throttles forward on the take-off roll. Rivas craned his neck anxiously only to see another Hunter thunder over him.

The F6 accelerated down the runway and lifted off. Rivas immediately tucked in the undercarriage, pulling the stick into his stomach as the powerful jet shot skyward. Once airborne, keeping the Hunters in sight was difficult as they turned into the early morning sun. Speeding to 490knots, Rivas remembered that he had not jettisoned his drop tanks. When he did get rid of them at such a high speed, he induced a porpoise movement but was somehow able to ride it out.

Charging in at 600knots, he closed the range to about 3km, just short of the right range for a missile shot. Both Hunters continued to bank hard left, still at 1,000ft AGL.

The missile lock growled in his ears. Rivas fired his first missile at the rearmost Hunter ... it failed to track spinning off into the distance. He fired again. The second missile flew into the ground with a huge cloud of dust from the impact.

The Hunter pilots seemed totally oblivious of what was going on behind them. Rivas decided to press on for a gun attack, his heart pounding with excitement. This was the moment that years of training had prepared him for.

Since things had been happening so quickly, Rivas had forgotten to charge his guns ... now he did so. He could see the Hunter clearly out in front of his tight turn. Pulling the stick harder, Rivas could feel the F6 pull inside his opponent, just right for a deflection shot. He fired the centre gun ... the fuselage vibrated alarmingly as the heavy shells punched out. He held the trigger until all its ammunition was spent. Still the Hunter remained frustratingly ahead.

Where is the lead Hunter?

While Rivas dived to position behind the Hunter, out of the corner of his eye he saw another Hunter manoeuvring to get behind him. Rivas snap-rolled inverted, then pushed the stick forward and pulling massive negative-g, climbing vertical with both engines in afterburner. The Hunter passed below him.

Seeing the Hunter continuing the turn, Rivas rolled over and swooped down to get another shot. The dogfight rapidly descended to a dangerously low height of 300ft, with three fighters flying in a very tight circle at a speed of 400kts.

The first Hunter was out of range, the second Hunter much closer. Hitting the throttle Rivas tried to pull in closer, to make sure.

DUFF, DUFF ... DUFF he tapped the trigger with his wing mounted cannons. Puffs of dust appeared in the red soil, well wide of the target.

Rivas cursed with frustration. The Hunter was so close he could lean out and touch it. Still the Rhodesians held the tight banking turn. Flicking wings level, Rivas pulled into a vertical climb, thumped back into his seat as he engaged afterburners.

3,000ft ... 4,000ft.

As he looked over his shoulder, he could still see the two Hunters hugging the ground below. Banking left, Rivas put the F6 into a dive, using his superior speed to line up on the enemy. As he went through 2,500ft he clamped the trigger, firing a long burst at the trailing Hunter. He was closing in fast, the Hunter growing in his gunsight ...

Come on, Come on ...

*

Zambian airspace 119km southeast of Lusaka

Green and Blue Sections were at their turn onto the third leg of their mission profile.

Canberra Navigator:	Turn left now.
Green Leader Pilot:	Onto?
Navigator:	Now, three-zero-four.
Pilot:	Three-zero-four.
Navigator:	We're going to have to climb a bit.
Pilot:	Ja. One bird! Three-zero-four. Rolling out now. How's our speed? We're holding about 290.
Navigator:	It's fine. Just check on these rivers. Go left ... about two degrees.
Pilot:	Three-zero-two. Roger.

The four Rhodesian aircraft were still in loose formation, the Hunters having to control their speed to stay in touch with the slower Canberras. The Navigator in Green Leader's Canberra was navigating by dead reckoning, checking ground references on maps and aerial photographs. The terrain was predominately flat, made up of thick bush interspersed by wide vlei lines.

Navigator:	We're a bit starboard of track.
Green Leader Pilot:	Roger. We didn't get round that turn as fast as I wanted.
Navigator:	Speed back 15 knots. On track. On time ...
Pilot:	Dead right.

The Green Leader pilot took a moment to look out the right of his canopy. The two Hunters were majestic in their green/brown camouflage, fuel tanks and ordinance hanging beneath their swept back wings.

Green Leader Pilot:	These Hunters with the bloody golf bombs here … painted bloody red. Awesome man!
Navigator:	Go two degrees left.
Pilot:	Roger, that makes us three-zero-zero. I was on three-zero-two.
Navigator:	Steer three-zero-two.
Pilot:	Three-zero-two. I was on three-zero-two.

The buffeting of turbulence at low level make the Canberra bounce hard, throwing the crew hard against their harnesses, forcing them to breath in short sharp gulps. Their speech sounded strained and laboured.

*

Lusaka Central Prison, Paul Banda Road, Lusaka

Jock McLean had heard the helicopters a good minute before they appeared, coming in low over the eastern horizon. They seemed to overshoot, then bank hard as they realised their mistake. They flew right over his head, the thumping WHOOP, WHOOP, of the Cheetah incredibly loud.

The Cheetah lined up on a piece of open ground that had been burnt out by a fire, throwing up a cloud of grey/black soot as it slowly flared into the LZ.

Loud cracks from the Bren gun in the main watchtower made Jock duck involuntarily.

'Stay in the car, keep your head down,' Jock called to Patricia Southwood lying on the back seat.

He lifted the RPG-7 to his shoulder, bringing the iron sights up onto the watchtower. As he pulled the trigger, the K-car orbiting above opened up with the 20mm cannon. The impact of the exploding shells distracted Jock for a split second. The rocket sailed over the top of the corrugated iron roof.

Cursing himself, he whipped another projectile out of his pack and locked it in place, lifting the launcher in one fluid motion.

The Cheetah had dropped its troops and was now lifting back into the sky, still taking rounds from the Bren gun.

Jock fired, the rocket shot out the 150m to the target, impacted one of the steel beams supporting the roof, cutting the lone guard on the Bren gun to pieces.

The K-car also found its mark, knocking huge chunks of concrete out of the walls of the watchtower, spraying the observation deck with shrapnel.

Six men in camouflage came dashing through the black dust. Jock tore off his wig, and ran across towards them, waving his arms wildly above his head, his AK slapping wildly against his back.

One of the Selous Scouts saw him coming, lifted his AK to shoot.

'NO,' shouted Jock, waving more vigorously.

'Who the fuck are you?' shouted the soldier.

'It doesn't matter, but you are here to get a man out of jail. I'm here to help.'

'I'm Warner.'

'I'm Ben Nevis.'

'Follow me. Do you know where your bloke is being held?'

'No idea, some where in there,' pointed Jock.

As Jock and the Selous Scouts raced around to the front of the prison, another group of people came running across the open ground in the car park.

'Fuck me ... who are these people?' shouted Warner above the sound of the orbiting helicopters, looking back at Jock. Jock shook his head.

Cephas Ngwenya recognised Warner immediately as he, Chiyeka and Sarah ran across the carpark.

'*Ikhanka* is inside,' blurted Ngwenya, pointing at the door. There was no time for pleasantries.

'Who's the woman?' asked Warner, nodding towards Sarah.

'She has been helping *Ikhanka* and us *Ishe*.'

Sarah saw that they were talking about her.

'We haven't got time for a debate, Wilson is inside we need to get him out,' chipped in Sarah.

Warner took a moment to study Sarah.

'You that reporter that Wilson pulled out of Zambia?'

'Yes, Sarah Burrell.'

'Okay, you wait here. Let's get going, blow the door.'

A Selous Scout had attached an explosive charge to the side door. They stood back against the wall, and the door was blown open with a loud bang.

Two Selous Scouts took up station at the entrance to take care of any arriving police or army.

The rest of the Selous Scouts were through the door followed by Jock, Ngwenya and Chiyeka.

'I said you stay here!' called Warner pointing at Sarah.

Sarah pulled the Tokarev pistol that Wilson had given her out of her fishing vest.

'Fuck you!' she said.

*

Zambian airspace 102km southeast of Lusaka

The formation of Rhodesian Canberras and Hunters continued their approach to their target. Their track took them only 7km north of Lusaka International Airport. This brought them onto the Lusaka approach radar screen.

Green Leader pilot: Oh shit! I hope the fucking wings don't fall off!

The Canberras were old, riddled with metal fatigue. The Rhodesians had done their best to patch them up but it was a losing battle. The pilots avoided any aggressive manoeuvres but even a harsh bump through turbulence could rip a wing off.

Navigator:	What's your speed?
Pilot:	275 … the 15 you wanted off. Do you want me to get down?
Navigator:	Yes. You can go down a bit.
Navigator:	Okay. We're on track, on time.
Pilot:	Dead right—it's about a minute and a half before the Hunters leave us.
Navigator:	Two starboard onto three-zero-four.
Pilot:	Two starboard.
Navigator:	No, make it three-zero-five
Pilot:	Three-zero-five. Okay.
Navigator:	Make it three-zero-six.
Pilot:	Three-zero-six. Okay, you've got it.
Pilot:	There's not a peep out of tower so that's going to be superb. We won't have to talk to him.

The attack aircraft were listening in on the Lusaka Tower frequency to see if they had been picked up on Zambian radar. It was almost time for the Hunters to accelerate ahead for their attack.

Navigator:	The Hunters will be going in about fifty seconds.
Pilot:	Roger.
Navigator:	Go right another two degrees.
Pilot:	Three-zero-eight?
Navigator:	Ja.

Just then the pilot's voice of an approaching Kenya Airways flight came across the radio tuned to Lusaka Tower.

'Hello, Lusaka Approach, Kenya 724, do you copy?'
'Kenya 724, Lusaka Approach, good morning,' replied the Air Traffic Controller at Lusaka International Airport.

A Kenya Airways flight, inbound from Nairobi, was calling Lusaka Approach. This sudden interruption distracted Green Leader for a split second.

Green Leader Pilot:	That's the bloody tower.
Navigator:	Okay, just stand by Sir, we're coming up to …

The pilot of the second Canberra chips in to be helpful.

Green 2:	I think we passed it—I think that rise on the right, is the one. That should have been our turning point.
Green Leader Pilot:	Fuck! Okay I've got it. Blasted tower. That Kenya flight is going to get a Canberra ups its arse.
Navigator:	Okay. Go Hunters. Go!
Green Leader Pilot:	Blue Section Go! Blue Section Go!

Blue Section applied throttle and accelerated away ahead of the Canberras, then banked away to the right to carry out their part of the mission.

Navigator:	Okay. They were spot on time.
Green Leader:	That's Okay. Roger … 270 knots. You've got it now.

*

Freedom Camp, Westlands Farm 15km north of Lusaka

The ZIPRA cadres shuffled into loose order on the side of the parade ground, situated just to the east of the farm house HQ. As the sun was still rising, they all faced towards the west to keep their eyes out of the sun. None carried weapons, just their reisfleck East German issue uniforms.

ZIPRA Brigade Commissar, Comrade Elijah Bandama stood up from his desk in the farmhouse and lifted his beret off the hook. His two Cuban advisors, Captains Juan Fernández Ruz and Eduardo García Vigoa were waiting for him on the veranda. This was their daily routine, an early morning muster parade, an explanation of the day's roster and training regime, dismiss the men to breakfast, then Brigade Orders for the miscreants.

'Another hot day Comrade?' said Ruz in his broken English as he saluted Bandama smartly.

'Yes another hot day ... but a good day nevertheless. We are expecting Comrade Masuku later. He will address the men this afternoon at 4pm,' replied Bandama as the three men stepped off the veranda to walk the short distance to the parade ground.

The phone began to ring in the office. There was only one working phone.

'Who could that be? Please Vigoa, will you answer it?' called Bandama over his shoulder.

Eduardo Vigoa trotted back up the stairs of the veranda into the office.

Bandama and Ruz continued on their way.

The ZIPRA Political Commissar ordered the men on parade smartly[87].

Dust lifted from their boots as the men rushed into position, lifting their arms to set their dressing. A song began from the rear ranks, the daily morale booster.

The men sang with gusto in lilting harmonies. Bandama stood watching his men singing along with them, a beaming smile on his face.

Ruz turned to see Vigoa running towards him.

'Comrade,' whispered Vigoa trying to regain his breath.

'Yes?' asked Ruz.

---

87   Would have been classed as an RSM in the British Army.

'The Embassy has issued an alert, we need to get away from here. We only have a few minutes.'

Despite Ruz's dark complexion he visibly paled.

'Comrade Bandama, please excuse us, we have been called away to our Embassy. We will get back as soon as we can,' said Ruz.

Bandama waved his hand in dismissal and continued with the song.

The two Cubans ran towards the MT yard in a manner that could only be interpreted as panic. They were running for their lives …

*

Air space above Mumbwa Air Base 100km west of Lusaka

In the melee above Mumbwa, Captain Alberto Ley Rivas was still trying to get a shot on the orbiting Hunters. His wingman Lieutenant Jorge Neto had freed his aircraft from the mud and had managed to get airborne. Rivas could not see him but assumed that he would have gained height before joining the attack.

'Falcon, Hunter on your tail, break … break,' called Neto

Instinctively Rivas broke right as a stream of 30mm Aden cannon shells drifted past his canopy. Another Hunter had joined the fray.

As he looked up the Hunter seemed to be right on top of him.

Sensing the critical situation, Neto continued to warn his leader to break off the attack.

A puff of thick black smoke appeared from the right wing root of Rivas' F6. The thump of the impact of cannon shells was unmistakable. Rivas' mind could not believe that he had been hit. He had been in complete control. He was in a position to kill an enemy.

The aircraft began to vibrate violently. Pulling wings level, more cannon tracer passed over his canopy, so close he could hear the supersonic crack. The stick was shaking in his hand, the rudder was not responding.

'Falcon … punch out, punch out,' screamed Neto.

Rivas lifted his hands to the handle above his head and pulled. The KK1 seat fired. He exploded out of the cockpit, the seat tumbling in the slipstream.

The aircraft rolled over and crashed in a huge ball of fire.

Captain Alberto Ley Rivas hung in his parachute harness, his neck broken from the impact of crashing through the cockpit canopy. It had not automatically fired off when he pulled the ejection handle.

*

Zambian airspace 91km east of Lusaka

The two Canberras were now flying on their own, the Hunters having accelerated ahead of them to the target. The formation was approaching their final turn to bring them onto their final attack bearing 281°. The distance would be exactly 87.7km to target ... 9minutes, 10seconds.

Navigator:	Heading now two-eight-one, sir.
Green Leader Pilot:	Two-eight-one. Roger.
Navigator:	When I give you 'doors', can you switch on at the same time?
Pilot:	Will do.
Navigator:	Okay! We're coming up to 40 seconds to turn, sir.
Pilot:	Roger.
Navigator:	We passed a river on our left here. We'll see the bridge fairly shortly.
Pilot:	We've passed two-eight-one. Shall I turn back on it now?
Navigator:	Yes, back to two-eight-one.
Pilot:	Two-eight-one we've got.
Navigator:	Can you bring the speed back—240?
Pilot:	Steering two-eight-one.
Navigator:	Two-eight-zero.
Pilot:	Two-eight-zero.

The repetition of the speed and bearing showed the tension building in the crew. Tiny adjustments to keep the mission exactly on time ... constant reassurance ... excitement ... anticipation.

*

Chalimbana Ridge, 35km east of Lusaka, 13km east of the threshold to Runway 28 at Lusaka International Airport

'What did the English officer want yesterday?' asked the Zambian Army Sergeant in charge of the Rapier missile battery.

He was asking about a visit the previous day from the Royal Air Force Regiment Officer responsible for their training. He had missed the meeting, as he was with a girl in a nearby village.

'He didn't say much, he just fiddled with the machine,' replied the Corporal sitting in front of the TV screen.

Happy with the answer, the Sergeant carried on eating the apple he had brought back from the village.

The quad mounted Rapier battery spun around to the east. The 'Dagger' surveillance radar gave a buzz ... it had acquired a target, it said a range of 15km. Two lamps lit up on the Selector Engagement Zone (SEZ), a box containing 32 orange lamps arranged in a circle about the size of a car steering wheel. The operator looked into the TV screen on the optical tracker but could not see anything ... *it must be too far away.*

The missile launcher made rapid adjustments as new tracking information was computed.

The Sergeant pulled up his binoculars to look out towards the east. It was a perfectly clear morning, the sound of powerful jet engines carried on the light easterly breeze. The ridge he was standing on was at least 50m above the surrounding countryside. The sound was increasing in intensity and moving to the north of their position.

The threat buzzer sounded more urgently.

The Sergeant picked up an aircraft through his binoculars. He could not believe his eyes.

'It is a Canberra!' screamed the Sergeant. 'SHOOT!'

The operator hit the launch button but nothing happened.

'SHOOT, SHOOT!'

The missiles stayed on their rails, turning slowly to follow the flight path of the Canberras as they continued on their way.

*

Zambian airspace 18km east of the target at Westlands farm

Navigator:	Everything is set up and ready.
Green Leader Pilot:	There's a school coming up. Roger, I have 310 knots, two-eight-zero, QNH 1019.

The crew were still listening on the Lusaka Tower frequency.

Pilot:	There's nothing from tower and I'm not going to call them. Okay?
Navigator:	Okey-doke.
Pilot:	It's going to be perfect.
Navigator:	Little dam coming up. We're drifting port. Go to the right. Two-eight-three. Two-eight-four.

Pilot:	Two-eight-four? Or two-eight-five?
Navigator:	I want to do a kink, sir, to get it spot on.
Pilot:	Tell me when to roll out.
Navigator:	Go left. Two-eight-two.
Pilot:	Roger, coming up to two minutes to run. Two-eight-two. Got two minutes to run. Perfect.
Navigator:	Go left a bit. Steady.
Pilot:	Two-seven-eight?
Navigator:	Two-eight-two!
Pilot:	A school coming up—acceleration point. Two-eight-two is the heading.

The formation passed over Kasisi Mission School, less than two minutes to the target ... so close now ...

Navigator:	Okay. We should start accelerating now.
Pilot:	Roger. Shall I go?
Navigator:	Just leave it in case they (the Hunters) are going to be a bit late— to the minute.
Pilot:	Okay.
Navigator:	Accelerate!
Pilot:	Roger.

At this stage, the tension is palpable. The voices of both the pilot and navigator go up an octave and they begin to speak more quickly, using short phrases.

Navigator:	You want to get your doors open.
Pilot:	Yes, as soon as I've got my speed.
Navigator:	Go left a bit. Go left.
Pilot:	More?
Navigator:	No. OK. Flatten out on two-eight-two. Quickly! Carry on. Flatten out ... Quickly! Carry on.
Pilot:	Roger.
Navigator:	Up there—target!
Pilot:	Beautiful. Yes! Switches. Speed up, or is it okay?
Navigator:	Speed's fine. Go left. Steady. Steady. Two-seven-eight.
Pilot:	Roger.
Navigator:	Steady. Steady. Left a touch.
Pilot:	Beautiful!

Navigator:	Steady. Steady. Left a touch. Steady. Steady. Steady. Can I switch the doors open?
Pilot:	Yes. Switch your doors.

The excitement in their voices was at fever pitch. The navigator could see the target through the perspex bubble in the nose of the aircraft. Adrenalin was pumping. Pilot and navigator were literally shouting at each other.

They realised that the strike was going to be right on target. The enemy below had broken ranks and were running in all directions. The sound of the approaching jets was unmistakeable ...

Navigator:	Right. I'm going to put them into the field.
Pilot:	Yes!
Navigator:	Steady. I'm going to get them. Steady.
Pilot:	YES! Fucking beautiful!
Navigator:	Steady. Steady. NOW! Bombs gone. . . They're running...
Pilot:	Beautiful! Jeez! You want to see all those bastards. The fucking bombs are beautiful!

*

Lusaka Central Prison, Paul Banda Road, Lusaka

Warner led his men across the courtyard towards the maximum-security section. The plans of the prison were imprinted on his mind. They stopped at the steel gate entrance, charges were set and the door blown open.

A soldier carrying an SLR appeared in the passage, Warner double tapped him to the ground.

A shot rang out from the courtyard as Ngwenya shot at another guard appearing from the admin block.

There was only enough room for one person at a time to run down the passage, with cells on either side. They stayed in single file, Warner in front.

'Can anyone hear me?' screamed Warner.

The gunfire from the courtyard and the helicopters orbiting overhead drowned out his voice. He slid open the hatches of each solid steel door, it was too dark to see if there were any occupants inside.

Another soldier appeared, shooting high, then ducked down a side passage.

'In here', came a muffled call.

Warner slid open the hatch, he could see someone sitting against the wall.

'I'm Ian Southwood.'

'Blow the door,' called Warner.

A small chunk of plastic and det were placed over the keyhole. They backed down the passage.

DUFF ... the door flung open.

Warner was first in. He took one look and he could see it was not Wilson.

Jock McLean appeared at the door.

'Jesus Christ ... Ian.'

He could hardly believe his eyes. Ian Southwood was virtually unrecognisable. He tried to stand but fell back. Jock lifted him onto a shoulder, helped by one of the Selous Scouts.

'We are looking for another man called Wilson, have you seen him?' called Warner close to Ian's ear.

The man shook his head ... he was completely disorientated ... blind from his swollen face.

'Blow as many doors as you can,' instructed Warner, dashing forward to the end of the passage.

Doors blew open one by one, some were occupied, others empty. All the released prisoners were herded back to where Ngwenya held the courtyard. The stronger ones helped those too injured to walk.

'There must be an interrogation room,' said Sarah, now at Warner's side.

'The plans I saw, showed a larger room at the end of this passage,' pointed Warner down a side passage.

Another guard shot at them.

Warner took out a grenade and threw it down the passage. A deep thud followed, showering the guard with shrapnel.

Shooting ahead of him Warner moved down the passage. Sarah was right behind him. The other Selous Scouts covered the main passage.

The door at the end was closed.

Warner tried the handle and it swung open.

A man sat on a wooden chair in the middle of the room, his black hair instantly recognisable. Sarah gave out a low groan as she rushed forward.

'Wilson!'

Wilson smiled as she knelt down in front of him looking up into his face.

'I knew you would come.'

Unable to say anything because of the shocking state Wilson was in, Sarah simply smiled back into his face.

Sarah lifted Wilson's arm over her shoulder, helped by Chiyeka appearing through the dust. He could not support his own weight, his arms and legs too damaged.

Unable to hold his weight Sarah had to stop, panting from the exertion. Ngwenya came into the room, took Wilson's arm from Sarah.

'Right come on people … back to the choppers,' called Warner.

Gunfire could be heard from the main gate.

The distinctive DUM … DUM … DUM … of the K-car firing, indicated that all was not well outside.

Ngwenya and Chiyeka were struggling to carry Wilson's dead weight. One of the other Selous Scouts slung his rifle and lifted Wilson's legs. The three men struggled back down the passage to the main courtyard. Released prisoners were milling around, uncertain of what to do.

Warner needed to think quickly.

'Follow me,' he shouted to one of his men as he raced across the courtyard to the entrance to the exercise yard that he knew housed hundreds of prisoners.

He shot his rifle at the gate lock but it would not give. He could hear the murmur of voices on the other side. His man came forward with another charge and they blew the gate open.

They were not prepared for what they saw.

The courtyard was full of half-starved emaciated men and women. There were also children amongst them.

'Come on, get out, follow me, come on,' he shouted.

The prisoners were hesitant at first, confused by a white man covered in camo-cream shouting at them.

First one walked through the gate, then another, then all pressed forward.

'Open the main gates,' screamed Warner.

The main wooden gates were pulled open by the Selous Scouts allowing the escaping prisoners to flood through.

Outside the prison gunfire intensified.

Trucks full of Zambian Police had arrived, shooting at the people flowing through the gate.

The Rhodesians had been instructed not to engage Zambian military or police. Shorty Korff was left with no choice. He pulled in above the police truck and his gunner pumped shells into it, trying to chase the Zambians away.

Sarah followed Ngwenya and Chiyeka as they carried Wilson through the gate. Jock Mclean was carrying Ian Southwood in a fireman's lift.

A Prison guard with an old .303 rifle came out of an office. He lifted it towards Sarah. She raised the Tokarev, shouting at him to put the gun down. The sound of gunfire, helicopters and the excited escaping prisoners was too much. The guard continued to lift the rifle ...

Sarah shot him in the chest. He was thrown backwards against the wall, sliding to the ground.

She stood transfixed ... unable to believe what had just happened.

The Selous Scouts were pushed through the gates, caught up in the flood of people making their bid for freedom.

The police outside had taken cover on the far side of Paul Banda Road, still firing into the crowd now milling about in the prison carpark. A few prisoners fell to the ground as they were struck. Screams of anguish rang out when the people realised what was happening. The crowd broke into panic and began to run in all directions. Women, many too weak to run, held their children to them. The noise was overwhelming. Children were crying in terror. The air was full of the sound of gunfire, helicopters above, the thud of the 20mm cannon and incessant rattle of twin Brownings from the Cheetah.

Warner led the group along the outside wall of the prison, back towards the LZ in the open field.

Ngwenya and Chiyeka struggled with Wilson between them. Sarah followed closely behind. Safety was now only a few hundred metres away.

Warner called McNeil on the radio to tell him that they were heading back to the LZ. McNeil could see the Selous Scouts moving along the western side of the prison. He made another orbit then lined up on the LZ, closer to prison buildings this time.

Shorty Korff in the K-car adjusted his orbit to cover the LZ.

'Sierra Lead, I have trucks approaching from the south, plenty of them, better get a move on,' called Korff in the K-car.

A convoy of army trucks were approaching the prison along Burma Road, probably from Arakan Barracks.

Dust picked up as McNeil flared for his landing. The Selous Scouts and their party of escapees had to shield their eyes from the stinging sand and dust being flung at them. As the helicopter settled the dust was so thick the helicopter disappeared all together.

'Move ... MOVE' urged Warner trying to shepherd his people

through the dust.

The man holding Keith Wilson's legs gave a loud groan and dropped to his knees, in the dust Ngwenya and Chiyeka could not see in front of them and they and Wilson fell over him.

The distinctive crack and thump of incoming fire sprayed over their heads. The Zambian troops were firing at the helicopter.

Jock McLean struggled forward with Ian Southwood over his shoulders saw the open door of the helicopter and hurled him in.

'I must fetch this man's wife. She is in a car over there,' shouted Jock in Warner's ear pointing across the road.

'Be quick man.'

Jock dashed off out of the dust cloud towards the VW Beetle. Patricia had sat up in the car. She saw Jock running towards her.

Bullet strikes appeared in the dirt in front of Jock as he ran. Putting everything out of his mind, he focused on getting to Patricia.

He called out to her to run towards him, beckoning with his hands.

Patricia got out of the car to run towards him. She had tears running down her cheeks, her hair flying across her face.

Jock grabbed her arm, bent down slightly, then flung her over his huge shoulders, running back towards the helicopter.

Shorty Korff was desperately trying to suppress the Zambian fire as it streamed towards the helicopter sitting helplessly in the open field.

'Stoppage,' called Korff's choppertech.

'Shit, can you clear it?' called Shorty, looking across at him.

The tech was feverishly working the gun's mechanism, lifting the cover. A 20mm round was wedged tightly in the chamber. He felt below his seat for his toolbox, lifted out a shifting spanner and gave the round a hard smack. It didn't move.

'Sierra Leader, I have a stoppage, you must get out, get out now!' called Korff, a hint of panic now in his voice.

On the ground below, Ngwenya was desperately trying to regain his feet. Wilson was too weak to stand up, instead crawling desperately on all fours towards the helicopter. Sarah was trying to help him to his feet but she could not lift him.

One of the Selous Scout rescue team had been hit in the leg, he was staggering forward dragging his leg behind him. Another returned to help. Warner came back through the dust, saw Wilson, and bent down next to him.

Warner lifted his arm, to drag him up over his shoulder. Sarah tried to help.

Wilson could feel his arms being pulled. He tried to call out as the pain shot through his chest.

'Sarah,' he croaked, trying to see her through his watering eyes.

Like a balloon, his lungs stretched as they inflated. The pressure of being pulled by the arms was the final straw. His broken rib jabbed through the lining of the lung. Air escaped into his chest collecting between the lung tissue and the chest cavity causing a traumatic pneumothorax.

Wilson sucked for air, in short sharp gasps. What was left of his strength drained away, his head fell forward. He could taste blood in his mouth as his punctured lung began to fill with blood. Too weak to cough, his mind began to swim, lights flashed in his head, a dark shadow drew across his eyes.

Sarah and Warner continued to drag Wilson towards the helicopter.

Ngwenya and Chiyeka emerged through the dust, hands grabbed at them hauling them into the helicopter. Ngwenya's head flashed left and right as he tried to pinpoint Wilson.

The sound of gunfire and the helicopter turbine drowned out everything. The thick dust made it impossible to know which way to run.

McNeil was waving furiously out the door, 'Get In, GET IN,' he screamed but nobody could hear.

Jock appeared out of the dust, pushed Patricia onto a seat and jumped up next to her.

The Selous Scouts, with their wounded comrade, appeared next to the door. Ngwenya heard the distinctive sound of bullets hitting metal. The helicopter was taking rounds.

Ngwenya jumped back onto the ground, disappearing back into the dust in search of Wilson.

Sarah could see the blood coming out of Wilson's mouth. She stopped. Warner turned to bellow at her to keep going.

Warner was hit. He staggered back, his eyes wide with shock. Sarah saw the blood spurt from his upper thigh as he went down on one knee.

'Keep going,' he waved at her.

'Sarah go,' pleaded Wilson with all his strength.

'I am not leaving you Wilson,' she dropped down next to him. He was deathly pale, coughing blood, his eyes rolling back in his head.

Ngwenya appeared out of the dust.

'Come we must go,' he called trying to lift Wilson. Wilson lifted his hand towards Ngwenya trying to speak but no sound came. Ngwenya bent down next to him to hear his voice over the deafening sound of the helicopter.

'Take Sarah and Major Warner, leave me now, there is nothing left for me,' whispered Wilson with the last of his strength.

'No. Wilson, you bastard!' wept Sarah, pulling at his arm.

'I am here with you *Ikhanka,*' pleaded Ngwenya.

'Go back to your family Cephas. Leave me now.'

Ngwenya sat back on his haunches everything around him seemed to be spinning.

'Go Cephas,' waved Wilson, his lips in a thin smile.

In a final gesture of goodbye, Ngwenya held his hand to Wilson's chest bending forward.

'*Sala gashle Ikhanka.*'

Looking up into the eyes of Rob Warner, Ngwenya came to his senses. He jumped forward, lifted Warner's arm over his shoulder, pulled him to his feet, and staggered off into the dust.

McNeil had applied full power, he was inching forward on the skids, praying Warner and Wilson would appear out of the dust.

Two men appeared struggling forward, hands hauled them into the helicopter.

There was no time left …

The Cheetah lifted back into the sky, clawing for height. Small arms fire followed it as it banked out to the right, skimming low over the rooftops.

The dust began to settle around Sarah and Wilson, left behind in the desolation of the LZ. All was perfect silence. Wilson lay on his back, his head held in her lap, her hand stroking through his thick curly hair.

His eyes had lost their focus … lips quivering. She could feel his body shiver.

Sarah pulled his face closer, 'It's all right … I am with you …'

Barely audible, he whispered, 'I love you Sarah.'

With a shaking hand he tried to touch her face, his strength gone, it fell to his side.

She put her face next to his, tears running down her cheeks.

'Its going to be okay, we will get you to a hospital.'

'I am happy to have known you Sarah.'

Keith Wilson died there … cloaked in red dust, the ice blue canvas of the African sky above …

*

Zambian airspace 20km west of the target at Westlands farm

The Canberra strike had gone in and Green Section were still flying towards the west at low level.

Navigator: Are we putting in K-Cars here?
Green Leader Pilot: Yes, they've got K-Cars there. They'll have a beautiful time. They are like fucking ants running around there. Jeez. That was marvellous. Shit!

The Pink Section K-cars were now orbiting Westlands Farm, shooting at the escaping terrorists on the ground.

Navigator: Straight ahead for one more minute.
Pilot Okay.
Navigator: Keep an eye open, sir.
Pilot: Yes, I was going to say—a big pylon.
Pilot: Just check the tape recorder while you're there. Otherwise just leave it.
Navigator: Okay. Still turning.
Pilot: Roger. Okay. Let me try and get this spiel off

Green Leader Pilot: Lusaka tower, this is Green Leader. How do you read?

...

Lusaka tower, this is Green Leader.

Lusaka Tower: Station calling tower?
Green Leader Pilot: Lusaka tower this is Green Leader. This is a message for the station commander at Mumbwa from the Rhodesian Air Force. We are attacking the terrorist base at Westlands Farm at this time. This attack is against Rhodesian dissidents and not against Zambia. Rhodesia has no quarrel, repeat, no quarrel with Zambia or her security forces. We therefore ask you not to intervene or oppose our attack. However, we are orbiting your airfield now and are under orders to shoot down any Zambian Air Force aircraft, that does

not comply with this request and attempts to take off. Did you copy all that?

Postscript

'A CRIME AGAINST HUMANITY'

One could be forgiven for imagining that this would have been a headline from an American, British, Australian or Canadian newspaper on the shooting down of a civilian airliner over Rhodesian skies on 3rd September 1978. This headline comes from the *Weekend Australian* on 19 July 2014 quoting Australian Prime Minister Tony Abbott on the shooting down of Malaysian Airlines flight MH17 over the Ukraine.

While MH17 is fresh in people's minds it is incomprehensible that anyone, no matter how depraved or demented, would want to shoot down a planeload of innocent people. MH17 is not a new or unique story, it all began in a little landlocked country in Africa, far, far away, a long time ago.

The story goes that soon after Air Rhodesia Vickers Viscount 'Hunyani' (RH825) took off from Lake Kariba, a group of ZIPRA terrorists (today's press might call them terrorists, separatists or rebels, while the same press in the 1970's called them guerrillas or freedom fighters) scored a direct hit on its starboard wing with a Soviet-made Strela 2M (SAM-7) surface-to-air infrared homing missile. The pilot attempted an emergency landing of the critically damaged aircraft in thick bush on the top of the Zambezi escarpment. The attempted belly landing would have been successful had it not been for an unseen ditch, causing the plane to cartwheel and break up. Of the fifty passengers and four crew, thirty-eight died in the crash; a band of terrorists approached the wreckage, rounded up the ten survivors they could see and massacred them with automatic gunfire. Three passengers survived by hiding in the surrounding bush, while a further five lived because they had gone to look for water before the terrorists arrived.

The similarities between the MH17 and RH825 disasters are stark. Both aircraft were flying over a civil war zone, both were shot down by a Soviet era ground to air missile, both were shot down by terrorists (if Ukrainian read 'terrorist', if Russian read 'freedom fighter'), both sets of terrorists were trained and supported by Russia (read Soviet Union). The significant difference, however, is that MH17 was probably a terrible mistake, a consequence of putting sophisticated weapons in untrained hands. In the case of Air Rhodesia flight RH825, the aircraft was shot down deliberately and premeditatedly by Soviet and Cuban trained terrorists[88].

Joshua Nkomo the leader of ZAPU, claimed responsibility.

There was, and still is, deathly silence on the shooting down of Hunyani RH825 in 1978 and her sister Umniati in 1979. It seems that atrocities perpetrated in the past somehow lose their horror. When speaking about RH825 today the comment ... 'yes, but that was a long time ago', is often proffered as some sort of justification.

Malcolm Fraser, the Australian Prime Minister in 1978-79, when questioned on the shooting down of civilian airliners in Rhodesia said ... nothing. The British Prime Minister of the time, James Callaghan together with the then US President Jimmy Carter, equally refused to make any comments on the shooting down of the Rhodesian Viscounts.

On 5 March 1980 Malcolm Fraser wrote to Robert Mugabe, the avowed Marxist whose party had just won a crushing victory in the elections for the new Zimbabwe Parliament: 'I am confident', Fraser wrote, 'that under your leadership Zimbabwe will make great progress in achieving your goals of peace, prosperity and unity'[89]. Fraser never, at any time, condemned the shooting down of the Rhodesian airliners, while peace, prosperity and unity were never on Mugabe's agenda.

In 2014, after the MH17 disaster, Malcolm Fraser tweeted: 'If any other country went to war killing as many civilians, women and children, it would be named a war crime.' Fraser appears selective in his condemnation of war crimes. Rhodesia was one example, he previously turned a blind eye to the invasion of East Timor by Indonesia in 1975 with the loss of tens of thousands of lives.

In the late 1970s shooting down civilian airliners didn't cause a ripple in international circles, much less UN resolutions, universal condemnation and talk of crimes against humanity.

The perpetrators of the Air Rhodesia disasters were never brought to justice, it is unlikely that the MH17 perpetrators will either.

---

88   Another separate terrorist band, closer to the crash site, went on to murder some of the surviving passengers.
89   National Archives of Australia (NAA): A1838, 190/10/1, part 27, f. 83.

In more modern times, there are a few lonely voices in the Parliament of the United Kingdom:

House of Commons - Early day motion 1029

VISCOUNT MASSACRES

Session: 2012-13

Date tabled: 05.02.2013

Primary sponsor: Kate Hoey, Labour Member for Vauxhall

Sponsors:

That this House notes that 12 February 2013 will mark the 34th anniversary of the shooting down of Air Rhodesia Viscount Flight RH827 (the Umniati) by members of the Zimbabwe People's Revolutionary Army (ZIPRA) in the former Rhodesia resulting in the death of all on board; further notes that this was the second such shooting down of civilian airliners by ZIPRA and followed the shooting down of Air Rhodesia Flight RH825 (the Hunyani) by the same means on 3 September 1978; further notes that the 107 victims comprised civilian men, women and children, some of whom survived the crash of the Hunyani and were subsequently murdered on the ground by bayoneting and shooting; further notes that the victims included citizens from Switzerland, Scotland, Belgium, New Zealand, the UK and South Africa; recalls that the failure to officially condemn these atrocities, as articulated in the sermon by the late Very Reverend John da Costa known as *The Deafening Silence*, was an act of moral cowardice and deplores such failure; and commends the work done by Keith Nell and his Viscount Down Team to ensure that these atrocities are not forgotten and their on-going efforts to alleviate suffering amongst the pensioner community of Zimbabwe.

Henry Bellingham	Conservative Party	North West Norfolk
Peter Bottomley	Conservative Party	Worthing West
Kate Hoey	Labour Party	Vauxhall
Kelvin Hopkins	Labour Party	Luton North
Dr William McCrea	Democratic Unionist Party	South Antrim
Jim Shannon	Democratic Unionist Party	Strangford

Why would ZIPRA Shoot down a civilian airliner in early September 1978?

The timing and circumstances of the shooting down of the first Rhodesian Viscount have always been a puzzle to me. There are a number of events on the macro-political scene that raise questions.

On 3 March 1978, Ian Smith the Prime Minister of Rhodesia signed the 'Salisbury Agreement' with Abel Muzorewa, Ndabaningi Sithole and Chief Chirau for the beginnings of an Interim Government moving towards free elections in late 1978. This agreement was rejected out of hand by some of the so-called 'Front Line States' (Tanzania, Angola and Mozambique), who called for an intensification of the war. The Front Line States were supported in this view by Malcolm Fraser in Australia and Pierre Trudeau in Canada. In early 1978 British Foreign Secretary, David Owen, vainly attempted to expand the Internal Settlement in Rhodesia to include the ZAPU leader, Joshua Nkomo. A series of clandestine diplomatic manoeuvres, using Nigeria as an intermediary, continued until September 1978.

On 8 August 1978 the Interim Government introduced the first major measures at eliminating racial discrimination.

Starting on 14 August 1978, Ian Smith attended secret meetings with Joshua Nkomo, the ZAPU leader, in Lusaka Zambia. He met the Zambian President Kenneth Kaunda at the same time. He was ferried to and from Lusaka in a private jet owned by the mining corporation Lonrho. Attempts were made to involve the ZANU leader Robert Mugabe but Mugabe would have no part in the talks[90].

On 20 August 1978 Ian Smith flew to Lusaka and put a further offer to Nkomo; to reconstitute the Interim Executive Council with Nkomo included, possibly as President[91]. According to the South African military historian Jakkie Cilliers, negotiations between Smith and Nkomo progressed well and 'seemed on the verge of success' by the start of September 1978. On 2 September, Smith and Nkomo revealed publicly that the secret meetings had taken place[92]. There was a howl of opposition from Julius Nyerere and other black leaders when news of Nkomo's meeting with Ian Smith leaked out.

The first Viscount RH825 was shot down the very next day ... 3 September 1978.

---

90 Moorcraft, Paul L; McLaughlin, Peter (April 2008) [1982]. *The Rhodesian War: A Military History*. Barnsley: Pen and Sword Books.
91 Matthew C White, *Smith of Rhodesia*, Don Nelson 1978, at 122.

92 Cilliers, Jakkie (December 1984). *Counter-Insurgency in Rhodesia*. London, Sydney & Dover, New Hampshire

Why did Nkomo sanction the shooting down of a civilian airliner at that critical moment in time? While previous unsuccessful attacks had been made on civilian aircraft early in 1978, the political circumstances in late 1978 had changed significantly for the better. Why would he, or his leadership team, sanction an attack when the Presidency of the new Zimbabwe was being handed to him on a plate? It makes no sense.

If the shooting down of RH825 was deliberate, with the full knowledge of the ZAPU leadership, then it means that Nkomo had no intention of ever reaching a settlement, and ordered the shooting down as the catalyst for the continued armed struggle. If this was ZAPU's strategy then why where there no attacks on Rhodesian aircraft between April 1978 and September 1978? Why was there a hiatus? The alternative view is that Nkomo suspended attacks while negotiations continued. He may have been forced, through outside pressure, to accept responsibility for the shooting down, and thereby kill further peace negotiations.

The timeline for negotiations with the Interim Government in Rhodesia and the intense shuttle diplomacy that was in full swing, places a significant question mark around Nkomo's knowledge of the plan to shoot down airliners after April 1978, by any means. Nkomo may have had no knowledge of the plan to shoot down an airliner.

Taking responsibility for the shooting down of RH825 put Joshua Nkomo at a severe disadvantage with the international community. When compared with Robert Mugabe he was seen as too radical, too unpredictable and his Soviet bedfellows, too dangerous. From the day that RH825 went down, Joshua Nkomo was never seen as a serious candidate for the leadership of Zimbabwe, he became marginalised and his talented leadership team marginalised with him. This begs the question; did Nkomo have any idea of the plan to shoot down RH825? With the negotiations at the time, and the offers being made to him, would he have sanctioned it? Was he in fact a victim of circumstances outside of his knowledge or control?

Military build up

At the same time that Joshua Nkomo was negotiating with Ian Smith, President Kenneth Kaunda of Zambia was calling upon Britain for more protection against Rhodesian air raids and incursions. Rhodesian agents from the CIO and the Selous Scouts were active in Lusaka during 1978. It was also rumoured that senior Zambian government officials were Rhodesian spies.

In 1977 the first Soviet military training camp for ZIPRA terrorists was set up at Luena (Vila Luso) in Angola, under the command of Lieutenant Colonel Vladimir Pekin.

Throughout the Rhodesian War, Nkomo had received considerable aid from the Soviet Union, Cuba and East Germany. This assistance included a number of advisors to his War Council that was located at his Military Headquarters in Lusaka. These advisors were attached to their respective embassies.

During the later part of 1978, the Soviets were convinced that they would emerge as the victors in the war against the Interim Government. The tenuous bonds of the Patriotic Front began to dissolve as Nkomo and Mugabe focused their plans upon consolidating their own power within Zimbabwe in order to seize control of the government once a victory was achieved. The one planned to destroy the other.

The Soviet Union increased its assistance to Nkomo in order to ensure his control of Zimbabwe, and to enhance their sphere of influence within Southern Africa. Nkomo and his Soviet sponsors became concerned over their lack of support amongst the black population in contrast to Mugabe's ever increasing popularity. In order to achieve these ambitious objectives, the Soviets took charge of training the ZIPRA conventional forces. Cuban instructors were brought in to support the Soviets.

New training areas were established. The first was at the former Zambian Army Barracks at Mulungushi, and the second at the Boma Camp in Luena, Angola, another at Westlands farm on the northern outskirts of Lusaka. In early 1978 Joshua Nkomo visited the Luena camp, said to have had a very positive effect on morale[93].

In order to counter Mugabe's influence, the Soviet and Cuban advisors to the War Council provided a complete revision to the ZIPRA Order of Battle within Rhodesia, and its long term military objectives. This revision outlined the necessity of developing a conventional ZIPRA Army while using its guerrilla forces to open the way for a full-scale invasion of Rhodesia.

On 29 March 1978, there were reports of the arrival in Zambia of a Cuban force estimated at 300 men, 250 tanks and 25 MIG-21 supersonic fighters[94]. In April 1978 China presented Zambia with 12 Shenyang F-6 (MiG-19) day fighters. These were to act as a deterrent to the Rhodesian Air Force regularly entering Zambian air space. In 1978 the Cubans maintained a force of over 30,000 troops in Angola

---

93   Vladimir Shubin, *The Hot Cold War – The USSR in Africa*, KZN Press 2008 at 172.
94   Matthew C White, *Smith of Rhodesia*, Don Nelson, 1978.

including tanks, heavy artillery and MIG-21 aircraft.

The Soviet plan was based upon the training and equipping of at least five battalions of ZIPRA soldiers that were task-organised following the model of Soviet Motorized Infantry Battalions. It was estimated that this would be the minimum force required to defeat both the Rhodesian Security Forces and Mugabe's ZANLA. The scheme of manoeuvre involved an assault along two axis of advance across the Zambezi River. The first was along the northeast border to seize the airfield at Kariba while the second would occur at Victoria Falls in order to capture the airfield at Wankie. Once this had been achieved Libyan transport aircraft would airlift those remaining ZIPRA forces in Angola and Zambia into Rhodesia. MIG-19, and 21's would be provided for air-support, and manned by Cuban pilots. It was assumed that Libyan volunteers would man additional aircraft if they were required.

The capital city of Salisbury remained the principle objective. Once the bridgehead was established at Wankie and Kariba, three armoured columns would speed toward the capital. The first would move directly from Kariba. The second would attack from Wankie via the city of Que Que. The third element would move from Wankie to Kariba in order to consolidate the northern frontier, and then advance toward Salisbury. The second largest city in Rhodesia, Bulawayo, was by-passed because it was in Matabeleland, which was Nkomo's homeland and base of power.

In late 1977, the first reported use of a SAM-7 missile in Rhodesia was an attack on a RUAC sightseeing aircraft over Victoria Falls. In early 1978 two more attacks were made against SAA 737s flying out of Victoria Falls[95]. The mind boggles as to the consequences had the terrorists been successful. South Africa would almost certainly have invaded Zambia in search of the perpetrators. In April 1978 a further unsuccessful attack was made on an Air Rhodesia Viscount landing at Victoria Falls[96].

On 15 May 1978 Washington (UPI) reported that the number of senior Cuban military advisers working with Rhodesian guerrillas in their Zambian strongholds increased to as many as 70, and some were bodyguards for Joshua Nkomo. The Montreal Gazette reported that Zambia was now 'the prime staging area' for Soviet-Cuban support for the guerrillas seeking to topple the new multiparty interim, 'power-sharing' government in Salisbury. The report stated that the Cubans were being guided by a senior Soviet adviser to Nkomo's ZAPU,

---

95 Group Captain PJH Petter-Bowyer, *Winds of Destruction* at 493.
96 Keith Nell, *Viscount Down* at 401

Ambassador Vassily Solodovnikov.

According to the October 1978 edition of Flight International, the Zambian Army had a single battery of Rapier surface-to-air missiles in service. The number of fire units was reported as four to twelve, but no details were available since Britain never officially admitted to having supplied the weapon[97].

The stage was set. In August of 1978, Nkomo was negotiating in earnest with Ian Smith to join the Interim Government strongly supported by the British Government. At the same time the Soviet Union had started a significant military build up in Zambia using Cuban and East German military advisors. The Zambians had both Rapier Missiles and the new Chinese J6s (MIG-19). The Cuban's had positioned MIG-21s at Mumbwa in Zambia and had supplied trained platoon and company commanders. The Rhodesians knew that their freedom to fly unchallenged over Zambia was coming to an end. Everything pointed towards a negotiated settlement.

Who or what shot down RH825?

In my view there are five options for the RH825 disaster: (1) Nkomo's men on the ground using a SAM-7 (range 4km); (2) a SAM-3 missile fired from Zambia (range 32km), (3) a British supplied Rapier missile (range 6km) (4) a Cuban / Zambian fighter aircraft, (5) the aircraft was old and crashed through some mechanical malfunction allowing both parties to use the crash for propaganda purposes.

The Sydney Morning Herald of 23 October 1978, quoting the English Sunday Telegraph, reported that a Rapier missile shot down the Viscount. The article suggested that Kaunda had asked Nkomo to admit responsibility so as to avoid his and the British government embarrassment. On 30 October 1978 the Glasgow Herald repeated the claim. On 2 November 1978 the Sarasota Herald Tribune made the same report.

Flight International in November 1978 published the following statement,' It is quite feasible that a Zambian Rapier unit might have tracked the airliner as a training exercise, but if a round had been inadvertently fired, the operator need only have stopped manually steering the Rapier optical tracker in order to cause the missile to miss its target. Since Zambian personnel can only rarely—if ever—fire live rounds, the noise of missile launch would almost certainly have provided enough distraction to disturb the operator's aim. Such problems are common with many manually guided missiles, even

---

97   Flight International, 14 October 1978.

when trained operators are employed[98]'.

This statement is incredible. It assumes untrained Zambian operators would have had their aim disturbed simply by the noise of the launch! The level of naivety, for such a respected journal, is appalling. They missed two important points, firstly, these Rapiers were fire-and-forget, radar guided, secondly, the Rapier did not have the range from any point in Zambia to hit a Viscount airliner flying out of Kariba airport. Even if it did so, the aircraft would certainly have crashed into the lake.

Another important consideration is that the Rhodesian Ministry of Transport reported within only <u>five days</u> of investigation that the airliner was shot down by a SAM-7. Only five days! They had none of the forensic capability of more recent times and they were working on an aircraft wreckage that was virtually completely burnt out. It seems inconceivable that a damning conclusion could have been reached in such a short period. Aircraft accident investigations normally take months or even years to reach conclusion. This particular investigation held the lives of a nation at risk, the consequences were, and have been ever since, monumental.

Another puzzling aspect for me was the position and height the Viscount had reached by the time the missile shot was made. The SAM-7 (Strela2M) has a slant range of 4,000m and an altitude limit of 2,300m firing at an angle from behind the target at between 45 – 60 degrees, would self-destruct after 14 to 17 seconds of flight.

My analysis shows that the Viscount, climbing at 1,280ft/min at 150kts, would have been at an altitude of +-2,100m (7,100ft) AGL after 5minutes 24 seconds of flight. This was at the point the Viscount crossed over Lake Kariba near Gache Gache Bay, the earliest point for the SAM-7 strike (see Diagram) 17km from the crash site. The attack area is between the edge of the lake and the bottom of the escarpment, about 3.5km in length. This is assuming the flight data and accounts reported in the book *Viscount Down* by Keith Nell[99] are accurate.

The terrorist band would have been standing very close to the shore of Lake Kariba in order to make the strike 5 minutes after take off. Beyond the shoreline, under the normal operating parameters for the missile, the aircraft would have been too high. After being hit the aircraft flew on for another 3½ minutes to cover the 17km to the crash site. If indeed the aircraft was shot down by a SAM-7, the missile was successful at the very outer edge of its capability envelope. It was an incredibly 'lucky' shot from the terrorist point of view.

---

98   Flight International, *Britain airlifts missiles to Zambia*, 4 November 1978.
99   *Viscount Down*, Keith Nell (2011).

The distance from the firing point to the crash site was at least 17km over very rough terrain. The terrorists who killed the surviving passengers could not possibly have been the same as those that fired the missile. They were simply opportunists living amongst the villagers in the nearby Urungwe Tribal Trust Land

Flight of RH825 flight path – missile-firing window

325

SCORPIONS IN THE BLUE
A STORY OF THE LONG RANGE DESERT GROUP (1941)

North Africa in the Second World War saw for the first time in military history the development of specialised military units designed to operate behind enemy lines. What little military glamour shone through the conflict was confined almost exclusively to these private armies. They were the stuff of which legends are made. We have all heard of the Special Air Service that had its genesis in North Africa, but possibly the most amazing of all these private armies was that conceived by the soldier-scientist who built the first and most successful of them all - Ralph Bagnold – his unit - The Long Range Desert Group.

In Europe Germany had rolled through Poland, the low countries and France. The situation seemed desperate. Bagnold convinced British High Command that he could a build a small force of men, with specially adapted vehicles, that could operate across 2000 miles of the Western Desert. There to reconnoitre, ambush and disrupt enemy communications and installations – as Bagnold himself described, 'How about some piracy on the high desert?'

These very courageous men were drawn from New Zealand, Rhodesia and British units, they braved the harsh deserts of North Africa, stretching endlessly for thousands of miles to all points of the compass.

Here is a story of the Long Range Desert Group – a story of bravery, hardship, camaraderie, determination and a steadfast commitment to get the job done – no matter what!

Due for release in 2016

Winner of the Bronze Award in the Military/Wartime Fiction category in the 2012 Independent Publisher (IPPY) Book Awards in the United States.

A DESPERATE COLONIAL STRUGGLE ON A CONTINENT TORN BY WAR

Set in an almost forgotten guerrilla war in what is now called Zimbabwe during the 1970s, this is a journey into the world of young men fighting and dying at the behest of their political masters. The strain of having to survive close-quarter skirmishes preoccupy the combatants, who helplessly find themselves caught up in a conflict spinning out of control.

Mike Smith, an insecure nineteen-year old national serviceman, is immersed in a bloody insurgency witnessing horrors that seem too much for a young man to have to bear.

Tongerai Chabanga, a commander of the liberation movement, must withstand political pressure from his leaders outside the country to prosecute the war in a manner he disagrees with. At the same time, he is faced with the atrocities perpetrated of a depraved Soviet Spetznaz military advisor who threatens to undo the work he has done.

A COLONIAL WAR IN SOUTHERN AFRICA SPINNING OUT OF CONTROL

Set in the country now called Zimbabwe in the late 1970s, the Bush War has escalated into a desperate fight for survival. In a bid to stem the tide of freedom fighters flooding into the country, the war has spilt over into neighbouring Mozambique. External raids by special forces, the Selous Scouts and the Rhodesian Light Infantry, are required to hunt down the leaders of the liberation movement. They are hopelessly outnumbered, jumping from ancient Dakotas and rugged Alouette III helicopters. Chinese trained freedom fighters mount sabotage raids on key installations from bases in Mozambique, aided by spies in high places.

This story follows the harrowing, day-in-day-out combat and relentless pressure put on the combatants. Cold War rivalry, political paralysis and undercover agents put the men on the ground, on both sides of the conflict, in mortal danger. They not only have to defeat the enemy on the battlefield, they also have to endure the mistakes, bigotry and self-interest of their leaders. On the Freedom Fighter side, the fighting men and women are subjected to unspeakable hardship and brutality. Death stalks them from bomb, bullet, disease, hunger and their own leadership.

This is the story of the 'Steely-eyed killers' ...

COCKY LOBIN OVER GERMANY

Daryl Sahli

YOUNG MEN FLYING BIG MACHINES INTO INCREDIBLE DANGER. COMPELLING, CHILLING, PART STORY, PART HISTORY, ALWAYS REAL!

It is March 1944, the Battle of Berlin has ground to a halt, both sides battered to submission. Bomber Command gathers itself for the next assault. This story follows a bomber crew from 44 (Rhodesia) Squadron who have completed their 15th mission, only half way through their tour. Follow the routine of their lives, their living conditions, the parties and the commitment of the dedicated ground crews and support staff. The squadron has lost more than half its number in only a few months, the chances of survival now seem impossible. These are young men from the four corners of the Empire, from the wild bush-land of Rhodesia, the endless bitterly cold rolling plains of Canada, the hot and desolate centre of Australia and the squalor of bombed English cities. These men were thrust together by force of circumstance, forged in battle, their relationship based on mutual reliance and determination ... to see it through ... come what may.

The bombers face a ferocious, determined and well organised enemy. On the next mission they face the latest in night fighting and radar technology, the odds are stacked against them as never before. The Lancaster Cocky Lobin, C-Charlie, must carry her crew through a withering aerial battle, radar predicted flak, fast and well armed night-fighters and the weather. This is a fight to the death ... a test, for men barely out of their teens, like no other.

CPSIA information can be obtained
at www.ICGtesting.com
Printed in the USA
LVOW07s0052200917
549349LV00001B/135/P

9 780987 156495